D1248040

A Vein of Riches

A Vein of Riches

JOHN
KNOWLES

An Atlantic Monthly Press Book
Little, Brown and Company   Boston–Toronto

FIRST EDITION

T 02/78

LIBRARY OF CONGRESS CATALOGING IN PUBLICATION DATA

Knowles, John, 1926–
   A vein of riches.
   "An Atlantic-Monthly Press book."
   I. Title.
PZ4.K745Sd   [PS3561.N68]   813'.5'4   77–10730
ISBN 0–316–49971–4

ATLANTIC–LITTLE, BROWN BOOKS
ARE PUBLISHED BY
LITTLE, BROWN AND COMPANY
IN ASSOCIATION WITH
THE ATLANTIC MONTHLY PRESS

Designed by Susan Windheim
*Published simultaneously in Canada
by Little, Brown & Company (Canada) Limited*

PRINTED IN THE UNITED STATES OF AMERICA

To Martha Winston
True friend, peerless agent

A Vein of Riches

one

In 1909 three families stood at the center of the great Middleburg, West Virginia, coal boom: the Cliftons, the Hayeses, and the Catherwoods.

The Cliftons, it was recognized, were even more central to it all than the Hayeses or the Catherwoods. They had come here over the Blue Ridge Mountains in Revolutionary times, acquired and worked the rugged land as farmers, and built the rough log cabin which still stood, much restored and gussied up, on their estate. When coal became king toward the end of the nineteenth century they became its princes, and the Spanish Mission–style country villa they built on the outskirts of town, with its stables and greenhouses, the show horses, the private railroad siding, the indoor marble swimming pool, the aviary, all reflected a Medician sense of the permanence of this uniquely West Virginia bonanza.

Next to this property, which they named in a futile gesture toward unpretentiousness Clifton Farms, was Clifton Manor, built by the founder's son. Clifton Manor was straightforwardly an Elizabethan half-timbered country mansion, leaded windows and all, formal gardens, about a hundred rooms, a truly beautiful if incongruous replica of life in the sixteenth-century English countryside.

The Hayeses were less expansive, being more cautious, more numerous, and less rich. They simply threw up big hospitable houses here and there around town, with wide porches for the children to play on, large yards for them to run in, and small stables for their ponies, the Episcopal Church where they could be baptized, married and sent to their reward. The Hayeses then contemplated their work and found it good: all future generations were provided for in this world and in the next.

The Catherwoods were different. First of all they were less numerous than the other clans. Clarkson Catherwood came back over the mountains from Baltimore with his bride and her heirloom piano in 1894 to investigate the minerals underlying some land he had inherited. The mineral underlying it was discovered to be black diamonds — coal — and by quickly and quietly buying a great deal of adjacent land, opening it up to shaft and strip mining, hiring cheap Italian labor, resisting any moves toward unionizing, and by expanding into real estate in the town, he became a multimillionaire when being a millionaire just once over really meant something. The year after his wife, Minnie, bore their first child who lived (another had died in childbirth), he erected Catherwood Castle, a necessarily drastically reduced version of the British royal family's residence at Windsor, gray stone crenellated walls, two towers served by spiral staircases, a dining room with a minstrel's gallery, a "plunge" in the basement (too small, by the standards of the Cliftons' marble marvel, to be called a pool), a billiard room, smoking room, library, and observatory with a telescope at the top of one of the two towers.

These three clans, and the two dozen or so families who surrounded them and participated to a lesser but still ample degree in the prevailing prosperity, formed, before, during, and after the First World War, a dashing, exuberant society, dedicated to money-making by the father, mothering by the mother, and fun up to and including hell-raising by the children. They were an open, unaffected, friendly crowd. Not for them the tight-laced traditions of Tidewater folk in Virginia; up here in the highlands, here in Virginia's "lost counties," up here where there had never been many slaves or plantations or old traditions, people knew their manners all right but they had no time for stuffiness, no tendency to mourn the dear departed past, not when all this money and the power it gave poured out of their hills by the trainload and spread the amplitude of vast opportunity in all directions around them.

The great houses came first, and then the great show horses, the long trips, the big ships, the most costly cars, the finest schools and the best parties.

President William Howard Taft descended in all his massive bulk upon the Cliftons of the Manor for one unforgotten house party. He arrived at the Clifton siding in the private presidential car on a glowing day in June 1909, and the people of Middleburg, thoroughly pleased to have the President of the United States in their midst but not overly awed — after all, Mountaineers Were Always Free and the Tafts of Cincinnati were just another downriver family — turned out to cheer and wave as he drove the short distance from siding to mansion in the great black and silver Clifton Rolls-Royce.

The house itself, with its oak wainscoting, the huge Italian marble fireplaces, parquetry floors, elegant glass-enclosed porches with iron filigree doors, the long hallways giving on a parade of guest bedrooms, the house, in addition to being a home for a family on the lavish scale of the period, was also very intentionally a symbol and a riposte; the Farms and the Manor were coal's answer to steel — the Carnegies; railroads — the Hills and Harrimans; shipping — the Vanderbilts; oil — the Rockefellers. These families presided over their basic industries from *their* enormous private

[5]

palaces in New York and Newport and Rhinebeck and Pittsburgh, and if coal truly had become king, then he must have a palace to equal those other sovereigns'.

President Taft was the apex of the established Republican power of the nation, and the Cliftons' invitation to him was intended to show these Yankees, the power lords of America, this new dignity below the Mason-Dixon Line, the great Middleburg coal barons, rulers of the biggest, the best, and the richest coalfield in the world.

II.

The coal in West Virginia was better than elsewhere; the seams were thicker, the coal was of higher quality and with fewer impurities, and it came in more varieties. It was easier to reach, either by stripping or by tunneling into the side of a hill. The expense and danger of sinking a deep shaft were rarely necessary. And there was enough coal to last through a very long time of the most intensive mining.

So the Cliftons and the Hayeses and the Catherwoods plunged ahead in the exploitation of this great resource.

It is significant that the President invited to inspect the Kingdom of Coal was Taft and not his more colorful and influential predecessor, Theodore Roosevelt. But T.R. was a villain to the coal operators in West Virginia, for he was a "trust buster," and the coal in the Maryland–West Virginia regions was hauled by the Baltimore and Ohio Railroad, which conveniently also owned a lot of the mines. President Roosevelt and the Interstate Commerce Commission found this an unfair and illegal combination in restraint of trade, and so in 1907 the Clifton interests bought the mines from the railroads one step ahead of the law, and joining them to their own holdings, overnight became the biggest coal combine in the world.

By 1909 all was in order and ready to be displayed to the new President Taft. The railroad continued to haul the coal but no longer mined it, and the Company was firmly established on top of the coal industry, with headquarters in Middleburg, a production schedule of twenty-five million tons annually, outlets through Baltimore to customers in Europe, the New East and Japan, and the great houses to crown it all.

Having entertained the President in June, Mr. and Mrs. Sanderson Clifton of the Manor decided in November to give a ball in their oak and crystal ballroom for, as Caroline Clifton put it, "no reason in the world except it's Thanksgiving time and we have such a lot to be thankful for." The ball was held on the eve of the holiday. At the carriage entrance on one side of the great Elizabethan house the few remaining carriages and the numerous sputtering and growling new cars — electrics, steamers, limousines, racers — deposited the gentry of Middleburg and environs, and a seasoning of guests from Baltimore and the Tidewater and downstate, into the great rooms of the mansion, awash with the music of the string orchestra and champagne and a supper of every delicacy the B&O could bring in in fresh condition, the best cigars Cuba could produce, the air perfumed from the bursts of Clifton hothouse flowers everywhere mingled with the ladies' best perfume and the gentlemen's most powerful witch hazel, the library for brandy and cigars and serious, basso discussions.

Virtually all of the men were between thirty and a hundred pounds heavier than their doctors would have liked. Behind the black silk vests those great bellies, some tending to points like promontories, others magnificently and symmetrically rounded like the dome of Saint Peter's, some carried high, others tending to droop, were all supported, at whatever

strain to the back muscles and spine, with prideful uncon-
cern by their possessors. Was not J. P. Morgan so fleshed out?
William Howard Taft? Every bank president in the country?
The belly, with an important watch chain draped across it
like the Order of the Garter, was the very mount of business
and financial success, the demonstration that its possessor
could buy and consume as much and as rich food as ever he
desired, whenever he desired, and that he had achieved and
was sustaining his affluent (and therefore, by definition in
1909, admirable) position in the community by nothing so
vulgar as physical toil or agility, which required a certain
litheness, but by princely contemplation and decision-making
from the comforting seat of an enormous swivel chair. Belly
to belly, cigar tip to cigar tip, the weighty men of the coal
world stood about in the great arching library of the mansion and rumbled about new mines being opened, fishing trips
off Florida, the great Ivy League football teams, interest
rates. Their sons on such evenings would in later years complain bitterly about the income tax, but these gentlemen, earn-
ing between $50,000 and $500,000 a year when a dollar
was a dollar, did not: there was no income tax.

In the card room, across the dance floor on which the
younger couples whirled to the music, the more mature ladies
settled onto settees and card chairs in this pretty blue and
gold antechamber and planned who should be maneuvered
into asking whom to dance, how the courting of another
couple was progressing, why a certain engagement had not
been announced and how to hasten the day, the plans for an
impending wedding, how a particular young married couple
seemed to be settling down together, *what* was wrong in the
household of X, whatever possessed Y to *carry on* so behind
his dear wife's back, and the poor, hopeless Zs, with his completely inexcusable ways, and as for *her*, why . . .

The string music swept on, the black men in their liveries
circled with more glasses of Moët et Chandon on silver trays,

the black maids in their pretty uniforms helped the matrons reassemble their elaborate hairdos when they threatened to fall. It had begun to rain and blow outside, but within the fires just roared higher in the marble fireplaces; and the warming wines of France, liberally mixed with the finest Kentucky bourbon, sustained everyone through the evening.

"I declare," said Thelma Hayes to Caroline Clifton, gathering her black velvet and fox evening wrap around her as she crossed the glass porch toward her Cadillac and her chauffeur, "that's the best *damn* party anybody ever gave around here including *us!*"

"It's no such thing. You all give grand parties. This big place needs a regular *regiment* of people to give it any warmth at all. I hope we managed some tonight."

"You just know you did. Why I haven't had such a gay time since Harry and I got kind of tipsy going to Europe on the *Kaiser Wilhelm der Grosse*. And *that* night we had the Grand Duke Michael or one of them of *Russia* at the next table. Honey, this was *better*. Well, I got to hand it to you and your Sandy and the whole family, you show us the way, you surely do. And I don't just mean parties. Everything. Why, this whole county, the whole state, hell, the whole *country's* beholden to you. Good night, honey." She left Mrs. Clifton with a happy trace of tears in her eyes.

Mrs. Clarkson Catherwood, in a white silk evening coat, drifted up to her hostess, heading toward her car, where her husband, Clarkson, who was impatient of a chauffeur, sat behind the wheel.

"Good night, dear," she said, smiling and blinking, "it was just like a fairy tale. It had everything. I almost expected a prince with a glass slipper. But then Clarkson there would turn into a mouse, wouldn't he? And the Packard into a pumpkin."

"Well, yes, dear." Mrs. Clifton was practiced at handling Minnie Catherwood, but always uneasy with her in her whimsical moods. "But you haven't turned . . . Your dress is still lovely —"

"Yes," said Minnie dreamily, "I haven't turned, have I, as yet."

How typical of her, thought Mrs. Clifton, to turn it all into a fairy tale; and how typical of her to make it all center around herself.

"Well, dear," said Clarkson Catherwood after helping Minnie into the car and returning to his place behind the wheel, "enjoy it?"

Minnie drew a long breath. "That house doesn't like me."

"Now Min."

"It doesn't. And it never will, never will."

III.

At this period Mrs. Catherwood — Minnie — always wore white. She was rather tall and slender, with delicate skin and chestnut hair gathered in a bun in the back, and she said, "White's the color of goodness, and I want my child to think about goodness when he looks at me."

The afternoon after the ball she and her six-year-old son, Lyle, were sitting in the upstairs sewing room, a late November sun pouring through a big window behind her, spreading a glow around her hair and long dress, making her look dazzling to Lyle, perched on a stool near her feet. He associated his mother with tales of magic — fairy godmother, a sleeping princess, wicked witch — and now, doing her needlework, in an aureole of sunlight, Minnie indelibly fixed in her son's memory this glowing vision of light and whiteness.

"I wonder how many steps I've taken today," she said in a characteristic way, aloud but not specifically addressed to anyone, "just today. I wonder if every footstep I took made a little imprint in the floors of this house, what they would look like. Why, they'd be all *black* with all the thousands — millions — of steps I've taken here over the years, coming and going, coming and going. Think of it!" (Even this phrase was not directed at the little boy at her feet.) "And *where* was I going, what was the purpose? Just this and that, year in year out, this and that, step by step, over and over. And . . . to what purpose, I wonder. And what *could* I have been directing my feet toward, if I'd stopped to take thought, aimed myself, had great, important direction . . . no *wasted motion* . . . I wonder about that. Instead, well, coming and going, back and forth . . ." She smiled faintly, unseeing, at little Lyle, who was too young to comprehend, she thought. But the little boy had not been.

Big walnut furniture with elaborately carved doors and drawers filled the Catherwood home, which they had tried naming the Towers but everyone called Catherwood Castle. The high-ceilinged rooms contained natural and hothouse flowers in cut-glass vases; there were colored glass lamp-shades with cut-glass pendants over circular marble-topped tables holding knickknacks and mementos and framed "silhouettes," cutouts in black against white of children in profile; there were sliding doors, burgundy-colored Oriental rugs, wicker, tall thrusting potted plants and trees; big, enveloping leather and plush armchairs and couches filled rooms shadowed by heavy velvet and brocade draperies, with a very grand portrait of Minnie in full evening regalia, egret feather starting up out of her hair, pearl dog collar at the throat, in a heavy gilt frame, dominating the front living room where no member of the family ever sat except under duress.

The exterior of the house, imposing because of its crenellated battlements lining the roof above the third story, and the two towers rising two stories higher, presented a rather formidable appearance, although softened by the big windows at each level and the full-length glass doors opening on the grounds. This exterior was faced by gray stucco on tile. Mr. Catherwood had wanted solid granite but been talked out of it. The four acres around it were taken up by a large barn, big trees, lawns, a goldfish pond, swings, and a sunken rose garden.

The Castle was first and foremost, despite its self-conscious exterior, a comfortable home for a family, which could not be said for the Clifton edifices, burdened with their heavy symbolic roles as replies to the Vanderbilts. Big heavy dinners — of chicken and ham and corn and sweet potatoes and biscuits and apple cider and roast lamb and creamed onions and squash and chocolate cake and homemade peach ice cream and pumpkin pie and vanilla custard and roast pork and applesauce with cinnamon and creamed lima beans and corn bread and chicken soup and potato salad and lemon meringue pie — were all paraded from the big kitchen and pantries and served upon the mahogany dining room table under the silently reflecting chandelier, with, in summer, the French windows open to the filtering odors of leaves and flowers, of mowed grass with a water sprinkler sweeping lightly across it, flinging up a fan of water like gossamer in flight.

There would be three main courses often — ham and duckling and scalloped oysters — with six or eight vegetables, and then there would be trifle and layer cake and homemade ice cream and fresh fruit for dessert. Sometimes there was loin of pork for breakfast. Always there were mounds and steaming platters and bowls full of succulent food, offered three or sometimes four times a day, with smaller repasts always available by merely ringing a bell to the kitchen. Among Middleburg's Hundred Millionaires it was unthinkable that anyone feel real hunger ever.

Winters tended toward gloom and moist chill in Middleburg. Coal dust quickly spread its glum grayness over festive snowfalls, although the snow was good for sledding on the many slopes around town. Alongside the Castle property a dirt road ran steeply down an incline toward a little creek in Raccoon Hollow, and the Clifton and Hayes children and their friends would come over for sledding there, and afterward Lyle would bring them into the Castle for hot cider and cookies in the pantry.

IV.

One thing that perplexed and even saddened Lyle when he was nine or ten was how many brothers and sisters all these families had, six at a minimum, twelve at a maximum. What fun, what variety, what fights, what secrets must be shared among them. These troops of brothers and sisters seemed to him to live in a real circus of intimacy and uproar, something doing at every second, so much experience whirling about them all the time.

One day Lyle asked his mother why their family was so much smaller than anyone else's she knew. "God's will, Lyle dear, just God's will."

Living was, for Minnie and ladies like her, easy, secure, with all the drudgery performed by servants. So what was a married woman to do with her time except to supervise her children? Go to work? The idea of Mrs. Clarkson Catherwood taking employment was ridiculous, no one would have approved of it or even understood it, and what's more Minnie had never been taught to do anything useful in that sense. She could play the piano, sing, she was an excellent needlewoman, spoke schoolgirl French, could stay on a horse, raise dogs, and take part in or preside at all sorts of social occasions. Those were her accomplishments.

V.

Lacking a large number of children, Minnie began to brood mentally, speculating during the endless hours in the big empty castle after Lyle was in school, Clarkson in his office or else out at the mines, sometimes until late at night, and frequently away in the southern part of the state, or in Kentucky or Baltimore or Cleveland. As "Uncle" George and "Aunt" Tot moved softly about the house bringing her a cup of mint tea or massaging her feet or brushing her hair or bringing fresh bunches of flowers for her to arrange, the silence of the house unbroken except when she put a roll on the player piano or one of the collies scratched for fleas, Minnie was left to roam down the halls and up the spiral staircase into one of the tower rooms and to ask herself those limitless questions which recede forever into infinity: What if I had a real direction in my life? What if I had devoted myself to God and serving humanity? Suppose I'd never met Clarkson?

There were calls on other ladies to be made and returned but they knew each other so very well that they were empty and sparse. There were good works at the church, but the real effort was consigned to others and only ceremonial functions left to ladies of Minnie's position. Children! That was what she was supposed to occupy her energetic years with, and she had but one. It was not enough. Often Minnie would retreat to her cluttered dressing room and simply comb her long chestnut hair by the hour, deliberately tangling it so as to have the task of combing it out again, before her big oval mirror, studying her pretty, resigned face and asking her limitless questions. And, although she knew she must be careful, she would eventually have recourse to her opium-based tonic, easily obtainable at the pharmacy, and then dream on, vague, veiled, but feeling, as though it were a heavy thumping in her chest, that life — thump, thump — was passing metronomelike and she was standing aside and watching, watching and failing and really forgotten.

VI.

For Lyle, his boyhood summers passed in a shimmer of happiness. Canoeing on the river, swimming in the pools, the flower scents and running outdoor games, hiding in haylofts, gave way in August to the marvels of the annual trip to the seashore, in a compartment on the B&O Pullman to Baltimore, then by hired car and chauffeur to Rehoboth Beach, in Delaware. There in the big wooden clapboard house with its wide porches and screened-in sleeping balconies, its wicker and big windows, the gorgeous white beach stretching away and the sea forever roiling and tossing, with picnics on the sand and cautious venturing into the sea, he came to assume that life was meant to lead and would lead to total bliss.

VII.

The Catherwoods were dutifully Episcopalian, although Minnie felt a strong tug toward the Catholic Church from time to time because of all the Catholic nuns and clergy and institutions in Baltimore. It all seemed so *elaborate*: the nun's habits, the church rituals, the candlelit and statue-filled churches themselves, the intimations of exotic lands such as France and Italy that clung to it, although the Irishness which overlay that rather dampened the exoticism for her.

Eventually, however, Minnie came to a standard Protestant conclusion: that the Catholics, or "R.C.'s" as they were called

in her circle, were full of popery and Jesuits and author-
itarianism and indubitably not for her. At Christmas, when
a midnight mass was celebrated in the vault-ceilinged, ornate
Catholic church in Middleburg, she would however feel an
urge, never fulfilled, to attend, a pull toward the panoply and
incense, the gold and the chanted Latin, the ancientness she
felt to be preserved there.

But surely there was somewhere a religious teaching more
compelling than the tasteful readings and homilies she received at Christ Episcopal Church. If her life was to be as
empty of life as it seemed to be, surely there was vast space
in it for God.

two

I.

S HE confided her search, her need, to Aunt Tot, and Aunt
Tot had a suggestion.

Nothing about life with the Catherwoods surprised Aunt
Tot, not their bursting prosperity in a heretofore poor region,
nor their virtual childlessness, not Miss Minnie's moods and
vagaries. She had seen it all in her sixty-two years.

Born a slave, Aunt Tot as a girl in her twenties had watched
this part of Virginia pass through the total confusion visited
upon a slaveholding region which nevertheless elected to
side with the *North* in the Civil War, watched counties, towns,
church congregations, and families split violently apart on
the issue and plenty of young men passionately choose the
gray uniform instead of the blue. She had seen the Confederate marauders gallop through Middleburg and burn the
old suspension bridge over the river and rifle and burn the
family home of Mr. Pierpont, who headed the Yankee rump
government. He was the governor of something called the
Restored Government of Virginia, although how he could be
that when he and his Yankee supporters couldn't fight their

way to within a hundred miles of Richmond was something Aunt Tot couldn't imagine.

The Confederates rode off and the Yankees swept in, taking everybody's produce and livestock, and pretty soon it seemed that all the pro-Confederates were now for the North and all the Yankees hated the Union and the whole thing didn't make any sense.

If there was one thing Aunt Tot always tried to make, it was sense.

Then, in June of 1863, President Lincoln did what had been only an electrifying rumor and hope throughout the slave population from one end to another of the South; he declared the slaves in the rebellious states free.

As always, it was not quite so simple in this part of Virginia, which had rebelled against the rebellion and entered the Union that same year as the State of West Virginia, a *slave* state. To Aunt Tot that was the limit in not making sense.

Gradually, though, with deals and compensations among the white men, the slaves here became free too, but Aunt Tot found she was still laundering white people's clothes and taking care of their children. However, after a while, over the long pull of the years, colored men got jobs in the mines and had money of their own, and there was a school set up for the colored children to go to, and *that* made sense to her and that really was a change from the old days. Maybe the school wasn't very good, as some people said, but then a lot of people said the school for the white children wasn't very good either.

Being free was different and it was also the same. You could quit and you could move and your children could go to school, but Aunt Tot still took care of white children — her niece did the laundry now — and that seemed to be the way it was going to be, which was the way it always had been.

She did think that some of the young colored men might make a change and do better, maybe work their way up in the coal companies and then some of them get more education and get to be doctors and lawyers, but she did not expect to live to see that, because she had grown up as a piece of property that could be treated the way a horse or a chest of drawers could be treated, and in her bones she knew she would never live to see things that much better.

Aunt Tot had always been religious, through two marriages and two dead husbands, five children born and two dead, and she still was. One day when Minnie was engaged in the single occupation which she diligently pursued and excelled at, needlework, she called Aunt Tot to come and sit by her in the sun-flooded sewing room.

"Tot," she said, not taking her eyes from her needlework, "how is it you get up in the morning? What makes you, what do you really get up *for?*"

"My little birdie, Lyle, you know that."

"No, yes, I know, but what really gives you the courage?"

"The Lord, of course, just like he does for everybody that believes."

"I — I want to believe, I do believe, but I don't think I have the right . . . vessel."

"Vessel?"

"Yes. Christ Church isn't the right vessel."

"It's one Almighty God up there over everybody. Don't matter so much what *room* you're in when you start talkin' to Him."

"It does to me, it does, I think it does."

"Well, Miss Minnie, I know what you're leadin' up to. It's *my* church, ain't it, that you been hearin' about."

"I *have* heard a little," said Minnie with care, "which, being a religious person, interested me . . . a little. It's a *new* congregation and a new preacher, isn't it?"

"That's right. Reverend Roanoke."

"It's out on the road toward Bennettown."

"That's right."

"What's it called, this church?"

"It's a whole new *religion* Reverend Roanoke brought to the folks around here. He's from Kentucky, and he's been to the hill people in Virginia and North Carolina, and now he's here and made a whole lot of new members, including me."

"What's this new religion called?"

"The Church of the Last Judgment."

"The Church of the Last Judgment?" echoed Minnie wonderingly. "Whatever does it mean?"

"That means" — Aunt Tot turned her alert, settled face directly at Minnie, who, half-involuntarily, met her gaze — "that you get into communion, *deep* communion with Reverend Roanoke and you find out your eternal reward. Or your eternal punishment."

"Here and now you find it out?"

"You find it out here and now. And then you *know*. And then you know."

"Tot, Aunt Tot, tell me, what did *you* find out, what's *your* eternal reward, or your — well, I know you'll be rewarded."

Tot rocked back and forth in her rocking chair. Then she said, "Mustn't tell, mustn't ever tell, *that's* between you and the Lord. And the Reverend Roanoke. *He* knows, that's natural."

"He knows," echoed Minnie, "he knows."

"But he don't tell either, that's natural too."

"No, he doesn't tell."

Minnie drew her needle through the linen pillowcase she was embroidering, and for a minute there was only the faint, violinlike sound of the thread slipping through the material. Then she said, "Is it only one big room, inside the church?

Mr. Catherwood's been by it and he's told me what it looks like on the outside."

"Outside looks like nothin' much. It's just a gray old barn. Inside . . . inside there is the Lord, He is there 'in spirit,' that's the way Reverend Roanoke says it. 'The Lord is among us in spirit.' So that makes it *different*, inside."

"Tot?"

"Yes, Miss Minnie?"

"Is it all just colored folks in the church?"

"Oh no. Reverend Roanoke explains, that is, he *says*, what he *says* is, well, that there ain't no color in paradise and there ain't no color in hell, it's all the same," and she eyed Minnie speculatively as she stated this.

"And he's so right," said Minnie. "Everybody's the same in the sanctity of the Lord, I'm sure. I've always felt that. It had to be."

"Yes'm."

"How many white members are there in the church?"

"Fifteen, twenty."

"And how many colored?"

"Must be sixty, seventy, like that."

"And there's no . . . difficulty of any kind in the church, during the services, no kind of nasty looks or any of that, between white and colored?"

"We're all in the spirit of the Lord in that church, and we — well, Miss Minnie, you got to *see* it to understand. I don't explain things like I should. You got to *see*" — thus handing Minnie the opportunity for which Tot was aware she had been fishing from the beginning.

"Yes," said Minnie, bending over her needlework. "We'll see, we'll see."

The Church of the Last Judgment had meetings on Sunday mornings, but its real turnouts occurred on Thursday nights at seven-thirty, when many of its members, who were servants, would be able to attend, as they could not Sunday morning when they were getting the families they worked for ready to go to the Episcopalian or Baptist or Methodist-Episcopal Church South.

The following Thursday Minnie had ordered the Model T Ford ready at 6:30 P.M. This was a car Clarkson used to visit outlying mines on bad roads. Minnie was not going to arrive at the Church of the Last Judgment in a Packard limousine. Uncle George would drive her, and Tot would accompany her. She did not lie to Clarkson about her destination: she said she was "going to visit Tot's place and see how it was," and as Tot had a cottage in Bennettown near the church, this story fell into place. Always glad when Minnie exhibited any initiative in getting out of the house, any interest in things outside of herself, Clarkson approved.

Minnie had never been on the road to Bennettown before. It was reddish orange brick bordered by strips of concrete, and was barely wide enough for two-way traffic. It climbed and fell and curved and plunged among hills and encroaching woods, and as dusk closed in Minnie began to feel creeping, gathering qualms, and behind the qualms a wave of hysteria uncertainly held back. She took an inhale of her smelling salts and felt momentarily, only momentarily, revived. To be afraid while heading only a few miles out of Middleburg with two of the most trusted, faithful servants in the world was absurd. And yet as dusk gathered and the rattling little flivver chugged along over the perilous road, and the trees, great dark profiles, nodded majestically — threateningly? — in the evening breeze, Minnie asked herself if she had been mad to commit herself to participating in this fly-by-night ceremony — there might be some voodoo or black magic in it! — and without her husband's permission, since she had deceived him as to her purpose. Minnie did not do things without Clarkson's permission.

She felt undermined. Impulsively she seized Tot's hand, beside her in the jouncing little back seat of the open car.

Tot said, "It's all the same Lord, no matter what *room* you're in when you talks to him," and Minnie felt calmer, because of the way Tot saw right in to her feelings. No need to tell Tot she was shaken and afraid.

At the bottom of a particularly steep hill, Uncle George turned off the brick road onto a dirt one which followed a little stream up a narrow hollow. Here it was even murkier and there was a gritty quality to the dirt under the car's wheels: Minnie was approaching, for the first time in her life, a coal mine.

Every stitch of clothes I own, she reflected, every mouthful of food I take, the very warmth that fills our house in the winter, I owe to one of these places, and I've never even seen one. How heedless of me. It was true that she had naively asked Clarkson, early in their marriage, to let her go and see, enter, *launch* in a sense, the Minnie Mine when it was opened. He'd looked at her with his usual quiet indulgence. "The men don't like women around the mine. They think it's bad luck. It bothers the men." And that had been that.

Now they rattled along in the car up a little incline and to the left of the dirt road there was a primitively hand-lettered sign painted on a piece of board: THE CHURCH OF THE LAST JUDGMUNT.

Uncle George turned the Model T up this bumpy, rock-strewn track — an old streambed, it appeared — to a small gray barn. There were two other flivvers like theirs, a number of horses and buggies, several lone horses and a couple of mules. Four dogs barked as they pulled up. There were no people; the congregation appeared to be all inside.

Ordering George and Tot to precede her, Minnie ventured in. A big, high-ceilinged barn interior confronted her, with several score people on kitchen chairs and benches facing a large square table with a hand-hewn cross on it and a large oil painting, primitive but striking, of an old man with a white beard, holding up his right hand as though in blessing.

His skin was heavily tanned or brownish or colored; with an involuntary shock Minnie realized that this must be a representation of God the Father, at the Last Judgment.

At the other end of the table was another oil painting of the same size. This was immediately recognizable as the Devil, horns, tail and fork, jabbing at the back of someone falling into flames at the bottom of the picture. The only difference between this representation of the Devil and others Minnie had seen was that he was by no means black, but rather a whitish gray, distinctly lighter than God the Father.

As Tot had said, the congregation was predominantly colored, although there were quite a few white people. The women wore simple brown or black dresses and hats planted squarely on their heads or else had their heads wrapped in bandannas: all were the picture of impecunious respectability. The men had on dark suits or country clothes or, in a few cases, overalls. Everyone was very clean. All of these people are here, thought Minnie, because they want it established that they are Saved. And if you are Saved you want to look Saved. Suddenly she realized that she herself, thoughtlessly indulging tonight as every night in her whim of wearing dead white from head to toe, must stand out like a beacon in this congregation.

Then to her amazement an organ burst out playing behind her. Wheeling about, Minnie saw that there was a pump organ in the hayloft over the door and that a colored lady was playing away, pumping with her feet. Minnie could not recognize any of the music; it seemed very lively to be played at a church service; you could dance to it, clap your hands.

Then Reverend Roanoke swung suddenly into view behind the table, broad-shouldered, broad-faced, brown, balding, wearing a long black robe like a graduation gown with a huge, beautiful insignia beautifully embroidered, her needlewoman's eye detected, at the breast, of a golden figure with upraised right arm riding silver clouds before glorious reddish gold rays of dawn radiating out from it. The Last Judgment! Surely it would come with such glory, she thought.

"It didn't come, did it!" the Reverend Roanoke burst out in a deep, full, cheery voice, his black eyes dancing merrily.

Instantly switched from its demeanor of soundless respectability, the congregation exploded with laughter.

"We thought it might!" his stentorian voice continued, "we thought it might! But it didn't come! Not *this time!*" A long, contemplative pause followed this rollicking opening. The broad face and merry eyes composed themselves into a visage of contained seriousness, and then the Reverend Roanoke said in his full, deep, warm voice, "But we know that it *will* come, and then the *true* life, the life of eternity, begins. And *we are ready.* Yes." Pause. "We . . . here . . . are . . . ready." Long pause. "We are, aren't we!"

"Yes! Yes! Oh yes! Amen! Oh yes! Yes! We are ready!" cried the congregation with the same sudden, unprepared-for spontaneity as their first outburst.

A long, pregnant, almost dangerous silence ensued. Finally, his face passing from serious to stern, his voice to a new depth, Reverend Roanoke demanded in a deep, even tone, "But are we all?" Suspenseful pause. "Are we *all!*" Uneasy silence, stillness. "Search your hearts, search your hearts!"

Minnie found her heart beating with such light, racing, irregular beats that to *search* it would have been impossible. Of all the questions she had put to herself for years, all the wondering and the contemplation and cogitation and longing, none had approached this in vastness. *Was she Saved?* All the years and the wondering and the wasted hours flashed through her mind and were swallowed up by the gigantic dilemma which now this prophet in his blazing emblem held before her: was she, throughout eternity, to be a saint or a devil? And with sweat breaking across her forehead she suddenly saw the huge question inside that: since Reverend Roanoke taught that this could be known here and now, was she *now* a saint or was she *now* a devil?

Was Mrs. Clarkson Catherwood, the mother of Lyle, a walking, mothering devil!

At this Minnie began to feel the room withdrawing from her; the roof of the barn seemed to be floating upward, upward — toward Heaven! — and the floor beneath her sinking — toward Hell! — and the laws . . . the laws of . . . uh . . . gravity being what they were she must inevitably sink . . . with the floor . . . toward . . . toward . . . A whirling downward plunge took possession of her, she was now completely helpless, terrifyingly possessed by some whirling power beyond nature, the Devil surely, whirling, spiraling downward toward the bottom of some infernal funnel; looking desperately upward she could see the reds and silvers and golds of God the Father receding from her as she was whirled into chaos.

Then stillness. A dim light began to suffuse behind her closed lids. Low voices murmured. Something cold and damp was gently placed on her forehead. She opened her eyes. Tot. George. A strange little room.

"Oh thank the Lord," Tot murmured to herself. She held a glass of white liquid to Minnie's lips. Minnie trustingly took a gulp. A fiery tongue leaped down her throat. "What is that?" she asked weakly.

"That's moonshine, Miss Minnie."

"Never tasted it before," she said vaguely.

"Well, I figured right now you needed it. You swooned in there, in the church."

"Did I? Yes, I must have. Did I — did I disrupt Reverend Roanoke's service?"

"Oh no. He just told everybody that this was a new sister — I — he called you a sister because —"

"Of course. Then what did he say?"

"That the vision of coming glory was just too powerful for

you, seein' it all at once like that. Said it was his fault, he should of realized that the new sister — all in white — mustn't see the glory all at once."

"The glory," said Minnie wonderingly, sitting up with Tot's strong arm for support. "The glory. Then if I — if he, if Reverend Roanoke says I saw the *glory* then that means — then *he* thinks — then I — maybe I'm one of the Saved!"

"Course you are, who could ever doubt it!"

"I" — she glanced dubiously into Tot's dark, aging eyes — "I had my doubts! Let me get up from here. I'm all right. What is — where am I?"

"Why you're in my daughter's house, Miss Minnie. We brought you here in the Ford when you had that spell."

"Yes'm," said George, who spoke as little as possible.

"Why," said Minnie, looking around her, shocked at what she saw, "it's . . . isn't it cozy!"

"Yes'm," said George.

The little house in which she found herself had thin, wooden, unplastered walls held up by a flimsy frame, as nearly as she could tell from the kerosene lamps here and there. There was a little open grate for burning coal. Feeling it her duty, she asked to "have a look at the house," immediately regretting it, and Tot — this was the way she had been brought up — had to smilingly agree to any request from this white lady. The open grate in this front room and a tiny wood-burning stove in the kitchen were the total sources of heat. It could get bitterly cold in the hills of West Virginia in the winter. There was a table in the kitchen with a piece of oilcloth over it, and two rickety chairs. There was a cupboard with a few plates and utensils. The third room, the bedroom, had a kind of blanketed mat on the floor for sleeping, and two penned-in little areas with mats, for babies apparently. Minnie knew that Tot's daughter, Youranie, had married a miner and that they had two babies. "Where are they?" she asked.

"Oh, they went to the neighbors' when we came with you. Figure too many people might be bad when you come around."

There was an odor of something musky and burned out, of oldness, immobility, of settled-in-until-death, in this frail little dwelling.

"Let's go back to the Castle now, Miss Minnie."

"Yes, yes, let's go back."

Her head full of salvation or damnation when she awoke from her faint, Minnie now saw around her what seemed to her to be damnation on earth. And if this was earthly damnation, then God knew she was one of the Saved here on earth. What was it the Bible said? It is easier for a camel to pass through the eye of a needle than a rich man (or woman, maybe even more) to enter into the Kingdom of Heaven. Mightn't that mean that the roles of saved and damned here on earth might be reversed in the hereafter?

Then followed a strange ride out of Bennettown Hollow, jouncing along the dirt road with the leaning, rustling, gigantic profiles of the overhanging trees, the uncertain lamps of the car picking out the bumps and ridges and the occasional scurrying game flushed by the unaccustomed light. There was of course no public illumination in the Hollow, and few motorcars came this way.

And the long, winding, uphill-and-downhill journey back to Middleburg and to Catherwood Castle now seemed to Minnie like a journey from the Underworld to the Enchanted Castle, and her own bedroom, with its shining mirrors and solid mahogany, the great bed with its marvelous sheets woven by nuns in Belgium, all of it embraced her with its reassurance, its safety, and, so it seemed, its permanence. And at the same time the vast bed reproached her, or made her bitterly reproach herself. Look at what *they* slept on! Pallets on the floor! And in the *winter*, what must it be like!

She circled the second-floor gallery to look in on sleeping Lyle. All she could see was a tuft of red hair showing above the white sheet on the white pillowcase. With only the light from the outside to illuminate it the room's cavernousness was emphasized, the fireplace, the casement windows, the hobbyhorse on the expanse of floor, the little figure lost in the great bed with its high bedposts. Two small bedroom slippers were on the floor next to it. His blue flannel bathrobe was flung across the foot of the bed. She could hear his faint, regular breathing.

Of course it was absurd for her to get so stirred up by this mountain preacher. She must get hold of herself, for her little boy's sake. It was absurd: Saved or not Saved. And yet . . . listening to his faint, innocent, breathing, she asked herself: What if she wasn't?

II.

Minnie did not tell Clarkson at once about Reverend Roanoke, for the very simple reason that she had not learned whether or not she was among the Saved. And if she was not, then of course she would never tell him, for telling would amount to going up to her husband and blurting: "You're married to a devil!"

Minnie knew that when she at last confronted the question of whether or not she was Saved in communion with Reverend Roanoke that she would be able to tell by his — his aura whether he was a charlatan or not. She would trust her woman's intuition as to that. She *thought* he seemed genuine, there in the little barn-church (What a good omen: where else had Christ been born but in a barn!), but then he had been on display, frankly performing; he might be just a very clever religious performer. But, face to face with her alone, probing the most crucial question she had ever unearthed in this life, in those moments she knew she would know.

And if he was a genuine messenger of the truth, and of her fate, then, well, her life by definition would never be the same. She prayed, how she prayed by herself in her bedroom alone these days.

And then, taking every shred of courage and willpower she possessed, she asked Tot to arrange a meeting alone with Reverend Roanoke.

"How is it done, Tot, how does he — tell me, find out and tell me?"

"You pray together, you go down on your knees and pray —"

"In his church."

"Don't matter where. Any room will do."

"Do you know where I would like to pray together with him then?"

"Where's that?"

"In your daughter's little house."

"There? Whyever there?"

"Just . . . because. Sometime when it's not inconvenient. Maybe in the afternoon while her husband's in the mine and she's got the children out playing."

Tot's eyes swung slowly to Minnie's exalted face. "That's all right then, Miss Minnie. When? What day?"

Minnie drew a breath. Reverend Roanoke was genuine or he was a fake. He could or he couldn't tell her whether she was Saved. She would or she would not believe what he said. The suspense of these indecisions was telling on her. "Soon. The soonest that it's possible," she said.

The day chosen was the following Saturday. It dawned with an overcast, threatening sky. Despite that, Minnie insisted on going ahead.

As she was going out the side door to the car Lyle came running toward her from the barn. For an illuminating, possessed instant she saw him as though caught by a photograph, framed, objectified: this little boy, the one who slept in that huge bed, the only heir to all the Clarkson coal mines. "Lyle," she called impulsively, "go in the house and put on your raincoat and cap. And some galoshes. We're going for a ride in the country!"

"We are!" Getting dressed as ordered, he joined her in the high back seat of the rickety car, with Tot and George somewhat lower in the front seat.

"Where're we going?" asked Lyle.

"We're going down to Youranie's house. You remember her, Aunt Tot's girl? Works for us sometimes?"

"Um-hum."

Noting that this did not particularly excite him Minnie added, "And we're going to see a coal mine."

"Up *close?*" asked Lyle, eyes upon her.

"Up pretty close."

"Can we go in?"

"Not today. They don't let ladies like me in coal mines."

"Somebody else could go with me. George."

"Ask Daddy to take you in someday."

With George at the wheel they rattled along the road to Bennettown. As they turned up the Hollow the sheer shabbiness and dirt, the scabby, paintless shacks, bits of tin used to patch a hole here and there, loose chickens, pigs, the shacks or cabins or cottages, whatever name they might be called, these tiny houses straggling every which way up the steep hillsides, all of it closed Minnie over in its bleakness. The overcast sky deepened the gloom.

The little car chugged on up the Hollow, past the Church of the Last Judgment, and on to a point on the inside of the hill which overlooked the center of Bennettown.

Here and there were public pumps where everyone came for water.

And that, Minnie surmised, with the little clapboard nondenominational church and the little school and a little recreation hall, was every last thing there was in Bennettown, except of course the mine, which growled and rattled away at the far end of the town, where the mouth of the mine could be seen, a twelve- by twelve-foot cement-lined hole in the hill, narrow rails coming out of it along which mules pulled the small mine cars to the tipple, a three-story, metal-walled, frail-looking structure, where their coal was emptied out, sorted, and dropped into railroad cars. "Good times," observed George. "Mine workin' on Saturday."

This steep-walled valley must have been very pretty, even beautiful, before the coming of the mine, with its rich foliage, tall trees, the mountain stream, full of every kind of waste now, running clean and clear. What a pity.

And then she caught herself. Who am I to say that! Why, for all I know, Clarkson owns this mine. I never thought to ask him. "Tot, whose mine is this?"

"Why, it's yours, it's Mr. Catherwood's. Didn't you know that?" And she laughed eagerly.

They made their way on foot down over the dirt to the back, uphill door of Youranie's house. In daylight it looked far more forlorn than at night. It had once been green but the paint had nearly all peeled off to leave it a woebegone gray. All Minnie could think of when she looked at it was that it had the flimsy structure of a matchbox. And then the bits of furniture, the mat beds, the oilcloth, the pathetic dishes. Lyle looked wide-eyed about him.

Taking his hand she went into the front room and sat down on the couch where she had come out of her faint on the first visit. Tot said, "I'm goin' to see my daughter and grandchildren down at the playground. Reverend Roanoke will be here directly. Come on, George. You want to go to the playground, Lylie?"

He sprang up to join her. For one instant Minnie's reflex was to intervene. Then she thought again. Lyle was six. In a year or two he would separate himself from playing with black children. The town, Middleburg, would separate them. The colored children would separate themselves from *him*. That was just the way it always happened. "Try not to fall down," she said.

This artificial barrier between white and colored is wrong and terrible, she thought. And I'll bet I'm the only white person in Middleburg who thinks so.

Minnie went to the window to watch them go, and to see the playground. It was at the bottom of the hill, a cinder yard with two swings and a seesaw.

After a while Reverend Roanoke strode through the front door. He was dressed just like any other clergyman, black suit, reversed collar.

She sat down on the couch again and he pulled up a chair and sat facing her, his broad, strong face in front of hers. Then he began describing to her what being Saved meant, that it meant the end of all the troubles of this world, all the worries, all the fears, all the sicknesses and the losses. Eternal beauty, flowers, fountains, the music you loved, and all the people you loved eternally with you, eternally happy, eternally loving you, all strife gone, misunderstanding, failure, disappointment, all, all gone . . . gone, and you and everything you loved eternally happy in this beautiful garden.

Then he told her what being Damned meant, fire yes, oh yes, fire, but the torment, torment, *torment* of seeing what you loved most, your children, your husband, your mother, your dog, all of them, *all* tortured and tormented *forever* before your eyes as punishment for *your* sins. All eternity, always, your torment and *theirs*. Minnie had begun to pant and quiver.

"Oh and how do you *know* that you are Saved?" she burst out. "How do you know?"

"Together," he said in his deep voice, "we will discover. Pray with me."

And then he began a long prayer Minnie had never heard, and she tried to mumble along with him when she could guess the next words, and the awful conviction stole over her that he *was* a true messenger, he was *not* a charlatan in any way whatever, and he *could* tell her! Oh God, what would it be!

"Amen," he intoned. Then for a long time he sat still and motionless, his eyes closed. He took her hands and held them between his. How large and warm his were, strong but somehow almost soft too. Minnie waited in an agony, breathless, knowing that if the wrong verdict were rendered she would fall dead there on the floor of the cabin.

At last he opened his black eyes and beheld hers. He stared unblinkingly into her eyes. Mortified, shocked, spellbound, Minnie, feeling in a part of her mind that she was being raped, nevertheless desperately returned his stare.

"Sister," he intoned, "I see you. I know you now. I see into your soul, I see. It is my gift from the Almighty Jehovah. It is my gift! I see you, into your soul! I see! It is effulgent, it is radiant! It is . . . glowing with the glory of God! It is beauty! All beauty! Glowing and radiant! You, Sister, you are Saved!"

"Oh my God oh thank God oh my oh thank God oh," Minnie mumbled, overcome, terrors exorcised, all the unspeakable visions of herself, devil, bearing and raising Lyle vanished, unimaginable horrors driven out and into extinction — Saved.

From the depths of her relief it penetrated to Minnie that outside the house it had begun to rain rather hard. Rising from the sofa, feeling suffused with a new power, a new certainty in herself, she moved to the window, Tot, George, Youranie and the children were milling around uncertainly in the dirt track, now rapidly turning to mud, outside the house. Minnie waved for them to come in. They entered, Tot and her family greeting Reverend Roanoke with subdued, profound respect.

She started to present Lyle to Reverend Roanoke, then stopped; she started to present Reverend Roanoke to Lyle, stopped again, thinking how ridiculous that was, humbly presenting this Messenger of God to a six-year-old because the Messenger had darker skin. A colored man with prestige: the Middleburg system of life simply had no place for him. It was all bad and absurd. Finally, she said flatly, "Reverend Roanoke, you haven't met my son, Lyle." Lyle cocked an eye at him with great interest; Reverend Roanoke looked down at the boy with smiling surmise. In some unfathomable way this tiny encounter produced a standoff, Minnie sensed.

George, Tot and her family stood in a respectful semi-circle before Reverend Roanoke. It was the first time colored people in Minnie's presence had shown more respect for one of their own than for her. She glimpsed then a different order of things, that among themselves, the colored had their own standards and hierarchies and values, and a second thought flowed from that: what they show us is just a performance. *This* is their life. Once that struck her the absurdity of thinking it could have been any other way immediately followed.

Well, she thought, sustained by her newfound certainty in being Saved, able to entertain this thought with some equanimity, I hope Tot's show of devotion to me isn't *all* show. I know it isn't. I'm sure it isn't.

But here, in her family and in her religion, here of course is where Tot's real life is, real devotion is. I'm just a side dish, a necessity, but a side dish.

Then as she looked at this rather tall, lean, somewhat bent gray-haired woman in her one Sunday hat and her plain gray dress, whom she had known and taken for granted for so long, she saw that Tot had far more to her, was much more complicated, than ever she had dreamed. She was a *woman*, thought Minnie, an older woman toward the end of a full and difficult and in some ways rich life. My Lord, she reflected, I sure have been living in a little cocoon of my own.

"We had better get on our way," said Minnie. "This rain isn't going to do that road in here any good."

There was silence and then for once George spoke. "Miss Minnie, can't drive no car on that road when it rains. All mud. We get stuck good if we try."

She blinked and clutched her net reticule. "Then what'll we do?"

"Have to stay here, Miss Minnie. Till it stop. Maybe a hour or so after, maybe we can try goin' on down it."

"My stars. Clarkson."

"Now Miss Minnie." Tot moved over to her. "You sit right down on the sofa, and I'll fix you and Reverend Roanoke a nice cup of coffee" — an uncertain glance at Youranie to see if there was any coffee — "yes, some nice hot coffee."

"Sister Antoinette," said the Reverend, "thank you, but I have other calls to make, other work. It doesn't stop for the rain."

That was how Minnie learned Tot's real name.

Turning to Minnie, Reverend Roanoke once again and with complete naturalness took both her hands between his, and said in his fine voice, "Sister, welcome, welcome to the Saved."

Minnie felt tears crowding into her eyes. "Oh Reverend, I — you must let me do . . . give . . . some endowment to your wonderful church!"

"If your heart so moves you, Sister."

"It — it *does*."

Her reticule was bare of anything except handkerchief, cologne, smelling salts. But she was bound that she would give generously to the Church of the Last Judgment.

He went out into the rain, which had transformed the bare, grassless, treeless, plantless slope into a bank of mud. Minnie then became aware that not only were the roads not paved, but there were no sidewalks, nor any sewers. The water flooded down and pushed the mud into new shapes and gullies. She could hear it rippling underneath the house, which was set on wooden posts. There was a wind with the rain and sometimes it blew the stench from the outhouse into the room. Surreptitiously, Minnie had recourse to the bottle of smelling salts concealed in her handkerchief.

Youranie, a thin, open-faced image of her mother, wearing a long, shapeless calico dress, put a bucket outside the back door. "Got to wash the baby," she said, flashing a warm smile at Minnie, which showed her neglected teeth. "This way I don't have to go all the way to the pump and back. The Lord provides!"

"That's because Reverend Roanoke was in this house," commented Tot.

Minnie reflected grumpily that the rain was certainly no blessing to her, and then she thought: maybe it is, maybe it is.

But Clarkson! Coming home to find her, Tot, Lyle and George missing! There was the maid Thomasina, but they had not told her of their plans. She must get a message to him, and so George was sent off to the mine, which possessed the only telephone in Bennettown.

"Call my husband's office," said Minnie, "will you, George, the number's nine-three, and say that we drove out into the country to see the foliage —" Why not in the big safe Packard then? Why lie? "I mean, we drove out into the country for . . . a . . . special blessing, yes, that's it, for a special blessing, and that we are very safe in Bennettown but caught in the rain. We'll come back soon as the road's clear. At home there's some ham and potato salad in the icebox — there is, isn't there, Tot? Yes. He's to eat that and not to worry about us at all."

Once Youranie's bucket was full she put it to warm over the stove. Then she set it down on the floor of the kitchen and replaced it on the stove with a bigger tub of water. Lyle tried to help her move them. Kneeling, she began washing her baby. Tot dandled the older one on her knee. This little boy, about three years old, seemed restless. "Give him a toy," said Minnie. Tot smiled, and went on dandling the child. Minnie then had a sad little shock: there wasn't any toy.

George came back, looking flustered. "Mr. Catherwood, he's comin' out here. Bringin' one of his big trucks! He says we got to stay put and not get into that Model T. Miss Minnie, he says you go to the superintendent's house right away."

"I'm not going to walk anywhere in all that mud . . . that is . . . if —"

"Stay here!" chorused Youranie and Tot.

"Your husband will be coming home."

That triggered a complicated set of feelings and reactions flickering through the room, and then Youranie said, "You sure is welcome to stay here, Miss Minnie, both from me and from James."

"That's sure," said Tot with decision.

"Then I'll stay here," said Minnie.

"The superintendent's comin' up right now."

"Go tell him not to do that. I'm fine right here."

Minnie took out her hat pin and removed her big white hat, putting it on the sofa next to her gloves. She loosened her boots. She thought about doing the same to her corset but decided against it. I know, she thought. I'll read to these children. Lyle always loved that. "Maybe I can help out with the children after their bath. I'll read something to them."

A pause, and then Tot said quickly, "Tell them a story. They like that better'n reading."

Another blunder, Minnie realized again too late: there was no book.

As she now had time to sit and absorb her surroundings,

Minnie found the bleakness of this little house becoming overpowering, perched on its posts above the river of mud, with stench and smoke swirling around it, the grit from the coal dust everywhere, everywhere you sat, on everything you touched, resisting, she was sure, the most ferocious housecleaning. She thought she could feel it getting into her teeth. In Middleburg it presented a certain problem, but this was unbelievable.

Then the great whistle at the tipple blew; quitting time. With the children bathed, Youranie was preparing the much bigger tub in the kitchen for her husband. "Sure do like this rain, savin' me goin' to the pump so much."

A half hour later James trudged up to the back door and removed his muddy boots. Then he stepped into the kitchen. The back door and part of the kitchen were visible from where Minnie sat in the front room and she saw him come in, a figure of blackness and grime from head to foot. He moved into the part of the kitchen out of sight where the tub was; there was murmuring between him and Youranie and she draped the piece of oilcloth from the table over the opening between the two rooms. There was a prolonged washing session, and then at last James came into the front room.

To her surprise Minnie saw that he was not hulking, as she had assumed all miners would have to be to do such work. He was about five feet eight inches, and weighed perhaps a hundred and fifty pounds. Wiry. He was wearing some black pants and a gray shirt. He was as clean as a prolonged scrub in the tub could make him, but bits of grime clung tenaciously to tiny corners and crevices here and there. Once they start to mine, Minnie wondered, are coal miners ever again able to get themselves clean?

She then heard herself mentioning that. "Well, you did have a good bath. That dirt from the mines must be right hard to get off."

James looked a little startled. "Oh that not dirt, ma'am. That's just dust from the work. Outside there, on the ground, *that's* dirt!"

Yes, I see, said Minnie to herself.

James, although she understood he was in his middle twenties, had still the look of the boy somewhere about him, in his eyes it was, a roundness to the eyes, slightly amazed still by life and what he saw in it.

He and Lyle greeted each other and he handed the boy his mining hat with the lamp on it. Lyle sat down on the floor and began to study it.

"I thought all miners were great big tall men," Minnie remarked with a laugh.

"It's better this way, ma'am," he answered. "Means I don't have to stoop over so far."

"You mean when you're shoveling the coal?"

"That, and I mean standin' up."

"Standing up?"

"Yes'm. In the mine. Roof's low in there, so I don't have to bend over as far as a lot of them fellows."

"You can't — it isn't high enough to stand up in?"

"No'm."

"Anywhere?"

"Oh. Few places. Not where we works."

"You can't stand up straight all day," Minnie pursued, beginning to feel dazed by the picture forming in her mind.

"No'm."

"That's why his back," said Youranie, "give him the misery so much. I rub it, got some stuff I *rub* it with, but it still give him the misery a lot."

Youranie and Tot then went to work in the kitchen, sending George on borrowing errands to the neighbors' and to buy extra supplies with scrip at the company store.

"What's scrip?" inquired Minnie.

"They give 'em that," answered Tot dryly, "instead of money."

"But what *is* it?"

"It's coupons. You use it at the company store for food and stuff."

"But why don't they pay in money?"

Shrugs.

"Can you spend it anywhere else, in Middleburg, for instance?"

"Oh no," said Youranie. "But then we hardly ever get up to Middleburg. Shucks," she chuckled, "gettin' as far as Jessie Mae's a big event for us." Jessie Mae was the hamlet where they had turned off the brick road to take the dirt road up the Hollow to Bennettown.

Truly a sealed world, Bennettown straggled up the hills on the two sides of its Hollow, the mine mouth gaped at the head of the Hollow, there was the church, the school, the "playground," the recreation hall, the company store, and that, in a material sense, was everything in the world there was for these people, except their shanties and the mine. Middleburg was much too inaccessible to visit except on the rarest occasions, and places like Jessie Mae had even less to offer than Bennettown. They had no books, no newspapers or magazines, no Victrola, no picture show. Did anyone here play a guitar, a harmonica; could anyone sing?

Youranie and Tot were working in the kitchen preparing what was sure to be a very atypical supper. Minnie sat on the sofa, and James had been standing in the middle of the little room talking to her. Why didn't he sit down? Did she have to ask him to? Here?

"I'll bet that's your chair. The one with the arms there."

"Yes'm, that's it!" he exclaimed, crossing over to sit down on it.

There was an uncomfortable silence, Minnie's shyness beginning to creep over her again, and then James asked Lyle with a grin, "You want to be a miner when you grow up?" (How they love our *children*, Minnie reflected. It's so obvious why: not allowed to love us.)

"Oh yeah," said Lyle, sinking his head drolly into the hat (fleas, diseases! shot into Minnie's brain: she drove them sternly out). Both Minnie and James laughed so hard at the sight of him that the others from the kitchen came to have a look. Tot began to laugh, and Minnie had never seen her laugh so hard.

Then James said, "You need more'un that hat. You got to have a pick and shovel, and some dynamite!"

"Some what?"

"Dynamite. To blow the coal loose. You know. Boom!"

"Goll-ee." Lyle blinked up at him, then at his mother. "What if the roof falls in?"

There was a short silence, and then James murmured, "Well, lotta times you got that. Maybe you better be a train engineer. Them railroad tunnels, they don't fall in so much." He laughed in a we'll-drop-the-subject way, and then Youranie came out of the kitchen carrying a steaming bowl of stew into the room. "You just eat this where you are, Miss Minnie," she said, preparing to serve her on the couch. Apparently she was going to eat and they were going to serve.

"I *will* not," she said, "not until we all sit down together." They eyed her uncertainly. "We will all sit down together, and ask the Lord's blessing on what I can smell is going to be delicious, and then we'll all eat it together like . . ." ("white people" was shockingly on the tip of her tongue, for that was the most everyday of Middleburg phrases, "We're going to do so-and-so like white people") "like . . . like . . . it's a party! Well, it is a party, isn't it? And Youranie, we just invited ourselves in and made you give a party. My, what a delicious smell."

Minnie began to feel that she had never had this much

possession of herself in her life before, saying and doing what she really felt. Before today, she might have vapidly let them all serve her, because of her own shyness and lack of confidence, suffering through every mouthful of the artificial, inhuman meal that would have been.

They sat around a little table in the kitchen, the children sleeping in the pen in the corner, Lyle on a stool next to her. Minnie, knowing that no one else would make any requests, asked Tot to bless the food, and then from her chipped plate with her tin spoon she ate some tasty meat and vegetables and gravy and dumpling stew.

They were almost finished, dusk was gathering, when George saw the big truck stop on the road above the house, and Clarkson Catherwood with two men climb out of it.

As Minnie made her departure with thanks and good-byes she thought: I believe I've found something, something really worthwhile, that I can do.

Could that be what being Saved means?

three

I.

BACK at the Castle, Minnie did a very uncharacteristic thing: she carved that day's date, July 27, 1910, into the molding of the woodwork next to her dressing table. She made the figures very small, and since a curtain fell over them they remained unseen by anyone else. But she knew they were there, and to her they had, or she hoped they would come to have, as much significance as July 4, 1776, had for the whole country.

But everyone else saw a difference in her for the simple reason that on July 28, 1910, Minnie Catherwood went shopping, and when her new clothes arrived the following week she put on a gown for dinner as though breaking out a new flag. It was a violet lace dinner dress, with an undersheath of violet silk, and with her rich chestnut hair set off with a purple silk band and a brooch, she fairly stunned this household which could not remember seeing her in anything except white. Now that she felt pure inside, Minnie concluded that the virginal white she had affected was a superficial symbol she could safely discard.

"You never mentioned the Bennettown Mine," she said to

Clarkson down the length of the crystal-and-silver-laden dinner table. "I didn't know you owned it."

"Sure I did," he said, "lots of times. Bennettown's what we call Number Three."

"Number Three? Oh, of course, I've heard you speak of it. Isn't that the one you call the 'weak sister' of the Clarkson Coal Company?"

"That's it," he said resignedly.

"Why do you call it that?"

"Well . . . we bought it from Abner Bennett back in o-two and it never was right. It's damp and then it's dry, we got some gas in there, those rickety houses, no drainage, no streets, the whole thing needs to be taken in hand, have some money spent on it, fixed up. Trouble is, Number Three's right on the edge of being unprofitable; the first time business drops off that's the one I close first. *So*, it's not the place to spend money fixing up."

"Close it? Then what happens to the miners . . . and their families?"

"Go to work someplace else."

"Yes, but is there, will there be work someplace else? If business has dropped off —"

"It all sorts itself out."

"None of these people has any savings, I'm sure. How could they have? Working only two-thirds of the time. What will they *do?*"

"They'll manage. Always have. There's always charities, the churches . . ."

Minnie knew about the organized charities, and she knew about the churches, just as she knew what a drop in the bucket was.

"Clarkson," Minnie began, having planned to wait until after dinner but impulsively deciding to go ahead in front of Lyle. After all, at six, he could begin to understand something of this, and she wanted him to understand, "I want to do something for Bennettown."

"What, for instance?" he asked guardedly.

"Well, first of all that playground —"

"What playground?"

"There's a sort of playground there," she answered, succeeding in eliminating almost completely a note of exasperation in her voice, "and it's really a disgrace. It's gravel! Children are *always* falling down in playgrounds, and they're bound to hurt themselves on gravel!"

"The kids out there, they play in the woods, go fishing, they've got all kinds of nature all around."

"Not fishing in that creek, I wager. Why, it's *orange* in color. Can't be a fish in there."

"Over the hill. Down the valley."

"And I'd like to do a . . . well, for instance, a milk distribution. Children always need lots of good milk, and it's obvious they don't get that in Bennettown."

"Now Min."

It was a tolerant, indulgent little expression of his, designed to soothe her since the first time they met, and it had almost always succeeded. Now she felt herself expanding in anger at the sound of it: "Now Min" indeed: it was the tone you would take with a child, a pet dog, a pat on the head, "Now Min, be a good girl, atta girl. Sit."

"Now Clarkie," she replied on a certain rising inflection, "you're far too busy to think of everything about your mines, and your miners' families. Why don't you, why can't I . . . help you just a little in this? Some soil for the playground . . . milk . . ."

"We'll see," he said, "we'll see," and Minnie felt another stab of anger on hearing this familiar phrase, which both she and Clarkson used so often with Lyle, its meaning being roughly, "You'll forget about this by tomorrow and be possessed by some other equally trivial notion."

[46]

Well, a decent playground and good nourishing milk were not trivial notions and she was not going to forget about them. As she gazed down the table past the bowl of fresh fruit, the silver tray with the linen napkin filled with biscuits, the pot of pure honey, the rich butter, the steaming bowl of fresh vegetables, to the huge, juicy roast leg of lamb set before Clarkson, she felt an emotion completely new to her in her life in Middleburg and in the Castle: she felt that the Catherwoods were endangered.

Minnie had not had the faintest inkling before of the emotion which now began to seep through her. There is, she sensed apprehensively, something dangerous in all this plenty we live amidst. It was not any possible selfishness or "social injustice" present in it, clear as those might be, it was . . . danger. There was a threat implicit in the silver and crystal, even in Tot and George, and in Thomasina who served at table, there was something dangerous, threatening.

She looked at brightly freckled red-headed Lylie and she almost shivered: it was he somehow who might be menaced, a little boy, herself and Clarkson too, but even more, this little boy who had nothing whatever to do with bringing about the danger. She could not free herself from this pervasive sense of alarm: this way of life is leading us into terribly real danger.

I must do something. Playgrounds? Milk? More drops in the bucket. Something fundamental must be done. And by me! But what? What?

II.

Clarkson of course knew that something new was at work inside Minnie's mind, and being devoted to her he set out to find what that was, to isolate it, and to destroy it.

Minnie must never be unduly disturbed again, the doctor had told Clarkson after the birth of Lyle. Minnie had had a brief interlude of amnesia at that time, and the doctor had suggested to Clarkson it would be "very advisable and prudent" for her to bear no more children. Sexual intercourse, not love and devotion, had then ceased between Minnie and Clarkson.

In the past he had thought to encourage her in outside interests, to get her out of the house, involved in some community activity, but now that that seemed to be coming to pass, Clarkson found that it was the other, the original Minnie to whom he was devoted, precisely that helpless, drifting, sheet-white wraith, that Episcopalian product of a Catholic convent education whom he had met and married, lackadaisical, moody, flighty, adrift, vague, yearning, parched, tentative Min.

And instead of this lovely, lost lady, another all in violet had come rather purposefully to the dinner table that night and begun poking her finger into how the miners lived in Bennettown! Something had gotten into her all right and Clarkson set out to discover what it was.

It was typical of him that he did not lead Minnie into the library after dinner and simply ask her. Had he done so she would simply have told him all about Reverend Roanoke and the Church of the Last Judgment and her being Saved, and about Youranie and James and their two babies and the sad little lives they were condemned to live in the sad little house in the mud. Minnie was living in a purity of spirit now and would have forthrightly laid any and every bit of information of her inner life out before Clarkson like a Sunday buffet supper.

But he didn't ask her. He asked around Bennettown instead. And he didn't even remark on her wearing a color instead of white for the first time in ten years except to say as she came into the dining room, "Oh. That's new isn't it?

[48]

Pretty dress." To do more, he calculated, would have shown his hand too soon.

To Tot, kneading some dough in the kitchen, "her" kitchen as it was always referred to, Clarkson said, "Tell your Reverend . . . Roanoke, is it? . . . your Reverend Roanoke to come and see me at my office. Wednesday will do, around three in the afternoon."

Tot's face became guarded; it was defensive and fearful and defiant and respectful all at once.

"Thought I'd make some kind of a contribution to what he's doing," Clarkson added.

Her face then eased out of all these tensions into a beaming smile. "Oh I know he'll be real —"

"And Aunt Tot, this is an interest I'm taking which is strictly confidential, just between you and me and him." Tot's aging eyes flickered over his face before returning to the dough. "We all know we have to keep Miss Minnie calm," he added.

"Oh we know *that* all right."

"Don't want her getting upset or having any kind of spell."

"No, sir."

"Have to watch that."

"Yes, sir, we do."

"So, what I'm saying is, any dealings I have with this Reverend Roanoke are to be confidential."

"Oh yes, that's right, Mr. Clarkson."

He then went out of her kitchen and Tot was left to reflect that a gift of money by Mr. Clarkson to Reverend Roanoke was the last thing in the world to bring on a spell or any other kind of misery to Miss Minnie. It would instead like to set her dancing in the streets. But of course Tot would no more question Mr. Clarkson's reasons to his face than she would slap little Lylie. She continued kneading the dough, uneasily, and tried to visualize Reverend Roanoke in Mr. Clarkson's office.

Reverend Roanoke entered the six-story First National Bank Building at two-fifty on Wednesday afternoon. The Clarkson Coal Company's executive offices occupied the three top floors. He exchanged greetings with Sylvester, the elevator operator, and went up to the fourth floor.

Through the frosted-glass door Reverend Roanoke went into the bustling outer office, where about twenty men and a sprinkling of women were filing, typewriting, or studying pieces of paper.

This Negro in his black suit and hat and clerical collar created a certain suspension of activity upon entering. The typewriting slackened, stopped. The woman at the first desk, whom he approached hat in hand, said that Mr. Catherwood was expecting him. Then she added, after some hesitation, would he care to sit down in one of the chairs opposite her desk?

Reverend Roanoke did so, placing his hat on his knee, and began looking genially about him. The typewriters stutteringly resumed.

After about ten minutes the lady told him to cross this outer room to the corner office where Mr. Catherwood would see him now.

Reverend Roanoke entered a rather large square room. It was dominated by big dark wooden furniture; there were shelves of thick books, brown and white framed photographs of coal tipples and groups of men. Two long windows on each of the two outer walls gave a sweeping view of Middleburg — town, bridges, railroad, river. It seemed that the man who presided in this office was in a position to dominate all of them. To be sure, one block up the street, out of sight of these windows, rose the Clifton Building, two stories taller than the First National Bank Building, and from there the Clifton brothers could dominate everything visible including this building as well.

Clarkson, in stiff collar and tie and gray suit, relaxed in

his swivel chair behind the heavy desk, his back to the view.

"Hello there, how are you? Have a seat," he said in an energetic voice.

Reverend Roanoke said, "How do you do, Mr. Catherwood," and sat down in the wooden chair on the other side of the desk, once again placing his hat on his knee.

"Well," resumed Clarkson, rubbing his hands together, "let me come right to the point."

"Good."

Clarkson glanced quickly at his face, slightly thrown off stride by Roanoke's rejoinder. Then he went on, "My wife has taken an interest in your — what you do down in Bennettown, very interested she is, and knowing as I do something about how religion works, churches I mean, the way churches work, operate, I felt as the member of the family who takes care of the accounts I ought to make a — some kind of a contribution to your — church."

"That would be most kind of you, indeed, Mr. Catherwood."

"And I —"

"May I just add, sir, in accepting with all gratitude whatever you see fit to donate to carrying on this work, that Mrs. Catherwood is a truly Saved spirit. To have seen that and prayed with her is enrichment indeed. Now, if in addition, you, acting for her, make a material contribution as well, then I am truly rewarded."

There was a silence while Clarkson, jaw set, contemplated him. Then he said, "Mrs. Catherwood has always felt drawn to all kinds of religions. We're Episcopalians, but my wife went to a Catholic convent school because her family thought they got better training there. More discipline. She's active in our church here, Christ Church. And now your — church. It is, that's the other matter, the building you use in Bennettown, that building happens to be on land belonging to the Clarkson Coal Company."

[51]

"Is *that* so!" Reverend Roanoke looked surprised but not perturbed.

"Yes. Somebody put up that barn there years ago and nobody bothered about it at the time. Now, however, I have some plans for that piece of land. More miners' houses. Expansion. We're going to do more with Number Three, Bennettown. So we'll have to repossess the barn you've been conducting your services in. Tear it down."

"I see."

There was another silence and then Clarkson said, "You are, I understand, a kind of traveling minister, isn't that so? Preaching for a while in one place and then moving on to another."

"That is so, yes. I had thought," he went on in a quiet tone, "that perhaps in Bennettown I had found a place in which I might, you might say, rest. That's what I was beginning to think. But I see, I see now, that that is not to be."

Clarkson was writing out a check.

"Perhaps," Reverend Roanoke went on, "it is God's will. Perhaps it is."

In any case it was clear that this was Clarkson Catherwood's will, and Clarkson Catherwood and four other men were as close to godliness in terms of sovereign power as one could get in Middleburg. Reverend Roanoke's past experiences had made clear to him that such powerful forces could not be resisted. If they opposed him, as they sometimes had in the past, then he had to carry his work on elsewhere. He always stayed in the mountains, however, for there he felt at home, and he never crossed the Mason-Dixon Line into the North, although he had heard that colored people were treated better there. He could only work among people he knew in his bones. And now the good people he had gathered aound him in Bennettown would have to go on without him, and he without them.

Oh, if he could only *fight* once in a while, resist, defy. But

[52]

he had concluded that this was not God's way, not God's wish for him. It was not the way of a minister of God. And it was not the way of a colored man in the South, not yet it wasn't.

Clarkson handed him the check. There were a few parting words and then Reverend Roanoke left.

Two days later Tot responded to the bell ringing at the front door of the Castle at five o'clock in the afternoon. There stood Reverend Roanoke in his dignified clerical black.

"Greetings, Sister Antoinette. I've come for a farewell visit, to you, to Brother George, and to Sister Minnie."

Tot's face fell into a muddle of feelings, confusions she had never envisaged dealing with: religious supremacy versus white supremacy, the Word of God versus the Power of Caesar. To whom to render what? Here, at one and the same time, was the Messenger of Eternal Salvation deigning to pay a visit, and a colored man coming to the front door!

"Why Reverend! Why, won't you . . . should I . . . we . . . Miss M —"

"Thank you, Sister," he said, stepping into the house, entering the two-story octagonal front hall with its stained glass, its suit of armor, its inner gallery on the second floor.

"Who's that?" called down Minnie from above.

"It's Reverend Roanoke, Miss Minnie!"

"Oh," her voice floated down, "how *wonderful!* I'm just finishing with Lylie, and I'll be *right down!*"

Reverend Roanoke seated himself in one of the heraldic chairs next to the suit of armor. He motioned to Tot to sit down on the carved walnut chest next to him. Uncertainly, cautiously, she moved over and perched lightly on it, as though prepared at any moment to take flight.

They began talking of things of the spirit. After a few minutes Minnie came sailing down the curving stairway from the gallery above. Her hair was escaping from the bun in back, she was in a gray smock and house slippers, she was concealed by no veils or feathers or jewelry, a good-looking woman in her thirties at the end of a somewhat hectic, hard, and worrying day.

Her face shone as she came up to Reverend Roanoke and he clasped her two hands between his. "Let's go into the" — library, she started to say, a warm room for real human exchange, but then the image of Clarkson loomed up in her mind, it was his sanctum really — "sitting room, come on, Tot. Where's George? Let's have some tea," and she led Reverend Roanoke into the still little front parlor. This is the wrong room, she thought to herself. There is no right room, no room for salvation, in this house.

Minnie seated herself on a long, hard, horsehair sofa, and he sat down next to her.

"Sister Minnie, I'm going away," he said in his warm, resonant voice, looking into her eyes.

"Yes, I know," she said unhappily.

"You understand, don't you?"

"I — I don't know if I do." She gazed a little piteously at him. "I know that Clarkson . . . called on you, he said he made the contribution I wanted to make. Then he said you were leaving. I knew that . . . I found out that he owns the land where your church is."

"The church too!" exclaimed Reverend Roanoke good-naturedly. "But in the end, it is all the Lord's, it is all the Lord's, in the end. Mr. Catherwood is the steward for a while of this valuable land, with all its riches underneath. I am not leaving because someone is the steward of the land and of the humble little barn we use. We can meet anywhere. See? We meet here, in your Castle! We meet in Bennettown, in Sister Youranie's little house. Anywhere. We need no church. I leave because I can tell others, see into their souls and so illuminate them, that's all I do, the light is there, the small — but *eternal* — light of goodness, I turn the little knob and — flash! — all the light spreads through them, they glow with

[54]

their own salvation, which I've made them see, feel! Wasn't it so with you?"

"Oh yes, yes! It just flooded through me, my — my salvation saved me!"

"There, that's the way it is. And this I must now do for others, other luminous souls in our glorious Appalachian hills and valleys and mountaintops, the colored and the white people alike."

"Yes!"

"And Sister Minnie, one thing I never told you. In the end, at the Last Judgment, when we all rise and face our Maker, there are no whites or blacks or reds or browns, we are all gold, golden radiance. That's our true color within, that is the golden glow of our salvation, and before our Maker on the Last Day it stands revealed, the *same* color for one and for all, glorious gold, shining through."

"Oh yes."

There was a light rap on the door, and then Tot and George came in with the tea things. Minnie got everyone seated and served, trying hard to make this farewell as pleasant and happy as possible, but trembling inside, lest the departure of Reverend Roanoke would take away, suddenly or gradually, her newfound sense of salvation, of worth, of, yes, competence, and she might lapse again into that drifting aimless spirit she had been, combing her hair, drinking herself with her special tonic into an unreal world of cushioning but uneasy dreams.

They all sat sipping their tea, speaking of God and the Last Judgment and Tennessee and Bennettown and then there were footfalls in the hall outside. Clarkson opened the door and looked in. "Hello, dear," said Minnie.

Tot and George sprang to their feet. Reverend Roanoke also rose. Clarkson surveyed the scene, a formidable figure in his vested navy blue suit with high stiff collar, watch chain, all the symbols of business power, even his florid complexion.

Clarkson at first looked surprised at this tea-party-in-progress, but he was used to masking his reactions, and came smiling into the room.

"Well, teatime," he said agreeably. "Fix me a cup, will you, Aunt Tot?" He crossed the room and sat down on a stiff little chair.

"Dear," Minnie began, "Reverend Roanoke has come to say good-bye. He's leaving."

"*Is* he?" said Clarkson with interest.

"Tennessee is waiting," said Reverend Roanoke forthrightly.

"Oh how we shall miss you," murmured Minnie, "and the church."

"There is no more need for me here — well, let us say, not as much as there is down there in Tennessee, where I have never yet brought my message."

There was a silence, and then Minnie said, "Clarkson, how much money did you give Reverend Roanoke?"

Both men began to make demurring sounds — in this tense little moment Tot and George disappeared from the room — but Minnie persisted. "Two hundred dollars? Five hundred? How much? I think I have a right to know."

"It was a very generous —" began Reverend Roanoke.

"Five hundred dollars," said Clarkson.

Minnie sighed lightly, indicating that she found the sum at least adequate. She sensed, although she would not say it, that this sum had served both as a contribution and a bribe, and that Clarkson had wanted Reverend Roanoke gone. She sensed why too: he did not wish for her to continue in the new independence and competence which she had found.

Well. Reverend Roanoke was leaving, so Clarkson would have his wish there, although Minnie felt certain that the Reverend had been on the point of leaving anyhow, what with Tennessee waiting and all.

But she *was* going to continue in her new way of life, and Clarkson she hoped would eventually come to like it, see how much better it was.

But whether he did or not, she was going to continue.

four

I.

LIFE had entered a new phase in Catherwood Castle. Clarkson remained its lord and master of course, but Minnie for the first time took her place as its mistress. She found ways to be helpful in Bennettown and some of the other mining camps, her opium tonic and her drifting days forgotten.

Clarkson still did not like it. To himself he explained the change as Min's getting older; he found her somewhat less attractive than before. Maybe I'm getting older too, he conceded to himself.

But in any case he was far too busy to brood much about his domestic life. The big years of coal — 1909 to 1914 — were succeeded by the fantastic boom years of 1915, 1916, 1917, and 1918 — years of enormous growth and profits, those leading to and through the Great War.

The Great War, in addition to bringing a vast increase in demand for coal, had one other momentous effect in the coalfields.

Like a quiescent volcano it had remained for the most part

beneath the surface until now: the earthshaking latent anger of mine labor. There had been strikes and fights and shootings and deaths before the Great War, but after 1912 these had subsided, for the men and their leaders had recognized that there was a war coming and then a war in progress, and so the hundreds of thousands of miners toiled on in what many or most of them considered miserable conditions for drastically unfair wages while there was this war going on, and while the Cliftons and the Hayeses and the Catherwoods were, as any fool could see, rolling in prodigious new waves of wealth.

The coalfields, then, were quiescent and hugely productive during the war years.

Then came Armistice Day, November 11, 1918, and then came Strike Day, April 1, 1919, when 453,000 bituminous miners went out on strike for higher wages, and remained on strike, ranks unbroken, for six weeks, until forced to return to work by a federal court order.

To the coal operators, the massiveness of the walkout and the discipline of the miners were ominous warnings of the men's anger, and the power of their unity.

Middleburg was the place where the Catherwoods had flourished. Minnie's omen at dinner that night in 1910 that there was some danger, some force threatening the family, had not dimmed through the huge prosperity of the war. It had increased. And she knew in her heart that her fresh-milk funds and new playgrounds could do nothing to fend off what she felt was approaching. Terrible strikes? Physical violence? Bolshevik revolution? She could not have said. She was not an analytical woman; she did not read a great deal. But she sensed that this apprehension of hers was grounded in real danger, and that the danger to herself, to Clarkson and their child was growing. Ten years of ever higher profits had gone by, and she felt even more urgently that they were living beneath some menace equivalent to the chief menace the men lived with in the mines, that for the Catherwoods too some kind of cave-in threatened.

Then in April of 1919 there had been this vast and militant and disciplined strike of every organized coal miner in the country, and only a federal court had ended it. And how powerful were court orders, she wondered. How powerful would they be in the next strike? Shouldn't the miners have been treated better earlier? Shouldn't they be now, when it was perhaps still not too late?

II.

That first great miners' strike had ended in the middle of May 1919, leaving a smoky discontent, like a mine fire beneath the surface.

And then, one year later almost to the day, it burst again with guns pounding and blood spurting into the light of day.

Around Middleburg most of the miners had quietly and peaceably joined the United Mine Workers during the war. The operators there did not like it, but it had kept the industrial peace and the mines working.

In the southern part of the state, however, where some of them, including Clarkson Catherwood, also had interests, they joined with the southern operators in flatly and totally resisting the union. It was un-American, anti–free enterprise, tied their hands, usurped their rights, and was going to be blocked.

The courts had recently put a bludgeoning weapon into their hands in fighting unionization. This court decision ruled that a miner living in a house he rented from the company employing him was not like other citizens with the usual Anglo-Saxon rights of occupancy; he was instead a servant of the operator, living on the operator's premises, at the operator's pleasure. The miner, his family, and his possessions could be thrown out into the street anytime the operator so desired, and every southern operator desired and enforced this eviction whenever a miner tried to join, or advocated joining, the union.

To work for what they considered low wages in dangerous conditions was bad enough; to be denied a union was worse; to be evicted from house and home, with every stick of furniture into the street, aroused an atavistic rage throughout the southern fields which was not to be calmed by any possible court decision. This was life and death, and both sides knew it.

These evictions were carried out by the sheriff of the county and his deputies, or else by private detectives — known to the miners as "tin horns" — of the Baldwin-Felts Detective Agency. The miners had mortal grievances against both these groups of enforcers: the deputy sheriffs were very often paid employees of the coal companies, openly and unashamedly so although this was illegal in West Virginia, and the Baldwin-Felts detectives were a collection of ex-convicts, hoodlums, and other bruisers who carried out orders in a rough, ready, and ruthless fashion.

One spring day in 1920, twelve Baldwin-Felts detectives arrived in the small town of Matewan, Mingo County, in the extreme southwestern end of the state, to evict some miners and their families for pro-union activities. In a sultry, tinderbox atmosphere, they were walking along the main street from the railroad station when they were intercepted by Sid Hatfield, the chief of police. The force consisted of himself and one other man, Ed Chambers. Sid Hatfield was described by an acquaintance as "six feet tall in height, about one hundred sixty-five pounds, had strong shoulders, high cheekbones, a dark complexion, and a smile that would not come off." The mayor of the town, also a young man, was C. C.

Testerman. These three town officials and the twelve detectives, all fifteen of them very much armed, confronted each other on Matewan's main street, a typical sleepy southern block of two-story brick and wooden buildings, telephone poles, a few parked cars. Hatfield ordered the detectives out of town, and told them they could not carry out the evictions. One of the two detective leaders answered that Chief of Police Hatfield was obstructing the execution of the law and that he, the private detective, was going to arrest him. Who was the law in West Virginia at this time was a hazy question, depending not always on who wore the badge but on what power controlled the county. The mayor said that no such arrest could take place.

And then the shooting started. The first victim to fall was Mayor Testerman, mortally wounded. Next, a gun in each hand, Sid Hatfield shot in the head and instantly killed the two detective leaders. Then gunfire burst out all around the dusty street, and in the end seven detectives, the mayor, and two striking miners lay dead. One detective escaped by hiding in a large wastebasket and then swimming the Tug River into Kentucky. After that, according to witnesses, a drunken orgy seized Matewan, with the bodies of the dead detectives being robbed and mutilated.

Later some union supporters made a movie of their defender, *Smilin' Sid*, and exhibited it at union meetings.

Others, however, made Hatfield a villain of Iago-like complexity. For while Sid and Ed Chambers maintained that the action which set off the killings, the shooting of Mayor Testerman, had been done by one of the detectives, the surviving detectives claimed that Hatfield had himself shot the mayor in order to achieve a strictly private end: to marry pretty Jessie Testerman, the mayor's wife. And in fact, whoever shot the mayor, Sid Hatfield did marry Jessie Testerman soon afterward.

Smilin' Sid was indicted for murder in Mingo County. The

chief witness against him was a kin of his, Anderson Hatfield. One night when Anderson Hatfield was snoozing on the front porch of his hotel in Matewan a bullet whizzed out of somewhere and killed him.

Smilin' Sid, brought to trial soon after, was acquitted by a jury described as "terrified."

Within the confines of Mingo County, Sid Hatfield was safe. Neighboring McDowell County, however, was a stronghold of the mine owners and their hired men, the Baldwin-Felts detectives. Soon after his acquittal in Mingo County, Sid was indicted in McDowell County for shooting up a mining camp there. This was widely believed to be a trumped-up charge.

The "Matewan Massacre" had occurred on May 19, 1920. On August 1, 1921, Sid Hatfield and Ed Chambers, who had also been indicted in McDowell County for the mining camp shoot-up, inexplicably actually appeared at the county seat, the town of Welch, to answer the charge. Sid had at least taken the precaution of seeking, and receiving, assurances of his safety while in McDowell County from Governor Morgan of West Virginia and from County Sheriff Hatfield, the Hatfields being a very widespread family in that part of the state.

Accompanied by their wives, they arrived by train in Welch, and went to the hotel, with their lawyer, to get a room. None being available, they used the lawyer's room to prepare for the court appearance. This preparation, according to the testimony of both wives, including divesting themselves of their firearms.

The four of them then proceeded down the street to the courthouse, an imposing, ivy-covered building. As they began to mount the steps to the entrance they saw that ten Baldwin-Felts detectives were lounging about.

What happened next, just as at Matewan, was disputed afterward by witnesses. What is certain is that a great many

[63]

bullets began to fly, and at the end of it all the detectives were unhurt, so were the wives, and Sid Hatfield and Ed Chambers lay dead, drilled full of holes. The two dead men were searched a few minutes later and found to be holding guns. Two dicta of the Baldwin-Felts Detective Agency appear to have been fulfilled: "Kill 'em with one gun, hand 'em another" and "Nobody ever killed a Baldwin-Felts man and lived long to brag about it."

W. C. Mitchell, chief of police in Welch, said he saw Chambers shoot at a detective, and later he took a "warm gun with six empty chambers" out of the corpse's hand, and another gun from Hatfield's body. Whether anyone believed that Chambers and Hatfield had been able to fire and with what is a moot point.

McDowell County Sheriff Hatfield, who had guaranteed Sid's safety in Welch, had not been there that day. Instead he had been resting at Craig Healing Springs, Virginia. "I was greatly surprised when I heard of the unfortunate trouble which occurred in Welch . . . I understand that some want to know why I was not in McDowell County at that time." Having pointed out how "greatly surprised" he was, Sheriff Hatfield then added that he didn't believe his presence in Welch would have made much difference, and that part was easily believed.

Three of the detectives were tried in Welch for the murders by a jury described as "terrified," and, despite the overwhelming evidence of guilt, acquitted.

This was the mass of emotion and violence roiling over the coalfields three years after the end of the war. Although the "Matewan Massacre" had happened in the old Hatfield-McCoy feuding country and involved members of the Hatfield family, it was clearly not a question of another mountaineer shoot-out. The issue was whether a man could favor unionization and continue living in his rented home, and whether, since martial law prevailed, any kind of meeting or statement advocating unionization could be made in the southern fields.

The issue was no longer wages or hours or safety regulations or health or the right to strike, it was whether a man could instantly lose his home because he was said to have an opinion offensive to his landlord, and whether all attempts to form a union could be blocked by the law. These issues were viscerally arousing to the miners; they did not have to think about them — they knew. They would take any violent action necessary to oppose evictions and the gagging of all pro-union sentiment by the law.

The mine owners were equally determined that unionization would be resisted by any and every weapon at their command, most especially eviction and martial law. The irresistible force and the immovable object were about to meet head-on.

Some dramatic act had been necessary to set them against each other, and the shooting of Sid Hatfield and Ed Chambers had now provided it.

five

I.

MIDDLEBURG rested in a serene aura of peace that summer of 1921. The mortal enmities, the street murders, the terrified juries, were far away at the other end of the state. Such were the conditions of the roads and all the other tenuous links connecting northern and southern West Virginia that Matewan and Welch sometimes seemed as far away as Moscow and Petrograd. Bands of men obsessed with killing each other were down there. Here, all was peace and plenty.

Lyle Catherwood had completed his senior year at Greenbrier Military School, and would enter the University of West Virginia in September. He was passing a summer of swimming, playing golf, driving his jaunty new Stutz Bearcat, sampling moonshine, going to semisedate dances with certifiably "nice girls" and slipping down to River Street with some of the fellows to have glancing encounters with "bad girls." And he was trying to puzzle out the rights and wrongs, the grievances and the legalisms, of just what the hell was going on down in the southern coalfields.

On this August evening the family sat out on the flagstone

terrace off Clarkson's library, Clarkson and Minnie in big wicker chairs, Lyle sitting Indian-fashion on the ground. Lightning bugs made their tiny noiseless signals here and there. The steady undertone of crickets' screeching soothed the sensuous evening air, which carried a heady mix of flower scents across the lawns. The inevitable water sprinkler played lightly over the grass. The collies snoozed. Peace and beauty, as they had for so many years now, settled over the Castle. Thomasina and George distributed coffee, cream, and sugar.

"What's a 'Yellow Dog' contract exactly?" asked Lyle.

"Well," drawled Clarkson, pulling on his evening cigar, "I don't know where you heard that expression, but it isn't *our* term for it. What those radical agitators mean when they talk about the 'Yellow Dog' contract we offer our miners is that when a miner comes to work for us he signs a contract not to join a union during the life of the contract. Nobody forces him to sign it."

Except, wondered Lyle a little guiltily, the hunger of his wife and children? "Uh, Dad, what is going on about all these *evictions?* It sure sounds strange, people out in the streets, children . . ."

Clarkson thoughtfully drew on his cigar again, and then in a patient voice set out to explain. "Well, you see, when we talk about mining camps, that's just what we mean. Camps. These places, like Number Three — uh, Bennettown, where Tot and Youranie live, that's a *camp*, like an army camp. It's there for ten, maybe twenty years, then the mine's worked out and the camp closes. So, we can't invest a whole lot of money in it. Anybody else, they *won't* invest in it. Who's going to build houses and rent them out when after fifteen, twenty years he'll have no tenants? Nobody. That's why we have to build 'em. They yell about 'company houses.' Hell, the men would be living in tents if it wasn't for that. They've got to have a store. Nobody else'll do it — oh, some fly-by-night people would like to come in there, run a store for a while, gouge our workers, and then move on. So, to have a good stable store we have to run it. Same thing with the school. We have to subsidize the teacher to get some kind of real schooling in there. We pay the doctor. We pay for the recreation. We build the church. It's like an army camp and has to be, because it's only there for a while, until we get the coal out, and then it's empty. That means it's got to have special rules." Another draw on his fine Havana cigar. "One of the rules, down in the southern fields, is, no union agitators. If we find one, we have to move him and his out of there. He might infect the others if we didn't."

"Yes, but Dad," Lyle pursued, "all the mines around here are organized, including yours."

"Ours," he corrected, looking across at him.

"Ours," Lyle murmured.

"Well, around here, you know as well as I do, the Company calls the tune, and the rest of us dance to it. Marcus Clifton decided letting the United Mine Workers in here would guarantee that the coal would keep coming during the war, so he let them in. Do you see what that means? Marcus is no dunce, you know, and *he* thought if he didn't let the UMW organize here they might go out on a strike, war or no war, shut down the railroads, shut down the factories, shut down the *Navy!* That's what he thought those union people would do in the middle of a war if he didn't let them in here. So he did. And what could I do? Sit around with my mines struck while the Company took over my customers? So we've got the union too." Another puff. "Here.

"But down around Matewan," he went on, "down around Welch, down in Logan County, there we've got operators who are ready to stick together and keep those union fellows out. Running a business is like running an army, there's got to be a commander. If there isn't, then there's confusion,

chaos, conflict, strikes, delays, increased costs, lost markets
— there's other fuels coming, you know, coal isn't going to
have it all its own way forever. If we don't stay competitive,
well, you may see these hills empty, or with just poor un-
employed people everywhere. The nineteen twenties are going
to be competitive, and whoever heard of a team that was
a good competitor if it didn't have one captain and obey
him!

"Maybe we'll all go broke around here in Middleburg
before the union fellows are through with their demands for
more wages and shorter hours, price us right out of the market. Well, down there in the southern fields we've got our
holdings" — Clarkson's voice became a little husky — "and
I figure I can keep . . . care of you all" — his eyes momentarily filled with tears, then sternly checking himself he
went on — "and keep everything the way I want it to be for
my family, and if Marcus Clifton has led us into a blind
alley around here, then we can go ahead with my southern
holdings and be all right. If we keep those union agitators
out of those fields."

There was an impressed silence. Lyle was impressed in
spite of himself. Only once or perhaps twice before in his
life had he seen his father close to tears. Obviously he was
fundamentally moved by what he was saying, that his stand
against unions in the South was a vital part of what he had
set out to do in his life; that Marcus Clifton had undercut
that role here, but that down there he would be able to be
his own man, and be it for his own sake, for Minnie's, and
for Lyle's.

"But maybe you're carrying the comparison of an army
camp too far," said Lyle. "What I mean is, you pay the
police in these . . . camps. So what kind of impartiality are
these . . . police . . . going to show? Aren't they just going to
do what you want?"

"I haven't taken you around a mine in years, have I?"

"You took me once, when I was about fifteen. That's all. Maybe one summer I ought to work in one so —"

"Out of the question," murmured Minnie with a regretful little smile at him.

"Impractical," growled Clarkson at the same time. "Too dangerous."

"But these men work there."

"They wouldn't accept you. Think you were a spy." He paused, chewing on his cigar, and then said, "Getting back to the police we have around the mines, what I'm driving at is that this is West Virginia, and that means that the men here are *armed*. They had to be armed when they came here as pioneers, they had to be armed to the teeth during the Civil War with both sides riding all over them, marauders and stragglers everywhere, and *they're armed now!* It's the way it always was here, and it's the way it is now. What you've got is a male working populace, mad as hell about imaginary injustices, and armed to the teeth." He ground his cigar out in an ashtray and then said, "Labor is one of our resources, like coal itself. We need to have full control of it. The men in the southern fields are fairly paid, right up . . . close to the standard of the union men here. Up till now we've had no work stoppages down there, such as they've had in some of the unionized 'closed shop' areas, and when there are work stoppages everybody loses, operators, miners, the public."

Lyle stood up and began walking around the terrace. "But these men aren't . . . *free* to join the union if they want to. If they try to join they're fired *and* evicted. I think that's what bothers them. They aren't free."

Clarkson replied, "What about our freedom, the operators' freedom? Why shouldn't we be free to hire nonunion men if we want to? Why a closed shop? Why should our freedom to hire whoever we want be destroyed?"

Lyle said, "Maybe that's different."

Clarkson said, "It isn't."

There was a silence during which the somnolent summer's peacefulness of the big house and the spreading lawns and trees and gardens reasserted its sway, an enchantment of natural calm cultivated by the devoted Italian gardener into highest cared-for order. Clarkson drew a deep inhalation of the odors, the heavy peace, the natural richness.

This, from his point of view, was the meaning of it all. It would be absolutely wonderful if the lowest, most inept miner out at Number Three could enjoy this same way of life. Life not being constructed that way, however, it belonged to those like himself whose enterprise and foresight and managerial skills made it possible for the miners to have jobs in the first place, and for the industrial system of the country to function.

"But having the mining camps controlled by private police you pay for," Lyle said a little uncertainly, forcing himself up from a drowsing daydream, "private armies, it's like the Middle Ages, isn't it? Why don't just the regular town police have that job?"

"What town police? In Matewan, there were exactly two men on the police force. We didn't even *have* any State Police in West Virginia until two years ago. And our National Guard. They came home from the war and disbanded and nobody's ever reorganized them. So what are we going to do? Let the miners, armed to the teeth, be the law?"

Lyle was silent, cogitating.

Minnie never stirred in her big wicker chair. She had changed little over the past twelve years. There was some gray in her thick chestnut hair, but she still wore it in a 1909-style bun in back. She had put on a little weight, but there was still an aura of girlishness about her as she sat, in a filmy, light green ankle-length dress. With her right hand she was slowly, meticulously exploring the network of wicker on the arm of the chair. If she could concentrate exclusively on that, then the rising clouds of fear she felt filling her throat might subside again, and the haunting vision she had wrestled with for years, the vision of sweptaway happiness, of life lost, shining opportunities dead, that vision might fade once again.

II.

The organizing of the miners of West Virginia into the United Mine Workers was completed in the Middleburg field, and had advanced southward to the Kanawha River, on which the capital of the state, Charleston, was situated. In this area the miners had also largely been organized, and the unions turned to the last unorganized coalfield remaining in the state, McDowell, Mingo, and Logan counties, in the extreme southwest corner, next to Kentucky. This was the old feuding ground of earlier days, hillier even than the rest of the state, and more isolated than any other part of it.

Although Clarkson Catherwood and other West Virginia operators had interests here, most of the coalfields were the property of "absentee owners," principally the Pennsylvania Railroad, the Girard Trust Company, the United States Steel Corporation, and some European capitalists.

No paved road had yet been built into this fastness; the only access was by railroad or on horseback. Passengers taking the train from Charleston to Logan were under surveillance from the moment they boarded the train; they never remained in Logan without being closely questioned as to their purpose in coming, how long they proposed to stay, and so on. If their answers were unsatisfactory to the sheriff of Logan County, Don Chafin, they were encouraged by any and every means necessary to return to Charleston on the next train. A stranger who seemed to be there on union business or to entertain union sympathies was of course not only sure to be sent away but was in the most serious physical danger.

Don Chafin, big and beefy, in boots and jodhpurs, a Mexican War wide-brim felt campaign hat, pistol in shoulder holster, and the manner of a military dictator, ran Logan County for the coal owners. By August 1921, he had sworn in and heavily armed three hundred deputy sheriffs. In addition, because he was the spokesman and strong right arm of all the owners in the county, all the economic power there, he effectively controlled what happened and what was said in the churches, the schools, the judges' chambers and the jury rooms. Sheriff Chafin's annual salary was $3,500. In 1921 he was worth between $300,000 and $400,000. More than a hundred pro-union miners and organizers were in jail in Logan. Martial law had been declared. Chafin's small army of deputy sheriffs were efficiently seeing to it that the mines, worked by one hundred percent nonunion labor, local and imported, were functioning normally and without interference from strikes, evicted miners, or union organizers; that anyone opposing this policy was run out of the county or jailed; and that no spoken or written opposition to this policy was publicly expressed.

As the hot summer of 1921 deepened in the hills, two facts were unquestionable: ordinary liberties and civil rights were being violated wholesale by Don Chafin throughout Logan County, and the union leaders all over the rest of the state were inciting their men to violence against him by every means.

```
┌─────────────────────┐
│         .           │
│        SIX          │
└─────────────────────┘
```

I.

O N August 14, it was announced that Frank Keeney, president of District 17 of the United Mine Workers, would address a meeting in Middleburg. This, Lyle Catherwood immediately decided, he would have to attend. Keeney had a reputation for being one of the leading hotheads of the union leadership. He was thirty-six years old, the father of six children, and a self-educated, aggressively Socialist fighter for workingmen's causes. He spoke often of "the class I was born into," which Lyle found particularly un-American. "Just about everybody was born into that class in some generation or other" was Lyle's comment.

The union meeting was at eight o'clock in the evening. At four o'clock that afternoon Mrs. Sanderson Clifton was having her annual tea dance in the Elizabethan mansion, the Manor, for the young people. Lyle was determined to attend both.

Over the parquet floor they glided and bounced to the accompaniment of the six-piece band; there was fruit punch from the famous Clifton crystal punch bowl bought in Venice, and a shot of something stronger for those who slipped out to the glass-walled porch. The girls wore short hair and flimsy dresses, the young men were in their floppy full pants legs.

In a semicircle in a room off the dance floor sat Mrs. Sanderson Clifton, Mrs. Harry Hayes, Minnie Catherwood, and other ladies of the older generation. In their silk and brocade dresses with matronly hemlines, their queenly hats, their physical amplitude, they seemed much different from their children than heretofore had been the case between generations. What had been a difference in degree seemed, in 1921, to have become a difference in kind. The very bodies of their daughters were different, taller, much leaner, showing no promise of the dignified bosoms of true ladies, looser in the joints — and in language and manners and clothes and morals — slouching, gone the rigidly upright posture of yesteryear. Looking on in dignified and concealed bafflement, the ladies of Minnie's generation beheld their dancing daughters, who were beginning to refer to themselves as "flappers," of all the unladylike terms. As for the young men, or "sheiks" as they called themselves, *they* simply lacked the *substance* young men on the brink of adult responsibility were expected to have. They were *giddy*. They were devil-may-care. They knew all the latest silly dances, they seemed to be sneaking alcoholic beverages into the most respectable parties and getting away with it, and these giddy young men would before very long inherit control of the major coal companies, and *then* where would Middleburg be?

On the young people glided and bounced and giggled and rubbed, and stiffer became the faces of the ladies. Minnie reflected to herself: here we are, the owners and their children, and we are in for perhaps the worst battles in the history of the coal industry, and we are a house divided. These Clifton youths, these Hayes boys, can *they* cope with five hundred thousand determined and militant United Mine Workers? These boys here, dancing the *tango!* And my darling, my poor darling Lylie, how could he ever do, arguing with that new union president, the one who looks like the most ferocious English bulldog in the world, what's his name? Lewis? John Something Lewis?

Fanny Carstairs to Joe Boy Clifton: Do you know how to do the Tickle Toe?
Joe Boy: I guess not. How does it go?
Fanny: Well, if you don't already know . . .
Joe Boy: You didn't know once upon a time, did you? Come on, show me.
Fanny: Well . . .

Benjamin Harrison Hayes III to Emily May Carruthers: Do you kiss?
Emily May: M-m-m-m-uh-uh-
Benjamin: Well? Do you or don't you?
Emily May: Now I call that cheeky.
Benjamin: It's something a fellow needs to know if he's getting sweet on a girl.
Emily May: Meaning?
Benjamin: Just what you think it means.
Emily May: I don't know what I *do* think.
Benjamin: Aw, come on.
Emily May (after a pause, pouting slightly): Maybe I do.
Benjamin: Do what?
Emily May: Do *what?*
Benjamin: *Oh!* I *see.* . . . Well, let's go out on the porch.
Emily May: Well . . .

Lyle Catherwood to Elizabeth Ann Hayes: What do you mean, I've changed?
Elizabeth Ann: You've just changed, that's all.
Lyle: How? Exactly how?
Elizabeth Ann: Well, like that. Pinning me down. "Exactly how."

Lyle: I'm not pinning you down.

Elizabeth Ann: Yes you are. You used to be sweet, sort of. And now I think you're getting very cynical.

Lyle (rather liking the sound of that): Well, a man gets older, sees more of the world —

Elizabeth Ann (murmuring slyly): Greenbrier Military Academy?

Lyle (bristling): I've also been to New York, Baltimore, Louisville, I don't know where all. (Getting angrier on reflection.) I guess I just start losing interest in local — things.

Elizabeth Ann: Oh really!

Lyle: Yes. Really.

Elizabeth Ann: Well!

II.

After sandwiches and coffee at seven, Lyle accompanied his mother the short distance on foot to the Castle, and then, saying he was going to the Hayeses to play cards, took the second-best car out of the barn-garage, a 1919 Hupmobile, and picked up Fanny Carstairs who was a Clifton on her mother's side and who had, in Lyle's opinion, a head on her shoulders. She was four years older than he was: Lyle always found older girls more interesting. Because of the age difference Fanny had refused to go out with him officially, but she had jumped at the chance for an escapade like this. Together they drove to the office of the newspaper, the *Middleburg Exponent*, to meet the labor reporter Lew Jenkins. He would more or less smuggle them into the union meeting with the influence of his press card. Fanny had put on a voluminous gray raincoat over her flimsy, beaded party

[77]

dress. Lyle still had on white pants and shoes, but he was now in shirtsleeves.

Lew Jenkins was middle-aged, red-faced, thin hair parted in the middle, wearing a rumpled gray suit and a straw hat. Fanny had never met him, and Lyle had only the slightest acquaintance with him, across a poker table. However Jenkins had indicated on the telephone to Lyle that since he and Fanny were, or someday would be, an important part of the local industry he would see about getting them into the meeting. "You ought to tell your dads some of the things you'll hear tonight," he remarked dryly as they passed into the hall. "Might do everybody some good."

"You're right!" said Lyle firmly.

Inside the big, low-ceilinged meeting hall what struck Fanny was the overpowering maleness of the group, the basso rumble of voices, the smoke from many cheap and not so cheap cigars, the number of suspenders visibly holding up pants, the general gruffness in the atmosphere. There were, she was relieved to see, a few other women present, but for the first time in her life she came face to face with the fact that as a daughter of the coal industry she belonged to one of the most thoroughly masculine enterprises in the world. The industry made exactly one concession to its women: it often named mines after them — Minnie, Idamay. These feminine names were totems, like the ladies' scarves medieval knights wore into their jousts. Nothing else feminine penetrated the virile world of coal: women were not allowed in a mine, no woman worked in an office capacity higher than secretary and telephone operator, and if the Cliftons were any example, no woman had any influence on managerial decisions. Men, men, she thought as she threaded behind Lyle and Lew Jenkins through the crowded floor of the room toward their seats. Anything controlled entirely by men was bad; she felt that instinctively. The Great War had been an all-male enterprise, and look what that had done! Bled England, France, Germany and Russia white, destroyed three empires, caused the Russian imperial family, including all the women, to be slaughtered in a cellar, and left the "victorious" Allies exhausted, contentious, and much worse off than when it all started. That was what an all-male enterprise led to. And here was another: the coal industry, with its men of labor and men of management at each other's throats. We're in for it, she thought, we're in for it.

She sat down on a hard little folding chair to the left of the stage, on which there was a lectern waiting for Frank Keeney, and two rows of chairs, now filling up with men, behind it. The milling groups of men on the floor began to settle into their chairs; some man took the gavel and banged for order, made some routine announcements, and then with no ceremony introduced Keeney. Heavy applause greeted him.

A smallish, taut, wiry man sprang to the lectern. Fanny felt that if someone made a provocative remark to this man, his first response would be to spring for the throat.

"There are probably persons here in the sound of my voice that in the last fall election cast their election franchise for the present executive of the state, and whoever did it is a red-handed murderer, for Governor Morgan is as much a murderer as any pirate who ever sailed the high seas."

Fanny entertained a small secret scorn for her mother's generation's weakness of occasionally swooning, but now for the first time she had a taste of how such a thing could happen. The vehemence of this man accusing *her* of murder, for she had indeed in her first chance to vote cast an absentee ballot for Morgan, seemed to drain necessary blood from her head; she knew she had gone pale. Gripping the sides of her little chair she heard the rest of his tirade pour over her as if at one remove; snatches of what he cried out in his high, harsh voice came through: women and children were being murdered in the southern part of the state, the governor knew this and refused to give protection . . . The coalfields down there were going to be organized if it took every man in the United Mine Workers to do it . . . The union had tried before and failed but this time it had five hundred men under arms in the southern part of the state and others were arming, and all Don Chafin's hired gunmen, and all the companies' thugs and all Governor Morgan's Cossacks couldn't stop them . . . If they *were* prevented anything could happen . . . Whatever did happen wouldn't be the union's fault . . . it could be laid instead at Governor Morgan's door . . . If the union met resistance in moving in to organize Logan County it would make the affair at Matewan look like a sunbonnet parade by comparison.

He moved away from the lectern and the hall rose and cheered and whistled; a roaring came into Fanny's ears, from the hall or from her own blood she could not be sure.

She found herself being propelled past the heavy shoulders of crowding men toward the stage, and then somehow Frank Keeney had been buttonholed and then Keeney, herself, Lyle and Lew Jenkins were in a huddle, and *Lyle* was questioning him. Somewhere Lyle had acquired a pad and pencil.

"Do you think your radical approach will succeed?" Lyle yelled over the hubbub at Keeney.

"Radical!" His taut, reddish face tightened. "They didn't call me a radical when I agreed to forget our contracts and work for Uncle Sam during the war. Now they call me a radical! Because I insist on holding what the miners in this state have gained. It's an old trick. They're merely trying to cover up their own determination to crush us."

There was something pedantic about this firebrand, Fanny thought, a schoolteacher or preacher concealed beneath the rabble-rouser; a self-taught boy, once upon a time, alone among his books in the library, dreaming of the crusade he

[80]

would lead, bitter at the injustices he, the bookish boy, hadn't yet been, perhaps never would be, able to correct.

"Don't you think there ought to be some kind of cooperation between the miners and owners?" Lyle shouted.

"I'm a native West Virginian," Keeney shouted back. "There are others like me working in the mines here. We don't propose to get out of the way when a lot of capitalists from New York and London come down here and tell us to get off the earth. They played that game on the American Indian. They gave him the end of a log to sit on and then pushed him off that. We don't propose to be pushed off."

"Why are you so *bitter?*" Fanny suddenly burst out.

"Little lady," he replied, "did you hear my speech or didn't you? Women and children are getting killed. The workingman and his family are getting trampled by thugs and Cossacks. And you stand there in your party dress and ask me why I'm bitter." Her coat had fallen open, she realized too late. "Take your party dress and get out of here. This isn't a Chautauqua lecture. This is real. Some of the men might get annoyed. Get out of here."

"Come on," said Jenkins, casting an apologetic look at Keeney. They edged and shoved their way through the sweltering hall and out to the street.

"You two kids don't know your place, do you?" said Jenkins sourly. "This is the enemy camp here, this isn't the country club. Better go on home. My mistake." He turned away from them and went back into the hall.

"He's got his nerve," said Lyle.

"Y-e-e-s," said Fanny reflectively. "He does have his nerve. He's not afraid of us, or my uncles or any of us. They're not afraid of us anymore, any of them." They started walking toward their car. "And I loved that," she added derisively, "about '*if* we're resisted in going in to Logan County to organize it.' If! Does he think Don Chafin is going to roll out a red carpet for the union organizers? If. I really love

that. That man is bloodthirsty. He knows very well bullets
will be flying in all directions. I think he wants that. I really
think he wants it."

III.

The following morning Clarkson left in the 1919 Packard,
Uncle George at the wheel, for Charleston. With him went
his assistant, Virgil Pence, and Lyle, to his surprise, was
also asked to go along. It was the first business trip of Clarkson's which he had ever been asked to join.

Clarkson privately felt that his only son Lyle was (a) still
a boy; (b) a lightweight. This latter opinion he guarded
closely in his breast, so that even Minnie with her sudden
perceptions and uncanny insights had never glimpsed it.
Clarkson barely let himself become aware of it, and then
only at widely scattered intervals. But when some issue presented itself where any kind of weight or substance or even
thoughtfulness would be required of Lyle, then Clarkson
tended to deflect it: Lyle wasn't ready; perhaps Lyle never
would be ready. Lyle was a good-natured, happy-go-lucky
boy, and, just in case he never did, never could, grow into
someone Clarkson could eventually trust the tumultuous
management of the coal company to, well then Clarkson was
making provision for Lyle's financial security. He was a good
boy, a winning boy, a warmhearted boy . . . but there it was,
inevitably, that inevitably repeated word: a boy.

"Dad," said Lyle, as the dignified limousine rolled over
the curving, narrow, bumpy road through the hills southward,
"what frat do you think I ought to join at the university
next year? Got any one in particular in mind?"

Clarkson sighed faintly. "Phi Psi," he then said dryly.

"You think so?"

"Yes."

"Why that one especially?"

"It's the best," said Clarkson.

"Oh well then ..."

Clarkson returned to an intense interior contemplation of this labor situation into which he was heading. On the jump seat in front of him Virgil Pence scanned some papers on a clipboard. All three of them, and George in front, had doffed jackets, collars and ties in the heat. Virgil was lean and lanky, but he had smilingly declined to ride on the rear seat with the two Catherwoods, father and son, saying that the little jump seat "helps me concentrate better."

There were barriers and gradations and distinctions; class lines and economic divisions shot all through the lives of Middleburg, from James in Bennettown to Marcus Clifton in the Farms. There were very few equals: for example, Clarkson was not Marcus Clifton's equal. Virtually everybody was above some, below others. It made for a fundamental streak of uneasiness running through the friendly, unaffected surface of life in the coalfields.

"I had a wire from the Aracoma Hotel," said Virgil. "They're holding rooms for us. Don't have too many travelers down there in Logan these days, boss."

"I guess not."

Boss: Lyle had never heard his father called that before. It sounded, well — funny.

"My wife," went on Virgil, "wanted to know, were we takin' bodyguards in there with us."

"*I'm* the bodyguard!" exclaimed Lyle.

Both men offered small, formula smiles to this flight of fancy.

There was a rather loud sound and then the back left part of the car, beneath Clarkson, began to ride even more roughly over the bumpy road. "Damn it, a puncture," he said with contained exasperation.

Uncle George maneuvered the gleaming midnight blue limousine off the paved road to a small gravel area.

The men concentrated on extracting the spare tire, jacking up the left rear wheel, and effecting the transfer in the broiling August sun.

The radiator was overheated, but this halt gave it a chance to cool, and with the judicious adding of cold water from a spring nearby, it cooled back down to normal. Cars occasionally rattled by, Model T's mostly, with country people who seemed inclined to help out until they realized that there were already four able-bodied men and all the necessary tools on the scene.

"It still beats train travel," remarked Virgil as they climbed back into the car. "It's cleaner."

"Trains burn coal though," said Lyle, "and in these here vehicles, the fuel money goes to the Rockefellers instead of us!"

"True," murmured Virgil.

"I like to take the road when I can," observed Clarkson, "and see the unspoiled countryside. Along the railroad right-of-way there's so much old shacks and warehouses and so on. This is just nature as it really is out here."

"No slag heaps," said Lyle.

Clarkson made a restive sound.

"This sure is a fine automobile, boss," said Virgil energetically. "She really handles beautifully."

"Maybe on the drive back you'd like to take the wheel for a spell," suggested Clarkson.

"I'll say I would."

"We won't bother George now," Clarkson continued. "He's *concentrating*. I can tell by those wrinkles along the back of his neck. But on the way back ..."

"Fine. I've never handled a car this size."

"It's different," said Clarkson, "from a runabout or a

roadster or any of those. It's different. Massive. Feels like nothing can touch you."

"Except a blowout," said Lyle.

"I think," Clarkson went on, "they've pretty well got most of the engineering solved with these new automobiles they put out since the war. Don't see much more they can do to them, I mean underneath. Of course they can play around with the body all they want, and that's just what they'll do, I'll wager. Have to keep people getting rid of an old one and buying a new one. That's where Marcus Clifton is smart with his Rolls. Just stays the same, year in and year out. I felt Packard was as close as an American car came to the Rolls tradition."

"It's a beautiful car," said Virgil.

Clarkson took out a cigar, offered one to Virgil who smilingly refused it, and biting off the tip, lit up.

"Ain't you going to offer me one, Pop?" spoke up Lyle. He often used slang colloquialisms these days.

Clarkson heaved himself around to look at his son. "You never smoked cigars."

"Always has to be a first time."

"Not," observed Clarkson, settling back into his corner, "in the middle of a sweltering August day on a rough road with gas fumes all around."

To himself he thought: if I'd let him he would have taken it and smoked it, and in all likelihood been sick and made a fool of himself in front of Virgil and George. Where's his common sense?

"There's one thing about the coal business," Clarkson began in a ruminative tone, unusual for him, but induced by the good cigar, the prospect of hours on the road with no means of working, telephoning, dictating letters, and a general feeling of well-being which had come over him as they drove along through the beautiful rolling hills, hills overflowing with trees and undergrowth, laced with shiny streams hurrying over stony riverbeds, spanned by covered bridges which had reverberated with Yankee and Rebel hooves for four desperate years. A pretty, no, a beautiful back country, unspoiled — there was hardly any coal between Middleburg and Charleston — and heavily timbered, freshly watered, sparsely settled, not really very good for anything, economically speaking, and this very fact induced in Clarkson a ruminative mood: here he was out of competition, as though in a great park, somewhere with nothing to do, nothing to calculate. "There's one thing about the coal business," he said aloud at length, "unlike the auto business we were talking about. People, the country, *really need coal*. We don't change the design every two years to make the customers buy a new one, do we? The very idea is ridiculous, you can't even say it. Buy a new one? It can't mean anything. Coal *is*. Country stops dead without it. We don't stimulate artificial demand, the way the car people are beginning to do, the way the people who make women's dresses are beginning to do, the way people who sell furniture are starting to do, and so many others. They've got to have coal and we get it for them and sell it to them at a fair price. *That's* why I love this business. It's honest. It's itself. It's like being a doctor. People couldn't live without us, couldn't keep warm, couldn't have jobs or money."

"Basic industry," murmured Virgil.

"That's it. We're basic. And I love this business." A long, thoughtful pause, filled by several draws on his cigar. "Or I have loved it up until this thing we're in now. I don't know, I really don't know, if the shooting starts, where it will stop."

At the end of a long, hot, dusty, bumpy journey they pulled into Charleston. It was late in the afternoon, and the little city was stewing under a humid canopy of summer heat.

After they had checked into the Daniel Boone Hotel they learned from an associate of Clarkson's that Charleston was also stewing because several thousand armed miners were encamped in the town of Marmet nearby; at any moment these men might set out for Logan, eighty miles away, and try to shoot their way into Don Chafin's stronghold.

That made up Clarkson's mind for him: "If there's going to be a battle I'm going to be on the right side of the battle line." He made plans to take the train, with Virgil Pence, to Logan the next morning. Clarkson told Lyle to return in the car to Middleburg.

"But Dad, I know I can help. Let me come with you down there."

"Your mother would never forgive me," was the only answer he got from his preoccupied father. "George will drive you back tomorrow."

"I'm not twelve, for God's sake, I'm eighteen," protested Lyle, to no avail.

The following morning, August 22, 1921, the three men got into the capacious back seat of the Packard and George drove to the railroad station. Lyle accompanied his father and Virgil to the little train, its four coaches and two baggage cars lined up toylike behind a miniature-looking steam engine. "You think that will get you through all those mountains?" exclaimed Lyle.

"I believe the line sticks to the valleys," said Clarkson. "It always has got through. Of course, this summer, who knows? Maybe the sky will fall."

"And I won't be there to see it," muttered Lyle.

"You go on back, look after your mother. For all I know, there might be trouble — even in Middleburg." Lyle noticed a curious look come over his father's face as he said the last word, a flickering expression of desperation and disbelief; it came and went in a second, but Lyle saw a depth of fear which even expressing such a possibility caused his father.

There was therefore no point in arguing further that he accompany them to Logan.

Good-byes were perfunctorily said — sentimentality not being any part of the code of the Catherwoods — the engine hissed menacingly, the whistle shrieked, and the 9:45 A.M. for Logan pulled groaning and hissing once more out of the Charleston station.

Lyle and George turned away. "Take me back to the Daniel Boone Hotel, Uncle George."

"You got your grip in the car, Mr. Lyle. Why'nt we get on the road for Middleburg?"

"No. I want to go back to the Daniel Boone."

The hot, heavy weather had lifted a bit since the day before, and sitting with the windows open in the sparsely occupied day coach Clarkson and Virgil Pence settled down to enjoy the journey. There was a certain amount of soot coming through the windows from time to time, but the air was fresh, and the view from the window, as they rolled through steep-walled valleys, past smokily green streams, was attractive. Thin houses on stilts clung to the hillsides here and there. At the little towns where they stopped the depots were as sleepy-looking as ever, no sign of tension anywhere. "Pretty country," remarked Virgil.

"It is, isn't it," said Clarkson. "And not good for much else, besides coal and looking pretty. These hills are so darn steep they say a man can fall out of his own cornfield."

"I believe it."

"Hard place for people to get together with each other. Never *see* each other. Can't see a thing down here, can you, except hills. Hardly any sky."

"Claustrophobic," remarked Virgil abstractedly.

"What's that?"

"Uh, closed in, feels real closed in, doesn't it?"

"Oh, yeah, yes it does." There was a short silence and

then Clarkson remarked, "Used to teach school before you came with us, didn't you, Virgil?"

"Yes, sir, that I did. Not too much money in school teach· ing. And also, well, the coal industry is what's important in this state, as you were saying yesterday. I wanted to be in the thing that was important around here."

"*And* make better money," observed Clarkson calmly. "Nothing wrong with that. Hell, what are we all working for, if not to make a decent living. What did you teach?"

"Seventh grade. Out at Mainchance."

"Enjoy it?"

"Couple of the kids were bright enough, showed promise. I only did it for three years before going to take some courses at the university, and then I was lucky enough to get hired by you."

"We were glad to get you. I think it's working out, I think it's working out fine."

A bulky figure stepped out of the coach ahead of theirs, crossed the open platform and entered their coach. He was tall and husky, wore a felt campaign hat, shoulder holster, jodhpurs, boots: one of Sheriff Chafin's deputies.

"You just entered Logan County and I'm Deputy Shuttles-worth," he said in a low-pitched, level voice. "Who are you folks?"

"I'm Clarkson Catherwood, president of — well, Clarkson Coal Company up in Middleburg, of Spruce Creek Coal in these parts. This is my assistant, Virgil Pence."

The deputy's face broke from its stern mask into a cordial, formula grin. "Oh, Mr. Catherwood, sir. Welcome to Logan. Have a pleasant journey?"

"Yes, we sure did."

"Good. Anything we can do for you in Logan? Your hotel —"

"All taken care of, thank you. How are things in Logan?"

The deputy settled a little on his heels. "I'll tell you this,

Mr. Catherwood. Those troublemakers try to shoot their way in here, or come in here any other way, we're ready for 'em. I figure you must think so too, sir, puttin' yourself in our hospitality down here."

"Sure do, of course I do."

The deputy touched his hat respectfully and passed on down the car.

"Seem to be watching everything, don't they?" said Clarkson.

"They sure do."

"Reassuring. Too bad any of this had to happen. But long as it does, reassuring to see our men right on their toes."

Checking back into the Daniel Boone Hotel, Lyle took George aside in the lobby. "Time for you to go home now, Uncle George."

"Yeah but Mr. Lyle your daddy said —"

"He was just suggesting. He really left it up to me."

"It didn't sound to me like —"

"But he *did*. That's just his way."

"I know your daddy since before you was born, and I know when he says what he wants, *that's* what he wants."

"Well, now you're getting to know me. And *I* want you to drive up to Middleburg and look after my mother."

George cocked his head. "That what *you* want?"

Lyle returned his stare. "Yes. And I want it now."

"You does, do you?"

"That's right."

They beheld each other, the reddish, taut eighteen-year-old and the seasoned, cautious, independent-in-his-fashion Negro. Finally George said with wry cheerfulness, "Well, Mr. Lyle, you pretty well growed up now and I sure can't *force* you to do nothin' you don't want. Just remember, *I tried*. You be sure and tell your daddy that, hear?" He hadn't told Lyle to "hear" for some years past; it was a token of the serious breach George felt was being forced by Lyle.

"I hear, Uncle George," muttered Lyle. Then, as though suddenly remembering something, he exclaimed, "Oh, there's one more thing. I bet you'll have some expenses you didn't plan on drivin' back, what with me not bein' with you and all. So here." He slipped a twenty-dollar bill at his hand; George's fingers slowly closed over it as he beheld it with a certain disbelief. "And — ah — when you do get back, just tell Mother I ran into the Jameson brothers here and we went camping over toward Gauley Bridge."

George looked from the twenty-dollar bill to Lyle's face and back again. Suddenly Lyle's nerve seemed to break; he whirled around, sprinted to the stairway and disappeared upstairs.

"Sheeee," hissed George in discouragement to himself, heading out toward the car.

$$\boxed{\text{seven}}$$

I.

VIRGIL Pence had promised to write his wife a detailed letter every day during his trip to the southern part of the state. Like many people in northern West Virginia she thought of Logan as a combination of the Wild West, the Hatfield-McCoy feud, and the last remaining active pocket of the Civil War. A lengthy daily letter, they concluded, would at least partly reassure her.

> The Aracoma Hotel
> Logan, West Virginia
> August 23, 1921

Dearest Doris Lee,

It is late at night now — I guess I should have dated this letter August 24th — and even though I put the electric fan in the window this room is more like an oven than a bedroom. Mr. Catherwood has a larger room next door, and there's a bathroom in between. Not very swell accommodations for the Master of Catherwood Castle, but I guess we're lucky to have a roof over our heads. Logan is mobilized! They're ready to shoot the first union miner on sight. And the miners, I hear, are ready to march straight across Boone County, straight at Logan. Do you want to

know what the sheriff of Boone County said when this miners'
"army," thousands of them, with guns and automatics and I don't
know what all, entered his county? It was in the *Charleston
Gazette*. "These men will meet with no resistance from me. There
are only three or four deputy sheriffs in Boone County." (Can't
he count?) "We have no means at hand with which to stop
them." (Swear in more deputies, the way Don Chafin did.) "So
far as I am concerned" (That's the *sheriff* talking! *So far as he is
concerned!* Thousands of armed men invading his county!!!)
"they are perfectly welcome to walk along the highways through
Boone County." (Lily-liver!)

So you see what that means. He's waving them right through,
right up to the Logan County border.

This is a strange little town. I don't know what the population
is, but it's a small town and it always will be, because the mountains go right straight up all around it. They're completely
covered with trees, and there sits the town like a saucer in the
middle of these steep hillsides, and — maybe I'm getting persecution mania from all the tenseness around here — but in this
town you feel like a sniper is sighting down his barrel, and all
set to pick you off. Even in the rooms of this four-story hotel,
the windows look pretty big and some guy with a telescope sight
or something might be ready to shoot me now!

I'm sorry, dear, that kind of statement wasn't the purpose of
these letters, was it. But it kind of helps to communicate some
of the things that go through my head down here that aren't too
pleasant. Being sniped at is one of them. And, I don't know,
there's something spooky, ominous I guess you'd say about the
town itself. Those hills overhanging it are one thing, and then a
river cuts it off on one side and the railroad tracks on the other,
and with the heat and all it just seems to sit there and *stew*, like
a pot on a stove, bubbling and hissing.

Heat or no heat, my head is drooping and I'm going to try
for some shut-eye. Thinking of you and Virgie.

Your loving,
Virgil

[93]

Aracoma Hotel
Logan
August 24, 1921

Dearest Doris Lee,

What a day, what a day! Do you mind, dearest, I'm going to tell you everything even though some of it will distress you — it distressed me, but getting it down on paper and sending it to someone dear to me relieves me a little bit . . . I wonder if they're censoring mail out of here? Does that sound crazy? Well it isn't. Newspaper fellows are beginning to arrive and everything they send out is censored. Maybe I'm taking a chance writing you all this, but I figure we're on the side of the angels around here, Mr. Catherwood and I. This town and this county are owned lock, stock, and barrel — and law enforcement — by the mining companies and I guess they won't censor the mail of Clarkson Catherwood's right-hand man. If they do, mail me a file care of the Logan County Jail (joke).

I saw a bad sight today, bad, it's why I wrote that nervous paragraph above, I guess. Mr. Catherwood had to have lunch at the superintendent's house and he didn't need me so I went into a little lunch place on the main street, a grim little street, narrow, two- and three-story buildings, gray. Well, I sat down at the counter and began to look over the menu. There was a quiet-looking man in a dark suit sitting two stools away. All of a sudden the door was slammed open with a bang and in came this big bruiser with shoulder holster, boots, etc. Don Chafin, to be sure, and two deputies. Chafin stalks up to this man and yells, "You belong to the goddam union, don't you!" The man, looking completely amazed, says, no, he doesn't. Then Chafin punches him on both sides of the head and says, "Get up, goddam you!" The man gets up, Chafin smacks him on the side of the head with a gun, and tells his men to search him. They find some credentials in his vest pocket. Chafin examines them, hands them back to this stunned-looking man, says, "Be goddam sure you do nothing here but preach!" and the deputies give the man the bum's rush out the door.

Do you know who that man was? I found out later. He's the

[94]

minister at the First Baptist Church in a place called Stone Branch. So you see, anybody can catch it around here, but don't worry I'm being very careful, and of course Chafin and all his men know I'm with Mr. Catherwood so that's all right. But I had to get that scene out of my head by writing it in a letter to you. I can't talk it over with Mr. Catherwood, it turns out. I tried to tell him about the beating up of the preacher but he just said, "Oh it couldn't have happened like that, there's some mistake there somewhere." Something I saw with my own eyes! He won't listen, won't believe it, doesn't want to.

Now and then, recollecting the look on that preacher's face and that gun slamming against his head, I can't believe it either.

Love,
Virgil

Aracoma Hotel
Logan
August 25, 1921

Dearest Doris Lee,

Well, honey, things are getting pretty hifalutin' around here. Yesterday Sheriff Chafin made a statement to the press and public. You know what his words were? "They Shall Not Pass!!!" Now ain't that something. Using the words Foch or Joffre or whoever it was said at Verdun! I mean, where's the sense of proportion?

But proportion is one thing Logan hasn't got right now, and I guess the miners marching through the mountains toward us haven't got it either. There are cocked guns everywhere, and sometimes one of them goes off.

For instance, there was some man, a bricklayer, who was heard to say something favorable about the union. Of course he was arrested and thrown in jail right away. That was yesterday. Today, the story Chafin's men are giving out is that the bricklayer got out of his cell some way, knocked the jailer down, went for his keys, and to protect himself the jailer was forced to shoot and kill the bricklayer. "Shot while trying to escape," they called that old one.

But it's not all so grim here. Yesterday's *Logan Banner* had an item about a man named Frank Olmstead. He suffered face cuts and an eye bruise when he tried to take the bullets out of his gun. The gun went off, the bullet hit the pavement in front of Guyan Valley Bank, and some chips of flying concrete scratched several young ladies standing nearby. That kind of thing happens a lot. If you're taller than a shotgun they hand you one, swear you in as a deputy sheriff, and turn you loose! Hell, the miners won't do half the damage stray bullets and accidental shootings are going to do around here.

If only those miners would get to the county line and the two sides actually get into it, a lot of pressure would be off. This way things just get tenser and tenser.

I think of you all the time up in Middleburg — it seems like Mars I feel so far away from you, locked in this hot little place with the steep hills all around and boys toting guns everywhere. If things have got to such a pass down here, can it be kept from spreading up there? I doubt it. It's one state and one industry and it's one union and what happens here is going to "kick" like a shotgun when you fire it, all over the state and, it couldn't surprise me, all over all the other states with big coalfields.

Well at least for the moment — Holy God! What's that! —

Later — 5:30 A.M.

What happened was that a siren and some whistles suddenly went off shrieking in the middle of the night. Nobody told me that that was the signal that the "invaders" had got up to the county line. Everybody rushed out to the courthouse, and they commandeered cars to go up to the "front line" on Blair Mountain, and some other men formed up in groups ready to set off for any other point at the "front" that was threatened. Just now two aeroplanes (!) took off for the front. You never saw so much confusion in your life, cars racing around, guns going off, and these aeroplanes! Mr. Catherwood advised me to come back here and get some sleep but who can sleep?

This is some kind of a little war, and people are going to get killed, and I don't know where it will end.

Love,
Virgil

II.

Once he had sent Uncle George on his way, Lyle went up to his room at the Daniel Boone Hotel in Charleston, and changed into a worn gray suit. This seemed to him a suitable disguise. Deciding that all newspaper reporters, which was what he proposed to turn himself into, wore straw hats, he went out and bought himself one. He bought some cigars, a pad and some pencils. He bought some bootleg Canadian whiskey from the bellboy. Thus equipped, he set out to find a story. And if he did find a good story and sent it back to the *Middleburg Exponent* he had no doubt that they would print it. There were such things as free-lance journalists, weren't there? Well, now there was one more: Lyle Catherwood. Oh, well, perhaps Catherwood was not quite the suitable last name for a labor reporter at this particular juncture in West Virginia labor relations. He knew that as a journalist he was supposed to be "objective," impartial, calling 'em as he saw 'em, without fear or favor. Catherwood would not be the ideal name for that purpose. He reflected. How about Jenkins? That had a nice classless sound to it. Lyle Jenkins.

Now. Credentials. Since he was a free lance, nobody could expect him to have a press card, could they? But how about a letter, from an editor, asking him to cover the miners' story around here? The name of the editor of the *Middleburg Exponent* was Neil Boggess.

There was a public stenographer in the hotel, and Lyle had her type up a letter, addressed to Lyle Jenkins, authorizing him to cover the labor-operator dispute in southern West Virginia for the *Exponent*. When he returned to his room with the neatly typed letter Lyle took a swig of the whiskey and then, with a flourish, signed the letter: Neil Boggess. There.

Now to find the story.

So in his straw hat and rumpled gray suit, with his pad and pencils and forged letter, Lyle hitchhiked to Marmet, a few miles outside Charleston, where the miners were encamped. He found they had set up a large area with tents and fires, crap games and poker, and they also had guards, in overalls, World War helmets, and rifles, posted around the perimeter.

"I'd like to interview a couple of your leaders in there," Lyle said, grinning widely, to the first armed guard he encountered.

"That right?"

"Yeah, I'm from the *Middleburg Exponent*, see, here's the letter. I want to tell your side of the story to our readers."

"We got an office in Charleston gives out stories to the newspapers. This here's a military camp. No visitors."

"Yeah, but it's just the atmosphere that our readers want. How the men are livin'. What they're doin'. Well, I can see for myself they're shootin' craps but —"

"You get on back to Middleburg, or leastways Charleston."

The tone was not very menacing, but it was final. There could be no argument. So Lyle took in what he could from where he stood — a whole lot of men, thousands it seemed, all with guns at hand, milling around, waiting, and, he could tell, in no mood to be interviewed by the likes of him, or, for that matter, anybody else.

He returned to Charleston, checking out of the Daniel Boone Hotel and into a small hotel on a side street as Lyle Jenkins. Then he sat down on the little bed in his little room to think of a better approach to the armed encampment at Marmet.

Tomorrow, better prepared with a better strategy, he would approach it again.

But the next day the encampment was empty, the men gone, on the march, the Armed March to Logan, singing, to the tune of "John Brown's body lies amolding in the grave," new lyrics: "We'll hang Don Chafin to the sour apple tree."

Lyle cast about for ways to follow. He was not going to lose his story.

III.

Aracoma Hotel
Logan
August 27, 1921

Dear Doris Lee,

It happened. There's a war going on here. Americans are lined up in organized military formation shooting other lined-up, organized, armed Americans. It doesn't seem possible — another Civil War! — but it's happening. Sheriff Chafin and three hundred of his deputies are up in trenches and machine-gun nests on Blair Mountain firing away at a few thousand armed miners in the valley below. Our side has had its first casualty, a man named John Gore, a deputy, shot and killed instantly. We don't know how many casualties there are on their side. How strange, talking about "our" side and "their" side.

I'm getting firsthand information about the fighting because there's a correspondent from the Associated Press here, an interesting guy about my age, and I've struck up an acquaintance with him. Think I feel lonely? This poor guy is from Providence, Rhode Island, and here he is in the depths of Logan County with bullets whistling by his ears, some from in front of him and some from behind and some from beside. Still, he's kind of hard-bitten, experienced.

He was up at the mountain today and got himself into a machine-gun nest which was firing on miners a thousand feet below. The miners were trying to advance to the right or left, but every time they moved the machine gun and rifle fire drove them back. On one of their sorties two of the miners were hit and lay still in the road. Here is the way his dispatch goes on: "The machine-gun bullets clipped the dust in front of and behind the two fallen men, preventing attempts at rescue. Later a band of about fifty men came down the road between two buildings. A heavy fire from the ridge, however, caused them hastily to retreat, carrying four or five of their comrades on their shoulders.

"The machine gunners had previously been instructed not to fire on certain houses in the valley below where it was reported a woman, a child and an old man had not been able to leave. Now and then the child and the old man could be seen in the roadway during lulls in the firing."

Do you believe it? Americans, and not even Southern versus Northern, these are *all* West Virginians and that means Southern *and* Northern, border state brothers, killing each other. Well, this always was a violent country, and now God help us it looks like it always will be.

I have gotten two letters from you. I guess the others are floating around somewhere in all this confusion. Your main good news is that all is quiet up there. And what you said at the end, that you never knew you needed someone like me beside you in bed until we were married, and now it feels "unnatural and empty and scary" not having me there, well that made me feel sad and very happy, both. Our first separation. I miss everything about you, especially, you with me at night, two people made one by love.

With all my love,
Virgil

Aracoma Hotel
Logan
August 28, 1921

Dearest Doris Lee,

With everything so grim and dangerous around here it's nice when something funny happens. This morning as I was coming out of the hotel a man with a pistol shot himself in the foot while trying to put it back in the holster. "My foot, damn it, my foot!" he yelled. "I done shot my goddam foot!"

Well, I guess ordinarily a man accidentally shooting himself wouldn't be funny, but somehow this event made me think that this little war maybe will eventually dwindle away.

Mr. Catherwood is busy and worried all the time, because on top of everything else Lyle Catherwood has disappeared! George, the chauffeur, got back there to Middleburg and said Lyle had gone camping with some friends. That kept Mrs. Catherwood calm for a day or two but then George got acting very queer and finally confessed that Lyle hadn't gone camping with friends but just took off by himself! He's the kind that takes off, I hear. Probably he's at Virginia Beach right now, swimming in the ocean. So Mr. Catherwood is trying to get long-distance calls through all the time, to try to trace his son, on top of all the business about protecting the property here, and not get shot! Of course he's nowhere near the front line and neither am I, but these rubes with their guns they don't know anything about can wing you anytime and anywhere.

I hear there are about five or six thousand — yes, thousand — armed miners trying to storm their way in here and Chafin's only got a few hundred men, and he's sending to neighboring counties for reinforcements and they're on their way! Just like in the picture shows!

My friend Hough, the A.P. correspondent, showed me a list he'd made up of events down in this part of the state which led up to this war we've got on our hands. I think it's worth copying down so when Virgil Jr.'s old enough I can show him how things were and why this happened.

Thatcher, W. Va.

A truckload of working miners was fired on while passing a United Mine Workers tent colony. Two of them were wounded.

Merrimac, W. Va.

Three U.S. soldiers, who were stationed at a mine in Merrimac, were fired on while walking along the county road.

Vulcan, W. Va.

Several men, who were at work outside the mine, were fired on from ambush.

War Eagle, W. Va.

Two members of the United Mine Workers assaulted a man at work.

Sprigg, W. Va.

The bookkeeper of the Crystal Block Coal Company was assaulted.

Rawl, W. Va.

A miner was shot at Lick Creek.

Rose Siding, W. Va.

An attempt was made to blow up the tipple.

Vulcan, W. Va.

Ernest Ripley, state policeman, was shot in the back.

Chattaroy, W. Va.

Three men who arrived to get work there in the mine were assaulted and driven away.

Matewan, W. Va.

Two miners employed by Red Jacket Coal and Coke Company were assaulted and badly beaten by three members of the United Mine Workers.

That's just a very partial list of what's been going on between the pro-union men on the one hand, and mine guards and non-union men ("scabs" to the UMW) on the other. And nobody's safe and a lot of people are on the ragged edge as far as money and food are concerned. Miners are just ornery! And so are Chafin and his crew, and if you get right down to it so are the owners. Mr. Catherwood is a gentleman and all, but when you get right down to it, when it's a choice between what *he* wants and *they* want, then he's ornery. And it looks like that kid of his got a lot of that orneriness too. We still don't know where he is. He checked out of the Daniel Boone and then just plain disappeared. Something tells me my idea of him taking off to Virginia Beach or someplace like that was off the mark (Can't help using *gun* language around here!). I bet he's mixed up in all this mess somewhere and let's hope he doesn't get his fool head shot off.

Excuse me for having to talk about so much violence in this letter. Let's hope President Harding gets busy and puts a stop to all this craziness, since it's plain Governor Morgan isn't going to do anything.

No more letters from you but I know you're writing them and it's just all the confusion. Kisses for the little one and

With all my love,
Virgil

IV.

Lyle was hot, hotter than he'd ever been in his life. He was walking along a dusty country road somewhere in Boone County, having hitched rides in four vehicles, rented a mule to cross a mountain pass, and now it seemed he'd been walking for an eternity. Up ahead of him somewhere must be the rear guard of the Armed March. People along the road had confirmed that the miners, thousands of them, had passed through. How had they behaved, he'd asked them. Had they commandeered cars, stolen food, beaten anyone? Faces had closed like jailhouse doors at these inquiries, mouths clamped shut, except for the occasional person who would allow as how the miners "were just folks passin' through like anybody else." One woman had finally said, "They got a job to do and they's doin' it." In the slim smattering of opinion he'd been able to garner in Boone County the feeling seemed to be that it was none of their affair, that hotheads to the east of them and fanatics to the west of them were going at each other, and that they themselves planned to stand well to one side and just see what happened. On his last ride a man had suggested that he "get on over to the railroad and hitch yourself a ride on a freight car," pointing out this dirt road. It had led up a narrow hollow and on and on, between steep hills.

Lyle felt what many people from other parts of West Virginia, let alone other parts of the country, felt on entering
this southwestern corner of the state: feud-fear. He knew
that the old feud had ended decades before and that his fear
was groundless, *probably* groundless, but all the same he
felt a reigning hostility closing around him. A bloody feud
had risen in these hills, and the families, the impulses, the
emotions would still be here. It was not that he himself would
have become involved in a feud here in any era; it had
raged strictly between native clans. It was just that a pervasive
sense of hostility hung over these gulleys and hollows and
hills, a stillness and a steepness and a waiting and a watching and a fear. Narrow-eyed watchfulness seemed to him at
the core of everyone he had encountered, everyone he tried
to "interview." Hell, interview! He'd barely got the time of
day; it was almost as ignominious as his attempt to penetrate
the camp at Marmet. Maybe he was just a little squirt after
all, playing at being grown up. The memory of being more
or less thrown out of the union meeting in Middleburg, and
scornfully thrown out at that, burned in his mind still. He
took off his new straw hat and fanned himself with it. Then
he looked at the hat, with its red and blue band around the
crown. No one else he'd seen since leaving Charleston wore
one of these things. By golly, maybe that was the problem.
He didn't look right. They saw him as a kind of city slicker.
He took the hat by the brim and got ready to send it sailing
down into the little country creek running along below the
road.

On the other hand Lew Jenkins wore a straw hat. Lyle
wasn't supposed to look like the people here; he was a reporter, a journalist, from an important paper in the northern
part of the state. He clamped the straw hat back on his head.
The hell with them. He'd be himself and also dress like himself, Lyle Catherwood . . . or rather, Lyle Jenkins, reporter.
Firmly strengthened in his resolve to be himself, that is, his

adopted alter-ego self, determined to "show them," he stamped on up the gulch.

V.

Aracoma Hotel
Logan
August 29, 1921

Dearest Doris Lee,

We got the air cops in here fighting for us! I guess it's not the U.S. Army Air Corps, but we've got two De Havilland three-man aeroplanes that take off and if they're lucky clear Blair Mountain and swoop down over those miners' lines and throw gas-pipe bombs down on them! Sometimes the bombs go off, too! My A.P. friend Hough took a flight with them yesterday — he'll do anything for what he calls "color" — I call it suicide but there you are, that's why I work behind a desk and he takes notes skimming along the treetops with machine-gun bullets flying all around him.

If this letter sounds a little excited, it's because I am! You can't help but be. I don't like it, but it sure is different!

The reason I'm kind of keyed up is that the Boss decided this morning he wanted to see some of what was really going on, so we got a Ford and a driver to take us up toward Blair and there along the road we saw a real war with real nurses and trucks with supplies and mules and machine guns, ladies dishing out food, just like the sort of life I saw when I was in the Army at Fort Dix, except naturally much smaller. I hear President Harding said in the White House that the "insurrectionists" must lay down their arms or he was going to send in federal troops, but I don't think those six thousand miners on the other side of Blair Mountain heard it, or if they did they paid any attention.

For one thing, they're scared. Hough says there have been raids by company police into union territory, women killed, babies, I don't know what all. I don't know if it's true and neither does Hough, but what he is sure of is that the miners *believe*

[105]

that it's true, that their womenfolk and children, not to mention themselves, are just going to be slaughtered if they stop fighting and lay down their arms, that Don Chafin will come in like the Kaiser himself with a bunch of Huns and wipe them out! So you see, they're desperate!

As for *our* side, well, we've got better guns and we've got those aeroplanes and with more men on the way I don't see how we can lose. They can't get past us, up these narrow valleys, so easy to defend, so hard to penetrate, and if they can't get past Blair Mountain ("They Shall Not Pass" as you remember Chafin-Foch declared) then they can't get to Logan and they can't win.

And, anyway, how can the country let them win? You know I believe in unions, just between you and me, sweetheart. But even the president of the United Mine Workers himself, John L. Lewis, said that the union leaders here "are trying to shoot their way into West Virginia" and that wasn't the way it should or could be done. So.

But they're desperate.

I got your letter of August 25th. I'm so glad to hear that Virgie has mastered the dog paddle. So I'm glad that for this summer there is *something* to show.

Kisses and loving thoughts,
Your Virgil

Aracoma Hotel
Logan
August 30, 1921

Dearest Doris Lee,

I mentioned in an earlier letter the first death on our side, a deputy sheriff named John Gore. This morning after I had something to eat in the coffee shop I came out into the lobby and Mr. Catherwood was there. He told me to go to the depot to get a package that had come in on the morning train. I walked to the depot, it's only a couple of blocks, and after I got the package from the stationmaster I was just passing the time of day with him when a closed car, a Buick, drove up and out got one of the local doctors. I already knew him by sight from when the Boss and I drove up to the front and saw him working there. He helped two ladies out of the back seat. One of them looked like an efficient kind of person, and she was holding up the other, helping her. The other one, a young woman, more or less still a girl, looked like she was going to die, woebegone, saddest face I ever did see. Then she started to weep softly. The other woman tried to comfort her. The train wasn't quite ready to take on passengers so they came in and sat on one of the benches in the depot. The doctor couldn't wait. No doctor can wait in Logan these days. He drove away and these two women just sat there. The efficient one kept trying to comfort this poor lost soul, weeping softly.

"Who's that?" I asked the stationmaster.

"That's Mrs. John Gore," he said. "She just got married up with him four months ago."

"She's really all broke up," I said.

He looked through some tickets, and then he said to me, "She's tetched in the head, that's what happened to her. The shock made her tetched in the head. They was childhood sweethearts. She was just stuck on him from the time they was playing hopscotch. I guess she figured he'd be there right on through." He kept fiddling with the tickets and never looked their way, so they wouldn't know we were talking about them. "That's a nurse with her, taking her to Huntington. Insane asylum."

So now this damn war here is driving people crazy!

I think Mr. Catherwood is beginning to crack a little bit himself under the strain of it all. First of all, he doesn't seem to ever sleep. He has about fifteen long-distance calls placed every day and they come through at any and every hour, including four o'clock in the morning. That happened this morning and he woke me up — apologized, always a gentleman but said it was important I take some notes for him. Well, to tell the truth it wasn't important. It was about some stock transfers and I wrote down some unimportant notes he dictated and to tell the truth I was feeling a little bit irked at Mr. Catherwood for waking me up in the dead of night to do some work that could have waited till we're back in Middleburg (Gosh, I like the sound of that phrase, back in Middleburg, what beautiful words).

Anyway, he asked me did I want a shot of Canadian whiskey.

Well, you know I'm no drinker, and *never* at four o'clock in the morning wakened out of a sound sleep, but something about the way he said it made me think twice and I said, "Sure, Boss, that would be fine." So he poured us each a shot, and he sat down in the rocker in his dark blue bathrobe and I sat on the edge of the bed in my pajamas — I had to put them on after he woke me up, you can't sleep in pajamas in this heat. Then he began to ask me about the kid, our kid. Was Virgie old enough to go to school? What plans did I have for him for the future? Did I believe in disciplining him, and how much? Like that. Well, of course, I knew he was thinking about that boy of his and finally the conversation got around to him. Do you know what he told me? He's got the Baldwin-Felts Detective Agency looking for Lyle! Hell, I'd rather have the kid trailed by mad dogs myself, although I suppose they'll be gentle, or try to, with an owner's son, if they can find him. I can see Mr. Catherwood is disappointed, real disappointed, in Lyle, and that he thinks this son, the only son he's got, will never be able to carry on the Clarkson Coal Company, not in *this* day and age.

I don't think he's had a very happy life, Mr. Catherwood hasn't. Here I've been working for him going on three years and I always just assumed that anybody who lived in a beautiful castle and had beautiful automobiles and took beautiful trips and had a real lady for a wife and a healthy son and was the Boss of an enterprise that pretty well coined money (for him, if not for everybody else) would just naturally be happy. Well that wasn't too intelligent of me to begin with, and now I know it isn't true. It isn't true because he had some kind of picture, like a vision, of things handed down, that he was establishing a dynasty, that he was a king (living in a castle!) and establishing a powerful institution that would go on unchanged from father to son and father to son, and now, here in the first generation, he sees that the institution itself, the coal business, is full of holes, that maybe it won't be King Coal forever, not even for twenty more years, and what was it, what was his life, all about anyway?

That's what he's brooding about and that's the real reason he woke me up at four o'clock in the morning, to tell somebody a little about his sorrow, about this scapegrace son running off and this crazy shooting war in the middle of the coalfields with people getting killed and women going mad. And when it's all over, he said to me, how will we ever get the poison out of every-body's system, the poison all this hate and shooting and fear are letting in?

Well, I sure don't know the answer to that one, and let me tell you when I finally got back to my own little hot room — after a second shot of whiskey, he insisted on that — and took off my sweaty pajamas and tried to sleep in the hot sheets, the sky was beginning to brighten up over the edges of those steep hills around us, and I went to the window to look out, the hills were all still black, and the streetlights were glowing in the street below, where it was still black too, and then suddenly a motor-cycle came roaring down the street by the hotel and off toward the "front" and then some other cars came tearing and roaring down the street and pretty soon the daylight filtered down onto those narrow, gray little streets and men and boys were every-where again, rifles and automatics and holsters and cars back-firing to make everybody jump like hell, thinking some fool had accidentally shot them, and here came Sheriff Chafin shouldering his way along in his big boots and campaign hat, trying to look like General Pershing or somebody but to me he just looked like the schoolyard bullies I used to have in school, grown up now and with nobody around anymore to make him behave decent.

Ah well, another day and life goes on.

Love,
Virgil

Aracoma Hotel
Logan
August 31, 1921

Dearest Doris Lee,

The reinforcements have arrived. Yesterday afternoon a train-load of eight hundred of them got here from Huntington, and we were treated to a regular parade down the main street. A lot of them are young American Legionnaires and they looked pretty smart and like they knew which end of a gun was which. Maybe some of the boys in their teens can be put on the retired list now, Chafin can take back their guns and give them baseballs instead, and life will become almost safe in this little town in the hills.

The good women of Logan had a hot lunch for these new troops, right in the lobby of this hotel, and there was a lot of general optimism, a feeling that things at last are coming to a head and will soon be over, one way or the other. I heard President Harding was going to send in federal troops, and if that's true I think that's the best thing that could happen. Somebody, something, something *big*, has got to separate these two fierce tribes — that's what they seem like to me, somehow, two tribes out after each other's blood. Of course we've got "the law" on our side, Don Chafin that is, but Don Chafin does what Mr. Catherwood and the other operators tell him to do and what kind of a law is that?

Anyway, the new troops are here, all riled up and aching to get up to where the shooting is, and up there the shooting is as hot and heavy as ever, people are getting wounded and getting killed, the miners can't get by Blair Mountain and nobody can get them to retreat from it either, and who ever would have believed this could be happening in this modern day and age, in this world we just finished Making Safe for Democracy. If this is safety and if this is democracy, maybe we'd better start looking around for something else. Those miners are just plain crazy, and the operators think they're the czars of Russia, and where is the common sense and the ability to compromise?

Are we going to have a coal industry anymore?

Should I have stayed a schoolteacher?

Questions, questions! Doubts and confusions! Excursions and alarums, as they say. Wounded people going by on the back end of trucks, nurses, women crying, terrified-looking children, scared dogs: it's miserable.

I know we'll be back in Middleburg soon, and may we not bring this conflict, like some epidemic, with us.

Love,
Virgil

VI.

When Lyle reached the railroad line it was at a little siding, a scraggle of mining shacks, the sealed mouth of a worked-out mine, a collapsing little tipple, and a sign saying that the name of this settlement was Mary Lou, Unincorporated, Population 942.

Well, all nine hundred and forty-two residents seemed to have moved on since that sign was set up. Steep, heavily forested hills rose behind it, crows and blackbirds seemed to be the principal inhabitants now, but the railroad tracks were slick and shiny, in frequent use. A train would surely come along soon. He had a sandwich and some corn liquor he had picked up in the last town, and sitting down on the railroad track, he ate a ham sandwich lunch not too heavily laced with whiskey.

Then he moved off the tracks, over beneath a shady tree, to await developments.

Lyle's plan was none too clear in his head and he was aware of it. He simply wanted to get to where the fighting was and see what he could see, write what he found to write, send it to the *Middleburg Exponent* where he visualized it appearing, under his own name: by-line, Lyle Catherwood —

EXCLUSIVE SCOOP ON THE ARMED MARCH
Youthful Reporter Penetrates Miners' Lair
Violent Shooting and Mayhem Described
Exclusive Interview with General-in-Chief
By Lyle Catherwood, Special Correspondent

That would make a sensational impression in Middleburg. They would see that he had resources and courage they'd never dreamed of, and, best of all, he would have obtained his sensational scoop of the *miners'* side of the line so that no one could say his father's influence had made it possible.

He took another small swig of the whiskey. If he got a story like that it would certainly be "put on the wire" by the Associated Press and printed nationwide, for he knew from yesterday's *Charleston Gazette* that the fighting here was getting heavy national publicity, that the White House was involved in trying to settle the conflict, that federal troops from Ohio and New Jersey were poised to intervene, that a flight of aeroplanes had been dispatched by the Army Air Corps to Charleston, and that all in all he was quite close to the biggest story of the day for the whole damn country.

But he had to get right into it! No use to be *close* to, almost there, nearly. He had to be right up where the bullets were flying. And exactly where was that and exactly how he was going to get there, now that he had laboriously hiked far from main roads and wound up in this ghost town lost in the hills, with nothing to report on except crows and blackbirds?

Then to his combined relief and uneasiness he saw a coil of dust rising from the dirt road he had hiked along. It was a car heading toward him, fast. The car, a Dodge touring car, pulled up to the siding and stopped with a jerk. Two young men got out of the front, and a portly older man got out of the back. None of them was dressed in the "uniform" the miners had adopted: overalls, army helmets, red handkerchiefs around their necks. The two young men looked like ordinary guys, in work pants and caps, and the older man looked just slightly like Lyle's father. They had not yet seen him, seated in the shade of the big tree. They stood beside the tracks and seemed to be talking among themselves in a desultory way. Lyle hadn't the slightest idea who they might be, but the fact that they had transportation and that they seemed to be going about something in a purposeful manner was enough to raise his spirits. He stood up and started walking toward them. Both young men saw Lyle at the same instant and both jabbed their hands underneath their shirts toward shoulder holsters.

"Hey, don't go for your gun!" he yelled, trying to sound cheery and friendly, "I ain't goin' to do nothin'." He held his hands out from his sides and advanced more slowly toward them.

The two young men were staring at him with the particular narrow-eyed fixity Lyle had seen so often as he made his way through these hills. The older man, executive-looking, regarded him in a nonplussed manner.

"I'm Lyle Jenkins," he said with a grin. "I work for the *Middleburg Exponent*. Reporter. Lookin' for the war!" He widened his grin.

"That right?" said the taller of the two young men. "Got any identification?"

Lyle fished out the forged letter and handed it to him. The three men studied it in an unimpressed manner. Then the spokesman said, "This here ain't a press card."

"I'm free lance, special correspondent. They don't give us press cards, because we're temporary. But I've got this assignment."

"Driver's license?" said the older man in an expressionless tone.

"That, uh, that got took off me, somebody done took it." Lyle instantly damned himself for using such English on them; they would now be sure he wasn't a real journalist.

"Done took it!" said the older man. "What kind of a paper is this *Middleburg Exponent?* The jailhouse newsletter?"

"Oh I try to talk the way some of the folks in the hills here talk, because then you find it easier to interview them. I guess it's getting to be second nature, I've concentrated on it so hard."

They now seemed a few degrees less suspicious.

"Well, son," said the older man, "you're making a big mistake wandering around alone and unarmed — you *are* unarmed, aren't you?" Lyle flung out his arms obligingly.

"Yes, well, you might just get shot through the seat of the pants first, and then asked for credentials later. You're close to Logan County and there's a war on."

"I certainly am aware of that, sir, and my problem is to get to where the war's going on. I . . . lost my transportation outside Marmet and I've kind of had to improvise up to this point. And now here I'm stuck."

The older man studied him, and then he said, "My name's McQuade, T. C. McQuade, of the Chesapeake and Ohio Railroad. This is Joe Harry Beutel and Earl Sattersfield. They're with the railroad too. Tell me, uh, Lyle, is it? Tell me, Lyle, what's your feeling about the situation here, the Armed March and all this, Don Chafin. What's your . . . or maybe I should say your paper's view of all this? Both. You and your paper."

Lyle spotted it: the opening. Something good could come out of this if he played his cards right. This man's an executive with the railroad, these other two are some kind of assistants of his, or else guards.

He cut his answer to suit the pattern he detected in them. "Well, sir, Mr. McQuade, I guess the miners have their grievances and they need to be heard from, arbitrated, nobody's perfect and that includes the owners. But this here Armed March! That's insurrection! We haven't had anything like that since the Rebels — since the Civil War, and there was a lot to be said for both sides in that. But a bunch of civilians getting armed to the teeth and *invading* Logan! It's a crime, that's what it is."

"And your paper," said Mr. McQuade. "That the way they see it too?"

"Oh yes sir."

"Um-hum. Well, Lyle, maybe you'll see something of this war. You stay with us, maybe you will."

Conversation tapered off, but by asking an occasional random question Lyle gathered that they were expecting a train

[114]

to pass, that they intended to flag it down and board it here and ride with it into the war zone. Great. At least the railroad was operating normally, and he could be transported right up to the front.

Almost an hour after the arrival of the three men Lyle heard the unmistakable, lonesome echoing outcry of a train whistle far down the valley. "That'll be her," said Mr. Mc-Quade. "Earl, light up these flares, and Joe, get ready to wave her down."

Earl set the flares fifty yards apart along the track and lighted them.

Joe made practice passes with his big flag.

Then the engine rounded a curve and swung into view, approaching them steadily, not speeding. Joe began energetically waving his flag. The train bore on down toward them, the powerful thrusts of its engine roaring and reverberating off the steep walls of the narrow valley.

"Why doesn't he slow her down!" yelled Mr. McQuade. "He saw those flares! Wave that damn thing!"

Joe wrenched the big flag violently back and forth and the train pounded on down upon them, the engine roaring and hissing as it passed, the engineer leaning out his window. Two men behind him held rifles pointed at the four men standing beside the track.

Behind the engine and coal car there were five flatcars, and miners sat and lay around on them, all heavily armed. Suddenly the train was braked; with a lurch the linkage between the cars slammed together; the train came to a halt. It stood there on the tracks, engine steaming, helmeted miners looking down at the four men. From the engine the engineer and the two men with rifles descended and began making their way along the tracks back toward them.

"I'll be damned if I know what the hell —" sputtered Mr. McQuade.

Earl Sattersfield began to reach inside his shirt. "Don't do that!" ordered Mr. McQuade in a tense murmur. "They'll cut us all down if you do. Keep your hands well away from your weapons, and if they ask for them give them up."

The engineer and the two armed miners came up to them. Mr. McQuade had apparently decided to take a hard verbal if not weaponed approach. "By what right are you operating this C&O engine on these C&O tracks?" he demanded firmly.

"That there's my right," said the engineer, pointing at the two guns behind him.

"Who are these men? I am Theodore C. McQuade of the railroad management. These are two of my aides, and this is a newspaper reporter. You're operating stolen property and this whole operation is in violation of the law."

One of the armed miners behind the engineer spoke to the other. "Let's put this tinhorn executive on the train. He's got a real big mouth. Be on the telephone next callin' up Harding in the White House."

"Yeah. Step ahead there, the four of you."

"Wait a minute," said the first miner, "maybe they're armed. You armed?"

After an indeterminate silence Joe Harry indicated his shoulder holster. One of the miners took that gun and the one from Earl. "You armed?" he said to Mr. McQuade.

"No."

"You?" to Lyle.

"Nope. Just with pad and pencil."

"That won't kill nobody. Get on up on this car."

The four men scrambled up on the car. The miners there made room for them willingly enough. Lyle was simultaneously thrilled by his sudden thrust into the Armed March itself, and scared, and a little indignant, at finding himself a prisoner.

"What did you flag this train for and let us all in for all this?" he demanded of Mr. McQuade.

"Didn't know it had been commandeered. We just had a

report a train was on the right-of-way off schedule and we figured it was some U.S. marshals or federals or something. Communications everywhere are in a mess, of course. Never thought the *miners* would take over the *railroad!*"

"We're takin' over the state!" said a big, Italian-looking miner next to him. "After that, we give you back your little railroad train."

"To play with!" yelled another miner with a laugh.

"They won't be laughing much longer," muttered Mr. McQuade.

Lyle wondered, wasn't so sure, wondered some more. Maybe this *was* the Bolshevik revolution. They had taken over Russia, hadn't they, and that was just as big a country as the U.S.A. Maybe *this was it*, maybe the Catherwoods and the Clarkson Coal Company and the Castle and the automobiles and good schools and trips were all coming to an end, right now on the back end of a C&O flatcar, and up at the Logan County line; maybe behind them in Charleston and Middleburg other miners were seizing owners' property as easily as they had apparently seized this train, disarming law enforcement officers as easily as they'd relieved Joe and Earl here of their guns, and speeding along just as the train was doing now, toward victory!

Lyle felt fear seize him. Everything might be slipping away under his feet, a social earthquake might be about to shake his world apart. Nothing, absolutely nothing, seemed secure or guaranteed or even momentarily safe. He didn't really know for certain who he was in this situation, since who he was depended so much on his being a Catherwood, on *having those mines* and *that big house* and being treated as something special, from one end of West Virginia to the other and many points beyond, just because of who he was. And now . . . who was he?

He was not even a real newspaper reporter. That was a fake. Who was he?

The train roared and hissed and clattered up the narrow valley. Lyle decided that the only thing he had left — his false identity as a reporter — had better be put to use, lest all identity desert him entirely. He turned to the big miner who sat beside him, shotgun across knees, chewing tobacco calmly, staring at the woods sloping steeply upward, and now and then expertly spitting clear of the train.

"I thought this was supposed to be an Armed March," began Lyle, "and here we are, ridin' to the war in style."

The miner went on staring at the passing trees. "You call this style?" he said after a while.

"Beats walkin'."

Silence.

"Where'd you get on this train?"

"Up the line."

Up the line, repeated Lyle sourly to himself. I thought maybe you *dropped* down on it, from heaven.

"Up where it started out?"

A long pause; then, "Yep."

"Where was that? See, I got to write a story for my paper, the *Middleburg Exponent*? You heard of it? We want to get the miners' side."

"I ain't got a whole lot of information."

"Just one man's story is plenty. The human side. Wanna tell me that? Ah — listen. How about a swig out of my bottle here?"

The miner eyed the bottle, sized up Lyle briefly, and then helped himself to a swig. Wiping his mouth he said, "That's good stuff," and they began to talk.

Lou — Luigi — Pantano had been born in the Pennsylvania coalfields, the son of immigrants from Calabria. His father had drifted down to West Virginia with his family and wound up in the Kanawha Valley, where Lou was now a miner, married, with three children. His explanation of the family life, both in his father's home and in his own, boiled down to one fact: there was never really quite enough of anything — food, heat, clothes, medicine, education, recreation, and above all there was never really enough of the thing that he saw as most precious of all: a sense of security. *Where* was next year's money coming from? How many days of work would he get? What if he got sick, injured?

"And them owners," he said several times, meditatively, "them owners with their big automobiles."

"Yeah," said Lyle.

There had been the United Mine Workers in Pennsylvania in his father's time, and the union had promised — and sometimes even delivered — a certain kind of security. And now the union was here, knocking at the last great bastion of unorganized labor in the coalfields, southern West Virginia, and Luigi Pantano meant to be part of the battering ram which would drive it through all resistance and conquer.

"But don't you think it's necessary to have the owners, the operators, management?"

"I guess so. Somebody to handle the papers. But we want our share, fair weighing, fair wages, conditions, health . . ."

"And you don't want the Baldwin-Felts detectives."

"I get a hold of one of them" — he clenched his big and knobbed hands together — "I fix him."

The train, dubbed the Don Chafin Funeral Special — words primitively printed on a long piece of white cloth hung to one side of the train — continued on its way through the hills, stopping at little mining camps here and there where other armed miners climbed aboard. A peppery little man, no longer young, sat down beside Lyle after one of these stops. His name turned out to be James McDonald, he was a native of Scotland, and on the issues of the day his mind was clear.

"The bloated capitalists and the economic royalists are bleeding the workingman here dry," he began in a rather

[119]

high-pitched, decisive voice with a pronounced Scottish burr, on the heels of Lyle's first question. "They're all absentee owners, living in New York and Europe."

"Not all. There's the Cliftons and — ah — the Cath —"

"They're all absentee economic royalists who've never been to West Virginia and just bleed us dry, sitting in their palaces on Fifth Avenue and in Mayfair. We're going to confiscate all their property here, workers' committees are going to operate the mines, and the profits divided among the men who actually do the work. All those hifalutin' economic royalists, and their lackeys, the Baldwin-Felts goons, they're all doomed. We'll wipe 'em out! It's all over but the . . . the bloodshed. It always takes some bloodshed. Look at what happened in the Soviet Union. Our comrades there were forced to shed much blood in overturning the decadent old regime. Same thing will prove true here. But, never fear, we workers will triumph! Look at us here, in control already of this great capitalist railroad, heading for the last capitalist bastion, Logan! It's all over, all but the bloodshed."

Late afternoon had cast this valley into deep shadow, and it was cooling off rapidly. Lyle longed for another swig of whiskey, but his bottle was empty. His stomach was empty too.

Why oh why had he ever undertaken this crazy project? He felt really alone, completely cut off from people he knew, defenseless. And *they* were defenseless too, his mother, his home. Why had he ever disobeyed his father? What madness. And all just to prove something to other people, to make an impression, to show off!

This was no game going on around here, no college-boy prank or Halloween trick, this was a civil war, a class war, an industrial conflict, and maybe the beginning of a revolution! His family and the people he knew were in the front line of it, the exposed position, and on the *other side* from where he was now, rattling along with a bunch of his family's mortal enemies into the night, alone, an impostor risking exposure at any moment, a stupid schoolboy and a deserter of his cause. Lyle sat by himself on the swaying flatcar, wondering exactly how this night was going to pass.

VII.

Aracoma Hotel
Logan
September 1, 1921

Dearest Doris Lee,

Well, something is finally going to happen about this civil war, it seems like. According to the paper a brigadier general named H. H. Bandholtz is due in Charleston today to take command of federal troops, thousands of them, that are coming in, and these federal troops are going to disarm the miners. We are all now under martial law here, and what that means is that we have to stay in this hot little hotel more than ever.

It's not all so bad, as a matter of fact. Mr. Clarkson Catherwood is not one to suffer too much. His manager down here, Henry Kincaid, has a nice little house with a big screened-in porch on the river a little ways out of town and we can go out there now and then and swim and cool off. But you still know you're in a war zone because the manager drives us out there in his car with a gun beside him, and he gets us back to the hotel well before dark, so he can be back in his house, everything locked up, when night does fall. Everybody is so damn tense around here that if those federal troops don't get in here and disarm everybody soon we'll start shooting each other here in Logan — on purpose I mean — just to relieve the tension.

And things in the rest of the state aren't much calmer, I hear. Here's an editorial from the *Charleston Daily Mail* Mr. Catherwood showed me:

How many of us would have suspected the ugly fact that in many communities are human reptiles, some of them with clean bodies and wearing clean clothes and walking up-

[121]

right like a man, who (as openly as they dare) lend aid and comfort to public enemies.

Did we of West Virginia fight to protect freedom from the German monster only to hand it over, when gained, to an armed mob organized within the very boundaries of the state itself?

Such cattle, *canailles* the French call them, belong in Russia. It is the one place in the world today where they would get that bellyful which they deserve of the miseries which society suffers when free government is overthrown by its enemies.

Last night there was a meeting in Mr. Catherwood's room of some of the other operators. He introduced me to all of them, and since the meeting was confidential and the names wouldn't mean anything to you anyway, let's just say that Big Coal and Big Steel and Big Capital were all represented. Mr. Catherwood circulated the bottle of Canadian whiskey and the Cuban cigars, everybody got down to shirtsleeves, the fans in the windows did what they could to keep us cool, and they talked over what they wanted to do over the long pull.

What they want to do is very simple: they want to destroy the United Mine Workers.

"Nothing but a bunch of out-of-state radicals and trouble-makers," was one view.

Some of the people at this meeting were out-of-state too, very out-of-state, but everybody let that go. That was different. Owners could be national, even international, because, well, that's the way ownership, big ownership, worked. But miners were local, were and would be and had to be, and any agitator from outside coming in here and stirring the men up, well, throw him to Don Chafin! That's what Don Chafin's for! That's why nobody asks any questions about Don Chafin's methods. He gets the job done.

They did say, one of them did, that the Baldwin-Felts "operatives" (That's what our side calls them, operatives, like they worked for the telephone company. What the miners call them I would never tell a lady), that maybe they were a little bit too "crude," that maybe they were "rough diamonds," but you had to fight fire with fire; breaking heads was the only language some of those rabblerousers understood.

Anyway, these men, all portly in their easy chairs, easy chairs gathered from all over the hotel for this meeting — in shirt-sleeves, with the whiskey and cigars, look kindly enough, talk in calm voices, say "It seems to me" and "My view of that would be" and are polite and qualify what they say and sound so reasonable, but at the end of all the politeness and all the reasonableness they *aim to wipe out that union!* And here is where they start, out there in the firing line at Blair Mountain: They Shall Not Pass, and after that they're planning to roll the union back to the Kanawha Valley, and roll it up and out of Middleburg and right out of the state.

And who should walk in in the middle of this meeting but Sheriff Don Chafin himself! All creaking with leather and clanking with keys. Very big. Never saw him before with his hat off. Never knew he could be so gentlemanly, butter wouldn't melt in his mouth. Deep but soft kind of purry voice. All smiles and confidence, charminglike. Said he thought the miners up on the line were getting all the action they wanted and a lot more than that, that his casualties were "the minimum you could expect," but that the miners were falling over wounded and even killed "pretty regular." Then he got real kindly and said he knew they had doctors and nurses and a hospital train behind their line and he was glad of it, to spare them from any "unnecessary losses." He knows how to handle these big executives. They don't want anything messy, they don't want to see it and they don't want to hear about it. Family men, all of them, pillars of their communities, give to charity. I'm not saying they're hypocrites I'm saying they're human; they want to have their cake and eat it too. They want to destroy that union and Don Chafin is the blunt instrument they're using right now and they want him to break it and they want him to do anything he has to do to break it, but they want to minimize any feeling that they themselves are doing anything bad. No, sir. That's for the other side.

Got another letter from you today. It took a week to get here but I don't care I was so darn glad to get it and see your handwriting again and read the news about the kid. You don't know, because you've never been in a peculiar, isolated war zone like this, how strange it can make you feel, lonelier than you could have imagined possible, sometimes. Just to see Mr. Catherwood's face, for God's sakes, coming toward me across the lobby of the hotel makes me almost choke up with gratitude — just because I associate him with Middleburg, home, you and the kid. Now I can see how men got "shell shock" in the war. It wasn't the shells so much as the godforsaken loneliness and strangeness. Of course it's foolish to compare this affair with the Great War, but it does give you some of the same feeling. Well, I sure was glad to have your letter in my hands and hear that the boy is fine and that the doctor says that trace of anemia that's been troubling you seems to be fading away. That's swell!

Gosh I'm tired.

All my love,
Virgil

P.S. It is now 5:20 A.M. and just after I finished writing the above there was a knock on the door and of course it was the Boss, asking if I wasn't too tired would I come to his room to help him "clear his mind" about some things by talking them over.

Well, what was I going to do? Dog tired or not, he is the Boss, number one, and number two I know just how he feels, the way I said in this letter, very lonely. So I went in there and had a little whiskey and we talked about the meeting with the other operators, and then he told me what he really had on his mind.

The Baldwin-Felts detectives have picked up Lyle Catherwood's trail! They have agents inside the miners' ranks, six or eight in the Armed March itself — I didn't know they were as clever as that. They got a report from one of these spies that a young fellow answering Lyle's description got on a commandeered train over in Boone County and was heading for the front! This fellow says he's a newspaper reporter — from the *Middleburg Exponent*, how about that! He sure sounds like Lyle.

The Old Man is worried, naturally, what with his son heading straight into the shooting. So he sent back an order to their detectives in the Armed March to arrest Lyle! But how can they do that? They've got no power to arrest anyone, and besides, if a Baldwin-Felts man showed his hand there those miners would string him up to the nearest oak tree.

I sure wish I could call you on the long-distance telephone and just talk for a minute and speak to Virgie. The line is open out of here, but so many newspaper folks and operators like Mr. Catherwood and Chafin's lieutenants have it tied up all the time that I don't get a chance.

Well, you know I'm thinking of you —

With love,
Virgil

Aracoma Hotel
Logan
September 2, 1921

Dearest Doris Lee,

Just a note to tell you I think it is just about all over! Federal troops are in West Virginia and moving up toward the front. By this time tomorrow I think the shooting will be stopped.

See you all real soon,

Love,
Virgil

VIII.

As night fell over the railroad line the Don Chafin Funeral Special pulled into another little mining town.

Lyle had dozed off, curled up on the floor of the flatcar, and awoke to see long tables set up near the tracks, and women-folk behind them bustling about: food! He clambered down with the miners and made for the food — chicken and potato salad and homemade pies and apple cider. Delicious. It tasted as good, better, than anything he'd eaten at home, but then had he ever been this hungry at home?

While he was finishing up the last of the apple pie, sitting on a baggage-hauling wagon, a miner came up to him and offered him a cigarette. Lyle was out of cigarettes as well as whiskey and eagerly accepted it.

"Gee, thanks a whole lot. I'm fresh out. Didn't plan this trip too well."

"That so? Where'd you start out from?"

"Mid — well, Charleston. I'm on assignment for the *Middleburg Exponent*, covering this here march."

"So I hear. You with their bureau in Charleston? Or you from Middleburg?"

"Ah no, I'm from Charleston, but they gave me this special assignment, the editor's a friend of mine."

"Seem kind of young to be a reporter."

"Oh I don't know." Then, to cover himself, Lyle thought it wise to add, "Matter of fact, I'm still a student at the university. This is just a summer job."

"You're acquainted with Middleburg, though, aren't you, seein' as how you're workin' for the paper there."

This miner seemed rather unusual to Lyle, with his prying questions and all. Lyle took a look at him: broken nose, overhanging brow, chew of tobacco in his cheek, wrinkled neck, big hands; he looked like any number of miners on the Armed March. Then why was he so much more friendly than they were, so much more interested in him? He had had enough experience of miners in the last few days, and enough general knowledge of them from life in Middleburg, to know that by and large they were like a special tribe, almost like Indians on reservations, special and suspicious and private and uncommunicative. And here was this miner offering him a precious cigarette and questioning him about where he came from, or didn't come from. Very peculiar.

"Where you from, Mister?" asked Lyle pointedly.

"Mingo County."

Lyle whistled. "Mingo. Now there's *another* hot spot."

A train could be heard approaching, coming from the direction of the battle. It passed slowly through the station, heading toward Charleston. In the illumination of the station lights Lyle saw that the four flatcars held stretchers and improvised beds, wounded men lying on them, nurses and helpers standing and kneeling nearby. There seemed to be several coffins on one car.

Here they were, the wounded and the dead, rolling slowly away from the firing and the death, and here was Lyle, heading into it.

People were getting wounded and people were getting killed. My God, he thought, one of those wounded or even one of those corpses could be me on the next hospital train out of here.

Well then I'll just have to accept that, he said to himself fairly calmly. That's what it's all about, isn't it, when you set out to report a war.

"That's pretty gloomy-looking," he said to the man next to him.

"You stick with me when we get up to the firing," the man said with a kind of quiet authority which changed Lyle's opinion of him for the better.

"You've seen some action before?" he inquired.

"Yep," said the man, "a lot. In the war and . . . other places. You stay with me."

Lyle decided to do that.

"You heeled?" asked the man.

"Heeled?"

"You got a gun?"

"Oh. No."

"I'll fix that. And I'll show you how *to keep the safety on at all times* except if you really want to shoot. That's the danger around here," he continued, almost to himself, "getting shot by some goddam fool who doesn't know a gun from an outhouse."

The word circulated among the miners as they finished their supper that they would all sleep here and leave an hour before dawn the next morning for the front. Women and children in the crowd began assigning the men to different houses for the night. Lyle found himself assigned to a bunkroom with seven other men.

Snores, smells, the primitive discomfort of the bunk, all were new and unsettling to Lyle: he slept badly. When he got up with the others before dawn he was groggy and tired and aware that he was going to pass through the most physically dangerous day of his life feeling as he did. Fatalistically he pulled on his shoes, planted his straw hat on his head, accepted the coffee and piece of bread a woman brought to the room, and with the man from the night before — his name had turned out to be Oscar Petersen — beside him, climbed once more onto the flatcar in the dark. Rather quietly for a steam engine, the locomotive pulled them slowly out of the station and up more steep-walled valley toward the war.

The war for Lyle began almost softly: ghostly, echoing rifle shots coming from somewhere far up the valley. The train had stopped at a siding, and these faraway shots could be heard reverberating down the valley. Hunters, they sounded like, out for a day of sport.

Lyle's newfound buddy ("Call me Bull," he had instructed. "Bill?" "No, Bull") said once again, "Stick close to me," and with the other miners, silent now, they clambered down beside the tracks.

"We're goin' straight up this here hill!" announced an older miner, apparently a leader, who remained standing on the flatcar. "On t'other side there's a little valley, and other side of *that's* Blair Mountain. We here are goin' to outflank that mountain! You all hear that?" A rumble of somewhat doubtful assent rose up from the men. "We go on up this hill," he explained again, "we rendezvous at the crest up

[128]

there, a whole bunch of other guys are already up there waitin', we join up with them, cross the little valley and come up right alongside them scab lines. Then we shoot the shit out of 'em!"

A much louder roar of assent followed that.

A tall, skinny miner with a face like a chicken's came up to Bull. "Ain't you somebody I used to know someplace?"

"Naw," said Bull gruffly, starting to move off.

"I think ya is," continued the miner, a true mountain man whose "think" rhymed with "tank." He continued to eye Bull narrowly. "I think," he went on in a louder voice, "I saw ya at Paint Creek back in nineteen and twelve. Ya was one of them tinhorn Baldwin-Felts bastards."

"You're wrong there, partner," growled Bull. And to Lyle, "Let's get on started up the hill."

As they moved past him the tall, skinny mountaineer's eyes followed Bull's every movement. "Ya was thar," he said in a level voice. "Now ya's here."

Bull kept moving and Lyle followed, disappearing into the thick foliage and the trees at the foot of the steep hill with the first wave of miners. "Didn't stay and argue it out," reflected the skinny miner aloud. "That's the proof." He took his shotgun off safety and headed into the trees.

IX.

Aracoma Hotel
Logan
September 2, 1921

Dear Doris Lee,

We got a report that Lyle's on a train with some of the miners' "troops" getting pretty close to the fighting. Mr. Catherwood is fit to be tied. There's a Baldwin-Felts man with him, though Lyle doesn't know he's a detective. Mr. Catherwood figures that if Chafin's men don't shoot his son in the front line, then the miners will find out that Clarkson Catherwood's son and a Baldwin-Felts detective have infiltrated their ranks and they'll both get lynched!!

But maybe it'll turn out like a picture show. You remember that one we saw, *Rifles on the Range* or some name like that? Where the cavalry comes riding in with their banners flying and saves the settlers. The federal troops are due here tomorrow morning, and then God willing it'll all be over and I'll be back home in a day or two with you and the boy and *then* will we have a reunion! You know something? I forget what you smell like! Ain't that awful, as they say down here. That fancy soap you use that I like so much, I can't remember the special smell of it. And that perfume you put on when we go out either. I never want to be away this long again.

All my love,
Virgil

Virgil finished writing this letter shortly after two in the afternoon. He went down to the lobby to mail it, and there encountered Clarkson Catherwood. "That train with Lyle on it has got near Blair Mountain. The Baldwin-Felts operative is going to try to bring Lyle through the lines to our side." Clarkson's face was flushed, sweating, and not just from the heat. "It's madness, suicidal. Tomorrow the whole thing will be over. They should just stay there and wait it out. But I can't communicate with that fool operative. Baldwin-Felts! That man must think we're going to pin a medal on him. Why doesn't he just lie low there with the boy until tomorrow! It'll be all over then. No. Oh no. He's going to *bring him through the lines!* If one side doesn't shoot them the other will." He mopped his face with a handkerchief. "This will send Minnie straight to Weston." Weston was the location of the state mental asylum. "She'll never recover. Oh my God. Well, there's nothing we can do. I can't communicate with that insane operative. He thinks I'll give him a reward, for rescuing my son. He's read too many dime novels. Well, let's go up to the front. Let's go on up. Maybe we can . . . we can . . ." His eyes glanced hopelessly over Virgil's sympathetic face, and he clapped him on the shoulder. "You're a good man, Virgil. Been through a lot here. Well, tomorrow it'll all be over. You'll be home with your family. Don't know what I would have done without you. And I'll need you more than ever for these next hours. After that . . ."

They were driven out of Logan and up to the base of Blair Mountain. "Well, we can't see a damn thing down here," said Clarkson. "Let's get on up toward the summit, maybe somehow we can . . ." And he left that sentence too unfinished.

On foot Clarkson and Virgil began tramping up the steep trail, full of men coming and going, toward the firing line at the summit.

X.

Lyle and Bull advanced stealthily up the steep, forested hillside. Miners were filtering upward through the trees on either side of them. Bull kept looking keenly to right and left as they crept higher. Suddenly he nudged Lyle and led him into a thicket. They both hunkered down; Lyle did not have to be told to remain absolutely quiet. He had a premonition, a knowledge, of what was about to happen, but he could not accept it, believe it, act on it. He felt himself in the kind of nightmare where running for safety is vital but your legs are incapable of movement. The miners were now more widely scattered over the hillside. After about a minute and a half the skinny miner, hunched forward, moved into view, twenty yards across the hillside from them. Bull raised his rifle. Lyle was paralyzed. There was a loud, sharp report: the skinny miner whirled away from them and rolled over several times.

"Come on," said Bull.

Lyle's mouth, open, dry, tried to form some words, some protest, some indignant question. He couldn't. All of this was not happening. It *was* a nightmare. He would awaken soon. Meanwhile he followed the heavy, hunched shoulders of Bull farther up the steep, wooded slope.

Looking back over his shoulder, Lyle saw that two miners had come up to the fallen man and were bending over him. He could not make out whether the man was alive. "Get movin'," said Bull in a gruff whisper. "Want to get caught?"

"Caught? How can the —"

"I'm with Baldwin-Felts. You're Mr. Catherwood's boy. I'm gettin' you outta here. Your father's orders."

"Then that miner did see you before, when you were breaking a strike!"

"Too bad he's got such a good memory. Move, boy. They catch us, they string us up."

What kind of a story was *that* for the *Middleburg Exponent!*

But there was no time to think about anything like that anymore. The firing from the top of the hill was growing louder and heavier. This was unquestionably the front, the goal of all his efforts since he saw his father and Virgil off on the train at the Charleston station, and now that he was here he found only treachery and deception and an ambushed murder, danger of lynching, the long arm of his father, and a tinhorn from Baldwin-Felts, a murderer, hustling him across to the other side!

This was nothing like what he had imagined! EXCLUSIVE SCOOP OF THE ARMED MARCH — *Youthful Reporter Penetrates Miners' Lair —.* There was to be no exclusive interview by Lyle Catherwood, special correspondent, of the miners' general-in-chief, whoever he might be. The only thing which might well make the paper would be Lyle Catherwood's obituary.

I won't die, he thought suddenly, instinctively, an inner voice, unheard before. Bull was leading him close to the summit; he could see a crowd of miners milling about, guns and ammunition everywhere, their red neckerchiefs defiantly worn, ready to cross the narrow valley, lost in trees below, and outflank the enemy on Blair Mountain, an imposing shape, equally heavily wooded, just across the ravine. Bursts of fire from its summit now and then poured down upon the miners' lines off to their left. They themselves seemed not yet to have noticed.

"We ain't goin' up with that bunch," growled Bull. "Too dangerous. We're gonna slip down the other side of them trees, cross the holler, and up the other side. I got what we need to be recognized over there. Scared?"

Lyle shook his head impatiently. He really *wasn't* scared. Tense, yes, taut, very alert. But not specifically scared. Challenged. That's what he felt. *Be* somebody, this visceral inner voice, newly discovered in him, spoke again. You haven't really begun to live yet. So how can you die? It's impossible. It's against nature. Why would he have been born and his mother and Tot gone to all the trouble of raising him if he was going to be shot down on a mountainside in Logan in a war over unionization! It didn't make sense; it couldn't happen. It was impossible. There was too much in him still bursting to grow, be let out, for death to strike him down, here, now.

His city shoes taking a beating, his legs aching, hungry and thirsty, Lyle plunged down the steep hillside behind Bull. So long, news story, he said wryly to himself. So long, Lyle Jenkins-Catherwood, boy wonder correspondent, so long exclusive interview, farewell Associated Press!

A bullet snapped through some leaves just to the left of him. "Get down!" snarled Bull. "Crawl! Fast!" Like two warthogs, Bull and Lyle crawled and slid and clawed down the hill.

"Where's the shooting coming from?" asked Lyle.

"Behind. The miners."

"They on to us?"

"Seems like they is, don't it," answered Bull with sour humor.

"Yeah. They following?"

"Don't know. Get up. Let's run. They can't see too much with all these thick trees and brush."

Lyle ran and stumbled and ran after Bull. They were in the little hollow, and then they were starting up again, still shielded by the thick growth. Lyle was panting and gasping for breath, but he was not going to become exhausted. That was out. He would keep on going. He was not going to get shot and he was not going to get caught and lynched. That was out too.

He and Bull clawed their way up the steep flank of Blair Mountain. This is no-man's-land, thought Lyle fatalistically; you might know that's where I'd wind up in this crazy war: in between, in limbo, menaced by both sides.

Firing was pouring down from the crest of Blair Mountain onto targets off to their left; behind them the redneck miners were presumably filtering down through the trees into the hollow, and preparing to follow them up this apparently undefended flank of Blair Mountain.

Then another thought struck Lyle: this guy here and I are going to give the miners' secret plan to the other side, if we live; we're going to block their sneak attack; we're going to be sort of heroes, if we live.

They clawed and scrambled upward. Now the firing from the top of the mountain, machine guns, shotguns, something that sounded like a mortar, was growing so heavy and so sharp that it seemed to be just out of sight in front of them.

Bull stopped, pulled two pieces of cloth out of his pocket.

"Tie this around your right arm above the elbow," he ordered. It was a wide swatch of white cloth. "That's *our* side's identification. Them rednecks got their kerchiefs."

Lyle tied it in place.

His head felt suddenly vulnerable, perhaps because of the unbelievable closeness of the heavy firing. The miners all wore Army helmets; the other side, "our" side as Bull had called it, was probably even better protected. He had nothing but this ridiculous straw hat which he now realized with faint surprise he had automatically retained through flight and scramble, a talisman. His head felt as fragile as a goldfish bowl, something a pebble could shatter. I can't die, he repeated. It's not going to happen.

Suddenly Bull froze. A single gesture of his hand caused Lyle to drop to the ground and freeze too. "Clambake!" Bull yelled in his deep voice. "We're friends. Clambake! Clambake!"

There was a movement in the underbrush above them. Lyle looked up cautiously from under the brim of his straw hat. Two gun barrels glared back down into his eyes. "Friends! Friends! Baldwin-Felts! Clambake!" bellowed Bull.

"Stand up, hands up or I'll blow you to hell!" A voice cut through the surrounding clatter. Bull, leaving his gun on the ground, obeyed; so did Lyle. Now I'm in no-man's-land and we're unarmed, thought Lyle dreamily. One false move and it'll all be over. I *will* die. Or maybe these guys are crazy or nervous or marauders or something like that.

"Come forward!" ordered the voice. They started to advance Indian file, Bull in the lead. A bullet zinged into the ground just next to them. "You! Get out from behind that bastard!" Lyle sprang into their sight, and proceeded forward alongside Bull.

They came up to the two men, rifles trained at their heads. Then one of the men said, in a calmer tone of voice, "That there's one of them Baldwin-Felts fellers, for a fact. What ya doin' out there?"

Bull explained to them who Lyle was, and quickly outlined their adventure, and Lyle thought, I think we've made it. I think we're safe. "Tell them about the attack," he said breathlessly.

"Yeah I know," responded Bull shortly. He had not known, he had forgotten, Lyle noticed without surprise. Stupid but aggressive, slow-witted but opportunistic, Bull would always grab any credit within reach of his big paws. They were hustled off along the trail just behind the crest of the mountain in the direction of the firing. They came to a little ledge with a small tent on it. Below it was a larger tent where men were lined up holding tin plates and mugs. Milling about the first tent were preoccupied uniformed deputies, and to his amazed disbelief Lyle saw that sitting there in a camp chair was his father.

He does look older, thought Lyle, sitting all alone like that, thinking and worrying, not knowing anybody's looking at him, older, tired, sort of discouraged.

Then his father looked up and saw him. A disbelieving flush of happiness spread over his face (My God he *does* love me, shot through Lyle's mind. Why didn't he ever tell me?), and he sprang forward. "Why son," he mumbled, "son . . ."

They grappled each other awkwardly. His father smelled of tobacco and witch hazel, so familiar. I'm safe, reflected Lyle, home, safe.

Bull was in close conference with Sheriff Chafin, a frowning, formidable figure Lyle took an instantaneous on-sight dislike to. A military school bully, thought Lyle, just a plain, ordinary, paradeground bully who's wound up in charge. Maybe the miners ought to win, if he's the commander of the other — I mean, of our — side.

Lyle said hello to Virgil Pence. Virgil looked pleased to see him but somehow embarrassed.

"I hope I didn't cause everybody too much trouble," Lyle said.

"Well, your dad did worry some," said Virgil, "especially when he found out you were coming through the lines."

"Some miners figured out who Bull was," explained Lyle. "They'd 'a strung us up if he'd 'a stayed." Of course the decision to come through the lines had been made before Bull had been recognized, but Lyle's tendency was ever to shape truth into acceptable, logical, congruent patterns, and if in the process truth was modulated into a different key, into something else, well at least everybody's mind was easy.

What was the truth, anyway? For instance, in this war, what was the truth, which side was right? What was Right? Did it exist? Or were bits and pieces of it scattered all over West Virginia, from the Cliftons' mansion to Bennettown's shacks, and wasn't this battle an attempt to impose arbitrarily one version of Right upon another, when bits of it were in fact everywhere?

"I'd like to meet this man Bull," said Clarkson.

Don Chafin was moving off, bellowing orders as he went, out along the trail toward the miners' flank attack. Armed men and boys trotted up the slope and out of clumps of trees to follow him. Two men wheeled a machine gun on a little gun carriage along the path. Others carrying ammunition followed along.

They're going to machine-gun those miners, Lyle's brain implacably registered. If it wasn't for us, those miners wouldn't get machine-gunned. No, but these fellows here would be outflanked and some of them would have been killed. Where is the Right?

Bull came up and Lyle introduced him. He sensed that both his father and Virgil had to overcome some block before taking his hand.

"Well, you got him here," observed Clarkson.

"Yes, sirree, I delivered your boy to you safe and sound,"

rumbled Bull, with a big, set grin. Where's my reward, demanded his fixed gaze upon Clarkson.

"You'll write to me in Middleburg with your address," said Clarkson coolly.

"Oh, yes sirree," said Bull enthusiastically. "You got yourself a fine, adventurous boy there, Mr. Catherwood. He don't panic. Takes orders real good."

Clarkson was silent for a moment. A sudden, savage burst of gunfire behind them indicated that the flanking attack was under fire.

Bull shifted from foot to foot. "Well, I guess I better get me over there and see what's goin' on. So long, young feller. We done good, didn't we?"

"Yeah," agreed Lyle.

"Now let's get out of here," said Clarkson. "All this shooting. It's a scandal. Well, this time tomorrow it'll all be over."

"It will?" said Lyle.

"Federal troops are leaving Charleston by train before dawn tomorrow, and they will disarm those miners and that will be the end of it. Disgraceful. All these days fighting. A civil war. You'd think this was Russia or somewhere. Bolsheviks."

They were heading down the steep path. "Uh, sir, when do you figure we can start back to Middleburg?" inquired Virgil deferentially.

"On the first train," said Clarkson. "Tomorrow. Day after at the latest."

"How's everybody at home?" asked Lyle.

"Fine. Worried, but fine. I, uh, didn't tell your mother you were with those armed miners. We won't tell her that."

"No."

Clarkson was walking in front, Lyle behind, and Virgil was bringing up the rear. Now and then two or three armed men would hurry past them, eagerly mounting the path to join in the repulse of the miners' attack.

They rounded a curve in the steeply descending path. Two men and a boy of about sixteen were hurrying upward at the curve. Clarkson stepped past them, then Lyle; as Virgil followed he lost his footing, slipped feet first; his feet hit the boy's; the boy stumbled forward over him; the large revolver he held in his right hand exploded with noise; blood suddenly burst from Virgil Pence's mouth.

Lyle, transfixed, disbelieving, stared for several unreal seconds at this impossible blood, the terrifying pallor coming into Virgil's face. Then he rushed toward him. By the time they got him to the bottom of the mountain he was dead.

XI.

By noontime the following day total peace had returned to Blair Mountain. Federal troops arrived from Charleston behind the miners' lines, and the miners readily surrendered their weapons to them, trotting one by one into tents to drop their firearms at the feet of the troops. If some miners melted into the hills to hide their shotguns and ammunition against the day of some possible renewal of shooting, that was just mountaineer cautiousness.

The guns were put away. Don Chafin and his men descended from Blair Mountain, not forward upon the mining camps as avengers of insurrection, but backward upon Logan, to resume their usual duties.

The case, the charges and countercharges, the accusations and appeals, all disappeared into the courts, where they simmered and bubbled for years.

Tempers settled down to normal: banked, silent resentment among the miners, uneasy, watchful triumph among the owners. They had won; Don Chafin's grandiloquent battle cry, "They Shall Not Pass," had been lived up to: they had not passed. "They" faded back into their camps, up the steep-walled hollows, down into the pits, unorganized, their United Mine Workers repulsed, redress of grievances at a standstill. A silence, that is, the absence of war sounds, descended over all of the counties of southwestern West Virginia. It was not peace; it was waiting, more waiting on the part of miners who had already waited for a long time.

XII.

George was on hand to meet Clarkson and Lyle at the Charleston station when their train arrived from Logan. A hearse from Middleburg was there to take the casket.

Clarkson and Lyle climbed into the rear seat of the big limousine after they, George and some porters had dealt with the baggage and the casket. Lyle had bought several big bunches of flowers in Logan, and these he rearranged on and around the casket in the hearse. Then the two vehicles, the Packard in the lead, set out on the long, wearying drive north to Middleburg.

"What am I — what are we going to say to Mrs. Pence?" asked Lyle agonizingly once again.

"We can only tell her the truth."

"How did she sound on the telephone?

"Stunned. Numb."

"She won't be by the time we get there."

"I hope not. It would be very unhealthy for her if she was."

"What'll *I* say to her?"

"All we have to deal with is the truth." Clarkson looked abstractedly at the back of his hand. "Sad as it is."

"He wouldn't have been up there at that damn front line except for me."

"Yes. Circumstances can't always be foreseen." Clarkson slowly peeled the foil from a cigar, methodically pierced it, deliberately lighted it. He did not seem, to Lyle, to be taking anything like his usual pleasure in any of this. It was more as though he was looking for something, anything, to occupy his hands, and by extension, perhaps, his mind as well. Then Clarkson went on, "He wouldn't have been there except for me too. I asked him to go up there with me."

Elbows on knees, reddish face sunk in hands, Lyle mumbled, "And *you* wouldn't have wanted to go up there except for me."

There was a silence in the car as George shifted gears to climb a steep incline. The big engine rumbled expensively.

"Am I just no good at all, Dad?"

"Now son, nobody ever said that."

"I think a lot of people think it, thought it before, and now . . ."

"What happened to Virgil was a pure accident."

Lyle didn't speak for a while. Then he said, "No, it really wasn't. It was the result of me acting like a fool."

They reached Middleburg after dark. At the Castle Lyle greeted his mother. She did not reproach him; there was very little conversation of any sort. Lyle fiddled with a supper prepared for him in the kitchen and then went to his room, at the back of the house, looking toward the barn. A little crenellated balcony opened off it. He stood out there alone a large part of the night, watching the sky — a stunning, limitless September night sky — until dawn began to edge the rolling hills with a pink-orange glow; the stars, more remote than ever, withdrew, and Lyle prepared to call upon Mrs. Virgil Pence, widow, and her child.

His father declined to go with him. "Tell Mrs. Pence that your mother and I will call on her later today if that's all right. You should make this call by yourself."

So that reduced Lyle's choices to two: to have a few drinks

before going, or not to have a few drinks before going. He was about to face the worst interview of his life.

Well he certainly could not appear *drunk* at Mrs. Pence's, adding insult to injury, mortal injury. On the other hand, to go there without any kind of inner reinforcement called for a kind of fortitude which he felt that, on this particular morning at least, he did not have. After he had gone to bed, banks of clouds had drifted overhead and now it was a lowering day, September rainfall promised at any moment.

Lyle went to his closet, removed a small panel in the wall at the back of it, took out a bottle of Canadian whiskey, gulped down several swigs, took a stick of chewing gum from a pack placed conveniently next to his cache of whiskey, and closing the panel, strode around the room briskly chewing to take the whiskey smell off his breath.

Then, dressed in a gray suit and a black tie, he went downstairs, out to the barn, and got behind the wheel of the little Ford. He was not going to arrive at the Pence house in a Packard or a Stutz racing car.

The Pences lived on Overlook Street, where the frame houses were set a few feet apart from each other, high on a steep hill close to the center of town.

There were several cars parked at the curb. Lyle went up to the front door and knocked. A young man came to the door, familiar-looking somehow.

"I'm Lyle Catherwood."

"Hello. I'm Earl Pence."

A younger brother. Lyle stepped into the small, dark front hall. On the right was a small living room, and laid out in an open casket there, framed by a number of baskets of flowers, was Virgil. Lyle felt an insane, suicidal desire to burst out laughing. I really am trying to destroy myself, some part of his mind reflected objectively.

Doris Lee Pence emerged from another dark little room, a dining room, and came up to him. She was rather tall, and her face was pale but composed. She had on a severe black dress, and its simplicity made Lyle notice her face particularly: it had a delicate shapeliness. They sat down on a small couch in front of a window. Through the window the neighbor's house was so close that Lyle was sure they could overhear anything said.

From this couch the raised casket lid was visible, not Virgil's body. "Mrs. Pence, I just came to express my — the family's — everybody's so very sorry. This is terrible. We're all so very sorry. I know that Dad . . . I know that . . . well, pensions . . . well I know this isn't the time I just have to say that I — anything I can do to be of help at all and I know sorry is a cheap word but I have to say that and I hope you can understand and someday forgive."

She was nodding slowly, looking at the floor. "I guess it was the will of the Lord," she murmured. "Sometimes the Lord is very hard to understand. But it's not for us to understand, I guess, just" — here her voice grew suddenly tremulous — "accept."

"Can you forgive?"

"Forgive? The Lord?"

"No, I mean, fate, and well, we uh — we, the family, the Company going to Logan with the shooting going on and —"

She sighed tiredly. "It was just some accident. Could have been hit by a car out in front here. The Clark boy was, just last summer."

"I see what you mean."

"The Lord's will."

"Mrs. Pence, I have got to tell you something. I feel like I'm responsible."

That raised her eyes — they were a kind of green, he saw, shapely, intelligent — to look at him for the first time. "How can you feel anything like that?" she asked.

"Well you see when Dad and Virgil went down to Logan I kind of felt left out. They left me in Charleston with George,

[143]

that's our driver, and said to come back here. Well that made me feel real left out and so I got an idea to pose like I was a journalist? A reporter? And I faked some credentials and I got up with the miners' army, right on the train with them and right into the battle zone. There was a detective there, a company detective, and he brought me through the lines, over to the owners' side. And Dad knew I was coming through and he was worried and he and Virgil — that's why he and Virgil, they went up to the front because —"

Mrs. Pence's eyes were on his, and she had been following what he said with gathering concentration and finally her hands came over her eyes and she cried, "Oh what does it matter! He's gone. He should have stayed a schoolteacher! That's where he belonged. That's what he loved! And they loved him, the children, but *I* — I wanted more things! Yes. Better clothes, I said. Our child's future, I said. All things like that, he couldn't argue against, not Virgil couldn't. So I was getting them, beginning to. We were going to build a house, out toward the country club. I wanted that too. I wanted the ladies to call on me. And now you see what happened. 'Coal's a funny business,' he kept telling me, 'dangerous.' 'But you won't be in the mines,' I said. 'It's safe in the office.' 'I know I'll hardly ever be in the *mines*,' he'd say. 'But it's a funny business. Lots of violence buried in there.'"

She drew a long breath. "If you're responsible," she said, "then I am too."

Lyle felt slightly and strangely shocked by what she was telling him.

Life certainly was a lot more complicated than he had realized.

Outside he set the spark and began to crank the Model T.

I'm not responsible for everything that happens in the world.

These words broke over him with the force of an epiphany. It just seems that way, to me. But I'm not. I'm just a cog, like everybody else. All attention is not always focused on me. In fact, it hardly ever is, for the simple reason that most people are thinking almost all the time about themselves.

I am not in any way, shape or form responsible for all the things, most of all the bad things, which happen in the world.

The glorious panorama of last night's sky recurred to him. There is *all of that*. And there is one small cog, me.

I am not responsible for all these things which happen.

eight

I.

IF Lyle was not going to be a great newspaper correspondent, what was he going to be? A coal operator?

It didn't attract him. He sincerely found a lump of coal itself beautiful, when it was washed clean as Clarkson coal was, blue-black, lustrous, truly a black diamond, and just as valuable when you stopped to think that it heated the whole country and made every train run from Maine to California.

But mining, coal mining itself, had made a radically different impression on him. Four years earlier he had finally persuaded his father to let him go into a mine, expecting he didn't know what, and finding a strangely dangerous netherworld of clammy deadness.

When Clarkson had agreed, at dinnertime four years earlier, Minnie's eyes had roamed over her fourteen-year-old son and had asked a little tremulously, "Should he, really?"

"He's got to see them some time," said Clarkson.

"Sure I do. Down at school the fellows want to know about them all the time." Lyle had entered Greenbrier Military Academy in southern West Virginia that fall.

"The boy's got to know a little of what he's talking about," said Clarkson.

Minnie cast a piteous glance at him and then looked away. "What mothers of miners must go through," she muttered.

Clarkson had planned to take Lyle into Number Seven, his most productive and mechanized mine, but that day he was called down to Number Three, Bennettown, and since Lyle had to return to school the next day Clarkson decided a quick visit to this old mine would have to do. "It's an old-fashioned place," he warned Lyle. "We have lots better operations. But it'll give you the feel of mining, anyhow. And James is down there. He can take you in. I'll have to do some work in the office."

James, to whom Lyle carried a pie from his mother-in-law Tot, was not on the shift working when Clarkson and Lyle arrived in the Hupmobile — the Packard was never taken to the mines — and so he took Lyle in charge.

Wearing work clothes and heavy shoes, James led Lyle into a little shed where he was given a cap with a lamp on it, which made him feel very professional. The coal being processed by the machinery in the tipple made a rattling background noise which filled the tight little valley, combined with the small, clattering coal cars rolling in groups into the mine empty and out full from time to time.

James and Lyle went through the entrance, a concrete-lined opening in the side of the hill, and instantly a chill settled over them in this black-walled tunnel, which was just a little higher than James's head.

The black seam of coal with the tunnel blasted through it sank into the hill more and more deeply. To Lyle it seemed that the massiveness of the black, clammy, rocklike walls around and above them shut out world and sky and grass forever, enclosing him and everyone in the mine in the crushing, sterile, dead weight of black rock, massive and pitiless

[147]

and cold. He walked cautiously farther into this inhuman, heavy, reverberating place, clammy and chilly and eerie, as seen by its scattered electric lights and the flimsy illumination from the lamps on their heads.

After walking about three quarters of a mile, turning into various branches from the main tunnel, they came to what James called a "room," off to one side, where two miners were working. The distance between the floor and the ceiling of this room was about four feet. At the far end of it was the wall of coal being currently worked, the "face." The men were lying down next to it, in a puddle of water, hacking away with their picks at the bottom of the face, to undercut it.

Lyle recalled how James had explained in a soft, deferential, sometimes apologetic way which embarrassed this fourteen-year-old boss's son what the men were doing, what the purpose was, what everything was called.

After undercutting the face with their picks, one of them took an auger, a rotating boring tool, bracing it against his leg, and drilled a hole into the rocklike coal. Then they rolled a piece of newspaper into a tube shape, filled it with six inches of dynamite, inserted it into the hole, pushed a thin copper pin into the powder, filled the front of the hole with tamped bits of coal, removed the rod, inserted a long fuse, retreated to the other side of the room and lit the fuse.

There was a muffled, mine-shaking explosion, and the coal tumbled into the room in a thick cloud of gritty smoke.

Now the real work began. They pushed a small coal car forward into the room, along a spur of track which they had laid themselves. This little coal car was extremely heavy and required great effort to push it into position. Lyle moved to help but was instantly checked by James. Then, amid the acrid smoke and dust of the blast, the men began shoveling the pieces of coal into the car. There was not much space between the top of the car and the roof of the room, and it took some skill to sling the coal into the car instead of against the side or off the roof.

Once loaded, the car was pushed up a very slight, but because of the weight of the car now loaded with coal, back-breaking slope, out of the room, where it then went onto a downgrade and into the main tunnel.

Here an art called "shoving the sprang" came into play. The sprang was a piece of wood which had to be shoved through one of the holes of the moving wheel and pushed against the bed of the car to slow it down. Without that, the car could easily derail, and putting it back on the rails was a time-consuming exertion in a class by itself.

"When do you eat down here?" asked Lyle.

"Round about the middle of the day."

"Do w—— do they pay you for that time?"

"Oh no, you don't git paid for time, you git paid for the coal you gits out."

"Oh."

"Rats sit an' watch us while we eat," he said smiling.

"Ye gods."

"Steal our food if it ain't sealed in real good."

"Gosh."

"Cute little critters."

"Rats?"

"Yep. Never will work in a mine without 'em. Bad luck. Rats, they know when the mine's gonna blow. Some says they even know when they's gonna be a *cave-in*. Rats leave a mine or part of a mine, some of the men, they leave too. Smart little critters. Cute too."

"Cute?"

James drew a long breath. "Down there, it gets cold, colder than this. It's wet too, lot of the time. Ain't nothin' grows. No sun, no air like outside, no nothin'. It just gets to be like some place *out of this world*, nothin' livin', just that there black rock, everyplace, black rock, it's cold, this funny air, *explosions* all the time, dust, it ain't like noplace on this earth, and nothin' livin' 'cept these cute little furry critters. They's pets like. We feed 'em if they ain't already stole enough for the day. They's *company*. *They's* down there with us.

"Got to watch out for them cold months down in the mines."

"The cold months? Why?"

"Don't know, Mr. Lyle. Nobody knows, I guess. But that's when they's dangerous. Somethin' about dryin' out, the mine dries out in the cold weather. Then, that's when they can blow.

"Cave-ins too," he added thoughtfully.

"Yeah, I've heard about some cave-ins."

James explained the work he had been doing a few weeks earlier, "drawing the pillars," when the risk of a cave-in was worst.

While the room was being mined, large square sections of coal, the pillars, were left to support the roof. Then when the mining of that room was completed, the pillars were "drawn," removed for their coal content, and the roof began to "work," settle downward with many ominous cracking and groaning sounds, still precariously held in place by whatever pillars had not yet been drawn and by wooden props. The roof, with all the weight above it, began to squeeze toward the floor, the "bottom," James called it, and the strange groaning noises increased. This could go on for days as the pillars were drawn one by one. Experienced miners — James said he wasn't one of them — could gauge by the increasing, restless, groaning noises at what pitch to withdraw and let the whole huge section of coal and slate collapse with a tremendous roar onto the bottom. Drawing the pillars, he said, was just something he wasn't used to yet.

This had been Lyle's single firsthand experience of coal mining. He knew that if he went into the coal business, the world and the dangers of those miners — and of James — would never be his. But, he also knew that he was going to be aware for the rest of his life that this labyrinth of clammy menace underlay every limousine, tea dance and dividend in the world above.

II.

He decided to major in history at the university for the eminently practical reason that he had heard it was easy.

At home in Middleburg his informal adviser in West Virginia history and southern history in general was Mrs. Ophelia McClellan Stallings, "Aunt Ophelia," who lived in a small, white, resolutely Victorian house near the Castle with her virtually speechless husband, Clarence.

Aunt Ophelia, no blood kin to the Catherwoods but an aunt by virtue of old family intimacy, was the lifelong, it seemed eternal, president of the local chapter of the United Daughters of the Confederacy, and her allegiance to the Cause of the South was equally lifelong, militant and ever vigilant. Now in her sixties, she discovered this new generation around her, Lyle's, and set out to see that they were firmly and deeply indoctrinated into the glory of all that was the South.

Clarkson Catherwood called her "the oldest southern belle still on her feet" and tried to avoid seeing her when, two days after Lyle's visit to Mrs. Pence, Ophelia Stallings came to call at the Castle. She was already established in the front parlor, toque firmly planted on her head, pince-nez slightly atremble, when he and Lyle, returning from a round of golf, passed the door to that room and were firmly and with evident relief hailed by Minnie.

"Come *in*, come in," she cried. "Have some tea. Look who's come to see us. Dear Ophelia. Never mind about your golf togs. Come in and have some tea." Smiling, grinding their back teeth, the two Catherwood men felt they had no choice but to comply. Clarkson had always acted, sometimes successfully, on the principle that the best defense against Ophelia was attack.

"Tell me, Ophelia," he began, stirring his tea importantly as he settled as far back as possible in an abrupt armchair, "I've always been meaning to ask you and never have. McClellan, McClellan. That's your maiden name, isn't it?"

"Yes, yes, it certainly is," she replied in her somewhat hooting tone, a little muffled by false teeth and southern accent. "The McClellans, yes, Jefferson County, over on the Potomac. Of course the family originally came from Charleston."

"Oh is that so!" exclaimed Lyle. "I was just down there. Gosh it gets hot."

"You were . . . were you . . . South Carolina, were you?"

"Oh I meant West Virginia."

A minute, complex series of tiny starts and tensions ricocheted through Mrs. Stallings's face and figure and then she hooted, "My family were all South Carolinians. Now Charleston, *West Virginia*, that's a right charming little city, *new*. Don't know much about it." It was clear that Mrs. Stallings had adopted West Virginia and all that went with it, including the state capital at Charleston, but that her real loyalties, the bedrock, lay immovably in the oldest of the Old South. Since she lived her life in West Virginia she was devoting herself to establishing its southernness, but just as a baronet could never be compared to a duke in the aristocracy of England, to which she frequently harkened back through her lineage, so West Virginia could never be ranked with South Carolina. First things first.

"What I was getting at," resumed Clarkson agreeably, "was how your family connected up with General McClellan."

Ophelia swung her pince-nez to behold Clarkson. "*General* McClellan! General *McClellan!* That Yankee no-good murderer! Why he's no more kin to me than" — "you are" clearly was about to cross her enraged, trembling lips — "than that cur there at your feet." The "cur" was Cleo the collie, beloved by every soul in the Castle; Ophelia sensed this, and referring to beloved Cleo as a cur was her revenge for the suggestion that the Yankee commander during the early part of the War Between the States could have had the remotest kinship connection with her and hers.

She suddenly rounded on him again, the color rising beneath her powder. "Why Clarkson, I do believe you are pulling my leg." Lyle started: pulling her *leg!* Pretty racy language for Aunt Ophelia; she wasn't exactly Queen Victoria after all. He was beginning to see that there was always a trace of earthiness in these southern ladies: Puritanism was for New England. "You know no blood kin of mine," she went on with spirit, "could have been a Yankee drummer-boy, let alone commander. And what's more, it was that show-off rascal McClellan that abducted these counties here away from the great state of Virginia and *railroaded* them into the Union. All illegal, unconstitutional, just tore them away from the mother state and thrust them at that grasping Mr. Lincoln in Washington. Why, these counties were as loyal to the South as . . . almost anyplace. *Of course* there was some Yankee sympathy here. There was Yankee sympathy in Georgia! But that scamp McClellan came through here soon as war broke out, the Southern Army was over in the eastern part of the state, winning that great victory of Manassas, chasing those Yankees clear back to Washington City, and so McClellan had hardly any opposition here. He *occupied* these counties. It was a crime. Scandal. Treachery." She fumbled in her purse for her inhaler, took a revivifying whiff. "I declare, there was nothing else like it in the War Between the States. How can this section ever have been Yankee? Why Stonewall Jackson himself was born and grew up not twenty-five miles from here. Call *that* Yankee! You think McClellan could have come through here if *Jackson* had faced him? Read your history. Nobody could go through Stonewall Jackson, everybody could stop McClellan. Trouble was, there was nobody here to do it. They were all over winning at Manassas. Do you recollect who commanded the Army of Virginia at that glorious victory at Manassas? Do you? Lyle?" He rolled his eyes to the ceiling thoughtfully and then admitted he didn't. "Stonewall Jackson, of Harrison County, West . . . as it now is . . . Virginia, that's who. So don't start talkin' to me about that . . . that buffoon McClellan, and don't try to tell me these were Yankee counties."

After a courtly, unruffled silence to allow for the shock waves of this squall to subside, Clarkson said easily, "I take it you're not related to him, Ophelia." As her proud bosom, perfectly designed for ceremonial sashes, swelled preparatory to another foray at him Clarkson went on, smiling disarmingly across at her. "The head of that 'illegal' government that joined West Virginia to the Union was born and raised even closer to where we are now than twenty-five miles — about five minutes from here as the horse canters."

"Pierpont!" she hooted. "There are opportunists and turncoats in every war."

"Most of the men from these counties served, I take it from *my* reading of history, in the Union Army, three to one, I seem to remember, Union over Confederate."

Ophelia was monumentally unimpressed. "Who do you think wrote those history books except dyed-in-the-wool Yankee Republican Easterners? You think anybody believes those numbers? Do you know when they did the countin'? Eighteen sixty-five, eighteen sixty-six, that's when they did the countin'. Well, what are people going to tell a Yankee Occupation administration around here, after Appomattox? Lied like troopers, that's what they did. All you've got to do, if you were as old as I am, is remember what the men *said* to

[154]

you, and to your daddy, or to recall which uniform they got out, when it was safe to get 'em out, to parade in, years after it was all over. Then you'd see. We are the South here, sir." Lyle almost exploded with amazed mirth at this totally unexpected "sir"; it rang with the defiant pride of a plantation lady addressing marauding Yankee soldiers about to burn down the mansion. "And we must hand down that precious heritage to our children and never, never let it be diminished. You remember that, Lyle, you tell your children.

"Of course, I have to say one thing. The slavery business, holding of slaves, that was wrong, an evil thing. There was twenty thousand of 'em in these counties when the war broke out. We had some, my people. We didn't approve of it. We didn't dare think of freeing any of them — only had ten or twelve. The neighbors around us, well if we'd freed 'em, Lord knows what they might have done. So many people in the South never approved . . . Mr. Jefferson for one.

"Well, the slaves did get freed, didn't they. The Yankee way. The Yankees just came in here and they destroyed slavery all right. And they destroyed our way of life too. And our property. And then they went away and the Negroes were free and poor as church mice with nobody to look after them and no plantation working anymore and no business operating and everybody in misery. That's fixing things by war and violence for you. Men's way. You men," she snapped at Clarkson, "that's the way you solve things. Send that McClellan to kidnap western Virginia at the point of a gun, end slavery at the point of a gun." She drew a lace-fringed handkerchief from her purse and daubed experimentally at her lips with it. A faint perfume escaped from the purse; Aunt Ophelia was all little handkerchiefs and little inhalers and vials of perfume and cachets of rose leaves and tiny pots of face powder. Having made this gesture to her femininity, she returned to the attack, head-on. "These miners, going to

Logan with their guns. That man of yours — what's his name? Claflin? — setting up his machine guns against them." She nodded abstractedly to herself.

The three Catherwoods, who had heretofore enjoyed and patronized dear, Confederate Aunt Ophelia, sat somewhat stunned, wordless. Lyle glimpsed that beneath the proper lady in her there waited a tough, hawk-eyed old bird. His father's baiting of her about General McClellan had released her. After all, she had lived from sometime in the 1850s until 1921 in a border state, struggling first through a Civil War and then through an Industrial Revolution. "You don't think any of that shooting down in Logan is going to solve anything, do you?" she finished.

"They attacked us," said Clarkson quietly. "What else could we do?"

"Hm . . . yes . . . well . . . yes . . . martial law . . . no free speech . . . evicting people from their homes . . . yes . . . well . . . times are different, that they surely are, they surely are." She blinked and smiled placatingly at the members of this important coal family. She retreated, as General Lee of sacred memory had so often done so effectively when necessary, drew back to the safety of her home territory, the War Between the States, after this tough little sally, just like one of Jeb Stuart's, into the adversary's camp. "You know what the most terrible year in the history of these counties was? Do you, Lyle Boy?"

Lyle raised his eyebrows in perplexity and then blurted, "This year? Nineteen twenty-one?"

"No. Certainly not. Of course not. What's been goin' on now, well, it doesn't compare with the worst year . . . That year, Lyle Boy, was eighteen sixty-three. That prancing peacock McClellan came through here in eighteen sixty-one, and believe me by eighteen sixty-three there wasn't a Yankee sympathizer in sight around here. Who likes to be occupied by

[156]

an army from someplace else? So everything just sort of collapsed. Confederate Irregular troops were operating right out of here in Middleburg. There wasn't . . . well there just wasn't any government. Houses got burned down, livestock run off, somebody waylaid the sheriff and took all his clothes away. Brother against brother. Violence. No rhyme and no reason." She paused. "I remember it, a little, over in my county. We buried the silver and everything valuable back near the grape arbor. I can remember my mama taking me over to sit down in the window seat and saying, 'Now remember, Ophelia Jane, when any strange men come here, if they should ask about the silver and any other valuable things — you remember my necklace you liked to touch? — things like that, *we sold them.* Now you remember that, hear? *We sold them.* Had to, because of the war. Everything was sold. And you will never mention anything about burying them.' 'Yes'm,' I said. And there were some bands of men came through, several times. They never found what we'd buried. I reckon," she added dryly, "that's why one band burned the barn, and another band burned down the house." She pronounced this last word as if it were "hose." "I was so scared, little bitty girl, and it just seemed like the world *was* coming to an end. Next thing I expected was an earthquake, or the Devil coming up out of our well! And to tell the truth of it the world was coming to an end, our world, it was coming to an end and nothing ever could bring it back. Not even prosperity. This . . . all this, all this here, the . . . you . . . what I mean, we all do admire the Cliftons and their *lovely homes* so very much, but, what I mean is, well, it's really not the same, not the same thing at all. We were *secure,* thought we were, sitting on our own land, our crops, our food, our people. Each plantation and farm was like a little world of its own. Didn't depend on selling coal to New York, or labor unions, things like that. That made us feel . . .

easy, safe. And now, my stars, nothing's safe in West Virginia, and it never has been since that monster McClellan came through here with his guns."

Ophelia McClellan Stallings took another sniff from her inhaler. "We had what you might call gentlefolk here in those days. And now, well, what we have here . . . what we seem to have here"— an apologetic, forewarning little cough — "buccaneers." She tittered in a way that sounded faintly hysterical around the edges. "Forgive me, Clarkson, dear. Don't know what's got into me today. Been having palpitations and, my goodness, my tongue runs away with me."

Minnie, who had been a study in pastels, lounging back in a Victorian settee, leaned intently forward. "Ophelia, dear, Clarkson isn't offended. Nobody is offended," she spoke with a subdued emphasis, "when they're hearing the truth, not if they're honest." Clarkson stared noncommittally into space. "You know that I've been trying to improve things around Bennettown and some of Clarkson's other towns for years. Oh in little ways, playgrounds, milk. My dear, you can't imagine the opposition, ostracism almost, I've met with. 'What do you mean going down there, a lady like you?' Thelma Hayes says that to me every three months or so. The other ladies over at the church, the ones with men in coal at least, think I'm the most interfering, bohemian, Bolshevik maybe, that ever was. 'But what *do* you do down there?' they keep asking me, screwing up their faces as though I'd just returned from Hell. 'I try to help out a little,' I tell them. 'But the churches have missions down in the mining camps.' It's always 'down' in the mining camps, never 'over' or God forbid 'up.' 'You don't *belong* there,' they say, and they're really puzzled, indignant in fact. 'My husband owns the company,' I say. 'But what's that got to do with it! That doesn't give you the right to interfere in something that doesn't concern you.' 'But it does concern me,' I tell them. 'I'm concerned because those people are so poor and have so little and we have so much.' That really riles them up. *But that's the way it's supposed to be!* Anything else is union radical talk, Bolshevism. It could destroy this industry, it could destroy us, our homes, our children. You are a dangerous woman and you don't even know it.' 'I'm not,' I say. 'I just think it's dangerous *not* to do anything.' 'No it's not,' they say, 'because this is the way it's always been.' "

"Fiddlesticks!" exclaimed Ophelia. "That's the way it's been for the last thirty years, that's all. It's piracy," she repeated, seized in spite of her manners by her vision. "You're trapped in it, we all are, here on top, in Middleburg. We've seized the wealth, you know, and now we have to fight to keep it. I say 'we'; Clarence's practice is all based on coal operators. We don't know anything else to do, do we, up here on top? We fight for every dollar we've won. It's all so big now, so expanded. We *have* to hold on to our big profits, otherwise . . ." And she left that sentence unfinished.

Otherwise, Lyle finished it in his head, I'll have to go out and work for a living . . . and what can I do?

Otherwise, finished Minnie, these walls will begin to crumble and Lyle will have to face a hostile world, and I . . . somehow I will be — oh — overwhelmed. Because I will have so dismally failed. I *saw* the injustice. I *knew* it had to be redressed somehow. But I *could not do it*, because I was too weak, too . . . too feminine. Too neurasthenic, too much a meek little convent-bred lady in her Castle.

Otherwise, Clarkson reflected, everything I've devoted my life to will vanish. But it won't. I won't let that happen. I will not. Because if I did, then I would just amount to nothing. Nothing at all. Not exist. Minnie and I would both wind up in Weston.

III.

Ever since his experience with the Armed March, since coming through the battle lines with Bull, since the impossible instant when he saw blood pouring from Virgil Pence's mouth and since Mrs. Pence's acceptance of what she saw as her share of guilt in Virgil's death, Lyle had been pondering what had risen in his mind as a result of this sequence: the essential selfishness of, it seemed, everyone.

Having reached this conclusion, he began to feel somewhat cheered about himself. God knew he was selfish! He wanted spiffy clothes and a swell car, a top girl; he rarely passed a mirror without sneaking at least a glance at himself, half in admiration half in critical appraisal, but *all* directed at and concerned with himself. He wondered about and dreamed about his future all the time: *his* future.

What little time remained from all those self-preoccupations was devoted to shooting pool, going to the picture shows, parties, running Cleo the collie, sneaking Canadian whiskey, playing golf, driving his car fast, sleeping, masturbation, flirting, and evading feelings of guilt as much as he could.

And now this last preoccupation was perceptibly lighter. Everyone was preoccupied with themselves. (Oh me, bad grammar.) Everyone was preoccupied with his or her self. School days, school days. How glad he would be when they were over, and nobody would bother him with things like grammar again.

What had the Armed March been but a bunch of miners determined to have their way, *their* way, by any and every means? And what had Don Chafin's defense been but the mine owners determined to keep what they had, *they* had, by any and every means?

And what had Aunt Ophelia been talking about but the South fighting to preserve its way of life, *its* way of life, and the North determined to change that into *their* way of life.

It was all willful self-interest — me, me, me — I want mine. It was, Lyle reflected wryly — another pristine thought — all pretty crude and unattractive and basically uncivilized and certainly un-Christian in any sense of that word which he understood. But even in Christianity there was the Golden Rule: Do unto others as you would have them do unto you. Do unto you. And: Love thy neighbor as thyself. As thyself. Love thyself. Christ, even *Christ* was selfish!

Lyle was beginning to get an inkling, more than an inkling, of something behind all his feelings, some assumption he had about himself that had always been a terrible liability to him. It was some feeling he had. It was why he drank, why he traipsed after rebelling miners, made asinine remarks, argued with girls at parties. But what was it exactly? He couldn't put his finger on it. But it was all around him, it was as though it was his skin, so much a part of him that he couldn't really feel it.

I know what I will do, he resolved. I am going to change myself. Anybody can do that if he makes his mind up to it. I am going to become different and be a big improvement everywhere.

And I am going to be unselfish, completely unselfish.

Maybe then the paralyzing vision of Virgil Pence — a really nice guy, not particularly selfish — lying in that curve of that path, the shocking pallor coming into his face, the terrible fount of blood, the sickening realization that Virgil would never have been on that path except that Lyle Catherwood had wanted to show off, *be* somebody at any cost — maybe that vision would fade.

He was going to be completely different now, and the first place in which to turn over his new leaf would be with his studies.

Lyle began spending much more time at the university in Morgantown. He exercised in the gym. He threw out the

[161]

cache of whiskey, both in Morgantown and at home, and broke off relations with his bootlegger. He gave up poker; at night he tended to be in bed by ten o'clock. He even began doing his academic homework. Weekends were spent at Morgantown, often working in the library or else running around the track.

Varsity football was too overwhelmingly important at the university to be ignored, and Lyle like everyone else attended the games there, but this struck him as not at all a dissipation or an act of selfishness, but instead as a ritual of almost religious seriousness. The Mountaineers of West Virginia were a football team to reckon with on a national scale. Seated in the cheering section at Mountaineer Field, a steep, U-shaped concrete stadium overlooking the Monongahela River, he was swept away by the sheer magnitude of it all, the glorious completed passes and long runs, the tragic fumbles, the appalling interceptions, the unforgettable victories. It was the most inspiring drama taking place in West Virginia as the twenties went forward, a field of epic struggle where, if he had been good enough, he would have played alongside miners' sons on football scholarships from Bennettown or Monongah or Logan; here equality was truly enforced, or rather, preeminence went to those with the most strength, skill, and dedication, with no reference at all as to who Daddy was or what kind of house you lived in, or even what brand of English you spoke. It was a great battlefield, fit for heroes, and these heroes were made and occasionally, heartbreakingly, unmade, Saturday after Saturday. Lyle watched, taut with excitement and involvement, as other young men, just his age, some of them friends, solved *their* problem of being someone, getting the limelight, becoming a star.

Well he himself had put all of that, at least the selfish part of it, behind him, and now he was determined to be good, syrupy sentimental churchy word though it might be. He would never to save his life have confessed such a nunlike ambition to another living soul, but in the innermost chamber of his own thoughts this was uppermost. He *had* to be good, very good indeed now, because he sensed with deep uneasiness that if he was *not* good now some kind of baleful, very peculiar, and extremely unhappy future awaited him.

He was eighteen years old, rich and indulged; this was the Jazz Age, in the midst of the greatest boom the Middleburg field had ever known.

IV.

One brilliant October afternoon Clarkson had George drive him to Morgantown for the football game. He had lunch with Lyle at the fraternity house and then they walked to the football field under gold-leafed trees, an autumnal wind flirting with their overcoats and hats. Lyle felt a throat-catching excitement rising from people hurrying by, and the echoing uproar rising out of the stadium.

Utterly unannounced, Virgil Pence's face flashed vividly before Lyle's mind's eye. I've got to say something to my father about him, he thought automatically.

"Dad, uh, whatever happened about Virgil Pence and you know his pension and insurance and things like that?"

After a pause his father replied, "I've investigated it. His widow will have an income from insurance."

"How big?"

"Ah — modest."

"Modest? Real modest?"

"Modest. Quite modest."

"Does he get a pension from us?"

"There was no provision for that when he was hired."

"Yes, but now . . . now that he's —"

"I am going to make some kind of settlement."

"What kind?"

Another pause and then Clarkson said a little testily, "Leave this matter to me."

But I *can't* leave it to you, Lyle wanted to shout. I've always left everything to you, and this time I can't because you aren't responsible and I am. And where will I be if I *always* leave *everything* to you!

Apparently sensing Lyle's continuing uneasiness Clarkson added, "We can discuss it later if you like."

"We have to, somebody has to, because she's got a young kid, and well, somebody has to keep them out of the poorhouse!"

Clarkson gave him a dry, sidelong glance. "Don't overdramatize things, son. Things don't usually work out as badly as all that. Or as well as we like to hope. Mrs. Pence will be all right. She's a young woman, an attractive young woman. Nature will take its course. She'll remarry, and some other young fellow will provide for her and that child."

Lyle was startled. Remarry: he'd never somehow thought of that. How . . . well, *ordinary* of her! What a run-of-the-mill undercutting of the whole tragic drama. Remarry! And devoted Virgil barely interred. That child growing up with some other father? It didn't seem decent somehow; it wasn't fitting. All the drama would drain out of it, *his* role, hers, the Armed Marchers', Sheriff Chafin's, his father's. Remarry?

Striding along beside his father in the exhilarating, balmy gusts of October's breezes toward Mountaineer Field, amid the expectant hubbub of the dressy, game-going crowd, Lyle experienced an odd visceral flash: he couldn't name it, yet.

They entered the ramp leading beneath the stands to their seats.

"Great day for a game!" somebody called across the throng to Clarkson. "We goin' to take 'em?"

"You bet we are!" Clarkson called back cheerily.

"Are you bettin' we are?" the other called out in an almost challenging voice.

"Sure am."

"Well then, me too. If Clarkson Catherwood puts his money on something, that sure is good enough for me!"

West Virginia did win that afternoon, and the man who had followed Clarkson's advice, "Moon" Mulvihill, a coal operator from Charleston, ran into them again on the way out and collared Clarkson for a quick business discussion. It took place in the back seat of the parked Packard, and Lyle waited in the front seat with George, a pane of glass separating them from the conferees in back.

It always seemed to be like that for Lyle, when his father and business were concerned. He could see it all transpiring, the mysteries of his father's wide-ranging and consistently successful dealings, but he himself seemed consigned to a soundproof compartment with the servants. In the back seat, whatever secret abilities and prophetic knowledge his father possessed was being transmitted to this other businessman, and this man, this "Moon" Mulvihill, a dirt farmer turned strip miner turned millionaire, would follow it, just as he had followed Clarkson Catherwood's football advice, and prosper some more. It all seemed to go *past* him somehow, past Lyle, over his shoulder, behind his back, ungraspable, not quite overheard, elusive as ground fog. He would never learn the mystery, the secrets, the techniques and prophecies himself. He felt he wouldn't. He suspected that it was as beyond him as scoring that spectacular touchdown at Mountaineer Field this afternoon.

What could be surer proof of that than his father's never really trying to explain any of it to him, retreating always behind a pane of glass for his conferences, leaving him at Charleston with orders to go home to Middleburg while he himself pressed on to the crucial Logan with Virgil Pence? His father was undoubtedly a brilliant businessman, everybody knew that, and if his *father* didn't see the beginnings of such abilities in Lyle, well then they probably weren't there. They just weren't there to develop. And that was that.

His spirits were now very low, all the buoyancy of the exuberant October football afternoon shriveling with the long shadows of approaching dusk, a gray-turning day in glum, steep-hilled Morgantown, its waste-discolored river, its scarred hills. Lyle got out of the car, bidding George, Mr. Mulvihill and his father good-bye, and trailed back to the fraternity house.

Coming through the door into the front hall the first person he encountered was Fanny Carstairs, wearing some kind of a gold-colored, metallic dress through which a good display of her legs slithered in and out as she danced. "Golly, I'm tuckered out!" she exclaimed to her partner. "Lyle Catherwood. You always have refreshments on you. Give me some refreshment."

Cursing himself for having done away with his supply of Canadian whiskey, Lyle scouted about the fraternity house and managed to buy a bottle of some clear fluid which, he was told, mixed with fruit juice would be very effective. Fanny and he then procured a can of fruit juice in the kitchen, mixed it with the colorless liquid, and began to regale themselves with the result in an alcove in the back hall. They offered samples of it to passing couples and were rewarded with gulps of what the passing couples had to offer. Lyle was finding Fanny much more fun than she usually was with him. Perhaps taking her to the meeting of the United Mine Workers had made him more interesting to her. She let him kiss her a couple of times, although she would laugh and say, "Now Lyle, don't think anything *means* anything!"

He wondered whether, if she drank some more of this heady mixture, she might not find herself taking him seriously, if only for a couple of hours. How far, as the classic question went, would she then be willing to go? What did she look like with no clothes on, he speculated, conjuring up an irresistible shapeliness which made him feel abruptly drunker. Actually, in the dress she had on, not a great deal of imagination was needed.

Later on they were dancing in the crowded front room. His head seemed to be in some way detached from his body and Fanny Carstairs seemed to be conveying to him, by her swaying skirt and rumpled hair and the heat of her body, that she was ready for him, this once anyway, to move his hands and his mouth over her in a way that would have been unthinkable before.

He maneuvered her into the little back den, closed the door and turned the key, and putting his arms around her began to nibble her ear and then moved his mouth down her neck toward her bosom. His left hand began to go up her leg and then there was a resounding slap across his face and her furious eyes were burning at him. "You sneak! Who do you think you are. Who do you think *I* am! Giving me that rotten whiskey and then trying — Let me out of here!"

He turned the key and she charged out of the room.

Oh hell, oh damn. Oh how he had bungled that! Too fast, too much, not allowing for the fact that she was four years older and innately convinced of her Clifton superiority which amounted, when it came to him at least, to untouchability. He was stunned and ashamed and indignant all at once from the arrogant, unpredictable suddenness of her repulse. Why couldn't she have said, "No, Lyle, please, stop that." Fanny Clifton Carstairs couldn't be bothered with such a modulation. Suddenly displeased, she let him have it right between the eyes. That was her way. Why should she be bothered with any other? After all, look at who she was.

Well, then, he thought to himself, taking another gulp of the concoction, to hell with her.

He ran into Pete Hayes and some other friends and they had concoctions of their own which he was encouraged to

sample generously. Then there seemed to be some more dancing and other people's concoctions to be sampled, and then
Pete Hayes said they should all now drive to Middleburg
and go swimming in the indoor Clifton pool. If the Cliftons
wouldn't let them in, then they would go in the Catherwood
plunge. Lyle agreed hilariously to that. How he would drag
this crowd and himself in the state they were in past his
parents, past Tot for that matter, was a question which didn't
penetrate his mind.

Driving to Middleburg seemed the logical next move to
everyone, and they all got into their cars. No one would ride
with Lyle, but that didn't bother him particularly now. Four
cars headed out of town on the road to Middleburg, Pete
Hayes leading in his Chevrolet roadster, Lyle behind him in
his Stutz, and two other cars, crowded sedans, following. It
was all original and fun and spontaneous, hurtling along
the twisting road in the dark, the night air rushing through
Lyle's open car. Then there was a curve and somehow the
steering wheel seemed to spring out of his hands, a tree
trunk spread itself hugely in his headlights, he swerved, the
right side of the car slammed against the tree, rebounded off
it, and Lyle was catapulted into the air.

When he came to himself he was lying on the ground and
some of the fraternity boys and their girl friends were shining a light in his face. Somebody was feeling along his legs.
This examination and Lyle's own established that he was not
injured physically. Somebody mentioned the possibility of
at least a mild brain concussion, but Lyle said his brain was
perfectly clear. Then he said it again. The car had gone
down an embankment, turning over several times, and would
not be worth anything anymore.

So Lyle got into a sedan and asked to be let off at one of
the speakeasies on River Street. A couple of the others suggested it might be better for him to go home, but he said he

was fine. So they let him off at the Blue Hawaii bar. He was known there and therefore they let him in. It was a dark room, there was jazz playing somewhere, the lights were reddish, dim. He supposed he looked pretty battered, but it was too dim for people to see that.

He had a couple of drinks and then a girl who said her name was Theda joined him and they danced a little. Then they went up to Theda's room a few doors away. There she agreed for forty-five dollars to get into bed with him naked. Her body was not unlike what he imagined Fanny's to be. Perhaps because of that he couldn't manage to get sexually excited. Theda tried a couple of tricks but nothing worked, and finally she grew tired of it, she already had his forty-five dollars, and she just laughed briefly and said, "Little man, you aren't there tonight. Better go home to, you know, mother, don't you think?" But in the end, for another thirty dollars, she agreed to let him sleep there the rest of the night, she herself returning to the Blue Hawaii.

Shortly after dawn Lyle woke up in this flimsy little room hanging over the edge of the river. The Monongahela slid by, smoky green, beneath the window, and it seemed that if it rose a few feet it would seize this rickety little room and take it swirling upstream toward Pittsburgh. He opened the window wider, urgently needing air, and the damp cool river air came up to him, evoking movement, travel, escape.

Gulping this unsettling air, Lyle turned back to the room. It was pinkish — a pink silk bedspread, pink feathers adorning a kind of canopy, white-furred bedroom slippers, mirrors. His single thought was escape. He looked into the mirror. An almost unrecognizable young derelict looked back at him. Swiftly turning away, he saw to his enormous relief that there was a telephone, and succeeded in getting Pete Hayes, in his home at the other end of Middleburg, on the line. Pete agreed to pick him up; then they would drive back to Morgantown. Pete had taken it upon himself to notify the State Police about Lyle's accident. They wanted to talk to Lyle. Later, he thought exhaustedly, later.

A half hour later Pete pulled up in the Chevrolet roadster and Lyle stumbled into it.

"You look as wrecked as your car," was Pete's first reaction.

"I'm worse. Let's go down to Morgantown. God forbid anybody here would see me. Drive carefully."

"How was she?"

"Who?"

"Whoever you spent the night with."

"The top," he said, "the winner."

"You mean it?"

"No, I don't mean it."

Through a crisp, bright, idealistic early morning, all fresh sunshine and pure air, they drove down the tortuous road. Pete stopped his car beside the big tree with the bruised trunk and they got out and looked down at the crumpled Stutz. It somehow made Lyle think of his own boyhood, or youth, his eager beginnings. It made him want to cry. Instead, he went down to extract the registration and insurance policy from the car, and then without a backward glance climbed back up the embankment.

It seemed to him that a door, the one opening on a room known as Good Clean Fun, was closing in his life.

V.

Back in Morgantown, Lyle was sitting in the broken armchair in his chaotic room in the fraternity house. Suddenly he felt an odd, elemental shaking sensation along his spine. He knew he was not moving physically at all; his innards seemed to be trembling, his liver, his gut, his essence. It was not something rising out of his brain, his thoughts, his memory, even his remorse. It was the snub-nosed elemental animal at the core, the he-beast: it was in terror, blind. It wanted out, out! It was as though, Lyle realized in a kind of fatalistic amazed horror, there was this elemental animal inside, his primitive self, and this animal realized that the being it was trapped inside, Lyle, was going to crash, wreak destruction upon himself. It desperately wanted out, wanted to save itself. Even my own inside self, Lyle reflected with quiet horror, wishes to abandon me.

I'm going to faint, he thought. No, I can't faint, what a pantywaist thing to do! Get a grip on yourself, old man, get a grip on yourself.

He was certainly going to have to do something. If only he were religious, like his mother. His mother: well, she was his mother and she was religious and maybe she could help him somehow. Someone was going to have to, and very soon, or else, he didn't know . . . So this was why, this was how people threw themselves off bridges.

Lyle went to the bathroom to shave. He looked at himself in the mirror. Pale blue eyes, uncertain expression, bloodshot. Reddish, freckled skin, but pale underneath, sallow, as though he was in the process of coming down with some serious disease. Dry lips. Unkempt red hair going in all directions. A derelict's stubble of beard.

He took a bath, brushed his hair, dressed himself in gray flannel pants, a striped shirt, and a thick white sweater. Collegiate. Then he reconsulted the mirror. Everything looked good, a healthy normal American college student, right up to the eyes. The illusion stopped there. He went out, borrowed Pete Hayes's car, and set off toward Middleburg.

One characteristic of West Virginia invariably noticed by daunted visitors was the quality of its roads. They were like no others in the country, with the possible exception of those in eastern Kentucky, eastern Tennessee, and Arkansas. They were everywhere recognized as breathtaking. The whole state was a panorama of irregular hills, upthrusting mountains, high-walled rivers. In addition to these natural disadvantages for roadbuilding, it was, despite the enormous coal boom, a poor state. Taxes were very low. Its governors, highway commissioners, and other key public officials were not famous for their probity. What money finally trickled down for the actual construction of roads was nowhere adequate to cope with the challenging geographic conditions.

Bricks had been patted into place side by side in earlier years to provide bizarre versions of the Wizard of Oz's Yellow Brick Road leading from place to place, with appropriately witty results. Lately, macadam had come into style, but the necessary grading and subsurface reinforcement was generally dispensed with, so that the hot tar dripped along ridges and through valleys provided only, when it hardened, a surface soon cracked and potholed as the road made its way, leaning dangerously along the flank of some mountain or, in the case of Morgantown to Middleburg, the edge of a cliff above the Monongahela River.

Lyle sped along this road, taking the numerous bumps, the inversely banked turns, the steep grades, as they came. From long experience, and as a game with himself and with others who covered this road as often as he did, he tried to maintain an average of forty-two miles an hour. Pete Hayes claimed to have averaged forty-five miles an hour on this road, but Pete Hayes had sustained a concussion of the brain from flying off it at one of its special curves.

This damn state doesn't *want* to be modern, thought Lyle. Everything here is against it. We all ought to be Indians or something. The swift rivers were great for canoes, the mountain trails had been passable enough on horseback.

He drove his car forcefully along the last bumpy patch and into Middleburg, over the bridge, through the busy little

[172]

center of town and out gracious, tree-lined Middleburg Avenue. The trees had all turned russet and red and gold and brown, and a late October wind made them wave — drunkenly it seemed to Lyle's eyes — alongside the fine solid brick homes and the complicated turn-of-the-century big wooden ones with their little turrets and stained-glass windows and glassed-in porches. The City of a Hundred Millionaires, so they said, and maybe it was true. Porte cocheres and Packards, four-square mansions with their long windows and pillared porches, colored women giving their little white charges a stroll, the streetcar screeching importantly up the center of the avenue, and overall the splendid trees, many-colored and swaying, shed an atmosphere of shelter and permanence and solidity. There was no trace of a coal mine or coal miner. This was the county seat and the industrial headquarters. Here lived the shopkeepers and the professional people and the gentry and, as they were called elsewhere but never here — an unpretentious sense of the ridiculous being too highly developed in this society — the coal barons.

Lyle swung the Chevrolet roadster through the open, wrought-iron gates of the Castle, up the driveway, and stopped with a screech under the porte cochere.

The solid gray crenellated Castle was beginning to acquire an illusion of age, with ivy creeping up its walls, the rhododendron and other shrubbery crowding its foundations, and the thick lawns sweeping away from it.

Inside, in the octagonal hall, Lyle breathed deeply the characteristic odor of wax, fireplaces, and flowers. It would forever evoke home for him, that charged combination not to be encountered in any other edifice in the world: wax; fireplaces, lately burning, waiting ashes soon to be rekindled; flowers, the fresh perfume from the soil, just cut from the flower beds and the hothouse.

Aunt Tot appeared through the kitchen hall door and told

him that his mother was in her sewing room in the tower. He mounted the curving stairway to the gallery above, and then the narrower flights two stories higher, emerging at the doorway to her sewing room.

Minnie was wearing a long, gray silk dress, ruffled at the neck and wrists, with skirts overlaying each other at different lengths down to the ankles. Lyle complimented her on it. "It's what's called a tiered skirt, dear. I'm so glad you like it. It's awfully dressy to be wearing at home while you sew, but today when I was getting dressed something just said to me, 'Put on something pretty, Minnie, somebody special may just drop in to call.' Isn't that a coincidence?" Minnie turned away from her sewing machine. "Sit over there in the rocker by the window. You're looking well. But what's wrong with your eyes?"

Lyle brushed his hand over them and shook his head impatiently. "I have a little cold." Then he thought better of that lie. "Well, I guess I don't have a cold. I — ah — I'm not feeling so well. I want to . . . I'd like to . . . well, talk to you about something."

"Good. Let's go downstairs and get some tea."

Lyle looked quickly about him. "Can't they bring it up here? I like it better up here." Up here was his mother's domain; downstairs, with its focus on the library, was his father's.

She gazed openly at him for a moment and then said, "Sure they can. The button's there on the wall."

He pushed it. "You're not feeling so good," she said appraisingly.

"Naw." He leaned forward, forearms on knees, punching one palm with the other fist. "I'm in a mess, Ma." Noting her look of alarm he added quickly, "Oh I don't mean with the cops or with a . . . a . . . young lady or anything like that. I mean . . . just inside my head."

"Those are the worst kind," she murmured.

"And also inside my, I don't know how to explain it, belly, my gut, it's as though . . . well . . . as though something is trying to . . . to tear me apart."

Minnie was frowning and nodding, a small troubled smile on her face. "We'll have to talk," she said, "Let's wait till we get the tea things." A few moments later there was a tap on the door. It was Thomasina. "We're going to have some tea up here, Thomasina. Ask Tot for a couple of slices of that angel food cake she was baking." Thomasina withdrew.

"Where's that old Reverend Roanoke?" blurted Lyle.

"You remember him? Isn't that something! Why, he hasn't been around here in ten years. More."

"I know. Where is he?"

"What makes you think I know where he is?" asked Minnie, a cagey, playful look in her eyes.

"But you do, don't you."

She adjusted something in the sewing machine and then said a shade defiantly, "Yes. I do."

"You hear from him, don't you."

"That's right."

"*I* don't care if Dad doesn't approve."

"My religion's a private —"

"Sure. I approve."

"Do you?" she asked a touch patronizingly.

"Yes. I approve of anything, and anybody, if they — if you get some kind of help with yourself from them."

Minnie turned in her chair to face Lyle. "I correspond with Reverend Roanoke. Don't need to so much, because he's already given me — gave it to me years ago — that help you're talking about."

"What did he do?" asked Lyle evenly, with quiet emphasis.

"He discovered," said Minnie, a luminous smile beginning to emerge shyly on her face, "that I was — Saved! Maybe you want to hear about it. But let's wait till they bring the tea."

Lyle leaned back in the rocker and contemplated this room with a sense of momentary inner peace, its curving exterior wall with the big bay window, its high white interior walls, dark, polished floor, its smallness, the high ceiling, all of it clean as a needle.

There were footsteps in the hallway and then Thomasina followed by George brought in tea and food. "Awful long way to make you climb," apologized Minnie, "but my boy here wanted to have tea with his mama in the tower!" The servants nodded and went out, and Lyle fell upon the sandwiches and cake. One thing he'd forgotten to do for a while was eat.

He took some tea. It was very refreshing and even a little invigorating. For the first time he realized why English people, men as well as women, made such a fuss about it.

When he paused for air and had time to speak he said, "Well, if you're saved I guess it doesn't have to mean your children are."

"What it is, Lyle, what is it?"

He ducked his head, nodding. Then he said, "I'm sunk, Ma, I can't make any sense out of myself."

"It's that poor Pence man you mean —"

"That, and all the shooting down at Logan, and I don't know anything about the coal business and Pa knows that, those union people, they're beyond me, I'll never know how to deal with those fellows. But then I don't understand the management part either and I don't think I ever will, Pa knows that, I can tell he's just made up his mind I'll never be able to work in the Clarkson Coal Company in any important capacity, let alone run it. And so just what in blazes am I going to do? How do I fit in?" He started, bitterly enraged at himself — everything he did made matters worse — to cry a little just for a moment.

"Oh Lylie, oh my Lyle, come over here . . . that's it . . . now, now . . . now . . . now. That's it, sit back down, have some more tea. That's it. Now then, now." She sat back in her straight-backed work chair and took a few deep breaths. "You know, I sit up here a lot. A lot, by myself, working but also thinking. I have a lot of time to think up here. Don't get restive, son, I'm coming to right what you're talking about." The light from the window caught her blue eyes and Lyle was once again struck by how idealistic they were. She's never compromised, he suddenly thought. Somehow she's never given up on her principles.

"Don't you know what's wrong?" she asked. "Well, I don't either entirely, but there's one thing that's got us all confused in this family . . . and in this town . . . in this state. It's the coal boom!" She drew a long breath. "It's . . . it's almost too much for us. It's really, you may not believe this, almost too much for your father. It's all too sudden, too recent, too much. These men here, Clarkson, the Cliftons, they're all suffering from what you might call the Midas Touch. Everything they touch turns to gold. What a responsibility. Think of the envy. Other people who want some of all this gold, and then all the conflict, the confusion, all the passion that gets stirred up here in this little backwater, this little hill country, West Virginia. Goodness, there was hardly anything here before, simple farmers, hunting, nothing else except in a few counties along the Virginia border where there was some plantation life. And then! My glory, the whole country depending on our coal! President Harding getting all het up in the White House if there's trouble in the coalfields down here!" She pinched the bridge of her nose, grimacing slightly. "All this thrust on some nice boys from the hills — Marcus Clifton, your father, Fred Hayes — who were . . . well they were just like you, or just like what you *would* have been if you'd grown up in a plain clapboard house instead of in this, well, silly Castle. Yes, it's silly. Clarkson and I were so young, even younger than our years, at the time we had it built. And look at Clifton Manor! Houses like that were

[177]

built for dukes! Back in Queen Elizabeth's time, three hundred years ago! So what does Sanderson Clifton do with his first two million dollars? Builds one of these mansions, only more solid, better, in Middleburg, West Virginia, in nineteen hundred and six! You're just like them, Lylie, the only difference is that this whole huge thing, the boom, the houses, all those miners, you grew up right in the middle of all that, you don't remember anything else. They grew up *alongside* it, if you see what I mean, so it didn't intimidate them so much. They saw it grow. *You* only see this huge thing, already there. It doesn't intimidate them so much, only now, now I think it's beginning to, I think it is. Every time they have to negotiate another contract with the union, every two years since nineteen sixteen, it's as though they're cowboys trying to break a horse. The horses are getting wilder, and the cowboys are getting older." She poured them each some more tea; Lyle thought of his cache of whiskey, destroyed, which had been hidden in his bedroom. How badly were his nerves asking for a drink? "You know," she went on, sipping cogitatively from time to time, "the Catherwood family wasn't anything special until this generation. Your Granddaddy Catherwood, remember him?"

"Not very well."

"Had that farm over near Winchester in the Shenandoah Valley. Ophelia once asked your father about what she called 'the Catherwood Plantation your people had over in the valley.' Your father said, 'Well, if that was a plantation then I was a field hand. I did the apple-picking and fed the hogs.' It was a farm, a prosperous farm most years. He got to go to the University of Virginia. Then his uncle, never married, Harry, you never knew him, left him these lands here and Clarkson came to see and there was coal everywhere under them and the boom was starting up and here we are! Here we are, and here I am. My people were just nice respectable Baltimore people. We didn't know the what you might call high society people in Baltimore. We weren't like that, didn't live that way, didn't have a lot of money, weren't what they called 'old family.' Believe me, I had to learn a lot when I found I was the mistress of this place with seven servants and trips to Europe first class. We all had to learn, the Cliftons and all of us. Entertaining President Taft. Well, basically what we did was just to stay ourselves although we had a lot of fancy, expensive accoutrements —"

"What are they?"

"Fancy things. Limousines and jewelry and furs. We took to it all — I think by and large we've enjoyed it all — but it didn't turn our heads, none of it did, until *now*." She began slowly to twist her engagement ring and wedding band. "Now it's all getting so unsettled. Your father never talks about business to me, might as well discuss it with Cleo, but I hear his voice on the telephone and I see it in his hands, the way he uses them now, kind of nervously, hesitant sometimes. Marcus Clifton reminds me of a man doing a great juggling act and everyone is amazed and applauding and he has a kind of . . . astonished air to him, very keyed up and excited and pleased and somewhere, somehow, scared to death! It's all so big and so sudden! So . . . no wonder you should feel disturbed . . . sensitive . . . you're like your mama in that."

"Well there's all that, I guess," Lyle said, his hands clenched between his knees, "and I know the Armed March and Logan and . . . the Pence the Virgil Pence, ah, death stirred me up and all, but it's more. More. It's . . . who am I? It's got something to do with faith. Faith in something. Faith."

Lyle had never opened himself to his mother in this way since he was a little boy and afraid of the dark, but she was not surprised. She was aware that he must have been shaken, threatened to the core of himself to come to her in this way, but she knew that deep perturbation, was unsurprised by it.

"I think, Lyle dear, that I'm going to ask Reverend Roanoke to come up from Arkansas and pay us a visit."

Lyle sat motionless and wordless, not knowing what to think.

"I do wish," Minnie went on with a little smile, "that you had been old enough to go with us when your father and I took that tour of the Mediterranean. It was just fascinating and I learned so much. I'll never forget Pompeii. Now don't fidget, I'm not changing the subject from what we've been talking about. You'll see.

"We arrived in the Bay of Naples — this was in nineteen hundred and seven — we arrived aboard a yacht! It belonged to an English nobleman named Lord Carven of Medford. He had mining interests in Great Britain and he and Clarkson were deep into some kind of negotiations. In fact, now that I think of it, Lord Carven was and I think probably still is some kind of a partner of your father's, in his Logan holdings."

Lyle's mind flashed from the image of a long, white steam yacht gliding into the Bay of Naples to the main street of Logan, as seen from a window of the Aracoma Hotel.

"The yacht was called the *Osiris*. It — 'she' they told me to call it, one of the many things I learned — she, the yacht, was all teakwood and leather, and it had wonderful fittings, at table, I remember, a place for the wineglasses, plates, salt and pepper, everything, all shining fittings, so that nothing would slide out of its place when the ship rolled. There was even a kind of box you could sit in and have a steam bath! Lord and Lady Carven had a masseur they took with them everywhere. They were very *strenuous* people, much too much for me, certainly in those days when my health . . . wasn't the best. They both rode horseback a great deal, they hunted, and they even rode on skis! In Switzerland, a village there, Saint something. Ice-skated. Tobogganed. He loved to shoot, of course, but then so did she! So they were in constant need of massages and steam baths."

"Mother —"

"I'm getting to the point, Lyle dear. It's just that in getting there it brings back that extraordinary trip, that world. *They* went plunging, right into the sea, wherever we put in in the evening, on the trip out from Gibraltar. Nothing daunted her, Lady Carven. I was envious, so envious. I believe watching her planted something in me, some urge so terrible that I *had* to fight my way back, as I did two years later . . ." A tiny sigh of relief, "the Reverend" she murmured to herself. Then, laughing suddenly and irrepressibly, Minnie cried, "I declare I know I'm getting you all riled up, Lylie, but I *am going to come to the point.*"

"Mother, I'm not in any hurry."

"Good. Finish the cake. So. Where was I? Oh yes, we landed in Naples and the first thing Lord and Lady Carven insisted on doing was hiring donkeys, for the four of us and also a guide, and ride to the very top rim of the volcano of Vesuvius! It was the only way to reach it, on donkeys. Maybe it still is. Why anyone would want to . . . Well, by now my envy of Lady Carven was such that I simply forced myself to go. Clarkson was against it, but I insisted and in the end, wearing a big sun hat and carrying a parasol, I got onto this strange little beast and began what turned out to be a really endless climb. At least the animal was docile! I've never been afraid of animals, you know, just, in those days, I was afraid of exertion! My doctors were afraid of it for me. That was half my trouble. Well, up the side of Vesuvius we toiled and I don't know . . . hours later, we did finally come up to the rim of the crater and look in.

"Now I know what hell is." Then her voice drifted off again for a moment. "I shall never see it, thank the Lord. A strange, horrible crust was on the floor of this . . . what they called the Fire Pit, and there was a place where the lava was flowing and steam escaping and it was unearthly, hellish, it was just terrifying. The Carvens said, 'It's worth coming up to see, isn't it?' and that was all they had to say. I had never made such a physical exertion in my life and I had never seen anything so terrible.

"It turned out that there was a second yacht, even grander than the grand one we were on, somewhere in the area. Now, as we were coming down the mountain — I felt such a relief, such a sense of accomplishment. You know, once you reach a difficult goal, it's so much easier coming back, a lark. As we were coming down the trail we saw a party mounting it, two ladies, with some attendants. Very impressive ladies — huge hats, veils, parasols — and as we got close I saw that one looked quite beautiful and the other perhaps less beautiful but very striking. Then Lord and Lady Carven began to bow, as low as they possibly could, I mean seated on donkeys clomping along and all, and the ladies nodded and smiled and passed on. One was really lovely, no longer young, but still very beautiful. Do you know who that was? It was the Queen of England! Queen Alexandra. And the other was her sister, the Dowager Empress of Russia! The King of England, Edward, he was much too fat to make this ride, the Carvens told me, so he was apparently back on the yacht. Imagine! I was thrilled to pieces.

"And I learned a new word. 'Incognito.' All these royal people were traveling 'incognito,' according to the Carvens, which meant they didn't have to go through official receptions and so on, and it all rather put my Lord and Lady Carven on the spot! To recognize or not to recognize? So they never spoke. No one spoke. But my, did they bow!"

The Queen of England, thought Lyle, the Empress of Russia. Yachts. Incognito. Don Chafin. Logan. Evictions.

"So you see we were, as they say around here, living pretty high on the hog that trip. But, let's see, I was going to tell you about Pompeii. In the next day or two we took a carriage out to Pompeii. Am I boring you to death?" she asked a little timidly.

"Course you're not," he replied. "It's funny, you never told me these stories before."

"I haven't thought of them in so long!" She smoothed back her hair on both sides from her temples. "You see, when Reverend Roanoke showed me my . . . inner light, well, I sort of put away and forgot about most things that had happened before, because this new adventure of the spirit held so much more significance, so very much more. But after all, some interesting things have happened to me, and that trip was certainly one of them. It surely was. Curious how you can close a part of your life, just as though it were a volume of your biography, close it and completely forget about it, never glance at it. Then one day something happens, your son comes to you and seems somehow in danger of . . . that he and in fact all of us . . . Well, I'm losing my train of thought."

"What were you going to say just then?" he demanded.

"I'm coming to it, I'm coming to it all." She drew a long breath. "We arrived, the four of us, and our own private guide who spoke excellent English, at Pompeii. You've read about it?" He shook his head. "It was a city of pleasure. It was for the wealthy, and they had splendid villas there, and there were beautiful theaters and baths and shops. They had lovely jewelry and vases, and you can be sure the food and wine were the best, and that they had plenty of wonderful servants — slaves. There was even" — she hesitated, then plunged ahead — "a . . . house of pleasure there."

" 'House of pleasure?' You mean a —"

"Yes. All the pleasures of the flesh were catered to in this city. It was a resort city, an unusual city, isolated, privileged.

"They'd erected it just below Mount Vesuvius, which had been sleeping, *sleeping* not dead, for a long time."

[183]

"Oh yeah. Now I remember. One day it erupted."

"Very suddenly and very enormously Vesuvius erupted. So suddenly and so enormously that there was no time to flee, to save themselves and their jewelry and even their pet dogs. Everything was buried under ashes from the eruption. All the people and all the pleasure and all the wealth was destroyed, wiped out."

Then Minnie fell silent, rocking very slightly in her straight-backed chair and gazing before her.

"Is that the end?"

She nodded faintly.

"But I don't get it, I don't get it. What's that got to do with me or anything?"

Minnie began to breathe rather deeply. "Lyle dear," she said quietly, rising, "I've got to go to my room now. I think I'm just a wee bit tired. I must lie down, say a few little prayers. I've rambled so, I'm sorry, dear." She drifted toward the door. "I will send for him . . . It will be all right . . . you'll see."

Lyle decided to spend the night at home and return to Morgantown the next day after he learned that his father had gone to Cleveland, where an important shipping operation for West Virginia coal was being set up. He won't be here today or tonight, Lyle thought. A kind of chronic burden lifted up from him at this realization: he won't be here in this house while I am here.

There was about this spacious, high-ceilinged mansion today a peculiarly gracious air of peace. Lyle felt it. Tot and George and Thomasina and the others softly coming and going, unhurried, aware that their mistress was incapable of addressing an unkind word to them, equally aware that in their quiet, unhurried way they were good at what they did and so were undeserving of unkind words. They were not in a hurry; they knew what they were doing. Confidence permeated the house.

Lyle came slowly down the flights of stairs to the octagonal hall on the ground floor and then wandered out to the pantry and kitchens. On a sideboard next to the big, gas-heated range Tot in her long, shapeless blue dress was rolling dough in flour.

"Biscuits?" he asked hopefully. "Some of your biscuits?"

"That's right, that's it, Mr. Lyle."

"How'd you know I was staying for dinner?"

"I knew."

"Biscuits," he repeated contentedly. Tot's biscuits were really the next best thing in this world to Canadian whiskey. Why had he thought of that stuff? Then he thought of the place down on River Street where in a few minutes he could be buying as many bottles of it as he wanted. Then he resolutely turned his thoughts elsewhere.

Lyle went out the kitchen door, across the latticed-in back porch with the garbage cans, the smell of decaying food rising from them, and out onto the lawn. This was Angelo's domain. He was not in sight at the moment, but the evidence of his devotion to the earth and what grew out of it, when lovingly tended, was everywhere: silken grass, flower beds with chiseled borders, trees pruned into maximum shapeliness; the recently painted, spotless gazebo.

Great golden-leafed trees swayed overhead; the almost unbearably nostalgic smell of burning leaves drifted to him — that was what Angelo must be doing behind the barn. How could he feel this overwhelming sense of nostalgia when he smelled autumnal leaves burning when he had hardly any past to be nostalgic for? It was as though he had lived before, somehow, and suffered terrible but insanely romantic losses; some irretrievable love, doomed, had passed through his fingers and disappeared. Jesus, he reflected wryly, they'd take me off to Weston if they knew what I was thinking. I guess I'm like Ma in a way, kind of like a dreamer with maybe too much imagination or feelings too strong or something like that. I wonder if this Reverend Roanoke guy is some kind of confidence man, asking Mother for a lot of money? Or could he be the real thing? Could he do anything for me? Exactly what do I need done, anyhow?

He sat down and then stretched out on the silken grass. The October breezes whipped and drifted over him, the smell of the burning leaves mingling so evocatively that he felt himself sinking almost into a trance of past romance and limitless, unfulfillable future possibilities. Unfulfillable future possibilities: that was the bitter crux of his problem. There was no possibility of achieving one eighth of what his inner spirit, the blind beast, was capable of. It was a total impossibility, unachievable as jumping over the moon, and so he was going to be condemned to a life of frustration and failure, terrible incompleteness, gorgeous dreams turning as sour as that stale food in the garbage cans. That was it: his life would drift from the wondrous odor of autumn's burning leaves to the rotting vegetables and scraps of decaying meat in the garbage cans.

After a while Lyle got up from the grass, talked for a little while to short, burly Angelo, or attempted to talk to him. Angelo spoke with his hands and arms and his back and he spoke nature; to people, in English, he had little to say and little vocabulary to say it with. "Nice," "good," "grow," and "beautiful" were the pillars of his speech. Then Lyle wandered on to the big barn, still with hay in the hayloft although all the horses beneath it had been replaced by the Packard, the Hupmobile, the Stutz Bearcat and the Model T Ford. You could still smell the horses.

I wish this were my house, he thought suddenly, and this unbidden thought had a vehemence which surprised him. What if this were mine? A blissful feeling flowed through him, something the best Canadian whiskey ever distilled couldn't begin to induce. This feeling surprised him too.

He and Minnie had dinner that night, sitting at opposite ends of the dining room table. It was a meal Lyle would subsequently remember as peculiarly charmed and, well, civilized, somehow linked to her stories of yachts and queens, the to him fairy-tale world she had once briefly inhabited, of lords and ladies, the Mediterranean Sea and the ruins of Pompeii, a world commensurate with the dreams induced in him by autumnal leaves burning: there were places where romantic ambitions could be fulfilled, had been, by his mother and father.

And it had all sprung up from his, Clarkson's, dominance of an important segment of the coal industry, of King Coal, in northern and in southern West Virginia.

They ate by candlelight, Minnie would not dine any other way, and the little flickering flames caught jeweled reflections in the crystal and cut glass, the silver and the mirrors, as Thomasina glided softly in with the baked ham and the yams, with the famous biscuits, with homemade peach ice cream and angel food cake.

Minnie even served a little wine. "This is an occasion," she said gaily, "having my boy all to myself at home. You know your father never liked wine, even hated having it around all the time during our tour of the Mediterranean. Said it was bad for your teeth! But lately, since Prohibition came in, he just, well, thinks it's the *principle* of the thing to buy it and have it in the house and sometimes serve it. Who ever heard of West Virginians not being able to drink if we want to!"

"Yeah. They're lucky we're not making it ourselves in the basement."

"Lots of people are. You must never drink any of that, Lyle. It's terribly dangerous."

If you only knew, he said to himself ruefully, remembering the strange disastrous liquids he'd downed during the weekend party in Morgantown, if you only knew.

"Gaston Hayes had to be taken to the hospital after he and his brother made some gin in their barn. Pony got into it. Killed the poor beast."

"Are you sure, Mother?"

"Word of honor. Fell dead."

"Well," said Lyle, sipping his wine in a worldly manner, "I think it's great to have wine with dinner."

"I do too. Your father," she went on smilingly, "thinks it's *foreign*."

"What's wrong with learning some good things from foreigners?"

She sighed lightly. "You're like me in a way. You take after me some, in the ways you think, ways you feel. Unless it was something to do with mining your father doesn't think we have anything to learn from foreigners. And he says we've been teaching them everything new even in mining for the last twenty years."

"Gee would I love to go to Europe."

"The Carvens of Medford . . . those people I was telling you about? With the yacht?" Minnie was mellowing, becoming a little dreamy from the wine. "They planned on sending their son soon as he finished his schooling at Oxford University on a Grand Tour."

"They did! A Grand Tour! Lord-ee. What is it exactly, a Grand Tour?"

"Oh, those English lords send their sons — not their daughters, just their sons — on a long trip, a really long trip, all over Europe. Paris, Florence, Athens, everywhere that is rich in history, culture."

And wine, women, and song, reflected Lyle sagely.

"— not just traveling there but staying in those places, learning what I remember Lady Carven called 'Restaurant French' for instance in Paris, and 'Museum Italian' in Florence."

"Sounds terrific."

She gazed the length of the table at him. "You get good grades at the university and maybe we can persuade your father to let you have, well, if not a Grand Tour then maybe a Petite Tour."

"A Petite Tour?"

"Yes, a little version."

"I sure would like that. Shoot, I've hardly been any farther than Logan."

And what struck Lyle and fixed itself in his mind were the ties of power, the links from that lost little mining town deep in the broken hills of southwestern West Virginia to the great world of London and the Continent. And the lines were power and money, and the owners, Lord Carven of Medford and, yes, Clarkson Catherwood of the Castle, had it and were fighting, with Don Chafin and with bullets and with aeroplanes if necessary, to keep it, and the United Mine Workers and Frank Keeney were trying to take it way from them.

How ridiculous he, Lyle, had been to stumble around on the miners' side of that battle. Hell, he should have been on the crest of Blair Mountain, right alongside Don Chafin. What if Chafin was a bully? You had to fight fire with fire and the miners' side wanted to take all that power, leading from Main Street, Logan, to the rim of Vesuvius, take it away from the Catherwoods and the Cliftons and just sort of *scatter* it all over the state! The hell with it. Lyle buttered one of Tot's immortal biscuits firmly and realized that he was just going to have to get a lot tougher, a lot more — as his father put it — *savvy*, learn the business and hang on to the power and realize *his* dreams.

But then a vision of some of those mining towns he had gone through on the train heading toward Blair Mountain including the one where he had slept, the grime and the unbelievable flimsiness of the houses where the miners and their families lived, the terrible streets, lousy drainage, his own visit with James to the mine, that vision rose up before his eyes.

"You thinking about something, Lyle?"

"No, well, yes, sort of. I was thinking about what you talked about, about Pompeii, the city of pleasure, buried under the ashes. I think I know what you were trying to say." He moved some food around his plate with his fork. "And it doesn't have to happen. Not here."

"We must not be too selfish, not in the future as we have been in the past."

But if you give in some, Lyle asked himself, then won't they take it all away from you?

And would he ever be the kind of man to keep them from doing so, after his father and Marcus Clifton and all of them were gone?

This visit to his mother lifted Lyle's spirits momentarily. It was uncanny how much better he felt just from his talk with her, his stroll around the place, and that dinner, just the two of them. It *renewed* him in some way, or gave him a shot of confidence. He felt capable, momentarily.

VI.

But upon his return to Morgantown, the chaotic room in the fraternity house, to his classes, to his attempts at reform, all of this infusion of strength drained away and he became his old struggling self again, ineffectual in his own eyes, the rich kid who showed no potential, even to his own father, of ever really growing up.

Somehow, the tremendously expensive Pierce-Arrow Race-about with which his father replaced the demolished Stutz almost without comment, as though he had expected as much, made Lyle feel subtly worse.

The following week Lyle received a letter. It was impressive-looking, in a long envelope made out of stiff paper, and addressed in handwriting of flowing, curlicued grace. The name on the envelope was "Master Lyle Catherwood." Master. Very curious, Lyle tore it open to see several pages of stiff white paper and a message in the same elaborate, graceful hand:

My Dear Master Lyle Catherwood,

I am in receipt of a missive from your esteemed mother and at her behest I am communicating with you. That lady, whose salvation it was my holy privilege to bring into the glorious light of reality and so suffuse her soul with all the virtues theretofore locked within her, has requested me to communicate with you to determine whether we should meet.

Should we meet? If we met, if your spirit calls for such a meeting, if such a meeting is sought by your spirit, then I am ready to join with you.

As a practical matter, and the Lord in His wisdom presents us with practical problems so that we may utilize His grace in solving them, I am in Simmons, Arkansas, and you are in Morgantown, West Virginia.

But see how the Lord works his mysterious ways? He has inspired your sainted mother to send to me a most substantial monetary contribution, more than enough for me to go to the depot and purchase a round-trip ticket from here to there. I have other souls there in those unforgettable hills of West Virginia whom I might join together with in prayer during such a visit. Truly I believe God brought you to your present spiritual crisis that your mother might be given an opportunity to display her Divine Generosity and that I might thus be providentially given this opportunity to return to my vineyards in the hills, my vineyards of souls, to pray together with them once more.

But it is with you that this pilgrimage will in the first instance be concerned, for these others I mention are all already within the Caves of God (as gathered grapes from vineyards are pressed, poured into casks and places in Caves, as Our Lord was born in a Cave, not a Stable as popular myth would have it, but a Cave, and buried in yet another Cave, from whence He rose); the others would be met with by me so that all might join together once again in a Prayer of Thanksgiving and glorification unto God the Savior.

But it is to you that I direct my inquiring thoughts. Do you desire to meet with me that we might pray together?

I say no more, not of the outcome of our prayer or of any specific purpose of such praying together. I simply ask in the Service of God whether such is your wish.

May God's transforming light shine ever more brightly upon you.

Yours in Jesus, in the Father, and in the Holy Ghost,
Ramsey Fullylove Roanoke
Minister of the Church of the Last Judgment

Strolling slowly across the campus on an overcast, windy November day, Lyle reread this letter. He read it a third time. The Reverend Roanoke: Lyle could remember what his mother had been like before the revelation, real or fabricated, by Reverend Roanoke, to know what a change had been wrought. He remembered her tentative touch, her thin, self-doubting voice, her wraithlike white dresses. And he recalled his latest visit to the Castle, her stylish clothes, her warm voice, her embrace. Verily, as Reverend Roanoke would undoubtedly say, verily a change had been wrought. And now she had sent him "a most substantial monetary contribution," had she? There was money involved between her and Reverend Roanoke, always had been. His father, he knew, had given Reverend Roanoke money too, paid him off, some said (Thomasina for one, who had never had any truck with the Church of the Last Judgment, being a hardshell Baptist born and bred). Was he a fraud? Was he a confidence man?

[192]

Or did he have the gift of seeing into souls? Troubled souls?

God knew Lyle had one of those, if — as he sometimes asked himself when his worthlessness became truly over-powering — he had a soul at all. At least Reverend Roanoke might be able to establish *that*, once and for all.

Lyle went back to his room and replied to the letter as follows:

Dear Reverend Roanoke:

I have received your letter of November 2nd. Of course my mother has spoken to me of you. And I remember meeting you long ago with her in Bennettown, although I was so young I really didn't know what was going on.

I don't know if I am in a "spiritual crisis" as my mother apparently told you I was, or what, but if you want to come up here, and I know a lot of people would be glad to see you in our hills again, then I will meet with you, and I guess we will "pray together" because I guess that's what you do, isn't it.

I can tell from your letter that you don't believe in making any promises and I don't believe in making any promises either, especially if I'm not sure I can keep them. And I don't know exactly what the result of us meeting together and praying is going to turn out to be, but I am willing to find out.

> Sincerely yours,
> *Lyle Catherwood*

When his mother reached him by telephone ten days later he knew the message would be about Reverend Roanoke. "He's here!" she called excitedly.

"At the Castle?"

"No, dear, he's staying out in Bennettown with some of his old parishioners. And he's looking forward to meeting with you, praying with you. Can you come up here tomorrow?"

"Ah — yeah, I guess so."

"Good," she said crisply. These days when his mother wanted something to happen she wanted it to happen.

"Why don't you drive up here in time for lunch and then we — I mean you — will meet with the Reverend."

"Where's Dad?"

"Your father will be in Cumberland tomorrow."

"Ah — do I have to do anything, anything in the way of preparing? Go on a fast, or something like that?" Lyle began to feel giddy, even silly. "Or take eighteen baths? Shave my head? Light candles —"

"That will be enough, Lyle. This is the most serious of matters."

"Yes, I know."

"You merely have to approach it with an open mind and a trusting spirit."

After hanging up, Lyle felt he possessed an open mind all right. But a trusting spirit? That he was far from sure of. Trust this Negro stranger who took money from his mother behind his father's back? Who wrote letters that sounded like enormous gusts of hot air?

For that matter, did he trust anybody? Including himself? Well, that one at least he could answer flatly. He sure did not trust himself.

And for that reason, he suddenly saw, he didn't trust anybody else. Couldn't.

Who knew? Maybe this black spellbinder really could break through all of this and disentangle Lyle's inner confusions. There was his mother, stark evidence that Reverend Roanoke had accomplished something unmistakably good.

Well, Lyle would just go up there to Middleburg and see.

What about some Canadian whiskey?

No, no, a thousand times NO.

VII.

When he arrived at the Castle, Minnie, in a blue wool overcoat with a big fur collar and a blue hat with a tight, frail
veil pulled over her face, was waiting for him, sitting beside
the suit of armor in the octagonal hall.

"I guess we're going to meet Reverend Roanoke out somewhere, is that it?" he asked after greeting her.

"Yes, George is bringing the car around."

"Just where are we meeting him?"

Minnie glanced upward, toward the big, bulbous chandelier
high overhead, then here and there, and finally answered,
"It's in the car, we're meeting him there."

"In the car?"

"Yes," she murmured quietly.

"But what a nutty place. Why?"

"It's what he requested."

That gave Lyle material for reflection. Did it mean that
here in West Virginia Reverend Roanoke felt he had to keep
moving? Or what?

George entered from the porte cochere side, in his full
black chauffeur's uniform cap and gloves, a getup he was
rarely expected to bother with except for Sunday church and
the most formal calls.

Minnie and Lyle got into the back of the Packard and it
rolled slowly down the driveway.

"Of course I won't be present when you and the Reverend
pray together," said Minnie. "I — I will be in the front with
Uncle George, and I will *not look back here*, and of course
we can't hear through that dividing glass. As Reverend
Roanoke always said, we can meet together and pray together
anywhere — in a great cathedral, in the great out-of-doors,
in a cave, a barn, or in —"

"A Packard limousine?"

"Yes," she said softly.

Lyle saw that Minnie was firmly resisting in herself any doubts or questions arising in her mind from Reverend Roanoke's strange choice of meeting place.

The rich grumble of the car's engine preceded them down Middleburg Avenue, through the center of town and out on the road to Bennettown. "We're picking him up out here someplace. George knows where."

It was another overcast, windy November day, the overhanging trees and thick-forested hillsides, partly stripped of leaves, swaying rather lugubriously in the wind. West Virginia, so fresh and radiant through the warm months, an upland after all, bathed in forest-cleansed air, settled during the cold months into days and weeks of brooding, clammy grayness and gloom. What happened to the dirty, sooty look of everything during the sparkling summer days, Lyle had often wondered. Now, in this glum November weather, he realized the answer: the light bleached it out. There was neither more nor less dirt and grit, but the fresh, glowing quality of the light redeemed it all. Now there was grimness, November to March, when the isolated settlers of old must have huddled in their log cabins and stoically waited it out, not the gales and blizzards of the North, but the gloomy chill and brooding deadness in nature of the Appalachian Mountains, wintertime.

They reached a particularly steep hill and the Packard went cautiously down it in first gear to the hamlet of Jessie Mae. There, where the dirt road leading to Bennettown went off to the right, stood Reverend Roanoke, broader than before, dressed in a dark overcoat and a derby hat, and, as the limousine rolled majestically up alongside him, he tipped his hat and smiled broadly.

After a confusion of greetings, exclamations of pleasure, exchanges of evangelical salutations, mutual congratulations upon fine physical appearance, passing expressions of regret that the countryside was not at its best, seating in the car was rearranged and Lyle found himself in the capacious rear compartment with the Reverend Roanoke on a jump seat in front of him but turned around in his direction. On the other side of the closed inside window, George shifted the car cautiously into gear and proceeded aimlessly, farther into the country, and Minnie rather ostentatiously buried her nose in a small leatherbound book she had produced from her purse.

Reverend Roanoke turned and reached just above the dividing window and pulled down a gray silk window blind. Lyle had never noticed it before. Then he began pulling down blinds over the exterior windows. Lyle helped him; he had never noticed these before either.

"Now this is all we need," Reverend Roanoke rumbled cheerfully in his resonant voice, "just any quiet private place where we can meet together."

Reverend Roanoke's strong, wide, dark brown head was about half bald, and the remaining hair, curly and grizzled. Otherwise he did not look as old as Lyle calculated he must be. He looked healthy, except that the whites of his eyes were yellowish, and there was an exhausted cast which flickered over them now and then.

"Why'd you pick the *car?*" inquired Lyle. "Seems like a very funny place, even if it is quiet and private. And it ain't really even that, not with the engine running and two people settin' two feet from you."

"Brother," Reverend Roanoke began, "and I feel that all of us are brothers and sisters on this earth, all of us who seek salvation — brother, there are problems in life. Some are easily soluble, as when your sainted mother sent me the wherewithal to make this journey. Some are more complicated. Here in West Virginia there are those who oppose my mission — I tell you frankly — who would seek to prevent me from going about my duties. The clergymen at the established churches here, they say I bring dishonor upon the cloth," he smiled beneficently, "that I am a charlatan." Lyle knew his face betrayed his amazement at hearing the Reverend Roanoke bring this charge up himself. "I see you have entertained that suspicion yourself. It is only natural. Who am I? Where do I come from? What is my education? What are my credentials? These are questions you would like to ask, aren't they?"

"Only about your education. You speak such . . ." "Highfalutin" was on the tip of his tongue. ". . . good English, so educated. Where *were* you educated?"

"At the Tuskegee Institute, and if I say so myself, the principal of the institute, Mr. Booker T. Washington, said that I had a better command of English than any of his other students. My mother was educated; she was a slave but she was educated. She was a *reader*. She read stories to the white ladies in the plantation house in Alabama. They didn't teach her to read. She taught herself, picked up books around the mansion and snuck them to her shack and read them. Then when the white folks found that out they didn't punish her as most of them would — slaves weren't allowed to get educated, you knew that" — Lyle hadn't; not allowed to get educated — "but these folks were kindly and *they* were educated and they decided to *use* her talent, instead of punishing it. So she taught me to read and to speak and I got to go to the Tuskegee Institute and Mr. Booker T. Washington himself encouraged me, said I could be the best Negro preacher in the country. And I could have been too. Only one thing went wrong."

"What was that?"

"I didn't want to preach to only colored people. White people needed to know about salvation too. And *I could tell them.* Ever since I was about twelve years old *I knew* who was saved! I just plain knew. Well, the colored folks had their churches and the white folks had their churches and ain't nobody, as colored folks say, wanten to go to a mixed church! And that's what I had to have. So they didn't want me as a preacher in the colored churches, I mean the ones that have a permanent roof over their heads and staying in one place and all, they couldn't use me if I was trying to bring white people in too. So" — he drew a deep, resigned breath — "I had to set up in barns and caves and *keep moving*, because if I don't I get into trouble. So we're moving, right now. Maybe I'll get me a bus. Moving gets harder when you get older. It gets a lot harder."

I like this fellow, thought Lyle. Do I trust him?

Nodding in an unemphatically proud way at him, Reverend Roanoke said, "Brother, are we ready to pray together?"

Lyle nodded, and matching Reverend Roanoke's gesture he joined his hands. They were facing each other. Reverend Roanoke's eyes closed; Lyle closed his. And then began a long prayer, recited in the Reverend's deep, confident voice.

He really is speaking to God, thought Lyle in awe. At least he is absolutely sure himself that he is. I can hear it in his voice. Oh boy, what have I got myself into! No, no, concentrate, *forget* yourself for a change, follow the prayer, pray! ". . . if You choose once again to confer upon Your humble servant Ramsey Fullylove the gift of seeing into another human soul, one soul which is seeking its salvation, striving to know that it is saved, if in Your infinite mercy and goodness You grant once more this gift, so that he can know that he stands beside his sainted mother in Thy eternal light, that he is joined with her in a confident expectation of eternal happiness with Thee in Heaven. Can he know that, O Lord? Will You deign to show to me, Your humblest servant, the pure light of Your salvation shining beneath the toil of this young and troubled soul? May I be granted the gift of seeing it? What joy fills my soul when once more I behold it. O what transports!" *He is in touch*, Lyle said tensely to himself. *He is speaking to God. He is going to be able to tell me.* Good God, how exposed I am. Great Christ, my mother is in the front seat!

There was a long, fervent silence. And then Lyle somehow knew he must open his eyes. He did so and a second or two later Reverend Roanoke opened his and stared into Lyle's eyes. The Reverend's pupils were black and bottomless, the whites their whitish-yellow color, the momentary exhausted look had vanished into a glare of concentration. Am I being hypnotized, Lyle wondered tautly. He had never felt so tense before, it was in every muscle, every nerve. He can see all those bottles of Canadian whiskey in my eyes, and all that rotgut I've drunk too, and my bad sex habit and the lies and . . .

And now, Lyle thought, I am going to be shown that all those weaknesses of mine don't matter, and that I am saved. And somewhere deep at the center of his brain a tiny voice concurred: he won't dare do anything else, not with the son of Minnie Catherwood.

Reverend Roanoke broke suddenly from glaring into his eyes; he glanced sideways, and then jerked his gaze once more back into Lyle's eyes. Then the Reverend looked down, looked sideways, pulled back. "I — there's nothing — I can't see if —"

"Don't lie to me!" Lyle heard himself demand in a constricted, authoritative voice, new to him.

Reverend Roanoke met his gaze for a moment again, then looked away. "I don't know," he muttered. "I can only tell those who are saved. I don't know if the others are . . . if . . . Only I can't see that they are saved. I just can't see it," he finished in a muffled voice.

That's it, thought Lyle fatalistically. I've always known it. Damned: I have been, all my life. I've always felt it. There's something broken in me. Even the blind beast wants out.

He leaned across and, raising the shade, rapped on the window.

"We can go back now," he said to Minnie and George, who continued staring blankly at him. Then recollecting, he wound down the window.

"It's over," he mumbled. "We can go back."

Minnie took a long look at him, and then looked away. "Look at that beautiful meadow," she said.

"What?" he asked thickly.

"Perfectly beautiful meadow over there. And a fine field beyond it. Farmland. Anyone can see how fertile it is. Isn't this a pretty corner of the county. Even on a day like this. I've never been this far on this road before. Beautiful. You know where we are, do you, George?"

"Yes'm."

"I want to find out about that land. I don't think it's being cultivated. Probably just for grazing."

What in God's name is she rambling about, Lyle demanded to himself.

"Let's go back, George," she finished.

George turned the car around, backing into a dirt track which led into the sloping sweep of farmland Minnie had been admiring, and they proceeded back along the road, Lyle lost in an air of total unreality. All the blinds in the back seat had been raised. With the dividing window lowered Minnie had turned around, her left arm along the top of the front seat, and now she began chatting about the countryside. She seemed completely at ease and was in fact turning this mobile prayer meeting into a Sunday outing kind of drive, no more significant than any other outing. Lyle felt in the depths of unreality and a strange alienation — she's saved, I'm damned — and an overwhelming sense of needing to run, run away, ship out on a boat for China, join the Marines, kill himself, get drunk, go work in a coal mine and get killed in a cave-in.

He was in oblivion already, always had been, only now this colored man had made him see it and above all feel it.

[201]

Why had he ever sobered up?

Minnie chatted along pleasantly about the countryside, then she mentioned a farm in Maryland where she had spent summers as a girl, her grandparents' place, and how Clarkson was a farm boy really, but then so were most Americans of their generation, Lyle being a member of the first generation in which so many grew up in towns or cities. "A farm is all there is, really," she finished cryptically.

Reverend Roanoke sat on his jump seat, hands clasped between his knees.

There are two blacks and two whites in this car, Lyle thought suddenly. They could attack us if they wanted to. The idea of Uncle George attacking him and Minnie was grotesque but still he thought it.

Slaves have rebelled before, he reflected cautiously. Uncle George was not a slave, he could quit tomorrow and go to New York, but still he thought it.

They reached the little hamlet of Jessie Mae again. Nodding apologetically to Lyle as he moved, Reverend Roanoke got out of the back seat. Minnie got out of the front seat. They stood for a moment in the road, communicating with some kind of spiritual intimacy. She thanked him for coming. She pressed an envelope into his hand. *More* money, Lyle thought.

Then Reverend Roanoke turned once more to the back seat. "Will you let me give you a blessing for God?" he asked Lyle soberly. Lyle grimaced. The Reverend raised his right hand and murmured a few words.

"We will save Lyle," Minnie then said in a tone Lyle had never heard, quiet but exalted, as though she were the Angel Gabriel and this were the Annunciation.

Lyle wanted to die on the spot.

Then she climbed into the back seat with him, helped by Reverend Roanoke, and with a last exchange of waves they drove off.

VIII.

The following week Minnie persuaded Clarkson to buy the farm she had noticed during this drive.

The weekend following the Doomsday Drive, as Lyle came to think of his excursion with Reverend Roanoke, he returned to Middleburg. He had spent the intervening week almost losing himself in Canadian whiskey but not quite. He had gotten some bottles of it, but he only took a bracing gulp once in a while, and offered some to his friends. In limbo, preparatory he now felt sure to his final plunge into Hell — the man was a seer, just as in an odd way his mother was — Lyle tottered but did not quite fall. What the hell, something might turn up. Hadn't Saint Paul been saved from evil on the road to Damascus? Anything was possible.

In Middleburg that weekend — raw, gusty, a liverish sky — Lyle took a solitary walk Saturday afternoon down Raccoon Hollow, a steep-walled ravine between two parts of town. He was proceeding down the dirt road, concentrating on kicking stones, when he saw, crossing the Fourth Street Bridge which spanned the ravine above him, a solitary figure, head slightly bent against the gusts of chilly wind. He knew he recognized her but couldn't immediately realize who it was. Impulsively he put two fingers between his teeth and let out the whistle which could startle horses at a hundred yards. She glanced down and he thought: good Christ, the Widow Pence. Covered with embarrassment and guilt, Lyle nevertheless felt he had to wave at her. She gave a faint wave back. He motioned her to come down, via a long flight of wooden steps set into the side of the ravine. He didn't know why he did that; it was just something to cover his embarrassment. To his surprise he saw that Mrs. Pence was complying. As she made her way down the long zigzag flight of steps with the wind whipping her rain hat and raincoat and skirt he noticed a certain grace about her. Willowy, that was the word they used for women like that.

She came up to him, a little out of breath. "I'm glad I ran into you. I was meaning to write you, I was going to today for sure. I — it was real nice of you. 'Not charity, debt.' I liked that, I understood it. It was thoughtful. So that's how I accepted it, and . . . thank you."

Lyle stared at her, nonplussed. "Ah — what do you mean, I mean, I don't know what you mean."

"The money order you sent. Five hundred dollars. And the note. I memorized it. You put it so well. 'Not charity, debt. Please take it. It will help me. With sincerest respects and deepest condolences, Lyle Catherwood.' "

Lyle's face worked through and past amazement in two instants, and then he burst out, "Oh, that! Yes, that! Why I — it was — well, yes, not charity, debt. Yes, you, then it was okay, was it? Good, great, well you never know, do you? You never do know. I . . . uh . . . I'm just walking on down the hollow. Your house is up the hill from the end of it, isn't it. Mind if I walk you home?"

"Of course not." They proceeded down the dirt road between the high walls of the ravine, scraggly leafless growth clinging to them. In her high-heeled shoes she was almost as tall as he was. "Do you come up from the university often?" she asked. Her voice was rather low-pitched, smoothed out, a little lower in her throat than that of other girls he knew. Older women sometimes had voices like that, but theirs had a quaver of age in them; hers was energetic and young, but with this low pitch. He kind of liked it.

And so to listen to it some more he asked her about herself. She had grown up in Poundville, an outlying mining camp, where her father had been superintendent of the mine. Then after studying at State Teachers College she had taught school, met Virgil, married, had a child, been widowed.

And, an unspoken sentence seemed to add, her life was now

over. But as she strode along beside him that did not seem to Lyle to be true at all. There was much too much vitality in her, and also a kind of breeziness which she herself seemed unconscious of. She just seemed to be, well, waiting, without knowing it, still shocked from the death of her husband three months before, but now unconsciously waiting for what came next. Something assuredly must come next, the second act in her life, for it was evident to the naked eye that Mrs. Pence had a good deal of living still to do, and that while the surface of her mind might have resigned itself to widowhood, child care, and gradual desuetude, the deeper layers of her mind, and the energy of her body, were preparing themselves for some more adventurous future.

"What would you like to be when you grow up?" Lyle suddenly asked.

"Wh-what?" she replied, glancing in a startled way sideways at him. *Green* eyes, he noted, very green, rather large.

He grinned uncertainly at her and said, "We're all still growing up, isn't that right? I mean when you get older, what do you want for the future?"

"Oh well, the future . . ." A gesture of her hand fragmented any future.

"Oh, come on. Everybody's got a future, you, your boy, me."

"My boy is my future. I'm going back to teaching. That's all I can do."

He walked on, kicking at likely stones. "I doubt it."

"You do, do you?" she said, her voice becoming a shade cool.

Lyle decided to plunge ahead. What had he to lose? After all, he'd given her five hundred dollars, he said to himself with boisterous self-mockery (Had it come from his mother or his father?). To her he blurted, "My dad says nature will take its course and you'll get married again."

She strode on silently for several moments. "Nature will

take its course, will it?" she then said with an undertone of disdain. A proud lady, Lyle decided. "Your father doesn't know me, does he?" she went on in this reserved tone. "Women aren't all alike, you know. Marriages don't happen automatically, like springtime. I doubt very much I'll ever remarry. I can't imagine it." She gave a slight toss of her head and added, "I doubt very much that anybody would ask me again, with a child, the town full of pretty eighteen-year-old girls. I doubt it." She pulled her coat about her against the clamminess of Raccoon Hollow. "Getting much colder, isn't it. Not much of a fall. How's it been at the university?" And seeing that she had closed the subject, Lyle told her how it had been at the university — just exactly the same as it had been in Middleburg — and they proceeded on briskly to the end of the ravine, and on up to her little house, where he took leave of her at the door. "I'll bet the neighbors'll think I'm courting you," he said teasingly.

"Oh no," she replied absently, "not someone so young."

They were facing each other, and as she let fall this condescending dismissal he was thinking, Good God, she's beautiful!

IX.

In the capacious barn set in trees across the lawn from the Castle, the former Harness Room had been converted by Clarkson, after the last horse to harness had been regretfully disposed of, into what he called his Research Room, but which the family simply called the Tipple. Tacked to the plain board walls were detailed maps of mines, showing which sections had been worked out, which remained to be mined, but these were not working plans, they were in the office downtown and at the mines. These were here for atmosphere, as Currier and Ives prints might be in other rooms, creating a congenial place for concentration. At a big piece of wood paneling mounted on two wooden horses with an engineering table lamp suspended over it, Clarkson sat on a stool and concentrated. His doctor might inveigh against the stool as aggravating Clarkson's back problem — virtually all the senior coal operators had back problems — but Clarkson insisted on a stool. "My clerks sit on them, don't they?" he would ask rhetorically. "You can think better uncomfortable."

He did not discuss with his family what he worked on there because Clarkson was a man of rather few words, and his own quick mind was so intolerant of being bored that he had a fixed resolve never to be a bore himself, and he never was. His work, he believed, was a bore to any except other technically minded coal men, and with them only would he discuss it. The geological studies he pored over in the Tipple, in which he searched out the coal possibilities in contemplated acquisitions, the dumbbells in the corner he used every day to perform what he called his "physical jerks," these occupations which gave him a keen, constructive sense of useful accomplishment were, he believed, unsuited for the essentially domestic and even feminine atmosphere of the Castle, and were besides Bores to Others. A combination of secrecy and consideration drove him to retreat with his reports, his dumbbells and his copy of *The Case of the Bituminous Coal Mine Workers to the President's Coal Commission, 1919* to his sequestered room in the barn.

Here Lyle found him after walking Mrs. Pence home.

"Hi Dad."

"Son." Clarkson had turned on his stool and was eyeing his son quizzically. Lyle virtually never came to the Tipple. If the library was his father's room, the Tipple was his sanctuary.

"I just wanted to ask you something about that . . . the

money, that five hundred dollars that went to . . . Mrs. Pence. It had my name on it?"

Clarkson's eyebrows had gone up, and now they came down. "How'd you hear about that?"

"I ran into her in Coon Hollow and" — he began to giggle in spite of himself — "she *thanked* me for it!"

"She did, did she?" Clarkson commented, the ghost of a twinkle behind his eyes. "She wasn't — uh — didn't seem offended at all, then?"

"Oh no. She said that thing 'I' said in 'my' message, 'Not charity, debt,' that made it okay. Why'd you sign my name to it?"

Clarkson placed his hands with their strong, square-tipped fingers on his knees and leaned forward a little.

"Well, you see that was why. In case she got offended we could say it was just impulsive, a boy's impulse. That's all right with you, isn't it?"

"Oh sure!" He didn't mind having the gift ascribed to him, far from it; he was delighted, especially as she had accepted it so well. What he minded was being called a boy.

Clarkson had begun to glance back toward the papers he was studying (Bored with me already, thought Lyle) when Lyle cut in, "There was one thing she *did* mind though. We started talking about her future and I told her you said nature would take its course and she'd find another husband. That threw her for a loss! Dropped back twenty yards on that play."

Clarkson frowned a little. "She was upset, was she? You shouldn't have said that to her."

"Oh I think she's just kind of high-hat in her own way."

"And her husband gone just three months. You shouldn't have been talking about it."

"Do you mean 'you' singular or 'you' plural?"

Clarkson grimaced at this saucy question and Lyle immediately regretted it; boyishness again. Shoot, he never would get it right with his dad. Also it was obvious that his father wanted now to get back to those reports about eight billion years ago in the Appalachian jungles, or whatever he was studying. If only he wasn't so damn smart! Or, he finished, if only I was smarter.

X.

From this first day Lyle felt compelled to see Mrs. Pence, see a great deal of her, but he realized that in the society of Middleburg, West Virginia, and its taboos that appeared to be next to impossible. She was a widow and must be at least twenty-seven years old, maybe even thirty; he was a rich eighteen-year-old college boy. Probably in New York or somewhere such a couple could meet, could go tea dancing at the Plaza Hotel, could take a carriage through Central Park, go rowing on the lake there, go to the Ziegfeld Follies, to speakeasies: all these romantic rendezvous would be possible in the great, carefree, sophisticated city. No one would raise an eyebrow. But here, tucked away in the West Virginia hills, with everybody staring down deep into the lives of everybody else, with the moves of your life laid out for you as carefully as a minuet, it just seemed totally impossible.

Take her to a country club dance? People would think both he and she were mad, and drunk as skunks besides. Go to the pictures with her? They would be seen; people would chatter like jaybirds. He would be indulgently dismissed as a boy sowing his wild oats; she would be branded a gold-digging adventuress trying to rob the cradle. It would be Mrs. Pence who would suffer. Hell, they would probably fire her from her teaching job: they would certainly do that, he remembered a similar case from a year or two before.

What a quandary.

And then very gradually it permeated Lyle's consciousness that this quandary simply might not exist. What if she
wouldn't consider having anything to do with him?

Now *that* was a thought. But of course she would, she just
naturally would. Of course she would. He might be a worthless son condemned to the fires of Hell, but he *was* an attractive guy. He would ask her.

Ask her to do what?

Go for a drive in his car, out into the country, back into
the hills. They would have a picnic. Nobody would see them,
they could just be themselves and get to know each other
better. Then somehow one thing would lead to another and
the future would work itself out.

Lyle returned to the university at Morgantown and pon-
dered throughout the first part of the week on just how to
issue this invitation to Mrs. Pence. God forbid that she would
say no to it. He would not be able to stand that. Spooky how
important this girl, well, this woman, had become to him,
but there it was. He couldn't help it.

In the end he decided it was much too easy to decline an
invitation over the phone — or even hang up on him! — so
he decided to write her a note:

Dear Doris Lee,
Is it all right for me to call you that? I feel we have something in common, a terrible event, and can stop calling each
other Mrs. Pence and Mr. Catherwood. I hope I'm right about
that.
I understand that your field is American history, and that
that's what you're going to teach at junior high. So you must
be an expert on it. American history is my major at the university and I'm sure having some trouble with it. Could you
give me a little helping hand sometime soon? Maybe just an
hour or two, a general discussion, would help me get things
straightened out in my mind. I know you're busy and have a lot

on your mind. And I know about what you have suffered. I do know, truly. I suffered from that and I still suffer, in my way, for my part. Well, I thought if we had this history discussion it could be during a drive out into the country a little ways, to "get you out of the house" — my mother says that's important for ladies. You could get some fresh air while I get some fresh ideas about all these history problems.

Do you think you would like to do that?

Respectfully yours,
Lyle Catherwood

Ten days elapsed before a reply came, ten days of maturing for Lyle, he felt sure, because he sternly resisted every single temptation to call her on the telephone and start cajoling, pleading, making a fool of himself. Thanksgiving came and went: he returned home for it and performed its rituals mechanically, never venturing to call her or even drive down her street. He resisted all such temptations and after ten glacially slow days he was rewarded with a note from her: graceful, delicate handwriting on thin white paper:

Dear Lyle,

I received your letter sometime last week and had to put it aside for the reason that I'm working on history! Funny coincidence. I have to brush up on it a lot, of course, to start teaching it again after a number of years, come January. So I am delving into the subject. If you think I can be of help to you then of course I can't refuse. If you'll let me know a few days in advance I'll set aside a couple of hours. What period in American history are you most concerned about? Any specific characters or events? Or is it just overall trends? We teachers kind of like our overall trends. So vague. Then we can really get in there and theorize, and so can you students!

Sincerely yours,
Doris Lee Pence

Well, thought Lyle exultantly, off to the races!

He decided that the car to take was not his Pierce-Arrow. It was now early December, damn it, and a sporty open car was hardly suitable. The Packard was too grand and besides George wouldn't let him drive it, the Model T was too dinky, but fortunately there was the solid sober Hupmobile, four doors, big running boards, a closed car, snug, substantial.

Wearing a gray fedora, which concealed much of his lively, boyish red hair and made him look older, he knew, and a pale yellow camel's-hair overcoat, which he felt made him look interestingly man-about-the-campus, Lyle called for Doris Lee at her home. She was at the door and came out as soon as she saw him stop in front of her house. She was wearing the same long tan raincoat and rain hat as the last time he had seen her. Today it was not raining, just blustery and chilly. Perfect for a picnic, he reflected sourly as she came toward the car. It was the ugliest time of year around here. Why couldn't all this have happened in June, October? No, just his luck. He had to go courting, taking rides in the country, in dreary December. Lyle came around to her side and handed her into the front seat. Then he went back and took his place behind the wheel. Doris Lee had a notebook and several books in her lap and was also carrying a fountain pen. "I hope it doesn't leak," she said lightly. "Hate to leave a stain on this nice upholstery."

"Oh it's —" "Nothing, we can buy another car," he had started to blurt. But he caught himself. He was just going to have to grow up. No boasting about the "coal baron's" money in front of Doris Lee Pence. "It's . . . it looks like a good pen. Hey, you're looking like a real teacher today."

She turned to face him then and he ate those words mentally: she looked like a madonna or something, the Mona Lisa. What eyes!

Starting the engine, Lyle proceeded slowly down the steep

[212]

hill from her house. "Where are we going for our history conference?" she asked pleasantly.

"It's not the greatest day in the world to drive," he conceded, trying desperately to answer her question, one he had been asking himself for days. How hemmed in they were in Middleburg! No big city within a hundred miles. The nearest real pleasure resort, White Sulphur Springs, was hopelessly distant in the southeastern part of the state.

"We'll go to Morgantown," he suddenly and decisively announced. "That's the right place for study. Get you out of Middleburg too. Change of scene. My mother says that's important. She went to Europe and it changed her life — that and — uh, a preacher. Before that she was kind of what they call a recluse. You think you'll turn into a recluse?" he threw jauntily, nervously, at her.

She laughed. What a laugh. It was rich and kind of throaty, and free. "I doubt it! Chasing my child up and down the street all day. You need *servants* to turn into a recluse."

"You'll have servants someday," he muttered wildly.

"Hmmm?"

"Nothing."

In order to reach the road to Morgantown they had to pass through the center of town. High in the Hupmobile they sat, expanses of window all around them. Lyle noticed out of the corner of his eye that she was sitting very straight, her fine pure profile high, almost haughty. He himself tended to crunch down a bit in the seat and try to hide his face between the brim of his hat and the collar of his coat.

He did not notice anyone he knew on the glum December streets, but as he piloted the Hupmobile through them a spark of complicity — guilt? — seemed to him to have sprung into being between Doris Lee Pence and himself. She had been aware of a certain . . . unsuitability in her going for a drive with him and that was why she now sat a shade defiantly.

[213]

·The idea blazed behind his eyes: there was a possibility of something happening between them. He knew it, saw it, felt it, was positive of it. Why had her chin gone up, why had she become silent, as they drove through the center of Middleburg unless she too was aware of just such a possibility, a possibility present in the minds of busybodies in the town, true, but also present in her own? She knew there was this possibility, and still she had come out with him, was sitting next to him now in the Hupmobile.

There it was, there it was. It could happen. And she knew it. Lyle felt so intoxicated he could hardly continue to shift gears.

They proceeded across the higher of the two bridges over the Monongahela River and set out on the narrow, wandering road to Morgantown.

Doris Lee settled more comfortably in the seat. "About American history. What period is giving you trouble? Or is it —"

"Well, as a matter of fact, it's the Civil War. Do you know Mrs. Stallings?"

"No, not personally. I've . . . read about her."

"Read about her?"

"In the *Exponent*. You know," she finished quietly, "the society pages."

"Oh. Well, she's a real expert on the Civil War, or thinks she is, and I've talked to her about it, and there's a course I'm taking in Morgantown and well it's just — well, who's guilty, who's responsible? I" — here Lyle began to lie and so his voice became especially sincere and convincing — "I've got to do this paper, 'The Civil War: Causes and Effects.'"

"Ye Gods, what an assignment! You could write ten books. How long is it supposed to be?"

"Oh. Medium. And what I'm wondering, when we sit down for our picnic —"

"What picnic?"

"Back there." He motioned to a hamper and thermos bottles on the floor of the back seat; inside the hamper, Tot, mystified as to where and with whom Lyle was planning a picnic, had nevertheless packed deviled eggs and cucumber sandwiches and cold chicken and potato salad and apples and sponge cake; iced tea filled one thermos bottle, and a concoction of Lyle's — rum and apple cider and cinnamon — filled the other. Doris Lee looked from these provisions back at Lyle in amused perplexity. "Where are we going to have a picnic at this time of year? In the bell tower?"

"Out at Cheat Lake."

"Cheat Lake. It'll be too chilly out there."

"Not if we stay in the car. Pretty, Cheat Lake."

"In the car? A picnic?"

"Why not? I told you I'm giving you a change of scene. Well, what's wrong with Cheat Lake?"

She shrugged faintly. "Nothing, nothing at all, it's just, well . . ." She turned to face the meandering, potholed road again; she surveyed for a minute the stripped hillsides, the mudbanks, the slatternly sheds and barns.

She straightened her rain hat. "The causes and effects of the Civil War," she said in wonder, almost to herself. "Where do you want to start?"

"Well, whose fault was it?" And hearing her start to draw an almost contemptuous breath at the scope and naiveté of this question, he hurriedly added, "Or, to put it another way, the first mistake, the basic one — who made it?"

"God, by making people different colors."

"And after that?"

She drew a long breath. "Well, after that, the South, let's be honest, for putting people in slavery, and keeping them there."

"Don't you think the North should have left the South alone, to work it out ourselves?"

[215]

"Oh I guess so. It's so complicated."

"What about the effects?"

"What effects?"

"The effects of the Civil War."

"Oh. Oh yes. We-e-e-l-l-l. I, ah, the effects. Where do you want to begin?"

"In West Virginia."

"Here. Well, here the effects were different from practically anywhere. I mean here the North had to pretend we'd been loyal Yankees and the South knew we were more or less southern and so, well nobody could get *at* West Virginia, if you see what I mean. There was no Reconstruction here, of course, and I don't know, folks just went on with their simple lives, now that first the Yankees and then the Rebels wouldn't come sweeping through and tearing everything up and burning everything down. They just went on . . . simple lives, till of course they found some oil and natural gas and then they found *a lot* of coal!"

"I'll say they did," Lyle agreed stoutly. "And," lapsing into a minstrel-show darkie voice, "thank de Lawd!"

Doris Lee gazed before her, some contained, ironic mirth struggling to remain concealed behind the pure lines of her face. "Where would we all be," Lyle went on blithely, "without it?" Doris Lee's face stiffened; Lyle then sensed the tactlessness of his words. "Gee I — you know — Lord, what a *stupid* thing to say. Oh me, I'm sorry —"

"No," she said quietly, "it's all right. I know what you meant. Truly I do. I, uh, well, yes, 'thank de Lawd' because without coal, this road here would be a sea of mud instead of the magnificent turnpike all the world knows it is."

Lyle had to admire her lightning recovery from the stark thought of Virgil and his death by coal, her quick return to banter, her control, her consideration of him. I love this woman, he thought solemnly, and tears almost seeped into his eyes. There's nothing else to say.

They reached Morgantown, and Lyle guided the Hupmobile deliberately through its steep, brick-paved streets.
Disappointingly, not one of the people he knew there was
on the streets to see him and his companion. For while being
seen with Doris Lee in Middleburg would cause much social
tremor and tension, being seen with her in Morgantown, it
seemed to him, would be a feather in his cap, boyish Lyle
Catherwood out and about with a mysterious, unknown
"older woman." Now that would be very smooth. Sophisticated. Worldly. But nobody saw them, damn it.

He proceeded through the town and out along the road to
Cheat Lake. "You'd never know that this was coal-mining
country around here, would you," she remarked. And indeed,
continuing through the wooded countryside and then down a
steep, tree-crowded incline to the sheet of water, a placid,
clear mirror set amid the hills, the prospect seemed to Lyle
almost Swiss in its picturesqueness. Someday he would know,
he would go to Switzerland on his "Petite Tour." They
called West Virginia the Switzerland of America, didn't
they? Secretly, almost guiltily, he suspected this description
to be undeserved. He had seen photographs of the Matter-
horn, and there sure as hell wasn't any mountain like *that* in
West Virginia. Still, it was a very, very pretty state, no,
beautiful, slag heaps and coal dust or no slag heaps and coal
dust, this big range of bumpy, tree-rich hills, these clear and
fast streams, this virginal lake here, small, clean, in a saucer
among the hills, unpretentious as all things were in West Virginia except the Cliftons' mansions and, well, he supposed the
Castle too. And that car of theirs, the Packard with the speaking tube and George in his uniform wearing his gloves, that
was snobbish all right, and Marcus Clifton's Rolls-Royce was
pretty bogus, not to mention his private railroad car — thank
God, Lyle suddenly thought, his own father hadn't gone that
far.

There was a little grassy place, where boats were beached

in the summer, just off the road, next to the water and the bridge across it. Lyle pulled in there and turned off the motor. Doris Lee pulled off her rain hat and shook out her thick auburn hair.

"Let's take a little walk," suggested Lyle.

They walked along by the edge of the water. The air was cold and clear but motionless and so not particularly chilly. Overhead, the sky was trying to clear: patches of innocent blue broke here and there through the accumulated gray cloud banks. Both Lyle and Doris Lee were wearing stout country shoes and so walking was a pleasure. "Not a coal tipple in sight," he said, and then could have punched himself. *Say something romantic!* Stop talking about *coal.*

"No," she agreed.

"Do you like water? The seashore?"

"Sometimes," she went on, pursuing her line of thought, "I wish I lived in some other part of the country. Arizona. California. I don't know. Somewhere very very different. I feel like I don't really belong here. When I was little I used to think I was the daughter of the Emperor of Austria or someone like that and I'd been kidnapped. Did you ever imagine things like that when you were little?"

"No," said Lyle very reluctantly, wishing he could have shared in these imaginings of hers.

"Of course you didn't need to," she said a little ruefully. "You already were the son of a great house. A Catherwood of the Castle. You didn't need to make up some kind of gorgeous background."

This confused Lyle. It began to trouble him. They were rich. Almost everybody else around here was poor. Virgil Pence had been and he supposed Doris Lee's father too. This uneasiness about his family's wealth, which he had all his life taken for granted and enjoyed in an absentminded way, this uneasiness which had first struck him as he drove up to Cheat Lake with her, now recurred with much greater force. The Packard, the Castle, his parents' travels abroad, all suddenly looked to him almost, well, not obscene exactly, just very inappropriate.

"It's the way things are meant to be," every member of the Middleburg Country Club would have automatically and sincerely responded to an expression of what he was thinking. They were *supposed* to be owners and operators who lived very well. *They owned it all.* It was virtually God's will, and any other was blasphemous. God made it that way. To question it was Bolshevik, as were all those labor leaders like Frank Keeney, godless and Communist and evil.

Virgil Pence had died defending that principle.

But it was no Bolshevik labor agitator who had shot Virgil Pence. Some kid, a gun put in his hand by Don Chafin, champion of the owners, had done that. Well, but Virgil Pence wouldn't have been there except for the labor agitators. And except for Coal Baron Clarkson Catherwood's princely son, the incomparable Lyle, trying to be somebody he wasn't. "Are you ever lonely or anything?" he suddenly asked her.

She strolled on by the chilly sheet of gray-green water, her profile as pure as ivory, and after a while answered, "I think everybody is, at least part of the time. Yes, you could say that I am."

I'm going to put an end to *that*, he asserted inside himself. To her he said, "Maybe you'll let me, you know, play cards with you or anything like that. To pass the spare time."

"But you're here in Morgantown."

"I come up to Middleburg all the time. My dad's away an awful lot. I keep Ma company as much as I can. And now it'll be Ma and you, if that's okay with you."

She stopped and turned toward him. "Mr. Cath—— "

"Lyle!"

[219]

"Lyle, you don't have to keep worrying about me. That check was really thoughtful. Thank you again. You have your life and friends . . . responsibilities . . . your mother and all. I'm not one of your responsibilities. Nobody was responsible, certainly not that poor little boy in Logan with that gun they gave him. The only thing responsible . . ." Her voice trailed off.

"Yeah? What were you going to say?"

"Nothing."

"Come on. Say it." Then, more urgently, "Please say it."

She glanced at him again, a flash of green luminescence in her perfect face. She seemed trying to detect something of his thoughts, feelings. Then she said, "The only thing responsible was, well, King Coal. After all, I guess I really am the daughter of a ruler, King Coal. He's responsible. The famous coal boom. *That's* responsible."

"Things like that can't be responsible for a . . . a . . ."

"Oh yes they can. And they are."

"Doris Lee?"

"Yes."

"I hope you and I are going to be real good friends."

She walked in her graceful, willowy way on beside the water. "We are friends." She then said, "Aren't we?"

"Yes, but I mean *really good friends*."

She remained silent.

She doesn't understand after all, he thought grimly. But then she broke her thoughtful silence to say, "Lots of people would think it is pretty peculiar that you and I are becoming friends. But then I've never cared too much what lots of people thought."

"Me either! Let's go back and have the picnic."

They strolled back to the car and got into the back seat. Lyle opened the wicker hamper and handed her some cold chicken and a hard-boiled egg. After a little while he passed her his rum concoction in the most offhand manner possible. Unsuspecting, Doris Lee took a gulp. "What's *that!*"

"That," he answered complacently, "is Riverboat Punch."

"Riverboat Punch, is it? What's in it?"

"Sugar."

"Sugar? Sugar and wood alcohol, I'd say."

"That's right. It's called rum."

She gave him an appraising, sidelong look. "Yes, I know," she then said dryly. "It's illegal."

"My dad says *Prohibition* is illegal. Against the laws of nature, he says."

"Well if you think I'm going to sit here in the middle of the woods by Cheat Lake and drink *rum* with you, Mr. Catherwood, think again."

"Oh, come on, just a couple of sips. Warms you up. It's chilly here."

"On the contrary," she murmured.

"Hmmm?"

"I think we ought to start heading back. Daylight's short in December."

"Youth is short too," he suddenly blurted.

"Whaaat! Oh please, 'Youth is short'? Please. Are you going to start striking poses?"

"Am I striking poses?"

"You were starting to."

"Is that what I'm doing?" he inquired humbly. "Just tell me when I'm . . . you know, acting like an idiot or anything."

She took a look at him. "You don't act like an idiot."

Lyle stiffened, and to himself he said fervently, Oh, but I do, I have, and you of all people in the world ought to know it.

XI.

The next day Lyle escorted Minnie to the service at Christ Episcopal Church. The interior of the little stone building was a tableau of highly polished wood, tall candles in burnished candelabra, expert fingers at the resonant organ. Dr. Masterson in his black soutane and white surplice delivered from the pulpit words of Christian enlightenment in his well-modulated and well-educated voice, the congregation a sea or at least a pond of furred, hatted, gloved ladies and collared, necktied, vested, watch-chained, florid gentlemen, and their extremely well scrubbed and stiffly dressed offspring. The creaking of pews, the fidgeting of the children, the rustle of silk and a general aura of contented, intent hour-long attention to Higher Things filled the silences between prayers, sermon and hymns.

What is Mother thinking? Lyle asked himself as the service proceeded on its well-ordered, unruffled course toward its foreordained conclusion. What can she be thinking, this far from the Church of the Last Judgment and Reverend Roanoke? Is this the way to be Saved, or is that? Or any of them?

Outside, having been greeted by Dr. Masterson at the door, they encountered Marcus Clifton, proceeding with his wife Macel on his arm toward his Rolls, as usual parked directly in front of the church door, with the Catherwoods' Packard as usual just behind it. He was wearing a Prince Albert overcoat and a homburg. She wore a black wool coat with a silver fox collar.

Lyle had always thought that Marcus Clifton looked like a bloodhound, bags beneath the eyes, sagging dewlap and cheeks, fleshy nose, full drooping mouth. But Lyle also thought he detected a twinkle in the watery blue eyes, as though beneath all his wealth and possessions and importance he finally thought there was something not one hundred percent serious about it all.

Mrs. Clifton looked as though the first stiff breeze would blow her away.

"Morning, Catherwoods," Marcus Clifton called in his crackly, semisouthern voice. "Where's the lord and master?"

"Cleveland again," replied Minnie. "*You* don't seem to travel as much as *he* does, Marcus."

"That's because they come to me, my dear," he replied with blunt satisfaction, "that's because they come to me."

"And will *you* come to *us?*" chirped Macel Clifton. "We're having a real old-fashioned Sunday lunch today, spur of the moment. A few of the southern people are in town." Lyle knew that "southern people" meant coal owners from Charleston or Logan. "Don Chafin's with them too, so we thought we'd get some people together. You know him, don't you, Lyle? Weren't you down around Logan during the trouble?"

Lyle nodded stiffly. The last person on earth he wanted to see was Don Chafin. He didn't know exactly why. "Mother, don't we have to be at home for . . . for . . . that call from Dad?"

"Your father didn't say he'd call this morning, did he?" she replied, blinking at him through the little veil on her hat. "I don't recall that he did. Anyhow, he'll call later. I'd like to get a look at this Don Chafin."

"A fine figure of a man," observed Macel Clifton.

"Oh well, commented Marcus Clifton, "he's *big*, if that's what you mean."

"Good head of hair," added Macel.

"It's what's under heads of hair," responded Marcus, "that makes the difference. After you're twenty-five, that is, Lyle. Before, it's all in the hair."

Lyle forced a smile.

Assisted by their chauffeurs they climbed into their respective limousines and swept across Middleburg Avenue to the gates of Clifton Farms. Here the black and silver Rolls turned with an expensive crunching sound onto the driveway which curved through lawns and evergreens up to the four-story Spanish Mission–style main house. Lyle noticed eight to ten other important-looking cars parked near the main entrance to the house, their drivers idling alongside.

Inside, in the high-ceilinged, long-windowed living rooms with deep couches, great fireplaces, the famous Venetian glass punch bowl dispensing eggnog, Lyle found himself elated once more to be at the heart of this most basic of industries. He had always thought of the living rooms of Clifton Farms as that. Now the thought struck him: this isn't the heart of the coal industry. That's far underground, at the heading in some tunnel, where somebody is just about to set off a charge of dynamite. This is . . . this is the top maybe, or the brains, or the steeple, or maybe it's the belfry.

Marcus and Macel's children had all been considerably older than he was and so there had been relatively few occasions when Lyle had been invited to the Farms. To enter this formidable but still gracious homestead, which, Spanish Mission or not, looked more homelike and more suitable for the town than Marcus's brother Sanderson's Elizabethan manor or their own imitation castle, to enter it had always struck almost a sense of awe in Lyle, or, no, it had not been awe exactly, it had been — he searched for the word as he accepted a cup of eggnog — a feeling of fitness, of completeness, this was the apex of the industry and it looked exactly right for its role, all comfort and solidity in the interior, the exterior an expansion and elaboration of an earlier Clifton homestead which had been built in the last century. This house was the past flowing and expanding into the great power and ever-growing wealth of the present, presiding over the boom as the White House in Washington had presided over, well, the Spanish-American War or something, dignified, old, always there. There were family portraits and large oil paintings of the Clifton show horses about. Macel collected silver: there were beautiful silver bowls and candlesticks and trays.

Next to some glass doors was planted the bulk of Don Chafin, in the flesh. To Lyle he seemed an impostor without his usual jodhpurs and boots and Mexican campaign hat; in a double-breasted navy blue suit he looked like a successful bootlegger. Clumsily holding his little cut-glass punch cup he also suggested a badly miscast actor in the wrong play.

What are you doing here? Lyle suddenly and silently demanded of Don Chafin. Who the hell let you out of Logan?

Chafin was in conversation with a group of the southern coal men; four of their wives were with Macel and Minnie near the punch bowl. Ophelia and Clarence Stallings came into the room, fresh from services at the Presbyterian Church, the only guests here, Lyle calculated, who had not arrived chauffeur-driven. Money, money, money: perhaps someday in Middleburg they would fill their swimming pools with dollar bills and swim in them.

"Why don't you go over and speak to Sheriff Chafin?" Minnie suggested to Lyle.

"Uh . . . I don't think so, no."

"But that would be rude."

He gave her a look. Rude to Don Chafin? It would be like insulting a shark. "It doesn't matter, Mother. He wouldn't remember me, so he won't feel hurt." (Hurt: through *that* hide!) "And I do remember him, and so I — I don't want to go over and shake his hand."

"Why not?"

Sometimes, for a part-time clairvoyant, she could be pretty dim. "Because, Mother, Don Chafin in Logan was like, well, he was like the Yankees marching through Georgia."

"You never told me that. Brutal?"

He didn't know the exact word for it. It was just that, seeing him here amid the chandeliers and draperies and rich rugs and murmuring servants of Clifton Farms, mingling with the, well, the classiest people in Middleburg fresh from Sunday church, Don Chafin linked, in Lyle's mind, all the squalor and persecution and death in Logan to his own heritage, of which he had always felt an unquestioning pride, in Middleburg. Supporting the show horses and the Venetian bowl and the Castle and the Packard and Minnie's yacht trip in the Mediterranean was, at the most basic level, this bully with his goons beating up workmen in the road, shooting prisoners in jail, giving guns to young boys who couldn't control them.

"Hello there, Lyle," the hooting southern tones of Aunt Ophelia interrupted, "how you?" Verbs sometimes dropped out of her phrases, but the mannerliness never.

"Fine, Aunt Ophelia. Hello, Uncle Clarence." Clarence Stallings mouthed a greeting.

"Been to church?" she asked rhetorically.

"Oh yes. Saved for another week."

She eyed him from beneath her purple velvet toque. "You fixed on bein' Saved, like your mama?"

"Isn't everybody in the world?"

She picked the pince-nez off her nose and began twiddling it. "Oh I s'pose so. More's the pity. Many are called but few are chosen. It's pretty clear who's *Saved* in this world, isn't it?"

"*Is* it?" Lyle stared at her. "*I* thought it was a mystery and everybody just hoped and tried —"

"That's because you're Episcopal. Come to my church sometime. Who's Saved, who's not, it's as plain as anything. That preacher, the Negro, your mother went to? Who's he foolin'? We know over at my church, we don't need to go to some barn in Bennettown and get hypnotized! *Good* people are Saved, it's written all over them."

"These people here," Lyle began, startled by what she had said, "well, *us* —"

"Course you are." He had never heard her say anything

more firmly. "Course you are. You think the Lord is going to favor *sinners*, the Devil's friends, the way we all are favored? Give us the leadership of the industry and the state and society and *everything* unless we were doing *His* work?" She for once enunciated every syllable. "Of . . . course . . . not. No." The pince-nez was back in place. She clasped her hands beneath her matronly bosom, as though about to sing an aria. "That's what it is, Lyle Boy. *That's* why those agitators you saw down in Logan have to be *put down*. They're the Devil's own, tryin' to upset the way things are meant to be. Marcus and your daddy and these other men built up this mighty industry, keepin' the whole *country* warm, and so they're God's specially favored servants. He showers his blessings on them, and on us too, on Clarence and me. We're blessed. We're blessed here, we're all blessed. And we got to keep it, guard it, that's God's own will."

Glory hallelujah, thought Lyle wonderingly. Now ain't that sumpthin'. I wonder if she's right? You've made yourself rich, you've made yourself powerful, *so*, you're Saved. He tested this principle within himself. There amid the chatter at the punch bowl at the Farms he tried to lower this idea deep within his mind, as deep as he could, to see what happened. If it was true he expected a profound reverberation throughout himself, such as his mother must have experienced when Reverend Roanoke told her she was Saved years ago; it must have so reverberated because the effect of that reverberation continued clearly to influence her every day of her life since then.

He lowered Ophelia's idea of predestination, of the Elect of God, down into his mind. His father owned ten mines or however many there were: therefore, he was Saved. They lived in the Castle; therefore they were Saved. Seven servants: Saved. Pierce-Arrow: Saved.

Nothing reverberated. There was no deep, visceral stirring. But the point was, the Presbyterian point was, if he understood it correctly, that *you* worked and built up a powerful industry and *by that* proved that you were Saved.

But what if you inherited it?

So he put this question to Ophelia Stallings.

"Same thing," she sniffed, "same thing."

But she did not say it with the same conviction. His father had put together the Clarkson Coal Company and prospered mightily. *He* was Saved. But what had Lyle put together?

As these thoughts flowed through his mind Lyle had been gazing blankly out of a long window into the garden. He turned back to the room and flinched almost visibly at seeing his mother, in her black hat with its little eyelid veil, head tilted back, looking up into the foursquare, cherry-red face of Don Chafin. They were standing at the next window.

"Are there a lot of miners still in your jails?" she was asking him in her ladylike, gentle way.

"Why no, ma'am, just one or two troublemakers. Logan's as peaceful as, well, Middleburg here."

"I'd love to drive down there sometime — my son tells me it's wild and beautiful country — this is my son: Lyle, here's Sheriff Chafin! — wild and beautiful country, isn't that what you said, Lylie. I'd just love to drive down there and have a look at it, but I hear there aren't any roads!"

"Well now, ma'am, we haven't got just the best turnpikes in the country yet. It's hard terrain to build on. All ups and downs. Hardly any levels except along the creekbeds and there we got farms! How *you*, son?"

Lyle could have swatted this galoot for calling him "son." Instead he murmured, "Not bad," and averted his eyes.

Ignoring that, Don Chafin plunged on. "Course, havin' country roads down home and nothin' but, we don't get too many *outsiders*, what I mean *undesirables* down there. Just folks as belongs there. *You'd* be welcome any day of the week, ma'am, goes without sayin'. And your fine boy here too."

[228]

Flustered, Lyle had to admit that Don Chafin had a kind of open country charm about him somewhere. The big galoot had more sides to him than just the bully boy; he was a clever, or anyhow a cagey, so-and-so.

"Well, Mr. Chafin," said Minnie airily, "maybe I'll take the train down there sometime with my husband. I hope it's *still* peaceful and quiet when I do, and that you have no miners at all in your jail. That way I'll feel safe."

Chafin's big face seemed to inflate to larger dimensions. "Why, ma'am, it's by puttin' the troublemakers behind bars that we can g-u-a-r-a-n-t-e-e your safety!"

"No," said Minnie quietly, "no, it isn't. That isn't the way."

XII.

Afterward Lyle thought of his afternoon outing with Doris Lee as a crucial watershed of his life. On one side of it, the side before this little trip, there had been Lyle Catherwood, lifelong self-doubter, indifferent student and athlete, eager for life and for being liked and being loved, stumbling awkwardly along and attaining really none of these things except that he believed his mother loved him, a self-doubter so entangled in his doubts that he even submitted to the revivalist rolling prayer meeting with Ramsey Whatchama-callem Roanoke.

That was one side of the watershed, and the other side was simply Doris Lee. And from the other side he now looked back across the ridge at the vale of wandering he had climbed out of and, amazed and wondering and pitying in a rather contemptuous way what he beheld there, his past self, he knew he had changed.

"How's Reverend Roanoke? Heard from him?" he asked

his mother one morning at breakfast in the breakfast room. This was a small, big-windowed alcove off the dining room with pale yellow walls, full of ferns and sunlight and the smell of freshly ground and percolated coffee.

"No," said Minnie quietly, raising her eyebrows and gazing down at her hard-boiled egg.

"I haven't either," he said shortly.

She then lifted her eyes to his face. "No," she said after a pause, "I shouldn't imagine that you would have. Now Lyle" — she put her spoon down and placed her chin on her fist, leaning forward — "I don't want you to . . . to take too much to heart what happened that day in the motorcar. He couldn't *see* your salvation, that's all, couldn't feel it. You're so young, it . . . it probably hadn't, well, *jelled* as yet. But because he happened not to be able to see it *doesn't mean that it isn't there.*" Her anxious eyes studied his face closely. "You do understand that, don't you?"

"Sure," he said, "of course. Can I have some of that Baptist cake?"

"*May* I have some of that Baptist cake," she corrected automatically. "You do, you truly do understand? You're not in despair?"

In despair! How absurdly the words now echoed in his mind. "No, Mother," he replied quietly, and it was his turn to gaze innocently down at his soft-boiled egg, "no, I feel fine."

"Well, I'm glad, son." Her anxious eyes still searched over his face. "You are sure? Because there is nothing to fear, faith can move mountains, and you *will* be Saved, you will be."

"Yes, Mother," he said absently, and the sole worry he had left in the world, the sole remaining fear, the sole gap in his self-assurance, was the memory of how he had been before he crossed the watershed, and, having once been such a spineless, fearful little pipsqueak, crying at his mother's knee and scared by fly-by-night preachers, whether he could ever fall back into that again. How had he ever let himself feel so worthless, weak, purposeless? That worried him, that alone.

"When are you going back to the university?" she asked.

"Ah, Tuesday."

"Don't you have any classes Monday?"

"No. That's a special day down there, Stonewall Jackson Day. No classes."

"I wonder why we don't celebrate it here," she mused aloud, and he was once again helped by her endearing vagueness, which saved him a lot of trouble at times, such as this one.

On Monday Doris Lee had invited him to supper at her house, "with my boy, pot luck, all right?"

Yes, it had been all right.

"Have you talked to Dad?" he asked his mother.

"He called last evening, feeling very sorry for himself at having to spend a weekend alone in Cleveland, but first thing Monday morning they are launching a great big barge, I believe he said, some kind of huge lakeboat, to take coal from the Cleveland docks clear up through the Great Lakes to Minnesota, where the iron is and the steel. A huge new market, if I understood it right. You know your father."

Will I ever? wondered Lyle. And does it really matter anymore?

"He does hate to talk business with the family, but it's some big new expansion of business, and the idea of the Clarkson Coal Company now being involved in shipping, I like that. Captains, first mates. Bells going off, not loud ones, ship's bells, precise, meaning something specific. I just loved the bells on the *Kaiser Wilhelm der Grosse* when we —"

"The *what!*"

"The ship we took back from Europe. The *Kaiser Wilhelm der Grosse.*"

"What an unbelievable name. German. What's it mean?"

"It means William the Great. Now don't make faces. The war is over. I know all about those Belgian atrocities and I was as" — here her voice became a little fainter — "as shocked as anyone. More." Lyle, looking at her, knew that she must have been. To his mother deliberate cruelty to an animal was an unthinkable horror. Deliberate cruelty to a human being was not within the realm of possibility; when she was forced to admit it existed, her suffering must have been great.

Making what seemed a deliberate effort of the will, Minnie wrenched her mind away from the horrible inflictions of the Great War and went on. "Bells went off, precise ones, melodious ones, frequently during the day on the *Wilhelm der Grosse*. I can still hear them in my imagination. They gave such a sense of order, and of serenity. A sense of safety too, because it meant, or at least I thought it meant, that it was the officers signaling the men to change stations, notifying the engine room about something. Then there was the sea air, the roll, they called that ship 'Rolling Billy' because she was very high and narrow and she did roll quite a bit. In the center of the ship there was a huge, marvelous skylight, stained glass, and the well below it went straight down through three decks. Oh she was spectacular. But really it was the sea, the swells, those great living moving mountains which lifted the *Wilhelm der Grosse*, grosse or not, as though it was a floating leaf, and then settling it down again into a trough. It was blissful! It really — it made me want to live, helped get me ready to take my chance at it. And inside, inside, in the evenings, in the corridors, the companionways, beautifully carpeted, with great potted palms and indoor trees, we ladies sweeping along in our gowns and jewelry, clouds of the best perfume, the gentlemen in full evening dress too, the opulence of it, like a castle on the Rhine, and yet always at sea, always at sea, step through a door out on deck and there was the overwhelming Atlantic Ocean, moonlight, waves just set into the sea, hundreds of them outlined in the moonlight, and then one of those orderly little bells would ring, a steward would come by with a little gong and we would know it was time to go down — if we wished, you could dine at any hour — down a sweeping ballroom staircase into a great restaurant for dinner."

XIII.

Dinner at Doris Lee's Monday night was in a little dining alcove off the small living room and separated from it by a wooden archway edged with latticework. There was a dull yellow light with a glass shade suspended above the oval table. The little boy, Virgil Junior, had been put to bed.

For dinner they had ham and yams and creamed corn, biscuits, apple pie, coffee. Doris Lee wore a plain blue dress. Her hair, looking black until the light striking it brought out the deep auburn, bobbed, hung thick along the side of her head, and she continued to remind him of portraits he had seen in an art book at home showing Italian ladies of the Renaissance. She was not Italian — Scotch-Irish on both sides — but her features were what he understood to be those from the world of Leonardo da Vinci. Her face was as though outlined by some artist in ink: all excess had been eliminated; there were just the ideally shaped outlines of eyes, nose, jaw, cheekbones. The mouth had its own fullness.

The dinner passed hazily for Lyle. They talked about history, about picture shows they had seen, his favorite star being Charlie Chaplin, hers the combined Lillian and Dorothy Gish, they discussed the League of Nations (he was against it, she in favor), about Prohibition (he was against it, she in favor), about what country they would most like to visit (both chose France). It was all easy and unimportant and vastly enjoyable. Lyle felt he had always intended to eat this particular meal. All the while he was thinking about her beauty and her living in this little house and teaching school and marrying Virgil and the whole puzzle her life and her fate presented to him, and the paradox of it suddenly came clear in his mind: she did not know that she was beautiful. No one had ever told her so, at least not in a way which would convince her that it was true. Then the subsequent thought: *maybe they don't think she's beautiful around here.* When he thought of Fanny Clifton Carstairs, round-faced, dimpled, round-eyed, vivacious — beside her Doris Lee, aquiline nose, curving cheekbones, might look kind of strange, a little remote, forbidding.

She didn't know she was beautiful.

But Lyle knew, and it amazed him that she was not out in California appearing in the movies, driving around in a white Rolls-Royce, instead of living up here in Middleburg, West Virginia, about to go back to teaching junior high history.

And yet, what luck for him! Would Doris Lee Pence, movie queen — no, her name would be LaBelle LeSeur or something — ever think of looking at a kid like him, inviting him to supper. Of course not. Lyle Catherwood simply was profiting from the strange oversight of the world; he was beginning to share the life, incredible as it seemed, of Doris Lee Pence.

When he got home from this dinner, relaxed, serious, domestic, uneventful, unforgettable, he went into his mother's solid and yet dreamy bedroom, where she was already in bed, reading.

"What's the book?" he asked offhandedly.

"*The Age of Innocence.* I have to read it. She won the Pulitzer Prize with it. You wouldn't like it, but I can't face another luncheon without knowing what it's about."

"What is it about?"

"It's not your kind of book, dear."

The age of innocence, he reflected. I'll say it isn't.

[234]

"Did you want to see me about something?" she asked, smiling.

"What makes you think that?"

"Well, dear, you never come in here before retiring unless you want to see me about something."

What a mother: either she was as vague as a moth, or else she saw right through him.

So now he had to back and fill, ask inane questions, seek her advice, until finally he slipped in the subject he wished. It was based on the premise, which he had established with his mother, that he had had dinner with Pete Hayes that night. "Pete and I were talking about the good-looking girls in town," he remarked as he idly fingered the silver comb and brush at her dressing table. "He says there's one that people have overlooked."

"Oh really. Which one's that?"

"Ah — the — you know, Mrs. Virgil Pence."

"Mrs. Pence? Oh yes. Hardly a girl. But yes, Mrs. Pence, yes, she's remarkably handsome, unusual-looking. Not everyone can see it. Yes, she's really a classically beautiful woman. Dresses so modestly. People don't somehow *see* it. Not out in society, never was. I look at her sometimes in church. I'm surprised that scamp Peter Hayes ever noticed. He must be more of an observer than I gave him credit for."

"Oh, he is, he is," said Lyle. His mother looked up questioningly at him. Lyle was full of high spirit. "Pete Hayes," he went on exuberantly, "is a great guy, one of the greatest guys in the world."

XIV.

Back in Morgantown Lyle walked from one appointment to another, up and down the rearing and plunging hills of the town, or took drives in the country and asked himself: What am I going to do about Doris Lee?

Not a move had been made, not a word said, which indicated that there was anything but a casual relationship based on her tutoring him, and yet he was sure that she sensed at least some part of his love for her. It was for that very reason that she dressed plainly, remained pleasant and rather impersonal.

What was he going to do? He had never felt so completely stumped in his life. Here he was in love — love — for the very first and he was sure only time in his life; here it was, what all the songs had promised, what everyone was always talking and singing and writing poems and crying and killing themselves about, here it was and what was he going to do about it? He could not take her out anywhere in public without making them both the laughingstocks of the town and causing her to lose her position at the school. To raise the matter with his father would bring on God knew what. He could discuss it with his mother, who would be sympathetic probably, but what difference would that make?

Lyle continued to return to Middleburg at every opportunity, and to see Doris Lee on many pretexts. These pretexts, once the history seminar idea had run its course and exhausted itself, ranged from repairing the wringer on her washing machine to shoveling her walk after a snowfall. This latter offer she refused. What would the neighbors think? was the implicit question behind her refusal of this job which had to be done out in front of the house for all to see.

What would the neighbors think? Lyle repeated to himself bitterly. The key and paramount and supreme question in Middleburg, West Virginia. *What would the neighbors think!*

Why, he asked himself, did everyone always have to think of what the neighbors would think? Why not ask: What was right? What was fair? What was *human*? No. Never. *What* would the neighbors think? How he hated that question, what helpless contempt he felt for that attitude. And he could do nothing to change it or modify it or affect it in any way, even with regard to Doris Lee.

Bleakly he began to suspect that what the neighbors thought could deny him his happiness with strangely beautiful Doris Lee.

Still, she continued to see him on many occasions. She was lonely. That might be the only reason she saw him; he was someone to fill in the spare time, fill a little of the gap in her suddenly diminished life.

They almost never discussed Virgil. Lyle was aware that somewhere in the depths of his mind the knowledge that he had been responsible for the death of Virgil was fused with his love for Doris Lee. He did not try to figure out the drives which created that fusion. He had not looked twice at Doris Lee until after Virgil's death, had never particularly noticed her in church. He had been just as oblivious to her beauty then as, apparently, most people were in Middleburg. Just how his guilt and his love were bound together he didn't know. He was aware that in some way they must be. And suppose through some miracle he won her, how would this bizarre link affect their love? He didn't know that either. He did know that loving her made him feel less guilty about Virgil, loving her was the answer for him, that was all, the answer to everything. He must join his life to hers. But how? Where even to start?

And then the idea hit him: he would take Doris Lee to call on Ophelia McClellan Stallings. After all, she was the most formidable social battle-ax in this part of the state; if she could be made to accept Doris Lee as a possible person for Lyle to escort in public, then everyone in town would follow along like geese heading south.

Lyle got in his car and drove out to Cheat Lake and had a couple of shots of Canadian whiskey on that, just a couple, two long shots of the stuff. He had to maintain his discipline as he prepared to lead Doris Lee Pence up to Ophelia McClellan Stallings.

The first hurdle was to think of a plausible reason for him and Doris Lee to call on her; the second was to persuade Doris Lee to make the call. He attacked the second problem first during his twice-weekly phone call to her.

"Doris Lee?" he began tentatively.

"Y-e-e-s-s?" she answered in the cajoling way she had. Out with it, her tone implied; you're leading up to something you don't know how to approach.

"Doris Lee, I wonder . . . Would you help me with something I've got to do?"

"What's that?"

"I've got to go see Mrs. Stallings."

"Who?"

"You know. Mrs. Ophelia Stallings."

There was a silence on her end.

"She's an old friend of the family's. I told you that."

"Yes," she said briefly. Lyle could positively hear her defenses going up all around her. She was not going to be put in a false social position or condescended to or made to feel inferior. She was as good as anybody and smarter than most. Lyle heard all this along the silent telephone line.

"And she did me a certain favor and I have to see her, Ma says I've got to and I want you as a special favor to go with me."

"But what for? Why me? I —"

"I want her to meet you because she sponsors all kinds of things, charity things and school things and your students will put on a show or a sale or something like that and you'll need a sponsor, and she's the best there is. It'll be a big boost for your class and make more money for the charitable cause you'll be putting it on for."

There was a thoughtful silence and then Doris Lee said

[238]

doubtfully, "Our having an event and needing a sponsor — I don't know if it'll ever happen."

"Sure it will. Besides, it'll be broadening."

"What will?"

"For you to meet her."

Another silence and then Doris Lee said, her voice a little constricted, "And for her to meet me."

"Yes! That's it. The two most remarkable ladies in Middleburg, meeting at last."

"But why would *I* be coming with *you* to her house?"

Lyle was all ready for that one. "History," he said with satisfaction.

"History?"

"She is one of the great unsung experts on local history, West Virginia history, and southern history. I'm a history major, you teach American history, and *we want her views.*"

There was an impressed silence. " 'We want her views.' You're getting pretty fancy in your speech there, Mr. Catherwood, pretty professional. You sound like Richard Harding Davis interviewing President Harding."

"Someday," he half sang over the telephone to her, "I will be." Then waxing fantastical, he added, "I wonder if Richard Harding Davis and President Harding are related."

"Richard Harding Davis died."

"They still might be related. Very unlikely people can be related. Mrs. Stallings is related to General McClellan, you know."

"Aunt Ophelia?"

"Yes? Who's this? Yes?"

"It's Lyle Catherwood, Aunt Ophelia."

"Oh hello, dear." All the old-woman irritation and doubt melted from her voice and her warm southern tones flowed over the phone to him. "How are you? You here in Middleburg?"

"I'm in Morgantown, Aunt Ophelia."

"Yes, yes, of course you are, studying. And is the curriculum proving interesting?"

"Yes, it sure is."

"I'm so glad. A little learning is a dangerous thing, but a lot of learning is the best thing there is."

"Yes, I know."

"I hope you're doing well and keeping fit at the same time."

Lyle knew that she felt a blood necessity to keep this conversation flowing pleasantly along all afternoon if necessary. If he was to get to the purpose of his call he would have to break in.

"Mustn't neglect your health," she continued. "Met any nice girls down there? One of my cousins in Jefferson County has a girl there, if I remember rightly. Her name's —"

"Aunt Ophelia, I want to come and call on you, and I want to bring someone with me. You've never met her. Mrs. Doris Lee Pence."

"That poor girl, the widow of —"

"That's the one. May I bring her to call on you?"

"Of course you may, dear. But is there anything in particular you want to see me about, or are Mrs. Pence and I just going to make each other's acquaintance?"

"She wants to talk about history, southern history, West Virginia history. She's going to teach it again, now that she's" — a sudden loss of breath; then recovering — "single."

"She's not single. She's widowed. There's a difference."

"Widowed."

"Well I declare I didn't know anybody of your generation was interested in all that. Oh — oh — Mrs. Pence. Dear me, she can't be, isn't your generation really now, is she?"

"Ah you see, no, she isn't. But then I'm — I'm just as interested in that kind of history as she is and I'm in my generation."

"Yes, dear, 'deed you are," said Ophelia a bit dryly. "You ... you been seeing Mrs. Pence, have you?"

"Tutoring, she's been helping me with my history. And now we both want your help, Aunt Ophelia."

"You do, do you?" she said pointedly, not unkindly. "Well, come see me. Sunday? Four o'clock?"

"Just great, Aunt Ophelia. Just great."

"Yes," she finished briefly.

Aunt Ophelia's house was on Middleburg Avenue, the best residential street in town. Clifton Farms, Clifton Manor and the Castle existed as species of Vatican Cities, socially extra-territorial. Any of them could have been put down in the middle of the "colored section," down by the river, and retained their status. But all lesser domiciles relied as much upon where they were as what they were for their standing in the town. Middleburg Avenue, broadly extending from the business section for a mile and a half until it reached the country, was the most prestigious address. Overhung by dignified maples, lined by imposing residences set amid well-tended lawns and clipped shrubbery, the avenue transmitted forcibly one impression to anyone driving along it: substantial homes for substantial people.

Here, in a white brick house with a turret on one corner, a porch circling halfway around its first floor, stood the home of Ophelia and Clarence Stallings. Having had neither children nor pets ever, the house had no scratches, let alone breakage or soiling. Immaculate as Ophelia's white gloves, cared for by a colored man and wife as soundless as Clarence Stallings himself, it functioned simply as a small but complicated late-Victorian setting for Ophelia McClellan Stallings.

Lyle and Doris Lee alighted from the Hupmobile at the curb, where a stone mounting block still stood: Ophelia had used it to mount sidesaddle as a young bride forty years before. All well-bred young ladies rode horseback in her

[241]

day, she maintained, naturally sidesaddle only, as riding astride could have rendered them incapable of bearing children and been unspeakably coarse as well. If a young lady could not ride it meant that the family had not kept a stable when she was growing up and *that* meant she had not been brought up in the proper surroundings.

Lyle wore a gray suit, a stiff collar, a maroon and blue bow tie, a fedora and the camel's-hair overcoat. Doris Lee was in gray too, a rather severe dark gray dress, gray coat, and a black cloche hat over her auburn hair.

"We match!" she said with slightly strained merriment as they mounted the steps to the porch and went up to the oak and beveled plate glass front door. Lyle smiled briefly and twisted the little handle in the door. Instantly an excited ring shot impudently into the interior of the house, and after a very dignified interval Ophelia's maid Dorothy, in black dress and white apron and cap, admitted them.

Within all was cool and polished and dim. Clearly designed for gaslight, the house seemed uncomfortable with its central heating. There was a shallow fireplace with a glowing electric grid in it in the front hall, and a somewhat less shallow fireplace, unlighted, in the front parlor. Various Victorian chairs and settees offered themselves as invincibly uncomfortable places to sit. "I'm going to sit on the floor," growled Lyle.

"You are not!" Doris Lee shot back in an undertone.

He settled for a undersized, rocklike chair, she for a rigid settee.

There were shelves with leatherbound books — the Harvard Classics, the Complete Works of Charles Dickens — which it was clear at a distance of twenty feet had never been touched since being placed there. There were wax flowers under glass bells. Above the fireplace and mantelpiece there was a head-and-shoulders portrait in oil in a dull gold frame of a rather dashing-looking man, his shoulders in some sort of military uniform turned to the right, his sharp-looking blue eyes glaring challengingly toward the left. This was undoubtedly an Ancestor. There was a harp next to the fireplace. The wallpaper, hundreds of tight little rose blossoms against a cream-colored background, provided a suitably artificial setting for all the wax flowers, unread books, unplayed harp, unlit fireplace, and uncomfortable furniture in the room.

Ophelia swept in, wearing a deep purple lace tea gown, pearls, her pince-nez dangling to her swelling bosom, three diamond rings and a look of considerable pleased anticipation.

"Sit down, child," she said after Doris Lee had risen to greet her. Lyle noted the "child"; Ophelia was going to treat Doris Lee with all her practiced plantation charm, at least at first.

"You do understand I hope, Mrs. Stallings," Doris Lee began with the faintest quaver in her quiet but definite voice, "this isn't a social call, couldn't be. The loss of my husband . . . mourning . . . It's, Lyle said, because of history . . . and the school . . . and, well, research. Work. But I really am so glad to make your acquaintance."

"Of course, I know. What a loss. Cousin Clarkson told me what a fine man your late husband was and we all express once again our *deepest, sincerest condolences.*" Ophelia placed herself in a crimson armchair nearest Doris Lee's settee. "But my dear," she said, leaning a little toward her, "you're so pretty!" Shamelessly, to Lyle's mortification, she lifted the pince-nez to her eyes and surveyed Doris Lee from head to toe. Ophelia thought staring at people was rude, ordinarily. But, Lyle surmised, she felt she had her prerogatives and this was one of them. "Pretty as a picture," Ophelia then said as her considered judgment. "Can't help thinking of your, well, your future! Handsome young woman. Your life will go on, my dear. I hope you don't mind someone like me, from the past, yes, it's true, from the past, speaking plainly out of all the years I've lived. Life does go on, and for someone like you, so pretty, I just can't help speculating on what will be your future, seeing you today with this handsome young man here . . . Dorothy!" What timing, Lyle thought with a kind of dazed objectivity, first her lobbing a shell into Doris Lee's position and then calling for the maid. "Lyle, pull that cord there. Dorothy's a little hard of hearing. Always have servants who can't hear too well. Cuts down the backstairs gossip!"

Doris Lee was digging into her purse for something, and then she said rather coolly and swiftly, "I never expect to have servants of course and no back stairs in my little house, but yes, yes, I guess Lyle is a fine-looking boy and he *can be* a good student besides. Some young girl will be lucky to have him when he . . . finishes . . . uh . . . his maturing . . ." her voice trailing off and growing fainter as she completed this thought.

Ophelia was gazing at her over the rims of her pince-nez, and then seeming to resolve something in her mind she said decisively, "Yes! Well. And now, here's Dorothy with the tea things." A table was wheeled in and tea and little sandwiches and cookies handed around. Into Lyle's distracted mind a little rhyme impudently leaped:

> *If I marry Doris Lee*
> *Would I always have to have tea?*
> *If Ophelia came to call,*
> *Would tea and cookies be all?*

Let's see, let's see, finish it, one more stanza:

> *Well I don't care for cookies or tea,*
> *For Lyle Catherwood, plain whiskey, see!*

And as he completed this verse the need for a long bracing shot of Canadian whiskey seized him with sudden force. This force surprised him, and then it began to alarm him. To be sure the interview was a tense one, what with Ophelia immediately probing for a— no, for *the* — romance between Doris Lee and himself, and Doris Lee, his own Mona Lisa, his madonna, coolly dismissing him as a boy who would grow up someday to find some girl who was currently presumably about twelve years old.

What a long, lukewarm gulp of Canadian whiskey would do for his mind, for his tongue, for his self-possession! Lyle suddenly decided to imagine he was downing such a gulp here and now, and telling himself to feel the self-confidence and invigoration flow into him, he sprang into the conversation.

"Well I don't know you see I may not be totally grown up in every way but my father wasn't so much older than I am when he married my mother and frankly I myself never thought *age* had so very much to do with when you got married or *who* you marry. I don't think Doris Lee really believes that either. Do you, Doris Lee?" She sat upright; Ophelia settled, suddenly deep in thought, back into her chair. "It's really the way you feel that counts, don't you think so? Whether you love someone and they love you, or learn to love you, even if they are a couple of years older than you are. My grandmother on my father's side was *seven years* older than my grandfather"— here Ophelia's pince-nez began to move and Doris Lee began unconsciously to strangle her white gloves — "and when the time comes to get married and the right person is there, well then" — he was running out of breath and out of the illusory self-confidence of the imaginary shot of whiskey — "then . . . you just do what's right."

The Stallings home was one of the most silent occupied residences in existence and now that sovereign silence assumed its baleful dominance of the room. There was a grandfather clock ticking portentously in the entrance hall. A Model T Ford rattled along the avenue outside.

Ophelia drew a long breath. "Lyle Boy, are you trying to tell me something?" Ophelia's speech always tended to become more down-home in quality in moments of stress. "You and Mrs. Pence here, you going out?"

"Of course not!" cried Doris Lee.

"Yeah, we are," muttered Lyle.

Doris Lee gaped at him, speechless.

"You know we are, Doris Lee," he said, "you know we are."

Ophelia drew another long breath; they seemed to be preserving her from fainting. "Well, you are or you aren't," she finally said brusquely.

"And we aren't!" insisted Doris Lee. "I'm a widow! He's a boy! I'm tutoring him! Of *course* we aren't!"

"Well then I don't know what to do with you, the two of you," Ophelia said curtly.

"You? Do nothing!" cried Doris Lee. "There's nothing *to* do. He's being ridiculous."

"I'm not," he said with quiet stubbornness, "and you know it, deep down you do, you know it."

"I never in all my born days," sighed Ophelia in desperation.

"I *know* it? What are you talking about!"

Ophelia looked at her for some time and then said almost sternly, "I declare, I don't believe he has spoken up for himself with you. You have not, have you, Lyle?"

He shook his head disconsolately.

Doris Lee began to look stunned.

"But I'm going to," he then said defiantly. "Right here and now."

Ophelia's head, which had a tendency to faint, involuntarily wagging when she was overcome with emotion, now began to wag. "I don't know what to say to you," she said, breathing audibly, "the two of you. A young boy, a new

[246]

widow, *years* older, his family— their position, and you come calling on *me!*"

"I want your help," Lyle said simply.

Now both women beheld him with equal speechlessness.

"Make it acceptable. You can, Aunt Ophelia. I want to take Doris Lee — after the mourning and everything — out to the picture show, even the country club. I haven't told her anything about this —"

Ophelia's eyes were narrowing behind the glass lenses. "What are you dreaming of? What are you trying to do to this woman?"

"It's insane," murmured Doris Lee, shaking her head and staring at her lap.

"Yes, it is!" agreed Ophelia tartly.

"But it's the one and only thing I'll ever want in my life. And I want you to help me to . . . achieve it."

Now Doris Lee gazed at him with a look of stupefied anger. "How can you ask *her* when you haven't asked *me!*"

Ophelia and Lyle turned to behold her.

"Okay," Lyle said in a collected voice, "I'm asking you. Will you go out with me once your mourning is over?"

"Of course I won't," Doris Lee replied hurriedly.

Lyle turned his pleading look upon Ophelia. "Is there anything so wrong, so impossible, about me wanting to go out with her? I mean really wrong!"

Ophelia's head wavered with emotion. "It simply isn't fitting, it isn't done, you run all sorts of risks, *she* does, your *backgrounds*, your *parents* — why, well, *me!*" She searched for a handkerchief in her bosom. "I — with all the appropriate young ladies here in Middleburg, in Morgantown, throughout the state, all over the South —" She dabbed at her face with the dainty little handkerchief. A faint aura of old-fashioned perfume filtered into the room. Then she turned to Doris Lee. "Mrs. Pence, you know I didn't ask for, didn't

[247]

expect, these revelations. Although I will aver that in the back of my mind the remote possibility that something like this was transpiring did linger. But since I've been drawn into this . . . this *unfortunate* situation I have to ask you . . . It's all so unsuitable! . . . But I do think I have to ask you, well, how to put it? *What are your intentions toward my nephew!*"

Ophelia's eyes, to Lyle, seemed almost momentarily to cross from the distress of finding herself framing this question in this way.

Doris Lee appeared to be collecting herself. "Mrs. Stallings," she said, leveling her green eyes at her, "Lyle isn't your nephew."

"Close family ties," she snapped. "Same thing. Don't quibble."

"My intentions, my intentions. Goodness, I didn't know I had any. Was 'designs upon' the expression you were looking for? Well, Mrs. Stallings, I haven't any of those either. It is up to you to believe that or not to believe it. There are people in this world who don't try to ensnare rich young boys — men — I don't know, this really is confusing. I think I'd better go home now, if you can take me, Lyle . . . oh, Mr. Catherwood," she corrected vexedly, "oh," then correcting again testily, "Lyle!"

XV.

At home Doris Lee went up to her bedroom, having fed the child, and then she wept, making scarcely any sound, barely moving, weeping so softly it could not carry through the thin partitions of the house. It was something like the way she had cried at Virgil's death.

She agreed to let Lyle pay her a visit the following Saturday. He came straight to the point, asking her to marry him. "When you're ready, and when I'm ready."

Doris Lee simply replied, as she did to her students when they asked for something inappropriate, "We'll see."

"You don't think I really mean it, do you? You think I'll change my mind, not want to marry you, in a couple more years."

She smiled a little sadly and simply repeated, "We'll see."

But her attitude toward him seemed to be softening a little and, pressing this advantage which he felt he was gaining, he brought her to the point where he was able to kiss her, then kiss her again more passionately, hold her in his arms, whisper thickly, "God how I love you," in her ear. After a little while she extricated herself. He was on the point of taking possession of her body; Lyle felt that she sensed this. She released herself from his arms and he was able, just able, to let her go and allow himself to be shown out of the house. "I'll come and see you next Saturday," he said, looking at her fixedly; she didn't reply, just smiled quietly.

The next day, Sunday, Doris Lee placed a long-distance telephone call to a former classmate of hers from the Teachers College who was on the faculty of a small private girls' school in Washington, D.C. This classmate, Vivien Cummings, had urged Doris Lee to join the school's faculty in her letter of condolence after Virgil's death. Doris Lee had not replied to the suggestion. Now on the telephone she did. She said she was interested. Vivien urged her to come to Washington for an interview with the headmistress, and this was arranged for the ensuing week.

Doris Lee Pence, Virgie being taken care of by Goldie, the Negro woman who had raised her, took a taxi to the Middleburg railroad station to catch the Washington-bound Pullman car at 2:00 P.M. on Tuesday.

Clarkson Catherwood was at the station, also waiting for this train. They fell, awkwardly at first, into conversation.

They discussed the weather. Doris Lee said that she had thought Mr. Catherwood and all men like him traveled with at least one assistant and probably more. "Don't you have a valet?" she asked.

"No, of course not. I can manage everything all right on my own during these business trips."

"Then why did ——" And she broke off.

Clarkson Catherwood cleared his throat and made several deep, muffled sounds before saying, "That was going to be a complicated business, negotiations, meetings with the other Logan operators. Had to. Or I thought I did. If only I hadn't."

"I'm sorry I brought it up," she said quickly. "It just popped out before I knew it."

"Yes. It has to be in your mind all —— or at least a lot of the time."

The engine, expanding from down the tracks, came pounding and hissing into the station. The Washington Pullman was the last car on the train. The porter helped them into it and Clarkson asked if he could come and sit in her section. "Get so bored on these trips by myself," he added, grinning. "And I've seen the scenery a thousand times."

"Please do," she said. He had Lyle's square shoulders, much enlarged with maturity. She took the seat facing the rear of the train, Clarkson sat across from her, and both of them began looking out the windows at the winterscape along the banks of the Monongahela River. It had snowed the night before and whiteness, not yet soiled by soot and coal dust, lay on the hillsides, outlining the flimsy trackside houses as they passed by.

"This isn't exactly pretty country, but it's important country," said Clarkson.

"How is it important?"

"Well, this B&O line we're going over, it was the first railroad in America. You knew that."

"Um, I suppose I did."

"It opened up what they thought of as the West back then, west of the Blue Ridge Mountains; that meant Middleburg and Clarksburg and Wheeling and, later, Ohio. Our prosperity, developing and shipping our coal, the B&O made that possible. It was a big issue in the Civil War, who would control this railroad line. It's a great railroad."

"I like it."

"Good waiters, good porters, good food."

"Basically southern."

"You can feel that. It's got a heart. Is that silly to say about a railroad?"

"I don't think so. I haven't traveled much, nothing like what you must have done, Mr. Catherwood, but I have been back and forth on this line several times and I always feel right at home on the B&O. The feeling of being away from home only starts when I get off in Washington or Baltimore, and especially, the one time I went there, in New York."

"Are you nervous there, in those cities?"

"Not exactly nervous, but I just feel pretty far away from Middleburg, not to mention Poundville, where I grew up."

"I know the feeling. And of course being a young woman . . . alone in a city . . . not too pleasant sometimes. Perhaps I can be of some help along that line in Baltimore."

"But I'm going to Washington."

"Oh," he said in a tone of surprise.

The train clipped along the right-of-way as dusk settled. They plunged with a slamming noise against the windows into the first of the numerous tunnels. Clarkson invited Doris Lee to accompany him to the dining car, which she did. Over the country ham and sweet potato he with some difficulty returned to the subject of Virgil.

"Very sorry . . . we all are . . . what a loss . . . anything I can do to help you?" Smoking was allowed in the diner; Clarkson asked for and got her permission to smoke a cigar. "I've been hoping for an opportunity to talk with you, informally like this," he resumed after lighting it, in the more relaxed, avuncular tone cigar-smoking induced in him. "I'm glad you understood that, ah, small present from my son, took it in the spirit it was intended. We . . . we . . ." Here Clarkson flushed slightly, his eyes watering a little. "There's no, uh, legal responsibility on our part. It was just a terrible accident, quite a few of them happened in Logan. There is no . . . legal responsibility on our part but —"

"No, of course not," said Doris Lee, looking at the tablecloth. "No legal responsibility."

Clarkson's sharp hazel eyes were studying her intently as she said this. Then as though snapping himself out of a temporary trance he continued, "But we naturally want to help in any way . . . feasible."

"Yes," she said. Then she fixed her eyes on his momentarily. "Besides, you believe nature will take its course and I'll remarry."

Flushing slightly again, Clarkson quickly rallied. "Oh yes, my son was tactless enough to repeat that opinion to you the time he saw you. Well, it *was* just an opinion."

She looked at the tablecloth again, eyebrows raised, blinking once or twice. Then she said, "I think I may be going to live in Washington. Teaching. That's why I'm going there today."

Clarkson looked at her with interest, then looked away. "Is that so? Where would you teach?"

"At a girls' school. Martha Washington Female Seminary. I have a friend on the faculty there. She's arranged an interview for me tomorrow. I — it seems better — if I perhaps didn't stay in Middleburg."

He paused and then said judiciously, "I can see that."

"Too many . . . memories and associations and . . . well, small towns, a widow, youngish . . ."

"Quite, as my English associate would say."

"My husband always wanted to travel," she said dreamily.

"Perhaps you will, in any case."

"Me? It seems unlikely."

"Times are changing. Women are changing, voting, going to work in new kinds of jobs. Would that appeal to you, working in business, for example?"

She considered. "Not really. I'm not very aggressive and businesslike and any of that. I know how to teach history and I know how to deal with children. But the business world, industry, especially frankly the coal industry, it frightens me. I'm afraid of mining and all that goes with it. You remember that there was the Poundville disaster."

"You lost someone in that?"

"No. Yes. My father was the superintendent of the mine at that time. Well, you see, Daddy wasn't in the mine, wasn't injured in any way. It's just, fifty-seven men killed, leaving forty-five widows and a hundred and thirty-one children — how often I heard those figures! Daddy used to repeat them, sit in his rocker looking out the window, usually on rainy days, and repeat the number of dead miners, and the widows and the children. They retired him six months after the explosion. I never knew whether he died as a man, lost his self-respect, will to live, everything because *he* thought he was responsible for the explosion or he thought *they* thought he was responsible for the explosion. All I know is that he was finished, finished with working around the mines, finished with working. He sat and he rocked. He died two years ago. The rest of him died."

"And your mother?"

"Mother got a divorce," she said shortly. "Turned Poundville upside down, Middleburg too among anyone who knew anything about us. A divorce! Kids stopped speaking to me in school. She just felt the man she married didn't exist anymore and so she got a divorce and married a mining supply representative and went to live in Wilkes-Barre, Pennsylvania. I went back and forth for a couple of years but she finally gave me my choice and I went back to live permanently with Daddy. He had to have somebody. Goldie, our housekeeper, had the right name, she was gold, through and through, but I felt I wanted to be there with him too. To be honest I don't think he would have lived as long as he did without that. Thank God I did it. Nothing," she said quietly, "worse than a life cut short."

Clarkson was contemplating her steadily. Then he said, "Do you see your mother now?"

"Once in a while. We went up there two years ago at Thanksgiving time. She has her own life there."

"And you have a child," he said almost to himself.

"Yes? What about him?"

"Nothing, nothing. I was just . . . wool-gathering."

Later, the Pullman's windows black as coal, the train hurtling along beside the Potomac, Clarkson and Doris Lee had returned to her section and again sat facing each other.

"I guess I'm old-fashioned," he said. "I can't get used to young women traveling alone, or old women for that matter, any woman."

"Everybody's doing it these days."

"I know, I know. It's even as they say respectable. But I'm old-fashioned, can't get used to it. Women of means like my wife never went on any kind of little trip without their maids. Women who couldn't afford maids always had a brother or some male relation or some older maiden aunt or someone to accompany them. And here you set out, cool as a cucumber it looks like to me, on a round trip of about four hundred miles with nothing but your suitcase! Times *have* changed."

"I think it's better."

"I know it's certainly different. I know a lot is different. My son is different from me."

"I kn—— I suppose he is, yes."

"Very different from me." Clarkson fell silent, eyes soberly focused in the middle distance.

Doris Lee said, "Mr. Catherwood, I know how important the coal industry is and how important you are in it. So tell me something: Why aren't you in a private railroad car? Mr. Clifton has his, the Cliftons have two of them, don't they? Where's yours?"

He looked significantly at her. "If I got me a private railroad car, don't you know what that would drive Marcus Clifton to do? Get himself a whole private train, that's what, engine, coal car, baggage car, diner, sleeper, drawing room and caboose! I'd hate to put him to all that trouble."

Doris Lee giggled.

"He's more important than I am and nobody's ever supposed to forget it. All men are *not* created equal, not in West Virginia, or if they're created equal they sure don't *grow up* equal. Marcus Clifton is the most important man in West Virginia and also the most important man in the coal industry, which is the most important industry in the country and in the world."

"Goodness."

"And I, frankly, am one of the I'd say ten most important men in the industry."

"My father," she said reflectively, "must have been about the four thousandth most important man in the industry, and well, my husband even farther down."

Clarkson grunted in what might have been wordless sympathy. Then he went on, "And there are the miners themselves with their own pecking order. Nobody is really anybody's equal. Everyone is ahead of some, behind others, everyone except Marcus."

"Who speaks only to God."

"And President Warren G. Harding, on occasion."

"I'm afraid of the coal business, I have to admit it, afraid."

"Very understandably," Clarkson muttered reluctantly.

"I believe I will take this position in Washington, if they offer it to me. I believe I should leave Middleburg and Poundville and West Virginia and all of it behind me. Just leave it."

"Perhaps," Clarkson said with some hesitation, "you'll let us keep in touch with you, if you should relocate in Washington."

Doris Lee leveled her eyes on his for an instant. "Of course," she then murmured.

"I have business there rather often."

She made no comment to this.

"I enjoy the capital," he said more expansively. "It's a fine monument to our system of government and to the capitalist economic system. Yes, I enjoy it. But, um, it is . . . rather boring, no, more, rather lonely, dining alone at the end of a day of meetings and business discussions and so on. My wife never travels with me. If the trip isn't to England or Palestine she isn't interested. What I'm trying to get at —"

"I know what you're getting at."

The eyebrows above the hooded eyes rose. Then he gazed at her more calmly. "I see. More modern woman. Direct."

She made no comment.

"Well, since you know what I'm driving at, are you willing, some evenings in the future after the, well, so regrettable tragedy of your husband has receded into the past to a greater extent than, well, your present sorrow can contemplate, would you then perhaps be willing to have dinner with me? It would relieve this boredom of mine mightily, the charm of your company would, and at the same time I could keep you in touch with your West Virginia roots."

"Those," she said quietly, "are what I'm trying to forget."

He drew a long breath. "Well then, perhaps you would dine with me just for whatever pleasure or change or some such my company would afford you."

She looked at him very quickly and then said, "Thank you."

"Thank you, yes, all very well," he put in with some force, "but does that mean yes?"

Doris Lee fidgeted a little and then said, "Yes, that's what it means."

The train, a clanging, roaring, singular monster when it had pulled out of the quiet little Middleburg depot, crept inoffensively in amid the giant engines with long, sleek parades of following cars, the clangor, the cavernousness, the heedless hustle of Union Station, Washington.

Doris Lee stepped down onto the platform, the porter giving her valise to a redcap. In her gloved hand she held the card Clarkson Catherwood had given her with the telephone number of his hotel, the Lord Baltimore, in Baltimore, "just in case there's any way I can assist you while you're in Washington." She had on her gloves, her subdued clothes; she looked at the back of the head of the redcap as he preceded her toward the gate of the platform. She did not look about her; she was in a city; she was a single woman traveling alone.

At the gate she slipped into a hug from Vivien Cummings, small, vivacious, waiting for her at the gate. "Did you really buy yourself your own car?" Doris Lee inquired in considerable wonderment. "You drive it around, do you, all around Washington, by yourself?"

"Of course," replied Vivien a shade condescendingly. "I love my little Ford."

Doris Lee gave her a quick, concentrated look. The car, a black two-door coupe, was parked outside the station. They set out in it toward Vivien's apartment in Georgetown.

On all sides the great monuments of the capital city shone in dead-white ghostly elegance, sculptural in their floodlights. Vivien had planned a route past them: the White House, of an unearthly whiteness, a symmetry of untouched mausoleum purity; the Washington Monument rising in its featureless and massive single-mindedness, all alone on a hillock, primitive, seemingly requiring worship and arcane rights; the Lincoln Memorial, pure imitation Greece, a temple to Athena inexplicably inhabited by a middlewestern homespun philosopher-politician, massively and broodingly seated, as though pondering how in the world the Kentucky log cabin of his birth had led to *this*. Floods of light haloed these and other shrines across the low-flying city; it was a rare sight, for normally the capital's monuments were not illuminated.

"What are they celebrating?" breathed Doris Lee.

"I wonder."

No new-fangled skyscrapers competed with the Capitol dome and Washington's needle for dominance of the night skyline: political power and past history were alone asserted and honored here; all else, especially the ostentatious temples of economic power, was relegated to other, northern cities.

Doris Lee beheld it all. "It's gorgeous," she breathed. "I've seen it before but not like this, driving from one to another at night."

"You will, you silly hillbilly, you will."

nine

I.

Early the following afternoon, at the time Doris Lee was being interviewed by the headmistress of the Martha Washington Female Seminary in Washington and Clarkson Catherwood was concluding a business lunch with two vice-presidents of American Coal and Coke, Ophelia Stallings paid a call on Minnie Catherwood.

Minnie received her in the Castle's front parlor.

"Too early for tea," murmured Minnie once they were seated. "How about some homemade root beer?" she then suggested with a smile.

"Now that's what I call down home. I'd just love a glass of root beer."

Minnie rang for it.

"It's fixing to snow again," observed Ophelia a shade nervously.

"Just so the B&O tracks aren't blocked," said Minnie.

"I don't believe *that's* happened in living memory."

"Clarkson's in Baltimore."

"Is he? He is so busy, so very busy. All our leading businessmen are."

"It's this *boom*. That's what they're calling it, the news-papers and the businessmen. The *boom!* Isn't that a curious name to use to describe everybody making a lot of money? Did you know that's what they call it?"

Ophelia preened herself discreetly. "Yes, yes I did, dear. Clarence makes frequent reference to it after busy days in his office. Attorneys are in on . . . attorneys are affected by this boom as well as others. Yes indeed they are."

"Oh, of course," said Minnie. "And," she went on, drawing the edges of a filmy handkerchief through the thumb and index finger of her left hand, "they'll all be affected too if there's an end to it."

"How can there be an end to it? Will there be an end to the railroad using coal, the steel companies, the utilities, *us* and everybody else in America heating their homes? An end to it? Hardly, I would surmise."

Minnie went on drawing her handkerchief through her fingers. "You must take a drive with me out to see my farm. Someday when the weather's nice."

"What farm?"

Minnie smiled for the first time in this interview. "I bought some acres, well, about a hundred acres, out past Bennettown. Belonged to some distant relations of the Jessups, an old couple, children not interested, both boys had gone into the bond market, daughter married the Hupmobile dealer. So, they sold it to me."

"To you and Clarkson."

"Y-e-s-s," said Minnie. "Of course Clarkson takes no interest —"

"He's *so* busy."

"Mm. He thinks it's another of my whims, like, well, religion and playgrounds. But I . . . don't . . . think . . . it . . . is. I don't think so. You grew up on a farm, Ophelia. I want you to go out and look at it with me. I've found a man to work it, be in charge of it, and now he and I are thinking about what to use it for. Cows and pigs and chickens, I think, and corn and vegetables."

"That's very down-to-earth of you, Minnie. The Cliftons use *their* farm to raise show horses."

"Yes," Minnie, "I know."

Ophelia shifted on her settee. Then leaning forward, pressing her hands into her lap, diamonds twinkling, she said, "What do you think of this Mrs. Pence, the widow of —"

"I know who she is. Very pretty. A classic beauty really, although nobody seems to notice. She looks well bred, good family —"

"I don't think she is. Poundville. Her father did something around the mine. Mother *divorced* him."

"Otherwise I don't know her. Why do you ask?"

Ophelia paused for several seconds. This drew Minnie to look at her fixedly. Noting that she had achieved this, Ophelia then began, "Because, my dear Minnie, I feel I have to tell you, as a devoted friend of yours and your family's, that your son Lyle is head over heels in love with her."

Minnie crumpled the handkerchief in her hand. "Don't be silly. He doesn't even know her."

"Head over heels in love with her, imagines he wants to marry her and all, just as I feared, behind your back and Clarkson's back." She then described the call Lyle and Doris Lee had made on her, stressing Lyle's ardor, Dorie Lee's dubious denials, her own disapproval.

"Children," sighed Minnie at the end of it, "what mysteries they are. Who can ever understand one of them?"

"I think," observed Ophelia, "my parents understood *me* pretty well."

"And mine me, for that matter. It's *this* generation, this boom! It's made everything so . . . unsettled, the money all coming in and the turmoil among the miners . . . Logan . . . and the death of poor Mr. Pence and *everything*. There's too much pressure on us all. *Too* much depends on Clarkson and

[261]

what he does and what he doesn't do, Clarkson and the Cliftons and the Hayeses, and in a way on me too and even on Lyle. I'm not sure that he doesn't feel it more keenly than any of us. And I suppose he's been secretly *very upset* about the death of Mr. Pence. And this must be his clumsy, his boyish way of trying to make it up to the widow. I — I'm touched by it, I really am."

Ophelia's eyes squinted shrewdly. "And you know, my dear, Mrs. Pence bears a definite resemblance to you."

"I don't see any."

"Oh yes, she does. Her eyes are green instead of blue. But the shape of the face and the general . . . demeanor. Something rarefied in you both. It's there, the resemblance. Boys learn about women from their mothers, don't they?"

Minnie shook her head in bewilderment. "What on earth are we to do?"

"Couldn't he go on a long trip?"

"In the middle of his year at the university?"

"Perhaps *she* can somehow be encouraged to . . . well, go away, to begin anew somewhere else."

"Perhaps," said Minnie, frowning. "Why," she mused aloud, "do we Catherwoods always seem to be sending *away* people we love? Isn't that a strange thing to do?"

Ophelia, wordless, gazed into the cold fireplace.

II.

Lyle drove up to Doris Lee's house in his Pierce-Arrow that Saturday. A tall colored woman with plain gold rings in her ears, a slender woman with something capable of being amused behind her gaze, answered the door. She told him that Mrs. Pence was away and asked his name. When he told her she asked him to step inside and then she left the room and

returned with an envelope. Lyle, as though it were some kind
of death sentence, tore it open.

Tuesday
Dear Lyle,
In an hour I am leaving for Washington. I hope to go to work
as a teacher in a school there. If you really do love me — and I
know it is just an early feeling with the real one, for someone else,
to come later — you will let me go out of your life, forget about
me. I will not forget how sweet and kind you have been to a
stunned widow. And believe me I *do not* hold you responsible
in any possible way for what happened to Virgil. That was
God's will, not yours or the United Mine Workers' or anybody
else's.

With all best hopes for your future,
Doris Lee Pence

Lyle stood rocking slightly forward and then back on his
heels, his fedora set on the back of his head, the rich camel's-
hair coat looking a little too large for him, and then he looked
up from the letter at the woman smiling in a can-I-help-out
way at him, and said, "When's she . . . Mrs. Pence . . . coming
back from Washington?"

"I don't rightly know. Couple of days. Don't like her
travelin' in this *weather*."

Lyle looked blindly out the single bay window toward the
street. Winter, he noticed blankly. Dirty snow everywhere.

"Did . . . did Mrs. Pence go to Washington by herself?"

"Yeah she did, Mr. Catherwood. I don't approve of that
neither. But she sure did."

"Are you, uh, I think she told me about you. Are you
Goldie?"

Now the smile, always threatening, broke. "That's me."
He continued to stand before her, crestfallen, until Goldie
said, "Can I do something for you? You like to leave a
message?"

"A message? I, ah, what message can I . . . Is there a message to leave? Here. Read this."

"Oh no. Oh no sir. Not me. No."

"Well she says —"

"And I ain't wanten to know what Miss Doris Lee *says*. That's for *you*. Don't tell me. No sir."

Lyle looked at her as though his last hope were sinking. Goldie looked at her apron. He drew an exhausted breath. "Well, tell Doris Lee good-bye and if she needs me" — he would not allow his voice to shake: no! — "I, um, she can, she knows how to call me up on the telephone."

III.

"Lyle," said Minnie, looking up from where she sat with her book in the bay window of the library, "what's this about you walking out with Mrs. Pence?" Her voice was inquiring and serious.

Lyle took off his overcoat and hat and, flinging them on a chair, himself lay down on his stomach before the fireplace on a thick burgundy and blue rug.

The smell of dead ashes from the grate went back to his earliest memories of life. It was linked in his mind to the smell of his father's dead cigars in ashtrays in this room. These burned-out remnants of logs and tobacco leaves evoked in him the past, the settled home of all his years, of being a son, a Catherwood of the Castle.

Lyle drew a breath, his chin on his fists, and then mumbled, "Aunt Ophelia been here?"

"She has. And she told me. Why don't *you* tell me something like that? Have I ever punished you for telling me anything?"

He shook his head abstractedly.

"Don't you want me to help you with problems you have?"
Lyle barely found the energy to shake his head again.
"You don't?"
"Oh, yeah. Yes, I do."
"Well then, shall we talk about it, Mrs. Pence and . . . what's going on?"
After a long pause Lyle said, "There's nothing to say. She's gone. And so that's it." Another long silence. "She's just gone. And I guess that's it."
Minnie, after gazing at him for some time, turned her eyes again to the page of her book. Without looking back at him she said, "You can talk to me when you're ready."
To himself Lyle contemplated his next move. Her letter had been like a bull kicking him in the stomach. But now, lying here on this thick rug in the warm room with its stale, reassuring ashes-smells, he began to get his wind back. He saw that he had to make a decision. There were two choices: write her the greatest love letter ever composed, expressing the inexpressible and doing it so persuasively, so movingly, that she would have to see the inevitability of their love, the pricelessness of it, the lift its realization would give them into the . . . into the . . . the *spheres*, the circling spheres of . . . Heaven itself.

Either write her like that, or *else*, go to Washington and kidnap her. Have a real old-fashioned shotgun wedding. True, usually the bride's father and not the groom held the shotgun at these weddings in West Virginia, so he understood, but this was *different*. "What're we having for dinner?" he asked, rolling on his side.

"Why," said Minnie, looking up in surprise, "I think Tot is giving us some roast beef. Dr. and Mrs. Masterson are coming, and their boy. And the Sanderson Cliftons."

It was Lyle's turn to look mildly surprised. "What's the occasion?"

"No occasion," said Minnie, looking at her book again.

"I just get a little tired of . . . well, it's nice to have menfolks here at dinnertime."

IV.

Doris Lee's interview with the headmistress of the Martha Washington Female Seminary went very well. The school's American history teacher had been ill throughout the autumn, and seemed unlikely ever to be able to return; the substitute teacher could not remain much longer; the headmistress was very anxious to find a replacement who, if she proved competent and congenial, would almost certainly be given the appointment permanently. Vivien Cummings had fitted in well at the school; her recommendation of Doris Lee carried weight. What was needed now were a recommendation from the Middleburg School Board and a letter or two from prominent members of the Middleburg community as to her general character and reputation. Who better for Doris Lee to turn to for this last than Clarkson Catherwood? He did not know her well, but their encounter on the train had certainly been cordial, and he had been her late husband's employer. In fact, obtaining a letter from him was almost indispensable and its omission might create doubts in the headmistress's mind. Vivien told Doris Lee that she must not be hesitant about calling Mr. Catherwood in Baltimore. Everything must be done as quickly as possible so that all the material could be placed before the headmistress and the faculty committee and the Board of Trustees while the anxiety about finding a replacement and the current enthusiasm for Doris Lee were coalescing. The result for her could be a formal offer of a permanent position, an escape from the coal industry and its tragedies, and a new life.

She reached Clarkson in his suite at the Lord Baltimore Hotel at 6:00 P.M. He would be honored to write the letter for her, he said, and should she need others, as for example a recommendation from Marcus Clifton, he was sure he could obtain that. Speaking of Marcus Clifton, he went on, would Mrs. Pence care to join Mr. Clifton, his secretary, Miss Maitlands, and Clarkson himself at a dinner two days later on the famous private railroad car, which would then be in the yards in Washington?

"What's its name?" inquired Doris Lee numbly.

"Its name?"

"The name of the car," she stumbled on, "don't they always have names?"

After a pause Clarkson said, "I believe they do. Yes. Let me see. Yes, it's called the Great Kanawha."

"I would like to," she heard herself say, and the engagement was fixed.

She had heard of private railroad cars. Everyone had heard of private railroad cars, because the activities and appurtenances of the rich were what people liked to read about, the papers were full of heiresses and dukes and ambassadors. It seemed that anyone who was in high society was not just privileged but also somehow charmed, specially endowed by destiny, even, some might say, the favored of God. That was the way people by and large saw the rich, as special beings who, because of their wealth, had to be better than others, and so more worthy of attention.

Like any reader of the *Middleburg Exponent* and *Vanity Fair* and the *Ladies' Home Journal*, Doris Lee unavoidably had a great deal of journalistic information on the lives of wealthy people. She had read about and seen photographs of private railroad cars.

Two days later she stepped aboard the Great Kanawha, Clarkson assisting her up the steps, and a colored man in a white jacket taking her coat and hat. She entered what re-sembled a long, rather narrow living room, very comfortable and even elegant, blue and gray, lamps, easy chairs, rugs, curtains, couches. A to her incongruous odor of smoke pervaded this salon. Clarkson, tall, broad-shouldered, ruddy, was wearing a meticulously tailored suit, something he would not have worn in Middleburg. This must be the other Clark-son Catherwood, the city man, the equal of the New York financiers, the one who traveled in Europe. Doris Lee hoped she did not look mousy in her demure black silk dress.

"Isn't it kind of strange in here when it's moving?" she asked. "A living room on wheels?"

"You get used to it apparently," he said, "I haven't traveled this way much."

"Mr. Clifton called up from the Shoreham Hotel," said the attendant. "He and Miss Maitlands will be here directly."

"There's a telephone here?" observed Doris Lee.

"Yes'm. We got a kitchen, bathroom, bedrooms, hot and cold running water, icebox. Everything."

He then went out and came back with a tray holding two glasses of sherry. Clarkson motioned her to a couch. She sat down: even the cushions felt wealthy. Clarkson took the ad-joining chair. The attendant disappeared. Around them there was only a subdued rumble in this corner of the railroad yards. There were several other private cars nearby.

"Did you get the position?" he asked.

"I think they're going to hire me, once they have the re-port from Middleburg and the letter you were kind enough to write."

"And you're pleased."

"Oh yes. It's . . . well, I guess if your life half changes then the thing to do is change the other half. Then it will match up."

He gazed before him and then said, "I never could."

"Pardon me."

"Do you mind if I smoke?"

"Not at all."

He lit a cigar. "You don't smoke?" he said with a twinkle.

"Me! Smoke? A schoolteacher? I'd be fired on the spot. And even, you know, as just a housewife. Smoke? I'm not, you see, well, fast at all, not at all."

"Yes, mmm, yes. Tell me about the school."

She told him about the pretty white and green Colonial-style buildings, the lawns, the two hundred girls — young ladies, as they were always referred to. She explained that it was less conservative than most girls' schools, that experiment was believed in. He questioned her some more with great politeness and show of interest, and seeing that he was not interested she waited apprehensively until he chose to broach some more urgent subject. Finally he said, "Mrs. Pence, may I tell you something about myself, my private self?"

"Mr. Catherwood, I —"

"At any point if you find it disagreeable just tell me to stop and of course I will. But I need to speak to someone on a matter of privacy and I know I can rely on your discretion."

Doris Lee looked at her hands.

And then quite simply and directly Clarkson explained his marriage to Minnie, and how because of her nervous condition, more critical in earlier years than now, he and the family doctor had concluded that she must not bear any more children, and that sexual relations — "married intimacy" — had ceased between them, never to be resumed. He had formed a relationship with a widow in Cleveland, but that had now come to an end because she had become chronically ill, bad lungs, and he had arranged for her to live in Arizona for her health.

He explained to Doris Lee, who sat wordless and motionless, that he was not infringing the boundaries of propriety in any way, but that he was seeking for her to understand his personal situation, with the hope that an entirely platonic friendship could develop between him and her. He needed such company from a member of the opposite sex, a lady, a woman of education, of admirable character, and, he had to admit, of personal beauty in order to alleviate the inevitable isolation and loneliness which his marital situation forced on him.

After a long silence Doris Lee said quietly, "I just don't know what to say. I believe I should have stopped you. The situation with your wife —"

"If you don't know what to say," he cut in kindly, "then don't say anything. I was the one who felt I had to say something. There's no need for your saying anything."

"I feel I should say *something*," she murmured almost desperately.

There was a little commotion at the end of the car and then Marcus Clifton made his entrance, handing his overcoat and homburg to the attendant, and helping Miss Maitlands out of her coat. Introductions were made. Miss Maitlands was tall and a little severe-looking, prim. Marcus Clifton's bloodhound face was flushed, as though from some good, bootlegged Scotch whisky, and the expression on it above an even more elegant suit than Clarkson Catherwood's indicated an expectation of further pleasant stimulation to come.

"Mrs. Pence, welcome to my little abode," he said banteringly, taking her hand in both of his. "They make you comfortable, did they? Give you a glass of something? Good. Now let's sit down here and get comfortable. Want to take your shoes off, Clarkson?" Clarkson gave him a look and Marcus grinned. "Just joking. But these big city getups make me squirm after a spell. You can take the boy out of the country, and so on. You enjoying Washington, Mrs. Pence?"

Doris Lee smiled and nodded.

"Fine city. Fine people here. And then there are the politicians. And now, right here in the railroad yards, I hope we're going to be able to give you all a fine dinner. That right, George?" The waiter smiled and nodded. "I think it's sort of an occasion tonight here. What with one thing and another. I think we'll have some champagne with dinner. We got some champagne, don't we, George?"

Oh Lord, thought Doris Lee. Champagne. What next? Tied to the railroad tracks before an oncoming train? The Perils of Doris Lee!

V.

So a friendship, special in its content and in its limitations, began between Clarkson Catherwood and Doris Lee Pence.

It was tacitly understood by all parties concerned that Doris Lee could not possibly return to West Virginia on the Great Kanawha. Clarkson did so with Marcus and Miss Maitlands, who radiated implacable respectability, the following day; Doris Lee took the day coach to Middleburg the day after that. By now her appointment at the female seminary was virtually assured. With help from the school a suitable apartment had been located.

It was all adventurous and rather unconventional: a single woman, even though a widow, transferring herself "without a protector" from a West Virginia town to a coastal city. "Without a protector" had been Vivien Cummings's phrase. It did not mean, not necessarily, without a lover; it meant literally what it said, without a male who was sufficiently established in the world and had sufficient experience and authority to protect a single woman from any and all pitfalls she might encounter. "You're without a protector," Vivien Cummings had said. "I suggest you *accept* this invitation to dinner on a private railroad car."

"But he's, don't you see, he's —"

"I know, I know. But he's a gentleman, isn't he? You won't be compromised. Think of him as an uncle."

And Doris Lee certainly did need a protector. And Clarkson Catherwood certainly had the qualifications.

And Lyle . . . and Lyle was a nineteen-year-old college boy, with an allowance.

So she had gone to dinner on the Great Kanawha, had heard Clarkson Catherwood out concerning Mrs. Catherwood and the lady in Cleveland and his loneliness and need for a certain kind of platonic female friendship, and by her failure to protest or to reject that friendship she had in effect accepted it.

And now she possessed it, whatever that might say for the future. For the present what it meant was that she now had the virtually indispensable addition to a single woman abroad or in transit, a protector.

She realized that there were ambiguities for everyone concerned. Clarkson was her protector in Washington, and she supposed in other places such as New York or Baltimore, but he wasn't to be in West Virginia in general and in Middleburg in particular.

As far as Clarkson knew, Lyle and Doris Lee were barely acquainted.

Doris Lee, to Middleburg, would convey the impression that Mr. and Mrs. Clarkson Catherwood were man and wife in every possible sense of the words. She knew Mr. Catherwood very slightly.

To Lyle everything was unknown.

VI.

Doris Lee had not had sex with anyone in her life except her husband Virgil. Since his death she had had no sex. She knew that beneath Lyle Catherwood's naiveté and his sweetness an almost frantic sexual desire for her beat away, seeking any path, short of offering her money, to be fulfilled.

She thought that beneath Clarkson Catherwood's worldliness and kindly interest an at least inferential desire for her also lounged. And he, in a sense, *was* offering her what in the relationship with his son was the unthinkable lure: money. The "platonic" friendship he proposed would begin with the kind of dinner she could not afford for herself and progress to trips she could not have considered, and then to gifts beyond her means, and end . . . where else could it end, if her reading of his mind was right, but in his asking her to become his mistress?

The one contradiction to this pattern she had outlined in her mind of Lyle, Clarkson, and herself was the check Lyle had sent her for five hundred dollars. It didn't fit. It was too, somehow, sovereign a gesture for Lyle to make, now that she had come to know him better. Suddenly and confidently he dispatched five hundred dollars to her with a suave note?

When Clarkson called from the Great Kanawha on the morning following their dinner to bid her good-bye before departing Washington for Middleburg, she said, "I wanted to ask you about something, Mr. Catherwood. Right after the loss of my husband I received a check for five hundred dollars and it supposedly came from your son."

A silence and then Clarkson said encouragingly, "Yes?"

"You sent that to me, didn't you."

Another short silence, then: "What makes you say that?"

"Woman's intuition. You did, didn't you."

"Yes. I did. I hope you aren't going to take offense *now*. I just thought —"

"I'm not offended. It was very thoughtful. It just clears up something in my mind. Thank you. Have a nice trip."

"I — ah — Mrs. Pence, I — in West Virginia, you understand — I —"

"Perfectly, Mr. Catherwood."

"I'll look forward," he then said cheerfully, "to the pleasure of your company the next time I'm in Washington. I want to discuss history with you."

Oh no! she thought wildly.

"West Virginia history especially. It's always been a kind of hobby of mine."

They said good-bye, or rather she said good-bye and Clarkson Catherwood said rather debonairly "*au revoir*," the first somewhat embarrassing thing he had done. It took her back to her courting days. The boys then had often acted asinine. Somehow Lyle Catherwood, trembling like a leaf inside, never embarrassed her. Every awkward thing he ever did had been so genuine. There had been no warbling "*au revoir*" to her over the telephone. That businessman's hat he wore to try to look older. His particular brand of nervous telephone calls.

Doris Lee returned on the day coach to Middleburg the day after the Great Kanawha had rolled grandly over the same tracks and through the same tunnels. She sat alone in her seat gazing out the window at the grim winter landscape — grime, snow, steep hillsides. It was certainly glum at this time of year, but it looked considerably better to her than when she had passed over these tracks a few days before. She was traveling alone, but this was not as daunting as it had been before.

A woman alone: that had been the dismal phrase in her mind ever since the day the news came from Logan. A woman alone. She had come to hate those words. They conjured up, first, decaying schoolteachers she had worked with, their hair grayer and more disarrayed with every advancing year until they disappeared from the school into some cramped retirement somewhere; or else, certain ladies, genteel in their spotless houses, drinking their lives away out of fragile tea-cups, except at certain times when they disappeared into their bedrooms for a week among the gin bottles; or else, self-sacrificial lay nuns, still in the world but not of it, doing good works tirelessly and cheerfully, year after year, having Christmas at relatives' tables, taking a short trip alone or with another maiden lady every three years or so, angels in a way, and no more suitable to life on earth. These were the prototypes her imagination had placed before her when she was forced to apply these words to herself. She did not know any woman alone in her own special predicament, that is, young and widowed and with a child and no money to speak of.

It had been in this state of mind, and with these specters of her future before her, that she had left for Washington. But now they seemed to be fading into clouds, losing their scaring power.

It seemed that whatever her future was to be, it was not going to lock her into one of these Iron Maidens.

Mr. Catherwood was an interesting man. He seemed to be a gentleman. There was a down-to-earth directness about him which matched something down-to-earth she found in herself.

A certain wry quality in things he said reminded her of Lyle. So did his square shoulders.

At her house she found everything functioning. How could it not, with Goldie in charge? She herself was a sort of ap-prentice who had learned about housekeeping, and mother-hood too, from Goldie.

"That Mr. Catherwood come by to see you," Goldie threw in while reporting other news.

Doris Lee hesitated, and then said, "He did? When?"

"Oh, three, four days ago."

"That can't be right. He was — oh, *young* Mr. Catherwood. Oh, of course. And you gave him the note I left for him?"

"That's right." Goldie continued to look at her as they unpacked her bags and put things away in her little slope-roofed bedroom closet.

"He . . . Did he say anything?"

"He didn't exactly say nothing. Just . . . looked."

"Looked?"

"Like he was gonna die or something."

Doris Lee briskly shook out a skirt. "Young boys never die of lo—— of infatuations. Never do."

"Less they take the hand to theyselves."

"Goldie!"

"None of my business. Didn't even read the letter. None of my business. He want me to because he was so like distracted. I won't gonna do it. Just, the look on that boy's face, that what I'm talking about. Now I'll shut up. You did ask me, did he say anything. And I was answering, he did, only just with his face. I was just answering —"

"I *know*, Goldie. Well, that's finished. Let's go down to the kitchen and have a cup of coffee."

The succeeding days were very busy ones for Doris Lee. Overshadowing everything else was the question of whether Goldie could be talked into accompanying them to Washington. Doris Lee was scheduled to begin teaching in the spring term. For without her Doris Lee did not see how her escape from the coal country could be carried out. Find some stranger in Washington to tend Virgie while she worked? It wasn't imaginable, nor, to be honest with herself, did Doris Lee see how it would work financially. Goldie was a part of the family, and one of the qualities colored "members" of white families acquired was a willingness to work for less. It was an understood and never-negotiated contract: the white families would look after the Goldies of this world right up to death's door, and the Goldies would work their lives out, for less.

Goldie was hedging, Goldie was indecisive, Goldie was nervous, Goldie was emotional, Goldie was frightened, couldn't be sure, devoted, momentarily tearful, wavering, wondering. *Washington!* When coming up out of Poundville to Middleburg had been a giant step.

Doris Lee, head bent against late winter's gusts, was wondering what on earth more she could say to Goldie to persuade her, and had just arrived at the conclusion that she could say nothing more, that who and what she was and her child was to Goldie would be finally decisive and she must just accept the outcome of that in Goldie's mind and heart, and having reached that conclusion during her walk down Fourth Street from Middleburg Avenue she began crossing the Fourth Street Bridge, head bent against the raw gusts.

Intermingled in the hiss of the wind she thought she heard something sharper, more preemptory: surely not, it wasn't, couldn't be. She shot a glance down to the dirt road in the ravine below and there he stood, in a pair of old pants and some kind of hunting jacket. It was *déjà vu*: the double images in her brain refused to clarify themselves. This was happening now, or was it many weeks ago, or was it both? She looked down again. She saw the figure give her an energetic wave of the arm, again, and motion for her to come down the stairs fixed to the side of the ravine.

Doris Lee turned dreamily, encased in an unstable double image of doing what she had done before, and made her way, the wind now urging her on, to the top of the stairs, and then down their zigzag course to the bottom, to the dirt road under the bridge. Always bridges here, she thought with a sense of estrangement, always ravines and hills and bridges.

"Hi, Doris Lee," said Lyle in his energetic voice, face glowing at her, eyes alive, although a frown lurked in the eyebrows. He's intoxicated, she thought, and I don't think it's from Canadian whiskey. I think it's from me.

"Hello, Lyle. What a coincidence, running into you here again."

"Been here," he mumbled, "most of the time the last few days."

"Oh," she said faintly.

"Mind if I walk you home?"

"Why no," she said uncertainly.

They started farther along the dirt road down the ravine. She sensed, she knew, that his head was awash with all the intoxicating excitements of unhoped-for happiness, far more intense than ever because of the likelihood of their being cut off forever in the next fifteen minutes. He was a taut force walking along beside her; she feared he might levitate. It was magical and it was unbearable. "Did you get my letter?" she asked in a false tone of voice.

"Yes. You knew that I did. She — Goldie — must've told you that."

"Well, yes, she did. I — you see, I'm moving to Washington." No response. "I felt, for little Virgil —"

"Children are better off in small towns than in cities."

"— and for me, for myself, the memories here —"

"My killing your husband."

"Oh *Lyle*. Of course you didn't and I've told you that and you know it isn't true."

"You were saying, the memories here . . ."

"Well, the just everything, I, everybody knows that starting over somewhere else is often the only way to begin again a life after it's been . . . broken."

"Yeah, that's one way. There's another way. Find someone else to start over with."

"Yes," she said softly.

"Yes, but that isn't the way you see it, is it," he said, using a harsh tone she had never heard. "I mean, you don't see me as the someone else, do you?"

"Oh, Lyle."

"I'm just, you don't see it like that, do you!"

"Lyle —"

"Oh listen, Doris Lee, listen I . . . why don't you just *wait* a couple of years, I'll do . . . *everything*, and then by a couple of years I'll be set in the world and your mourning will be over and, why, everybody will approve, even Aunt Ophelia, and if they don't the hell with them. Listen, we'll *both* go to Washington, or why not New Orleans? I know somebody —"

"Lyle, it just isn't — I just can't —"

They had stopped walking and were facing each other in the ravine, and she glanced at his eyes and there was a look in those bright eyes of such a drive to break out of or through something, a naked, trapped, anything-must-be-done glare in them, impersonal, not somehow related to the Lyle she knew or even to herself, elemental, that a chord of fear sounded within her and she became aware of just how alone and out of sight of everyone they were deep in this empty ravine on this blustery winter day.

"You will," he said flatly.

"Will? Will what?" she asked breathlessly.

"You can't do this to me and to us."

"But I — Let's go on, to my house. You'll come in and we'll talk.

He stood motionless. She did not dare move. She then ventured, risked, to look at his eyes again. They held a blank glare, not exactly looking at her.

"I'll always love you in my way," she murmured.

Comprehension came slowly back into his eyes and they looked into hers. "There's someone else, isn't there," he said in quiet amazement.

"Why do you say that?"

"There's someone else," he repeated wonderingly. "That's it. There's *someone* else."

Doris Lee kept looking into his eyes, feeling that if she did so she would hold the comprehension that was in them and not allow it to withdraw, leaving the impersonal, possessed glare she had been harrowed by.

"Let's go on to the house," she urged quietly, "and talk."

The comprehension did not fade from his eyes. After a long silence he said in an even, unusual tone of voice, new to her, older, "There isn't anything else to talk about, Doris Lee. There's someone else. Older. Bigger. More money or something. And you've decided." He said these words as though they were in a foreign language he was just acquiring. "Well," he added almost diffidently, a boy again, "I guess then that's it. I guess that is it." He began walking farther along the ravine road, she beside him. He kicked a stone. "I . . . guess . . . that . . . is . . . it."

VII.

Doris Lee Pence moved to Washington, D.C. on March 3, 1922. Clarkson Catherwood was awaiting her at the cheerful little apartment in the northwest part of the city. Since the apartment wasn't nearly clean enough to suit Goldie, Clarkson installed the three of them in the Shoreham Hotel nearby. He himself was staying at the Mayflower downtown.

The apartment, on the sixth floor of a red brick building, had a view of Rock Creek Park. By the time she moved in on the sixth, two colored women under Goldie's implacable direction had brought it to shining perfection. The windows shone, the white frilly curtains were spotless, the floors were newly waxed. Sunshine poured through the windows.

"It's so high up we can't hear the noise from the street," Doris Lee said to Clarkson the next afternoon over tea in the bright little dining room. "Six stories is getting pretty high for a girl from Poundville."

"I hope you won't be lonely here," he said, "new to the city as you are."

"I guess I'll be too busy for that, teaching, Virgie . . . just getting to know Washington . . . everything."

"I wonder if there's anything more I can do," he said, almost to himself.

I really am beginning to like this man, she thought. And the reason was simple: he seemed to be beginning to care for her, in both senses of the word. And his intention did not seem to be, not yet, not specifically, sexual.

Doris Lee began teaching on the eighth, when the new term began. She quickly established herself as a disciplined teacher so popular with the students that several of the adolescent girls developed crushes on her.

Clarkson was frequently in Baltimore and Washington throughout the spring of 1922. The coal business had never been so good. The postwar boom moved on to even higher levels of demand and productivity. The Cliftons and the Hayeses and Clarkson felt encouraged to expand their operations in southern West Virginia further and to begin opening up remote but even richer fields in eastern Kentucky. The enormous financial outlay needed to make these expansions was swiftly, even jovially, met by the bankers of Wall Street, the Hanna interests in Cleveland, the Mellon people in Pittsburgh, and by investors abroad.

Even more encouraging, peace with the miners seemed to have been achieved in the state. The owners ruefully but stoically accepted the organization of the men by the United Mine Workers in the northern fields, and the United Mine Workers appeared to resign themselves for the time being to leaving the southern fields unorganized.

Everyone was making so much money. Every man who could see straight and had an even reasonably strong back

[281]

could find as much work as he wanted in the mines, a full week's work. So often in the past, from strikes, coal car shortages, overproduction or whatever other reason, that had not been true. Sometimes the miners had just taken off to go fishing: the result had been two or three days' work a week on the average, and subsistence living. But now there was a solid week's work at top wages. Rumor up and down Middleburg Avenue had it that the miners were truly content and even grudgingly inclined to give the owners their due in the all-encompassing prosperity. The miners, it was said, recognized that the owners were finding the good seams of coal and the good customers to buy it, and so everybody was benefiting, each on his level. After all, the men, and UMW, were not set up to perform these functions; cooperation was necessary and it was succeeding. Ideological radicals such as Frank Keeney might denounce the injustice of the Cliftons living in their mansions versus themselves in simple frame cottages in mining camps and demand socialism, but with their full-pay envelopes few miners listened. They did not *expect* to own a Rolls-Royce, never had, saw it as not in the cards. They wanted what they felt was their due, a full day's work for fair pay, and this they were getting.

Peace reigned even in Logan. The conflicts and legalisms of the Armed March had disappeared into the courts for years of litigation, the men jailed by Sheriff Chafin were gradually released, either to accept things resignedly as they were in Logan or to move on to less rigid jurisdictions.

VIII.

Minnie Catherwood took an ever-increasing interest in her farm. With her professional farmer she arranged for a pigsty, chicken coops, a big vegetable patch, corn, cows. When asked what she was going to name the property, Minnie replied, "You don't name places like that. The Castle, now that's a place that needs a name. It's for show. This is just a little hill farm. Maybe we could call it 'Minnie's Farm.' "

Lyle Catherwood continued to study at West Virginia University. He managed to attend many of his classes and to maintain a more or less passing average. He went out for the track team for a while. He was the life and soul of festivities at Phi Psi fraternity. Everybody seemed impressed with his Pierce-Arrow Raceabout, a formidable land yacht approximately twice the length of the Stutz, a massive two-seater racing machine (a third thronelike seat was behind the other two) with a great black detachable trunk with three spare tires fixed to it. The overall effect of its maroon and black presence put people in mind of steam engines and battleships. It was too powerful and huge to be driven at anything approaching top speed on any road in the state, but there were racecourses where Lyle could open it up, and of course it looked overwhelmingly impressive wherever it was parked.

Physically Lyle was maturing, his narrow face filling out a little, his spare frame acquiring more muscle, angularities fading into solidity, and the wild, eager surmise of his eyes settling into a more level look.

But his life in Morgantown and around the state was proceeding for him in an atmosphere of gathering unreality. What did any of it really *mean?* What difference did American history make? Who cared if the thirteen colonies became independent, or if King George III continued to reign over them? So what if the North won the Civil War? What if the South had won, what difference would it have made? What if the Civil War had never happened? Hundreds or thousands of men would not have died and limitless civilian suffering been avoided, but what difference would *that* have made?

If that woman with the green eyes and auburn hair who walked in that willowy way and who incorporated within herself the whole potential for his future life and happiness did not accept his love, that woman who in some way did love him but gave her love to someone else, why then there could be no meaning or sense in anything anywhere, and whether he got straight *A*'s and made Phi Beta Kappa or flunked out of West Virginia University was immaterial, the excitement over whether the Mountaineer football team did or did not beat the Pitt Panthers was like a sparkler on the Fourth of July — destined to fizzle out into a bent piece of hot, silly metal — the spread or the checking of the United Mine Workers was laughable in its irrelevance. Would the Clarkson Coal Company's profits continue to increase? Who could conceivably care? He would lose his Pierce-Arrow, he supposed, his allowance, way of life, daily bread. How could that possibly matter? Daily bread kept you alive. And why should he, fundamentally, want to be alive?

But there was an innate, blind instinct to continue which kept Lyle functioning, prevented his expulsion from the university, kept his drinking within sane bounds, and conducted him, mutely protesting and despairing all the way, willy-nilly into the future.

He thought frequently about Reverend Roanoke. No wonder he hadn't been able to foresee Lyle's salvation. It didn't exist. What had awaited Lyle, and maybe Reverend Roanoke in some way had foreseen it that day in the limousine, was having his whole life and hope and love slide into a swift-flowing stream, name of Doris Lee Pence, glittering and pure-seeming and slippery and sending him right over the falls.

What have I got, Lyle would sometimes ask himself. I've got a big allowance, a rich father, Pierce-Arrow Raceabout, Canadian whiskey, a whole raft of buddies and several girl friends at the university. And what does that add up to,

Lyle Catherwood, he would ask himself. And then he would answer: that adds up to nothing, sir.

Ophelia McClellan Stallings began to complain more publicly about the "falling standards" of the young people. She said among other things that young, unmarried women who wore dresses exposing their knees were ruining themselves forever, that the young men 'were throwing away their masculine authority by tolerating and even encouraging such things in the young women, that the older generation did not know how to control their money or their offspring. She stated that even in the great days of the plantation aristocracy it had been the *arriviste* planters of the Mississippi Valley and not the old families of Virginia and the Carolinas who had made and flaunted large sums of money; the older families had plowed most of their profits back into the land — "gracious living and *not* ostentation had been the way the First Families lived." Once you were above a certain level economically, affluent enough to show that God really cared, then who had more money than whom was a vulgar consideration. As for today, for a family to possess more than one large and one small automobile was tacky. Boys should be put to work in the family business the moment they had as much education as they could absorb, and girls should sit at home with their mothers until married, and not go gallivanting around Europe exposing themselves to God knew what dangers.

Minnie listened to all of this, and observed what was happening around her, the young people swamped by bootleg liquor and fast cars, interminable parties, skimpy and expensive dresses, restless fun and frolics and perhaps far less innocent goings-on, while their parents — herself, Clarkson, the Hayeses, Cliftons and the others — financed all of this out of their own overflowing incomes and a certain sense of guilt — hard to place, hard to fathom in oneself: guilty of what, against whom? Minnie felt that she and the other parents were sitting back, rather disapproving of what they saw unrolling in its gaudy, youthful, heedless way before them, unrolling in their homes, in the streets and lanes of Middleburg, at the university, everywhere, and she and the other parents were powerless, because both unwilling and afraid, to put a stop to it. Was it not an artifact of their success, their high accomplishment, their station in the world that this unprecedented explosion of youthful extravagance and glorious heedlessness could be taking place, here in the back country, the always-before-penurious hills of West Virginia. On with the party! It had been wrested from the earth itself. What was money for?

Doris Lee Pence did not return to Middleburg and soon dropped out of people's minds and conversation there. Not long after her departure, Minnie, who had kept what she thought of as Lyle's "shine" on Doris Lee Pence to herself, hoping it would just disappear, decided that it had and mentioned it to Clarkson one evening. After all, sharing and honesty were everything in a marriage. She broached the subject, but Clarkson confronted this information with such blank incomprehension, such scoffing disbelief, that she said no more about it.

Doris Lee continued living and working in Washington, and seeing Clarkson frequently. Their relationship progressed as she had foreseen it would, going to the theater, short trips, numerous expensive dinners, tasteful presents.

No other man seriously entered her life, although she had endless evenings to herself and Clarkson had never as much as hinted that she should not see, that he would prefer she not see other men.

This continued through the winter and into the spring of 1923. One evening in April at her apartment Clarkson told her that he was sailing for London in July on the *Aquitania*, mentioning it rather casually.

"The *Aquitania*," she repeated. Doris Lee did not read the newspapers and magazines for nothing. The *Aquitania*, she knew, was the most elegant, the most fashionable, the most luxurious transatlantic liner in existence, famous for its food and service and passenger list. To cross on her was one of the choice experiences available to the people with the time and the money to do so. And the style, she supposed: probably if you weren't stylish in the right way they wouldn't let you set foot on one of her decks, not in first class at least.

"I would like to book a stateroom for you too. We could meet for meals and for — for shuffleboard," he finished a little lamely.

"Shuffleboard!" she blurted, half-laughing in spite of herself.

Shuffleboard! If she accepted this invitation, to cross the Atlantic in the *Aquitania,* she knew with all her intuitions — it was obvious — that she and Clarkson Catherwood would meet for something much more basic than shuffleboard.

He looked at her quizzically, and then went on, "In London you might stay at the Hyde Park Hotel. I always stay at Claridge's."

"What would we meet for there?" she asked innocently.

He cleared his throat. "Why we could go to the theater. I — I think you're laughing at me."

"Oh no, not laughing. I, well, ah, may I have a few days to think about it? It's such a *wonderful* invitation. I'm overwhelmed. Who wouldn't be. But Virgie —"

"Of course, my dear. You have your responsibilities. And you — for all I know may have some friend here, an escort, someone you might not want to leave."

After a short silence she said, "No, there isn't anyone like that." She didn't know whether it might not have been cleverer to lie and say there was, but Doris Lee felt herself tossing in unknown seas; she was much too confused to think of lying or manipulating or trying to be clever. She would hold on to the strict truth, cling to that, and hope to reach safety, some safety or other.

That night, on leaving, he kissed her firmly on the mouth, held her there. He had not done that before.

As she closed the door after him she knew, his kiss had been his own straightforward notification, that if she accepted the crossing on the *Aquitania* they would arrive in England as lovers.

Doris Lee wandered back through the apartment, turning off lights as she went. She looked into Virgie's little room. He was sleeping soundlessly. She could hear Goldie snoring through the next door. She continued to the end of the little hall to her own bedroom, overlooking the park.

Tiny points of light were scattered here and there in the darkness below. What a snug little household she had established here in Washington, snug and safe and orderly and conventional.

None of this would have been possible except for the loans she had finally accepted from Clarkson. She had vowed to pay them back and she would pay them back: that is, unless she were to become his mistress, and then abruptly all the conventions and the proprieties and the limits would collapse.

She began to undress. Virgil surged to the front of her mind, his gentle young lovemaking, the naturalness and inevitability of it, the unquestionable rightness of it, the child who sprang from it.

And now: Clarkson Catherwood, forty-eight or fifty-two years old or whatever he was, a married man, with a more or less grown son.

And what about Lyle? Doris Lee, before pulling on her nightgown, stood for a moment nude before her full-length oval mirror. She noticed with satisfaction that she was as long and slender and lithe as ever, nothing sagging, nothing wrinkled, nothing fat. She supposed that she was a woman with allure, and that Clarkson, and of course Lyle, felt that. These Catherwood men seemed to have her in their blood!

Virgil. He had possessed her as naturally as a stream flows down to the river, as clean and swift and exhilarating as a fast-flowing mountain stream.

Clarkson. A kind, considerate older man without whose interest and support she might have lapsed back to Pound-ville and a hopeless life in a mining camp. And there was an upright, square-shouldered look to him that pleased her.

What else could she possibly do?

She took the framed photograph of Virgil off her dresser and after gazing long at it, closed her eyes and, feeling her way, put it in the back of the closet.

I'll never forget you for a moment as long as I live, she promised. But I can't look at your face, not while I'm trying to make up my mind about this. And if I do become Clarkson Catherwood's mistress, I'll have to leave that picture of your dear, dear face there.

IX.

They sailed on the *Aquitania* at midnight on July 7, 1923. Seeing the gigantic hull tied up at the Cunard pier in the Hudson River in New York made something catch in Doris Lee's throat. She had never seen anything like it and never expected to see anything like it. An immense, soaring slab of curving black steel rising up from where she stood toward Heaven, a wide, covered gangplank waiting for them to walk into it, a band playing gaily somewhere, streamers, her new silk evening dress, her fur, the bustle, the flowers, the hurry, the laughter, all of it swept her into a euphoria unknown and unimagined before. On board, the wide, busy decks, her spacious stateroom with the impeccable steward and his impeccable English accent, the unbelievable blast of the ship's whistle, a blast deep enough to raise the drowned; on the deck with Clarkson at the railing, champagne glasses in hand, they watched, holding hands — for she at least felt like a child — as the ship, this vast V-shaped steel city, pulled with awesome deliberation away from the dock and toward the center of the river; New York's jewellike night skyline hung fragile and glittering behind the docks as the tugs began very slowly turning the great bow downstream toward the Statue of Liberty, toward the sea, and Europe.

Cut off from America now, from letters, from humdrum life, at sea, with these glittering stranger-passengers and this faultless crew, they moved across the harbor, through the narrows, and, as the ship began a certain slight rhythmical rolling, into the open sea. A fresh blast of warm salty air hit them. Doris Lee turned, threw her arms around Clarkson, and kissed him long and tenderly on the mouth. He was enlarging her life beyond her dreams.

It was on the third day out that in her darkened stateroom Doris Lee, feeling herself another being, a deck strider, a sea sprite, reborn under the sign of Poseidon, joined her body as tenderly as she could to an experienced and considerate Clarkson.

Afterward she felt that their lovemaking had been what he had ultimately wanted and that it had made him happy. For her it had no resemblance to Virgil's. It was jarring, but in one way satisfying too: she had done what, looking at everything from every point of view, had to be done. AQUITANIA AS IN ACQUIESCE, she cabled Vivien Cummings.

X.

In August 1923, President Harding died, his administration inundated with financial scandals and corruption, and Calvin Coolidge succeeded to the presidency. The boom's enormous productivity and bursting prosperity continued: the demand for coal surged forward. None of the owners and operators wished to be left out or crowded out or frightened out of this by his competitors; it was necessary to go after coal which could not be mined so economically; new seams and new investments were swiftly approved.

Business was triumphantly in the driver's seat, in the White House, on Wall Street, and in the coalfields.

The young people of Middleburg continued on their seemingly permanent spree, and now the miners began to go on a spree of their own. The strip of buildings along River Street in Middleburg swiftly blossomed forth into one of the busiest hives of speakeasies, gambling dens and whorehouses this side of the Mississippi. Lyle Catherwood began to wander down there. The Mafia moved in decisively, and all appeared to be flourishing, from the cheapest floozie and the shadiest bootlegger on River Street to Marcus Clifton at the Farms. Don Chafin's own particular brand of joviality and boys-will-be-boys tolerance, based on now having everything his own way, surfaced in Logan, and from one end of the state to the other the heady combination of maximum industriousness and uproarious fun prevailed. Middleburg, the City of a Hundred Millionaires, was "on a party." And if Middleburg began to pall, then on to New York or Florida or Europe, or somewhere. The older generation looked on in their combination of half disapproval and full awe as the flow of money and of hilarity swept on. "Young girls of good family reeling drunk in public!" hooted Ophelia Stallings. "It is Sodom and Gomorrah!"

Clarkson Catherwood now possessed apparently almost

limitless prosperity and the now-complete, as he saw it, affections of Doris Lee Pence. That comprised the positive side of his life. On the other side, not the negative side, just the "other" side, there was Minnie, special as always, his first love, mother of his son, a rare spirit, and separate from him; and there was Lyle, uncommunicative and irresponsible twenty-five miles away.

Minnie had her perceptions, her sweet, devoted, and wayward boy, every material thing she could wish for, the servants, the automobiles, her unassailable social position, her private sense of salvation. And she had her farm, and she watched with care as pork and chicken and vegetables began to come from it to her table.

Doris Lee Pence had her growing son, now shaping more and more into an individual, she had her interesting classes to conduct at the seminary, evenings at bridge or occasionally going to the theater with other faculty members, and she had the kindly rich man from West Virginia who was devoted to her in a strictly limited way: within her compartment in his life she was a queen. He would certainly have supported her in leisure and in style had she permitted it, but Doris Lee resented this, became angry when he once ventured to suggest it. *That* was not the kind of woman she was. Her anger was such that it left him shaken and apologetic.

And Lyle Catherwood had, as he saw it, nothing.

ten

I.

URING the first part of the month of April 1924, an early and particularly beautiful springtime in West Virginia, Clarkson Catherwood, the Hayes family, and the Clifton brothers began receiving more and more ominous reports.

The coal was not selling.

Refill orders were coming in much more slowly than usual, and new business for several months past had been next to impossible to find. And then almost literally overnight the price of coal fell, plummeted, nose-dived, and at the end of the second week in April coal was selling at one half of what it had been selling at a few days before.

Customers had been switching to cleaner, easier-to-handle oil, that was one problem; but first and foremost and glaring them in the face was one word: overexpansion.

On the Friday of the second week in April the four Middleburg tycoons sat in their offices overlooking the bustling town in all its busyness, the streets pulsing with expensive new cars, customers moving briskly in and out of the stores, the purposeful comings and goings at the domed, pillared courthouse — so many contracts to be registered, so much litigation over mineral rights, so many deeds to register, so many marriages — everyone hastening from one productive deal to another. These four dominant figures in their town, their state, and their industry could look down to the river-bank and its endless chain of coal cars moving along the B&O line, and in the river itself, barges, the water close to the gunwales from the weight of all the coal, being pushed by riverboats toward Pittsburgh and its steel furnaces. On the other bank, on River Street, truant miners and overworked prostitutes were already anticipating nightfall in the saloons; the City of a Hundred Millionaires was dynamic with its daily multiplicity, the local stocks and bonds parlor doing an optimistic business because Wall Street was continuing its apparently never-ending climb to paradise and quick profits were being turned today as most days; out dignified, tree-lined Middleburg Avenue the sturdy homes stood like so many banks, and just as impregnable. At the great parade of piked-iron fence protecting Sanderson Clifton's Elizabethan manor autos were drawing up to discharge ladies attending one of Mrs. Clifton's elaborate luncheons, this one honoring Mrs. Robertson Merryweather III of New York and Palm Beach. Mrs. Merryweather, and her husband, who was him-self being entertained at lunch at Clifton Farms with senior executives of the Company, were scheduled to return to New York that night on the Great Kanawha.

At his luncheon Mr. Merryweather, who represented many millions of eastern dollars invested in the coalfields, was not told that as of that day every one of the thousands of tons of coal being mined would cost the owners several dollars in losses and that, unless there was a drastic change in price upward — and God knew where that would come from — the Company, the Clarkson Coal Company, the Hayes Coal Company, and every last one of the Hundred Millionaires would be in default on their loans, unable to meet payrolls, and then bankrupt and penniless in an amazingly short time.

Mr. Merryweather would learn this news soon enough. Nor was there any point in ruining his lunch — Chesapeake Bay oysters, saddle of lamb, Brussel sprouts Greenbrier, country-baked apple pie with Farms-made ice cream, Alsatian white and Burgundian red wine with Veuve Cliquot champagne — by telling him of the catastrophe, for there was nothing he could do about it. It was an avalanche, a gigantic hurtling descent which, unless miraculously reversed, would sweep away mansions and limousines, profits and payrolls, union dues and food from the tables.

Clarkson Catherwood had been invited to this lunch for Mr. Merryweather at Clifton Farms. He sat at the broad dining room table covered with its superb linen in one of the high-backed, thronelike chairs as he so often had before in this spacious and dignified room, its long windows giving a view of the terraces and balustrade and rose garden, sideboards gleaming with Macel Clifton's collection of silver, the colored servants moving quietly about the room as they always had, this apex of life as Clarkson had always known it. The conversation went on about Calvin Coolidge and the opening of the baseball season and the stock market and bone fishing in Florida. Clarkson watched as Marcus Clifton, the high-humored, enormously self-assured embodiment of King Coal, kept the conversation moving along in a friendly, unorganized way and did not lie exactly but casually evaded points about sales and a fatal question or two with friendly and disarming non sequiturs. Clarkson saw that it was going to be a successful lunch, a reassuring lunch; Robertson Merryweather would feel very well fed and satisfied and confident of his investments and those of the people he represented. Later this afternoon by long-distance telephone from his office in New York, or at the latest on his return to the city tomorrow, all these friendly and gratifying and reassuring impressions would be wiped out and not just wiped out but reversed. *Why* had Marcus Clifton wined and dined him and not told him that the bottom had fallen out of the country's greatest basic industry? What kind of fool was he!

But Clarkson believed he understood. Marcus was, as they said in medical circles, in shock: he was sleepwalking, going through the motions he had been born to, unable to learn new lines and a new role, a new self, not yet, not so quickly, probably, Clarkson suddenly surmised, never. The role of grand seigneur had suited him, he had played it so naturally and good-humoredly and well. And could he, Clarkson, ever successfully embody any personality except that of Clarkson Catherwood of the Castle? Were they to become fossils?

"And I tell you, Robby," Marcus was saying to Robertson Merryweather on his right, "show horses are just like yachts: if you ask how much it costs to keep 'em you can't afford 'em."

"You've got some beauties," responded Robertson Merryweather. "I'd be afraid to get up on one and walk around the ring. Afraid something as delicate as that might break under me."

"Have some more of this down-home pie," urged Marcus hospitably. "You never *will* make jockey weight, so go ahead. I am."

He signaled the servant who gave them each another wedge. Coffee and liqueurs were being served. "One thing about the Democrats," said Mr. Merryweather, "if they get in in November we'll have no more of this goddam Prohibition!"

"You know," said Marcus, "we — I mean the state legislature — voted Prohibition into West Virginia four years ahead of the rest of the country, in nineteen fourteen. Don't notice how it's made any difference *yet*. Am I right, gentlemen?" Everyone chuckled and concurred and raised their Venetian glasses, feeling that some sort of toast was in order. Then Clarkson Catherwood heard his voice fill the semi-awkward pause as everyone waited for something to be proposed. "To the future," he said. Christ, he instantly thought in mortification, I really *am* Lyle's father!

There was a muffled grunt, a swift intake of breath here and there, and they all drank to the future.

II.

George was busy that afternoon. He got himself up into his full uniform, gloves, cap and all, and drove the short distance up Middleburg Avenue to Ninth Street, turning in there and along it to the entrance to the Farms, sweeping up the curving drive in the Packard to park near the porte cochere among the Cadillacs and Pierce-Arrows, the Clifton Rolls, and the others.

When the gentlemen came out, in hats and overcoats despite the balmy April weather because they had their city guest and going bareheaded would have been very unsuitable, George opened the door for Mr. Catherwood and drove him down the length of Middleburg Avenue to his office.

Clarkson did not speak during this drive, which was very unusual: nothing about his cars or Lyle's Pierce-Arrow Raceabout or goings-on on River Street or even a remark on what an especially nice day it was.

The odors of the maples and the burgeoning shrubbery along the avenue, the perked-up flower beds, the window boxes of ferns, all the hopeful mingling of scents of April in the hill country failed to evoke a single observation from Clarkson Catherwood.

After leaving him at his office on Main Street George circled the cheerfully busy block of stores, past a church and the firehouse, and then back out Middleburg Avenue to the big wrought-iron gates standing open at the side entrance of Clifton Manor. He pulled the Packard into another line of

Cadillacs and Pierce-Arrows and more Packards, and soon Minnie in a straw hat with flowers on it and a green dress came out. Ophelia Stallings, looking like a piece of upholstery, was with her, and George helped the two ladies into the back seat.

"Wasn't that a lovely lunch," observed Minnie. "Spinach soufflé! Would you dare serve that for thirty people?"

Ophelia chuckled throatily. "I'd never serve it for *anybody* except Clarence and me. But then with her cook, and I don't know how many on the staff, in the kitchen —"

"Yes," agreed Minnie, settling back. "Isn't this a perfectly *gorgeous* spring day? George, do we have time to drive out to the farm and have a look around?"

It was now 2:45 P.M. George had orders to pick up Mr. Catherwood at 5:00 P.M. It was a thirty-minute trip to the farm each way. With time spent there he could just about make it. He took his time about answering "Yes'm," which was a clear signal to Mrs. Catherwood, one she would never mistake, that although this excursion was possible it was inconvenient and might interfere with other duties of his. But for once Minnie, usually considerate to a fault, stuck to her plan. So George headed the long, heavy hood of the Packard — the oval thermometer over the radiator like an enormous eye, or a great jewel — once more down Middleburg Avenue and out on the road to Bennettown.

Along the steep and curving road the hills shone beneath the April sun, their blossoming trees of delicate early green promising future fulfillment, the wood scents and wildflower odors, the fresh earth smells, all mingling in an exhalation from the renascent earth. "It's going to be a beautiful summer," breathed Minnie, "just beautiful."

They arrived at the dirt track leading up through Minnie's new cornfield to the barn. It was rutted and bumpy and George had only previously negotiated it with the Ford and, once, with the Hupmobile. Drive the Twin-Six Packard limousine over that mess? He stopped the car and turned to Minnie, looking at her.

"Yes? What is it, George?"

"Can't take this car over that road, Miss Minnie, ruin the springs."

"Springs? Well, it doesn't matter. I want you to see this place, Ophelia, feel it. Let's walk."

Ophelia managed to transform herself from a piece of upholstery into a battlement. "In my formal luncheon slippers? Not on your life."

Minnie, intent all her life on pleasing everybody, now found herself in a not unfamiliar quandary: two colliding positions, equally reasonable, to be resolved by her.

She sat back in the seat. "Drive on, George."

Silence from the front seat, and then George said, "This here's a *city* car."

"George."

Very slowly he let the clutch out and with its wealthy purr the big engine engaged and the white-walled tires began their unaccustomed exploring of country ruts and bumps.

The rows of young green corn curved away from them on both sides as the car crept upward to the big, old, slatternly barn with CHEW MAIL POUCH TOBACCO painted in looming yellow letters on a black background. Under that, in slightly smaller letters, had been painted: *Treat Yourself to the Best.*

"That unsightly *sign* on your barn," remarked Ophelia.

"Is it unsightly? We get a little premium from the tobacco company for having it there. Not much. Mr. Eubanks, he's my farmer, takes care of it."

"Can't be anything that makes a difference."

"The henhouses," said Minnie, "are on the other side of the barn. Cows are in the upper pasture. If only this land was flat Mr. Eubanks says we'd have a 'right fine spread' here. But then, what's flat in West Virginia?"

"Greenbrier County. Jefferson County."

"Not really. They just have old houses there."

"Plantations, you mean."

"Mmm. This is just a little hill farm. No house here. Never was. Mr. Eubanks lives in his house farther up the road. He and his boy work this for me and take some of the produce and . . . it all works out to be favorable to everybody."

George maneuvered the Packard into an untidy barnyard and looked about him with mock amazement.

"*Now*, Ophelia, you've got to step down. Don't you want to see the cows and pigs?"

"The pigs! Really, Minnie. Get a hold on yourself. You're a rare, uh, bird, *rara avis*, yes, but! Get down into a filthy barnyard to see the pigs! In my formal luncheon slippers! Dear, that goes way beyond originality. That's — as the young people would say, that's *bogus!*".

They gazed at each other in mingled perplexity and deepening comprehension.

Then Minnie said, rather more firmly than ever before, "George, please open this door. I've got to speak to my farmer."

George opened his door and after hesitating on the broad running board stepped gingerly into the sloppy barnyard and opened the door of the rear seat. Minnie quickly stepped down and, crossing the yard, entered the barn. It was empty of both cows and Mr. Eubanks. A hound dog roused itself from a corner and came forward to sniff at her hand.

Minnie proceeded out the other side of the barn, past the chicken coops, and was heading down a slope toward the pigs when she saw Mr. Eubanks coming down from the upper pasture, leading one of the workhorses.

"Early spring we're having, Mr. Eubanks!" she called as he approached. "Ought to be good for most everything, oughtn't it?"

"Ought to," he concurred, squinting at her in the sunlight,

his face turning into a mass of fine wrinkles. "Lessen we get some flash floodin'."

"Pretty high, here, aren't we?"

"What I mean is, a *rainstorm* flood. Not the river or the creeks. The sky. Deluge. Ever been through one of them, missus?"

"No, not like that. Have you? Here?"

"Don't remember it, I was just a little runt, two, three, but I heard tell of it from my folks. Had to float out of our house, one we had before this one. Swept the whole valley clean."

If Mr. Eubanks had been through two or three, Minnie calculated, then this deluge must have happened about 1870 or so. "Ever happen again?" she asked.

"No like to that. Not like to that one."

"Then we won't worry *too* much about it, because I think we're going to have a lot of good vegetables —"

"Cows are milkin' good."

"And milk and butter. And bacon and all. I hope I'm right?"

After a calculating silence he allowed, "There's a chance."

With that straightforward expression of optimism, stronger than any Minnie had heard from him before, she contented herself. She gazed around her acres. Not the best farm in the county by a long shot, dirt farming she supposed it was, hill farming. Still, you planted things and tended them and they came up, produced, could be eaten. You could do this year after year. Renewal. And standing there in her ruined luncheon shoes Minnie just then realized why she had acquired this farm. It renewed itself.

Coal came from nature's raw material, buried underground for millions of years, and then one day Clarkson dug it up after these millions of years of gestation and he sold it and made money from it and the customer burned it and it was gone forever.

This little hill farm, modest as could be, nothing to even mention beside the Clarkson Coal Company, let alone the Company, nevertheless, properly treated, was indestructible.

"Want some lettuce?" said Mr. Eubanks. "Take a couple head."

He pried four dirty heads of lettuce out of the soil and handed them to Minnie, who juggled them in her arms against her green dress. "Why thank you. First this season."

She made her way back through the dirt and hay and horse dung to the limousine. George helped her in.

"You're a sight!" exclaimed Ophelia.

"Oh?" said Minnie vaguely, laying the heads of lettuce on the ample space of floor before them. "Sometime, Ophelia, put on a pair of, you know, walking shoes, country shoes, and come on out here and let me show you around."

Ophelia fingered her pearls. "You know, Minnie, I grew up on a country place. We had field hands did the work. Once in a while my mother would drive out in a little buggy to see things and speak to them. Sometimes I rode along with her. The one rule Mama had was, 'Ophelia, never take off your white gloves.' And I *never* did."

"Mmm, yes, well, that was long ago, and far away."

"Far away? Jefferson County?"

"Long ago," sighed Minnie, wedging the dirty heads of lettuce against the folded jump seats so they would not roll around from the motion of the car, "and far away."

Back in Middleburg George handed Ophelia down next to the mounting block in front of her house and then drove on the shorter distance to the Castle, depositing Minnie and the four heads of lettuce.

It was four forty-five. He headed the Packard once more down Middleburg Avenue, as the Hupmobiles and Buicks and Essexes and La Salles and Fords moved up and down the avenue with him. There were plenty of open touring cars

and topless roadsters with people out enjoying the excep-
tionally fine April afternoon. On the lawn in front of the
Morrison house a croquet game was in progress, and on most
of the front porches, some of them pillared in nostalgic echo
of plantation life, the ladies of the house were taking the
air in light-colored, summery dresses. It was lemonade-
sipping time again. Children were playing in the sun porches
and in the yards, and hopscotch flourished on the sidewalks.

Clarkson, once again uncharacteristically on this excep-
tional day, was standing on the sidewalk in front of the office
building, his fedora at an angle, his suit coat off and casually
draped over a shoulder, talking to three or four younger
businessmen. There was an air of bonhomie about him that
he normally didn't have time for during the Middleburg
business day, a certain unbuttoned quality which was drawing a surprised and cordial response from the young men
surrounding him.

"Well, here's my car, fellows," he called cheerily as
George drove up. "Can I give anybody a lift? No? All right
then, see you all soon."

He stepped into the back seat and slumped into a corner.

"Who's been muddying the floor back here?" he demanded.

"I'm sorry, Mr. Catherwood," George replied in a clear
voice. "Miss Minnie was set on goin' out to her farm and
takin' this car right up into that barnyard and she got out
and —"

"I see," said Clarkson glumly. "Don't go on."

"I told her this with the city car."

"City car," repeated Clarkson in an ironic tone.

"You do want to go home, is that right, Mr. Catherwood?"

"Hum? Oh, yes, George. Home," he responded wearily,
pronouncing the final word as though it too had some ironic
significance.

George drove at a deliberate rate of speed one final time
along Middleburg Avenue, where the solid and ample houses

were now receiving the head of the house home for the day, and offering him the afternoon newspaper and a refreshing glass on the front porch. The children's games were getting faster because the call to dinner was not far off.

George drew into the Castle driveway and circled to the porte cochere. Angelo was out among his roses. The lawn had sprung into freshest green life, and the shrubbery arched with renewal beneath the great, half-leafed trees.

Clarkson struggled out of the corner of the big car, stepped down and then up again a few steps and into the side entrance of the house.

Inside, the big windows and French doors had been opened, there were growing ferns and cut flowers in profusion, and percolating through to his library came a trace of the odor of one of Tot's best baked ham dinners.

Clarkson tossed his hat and coat into a chair, loosened his necktie, and then thinking better of it, ripped off necktie and stiff detachable collar, and in his white collarless shirt, his loose neck exposed, he suddenly looked dispossessed. He sank into one of the two wingback chairs flanking the tall fireplace.

Minnie came in wearing a long gray chiffon dress with white cuffs and collar, dressed for dinner. Her hair had been carefully brushed and pinned by Thomasina and she had put one of the new rosebuds in it. Looking mildly surprised at Clarkson's unusual state of undress she greeted him with a kiss on the forehead and then crossing to the bay window sat down on the couch in front of it.

"Where's Lyle?" he asked almost gruffly. "Isn't he up from the university?"

"He is. He'll be down directly."

Clarkson stared before him.

"What would you like?" she asked. "I'll ring."

"Scotch. Ask him to bring the bottle and some soda and ice. Lyle been drinking today?"

"No," said Minnie with careful casualness. "I've almost never known him to drink during the day, except you know football weekends and special occasions like that. He's got some examination coming up soon. Then, just think, next September he starts his senior year. Lylie, a college senior. I just — Oh, George, bring Mr. Catherwood some Scotch. Just make up a tray with the bottle and the soda and ice, and put it there on the sideboard. And I'll have a glass of sherry. And, well, bring that bottle of bourbon. And if Tot has something for us to nibble on, bring that too."

George went out and the room fell silent.

"Do you want to close that window?" said Clarkson. "It's getting chilly." Again mildly surprised, Minnie got up and closed the long open window next to the bay window.

"We haven't even got our screens in yet," she observed. George'll have to get after that tomorrow." Clarkson made no comment. "Spring came so suddenly this year, just all of a sudden upon us. I went out to the farm today —"

"Where is that boy!"

After a pause Minnie said, "He's coming, dear, but if you want I'll call up and hurry him along."

George came in with the tray of drinks and one of the collies slipped into the library with him and settled proprietarily in front of the fireplace.

Clarkson slopped some Scotch into a glass, dropped in two cubes of ice and hissed a tiny jet of soda on top. George handed the sherry to Minnie. Then the hall door opened and Lyle walked in.

His face had filled out a little, his red hair was under somewhat better control. He had gained enough weight so that he looked less windblown. In white pants, dark blazer and striped tie he seemed to be the personification of Country Club, 1924.

"Hi Dad. Oh. What're we doing, undressing for dinner?" He pantomined ripping off his tie.

Clarkson raised a speculative eyebrow to contemplate his son. Usually Clarkson approved of seeing Lyle carefully and appropriately dressed. This evening, however, it aroused a strange feeling of contempt in him.

"Sit down," he said. "Or, I suppose you want your belt of bourbon first."

"Uh-mm, yes, I guess so." Lyle made himself a bourbon and soda and took the wingback chair across the fireplace from Clarkson's.

"I've got something to tell you," began Clarkson in an unfamiliar voice, nervous, a little reedy, "and I don't know how to lead up to it, or prepare you for it so I guess I'll say it straight. The coal business has become very, very bad. Very bad. The price of a ton of coal has been cut in half in the last seventy-two hours. I have been on the phone with the coal brokers, I've been in consultation with the Hayeses, and with Sanderson and Marcus. We've talked to New York, we've talked to Cleveland, we've talked to Pittsburgh. We've talked to Illinois and Kentucky. We've been in touch with London. The price of coal has been cut in half in the last seventy-two hours, and there is not one sign in hell that it's going to recover by as much as one cent in any foreseeable future. I lose . . . I lose several dollars, as of the day before yesterday, on every ton of coal I mine. If this keeps up in three or four months I . . . I and the Cliftons and the Hayeses and every last coal operator in West Virginia and in the country, I am . . . we are . . ." The downright quality he had achieved in his narration now began to falter, not because he could not bear to tell his family what came next, but because he could not bear to say these words themselves, give the facts as he knew them the dignity of being spoken aloud and so endowed with greater authority, permanence. "We," he resumed with grave deliberation, hands clasped between his knees as he hunched forward, a collarless, flushed, aging man, skin loose under the chin and on the neck, the authority none of them could ever remember seeing him without now missing, "we . . . will all have . . . to . . . take . . . bankruptcy. There . . . will . . . not be any . . . money left. No money left . . . We . . . will probably . . . not . . . be able to . . . continue . . . to live . . . in this house. The cars will . . . have to be sold. We can probably keep . . . the Ford. There won't be . . . any money . . . for . . . servants. You . . . well . . . you just . . . won't be able . . . to recognize . . . the life we will . . . have to lead."

"How could anything happen so suddenly?" Minnie asked in a stunned voice.

"It hasn't been so sudden. It's been happening behind our backs. We never turned around to look. Oil is coming in. Cleaner. Easier to handle. There's more of it available now. It's competitive, better than competitive, in price. It was. Now we're underselling it. And losing our shirts. And you see we" — and here he suddenly looked like Lyle, caught out, immature — "we all wanted our full share of the market, and so we expanded and borrowed and expanded and borrowed and now we owe a . . . whole lot of money, and the bottom has dropped out of the market."

Minnie sat with her hands in her lap. "Greed," she then said quietly.

Clarkson looked at her and for a while no one said anything. Lyle looked dazed. Minnie seemed lost in thought. Clarkson appeared drained.

"Is it all really inevitable?" Minnie inquired quietly at last.

Clarkson drew a long, pained breath. "Nothing is ever one hundred percent certain. There is going to be a meeting at Clifton Farms tomorrow morning at ten, and I wouldn't be surprised if that meeting went on right through the weekend. We are going to examine every possibility. Maybe someone will think of a miracle."

George came into the room. "Dinner's ready, Miss Minnie."

"We can't," breathed Minnie, "let it go to waste."

"Maybe I can drive a truck," observed Lyle. "Do they handle like Pierce-Arrows? But then, what truck? Trucks around here carry coal. But who's going to want coal?"

"Let's all go in to dinner," said Minnie, "and take this up later."

At the candlelit table, set with linen and silver and crystal, Minnie said grace, as always the one she learned in the Catholic convent: "Bless us, O Lord, and these Thy gifts, which we are about to receive from Thy bounty, through Christ our Lord." And the other two Catherwoods this night all contributed an audible "amen" to that.

Minnie had served wine with the dinner, and after the meal when Clarkson withdrew to his private office in the barn he was rather drunk.

There was a separate telephone line there with no extensions in the house. On it he placed a long-distance call to Doris Lee Pence.

Clarkson did not know how to break bad or shocking news any way except immediately and bluntly.

"Doris Lee," he began, "how are you?" When she replied that she was well and asked how he was he said, "Well, I'm afraid I'm going to have to retrench, completely retrench, we all are, the Cliftons and so on. Bottom's fallen out of the coal business. No recovery in sight, and so, my dear, I, uh, am going to ask to release you from our — whatever our connection is, you understand — devilishly hard thing to say —"

"I —"

"But the long and short of it is I've got no money, won't have, none of us will have, very soon now. So I, well, must release you from any tie you may feel to me, any responsibility and you know loyalty and, even, any connection if you see what I mean. There's going to be very little travel for Clarkson Catherwood from now on and, uh, I fear really no money to entertain you and treat you —"

"I didn't," she began with asperity, "see you, Clarkson, because of your *money*. Now please. If you're having difficulties, if you're I don't know bankrupt, I will still be your friend, more than ever, because —"

"I understand, my dear, but it isn't feasible for us to see one another. I can't keep going to Washington and staying in hotels. I am going to be just a small-town I-don't-know-what, a man who, well, doesn't have, can't afford, doesn't live as a man with a beautiful, well, lady friend in another city."

After a silence Doris Lee said, "I see."

"Are you, well, hurt?"

"No, I'm not hurt, Clarkson. "I'm a little *shocked*, any West Virginia girl would be. The bottom's falling out back home, the way of life we all assumed was forever . . ."

"Our lives, mine, Marcus's, Sanderson's, Pete Hayes's, are going to be unrecognizably different. Small-town I-don't-know-whats, that's what we're going to be. And because of that, I have to bid you good-bye, and offer my apology."

"There's no possible reason for you to apologize to me."

"And you are a beautiful being, and I'll never forget you."

"I'm so sorry this is happening to you."

Silence ensued along the line from the barn in Middleburg over the Blue Ridge Mountains to the apartment in Washington. Then his voice sent the word "good-bye" and she said "good-bye" and the connection was cut.

She sat moving the telephone receiver back and forth in its cradle, staring in front of her, hair in curlers, cold cream on her face, in the older of her two bathrobes. And so, she reflected, I am going to be a single woman after all.

III.

Clarkson remained immersed in conferences at Clifton Farms throughout the weekend, but did appear for supper Sunday night. Sunday night supper was a pickup meal: George and Tot and Thomasina were off, and the family forgathered in the big kitchen, rooting out potato salad from the icebox, some cold ham, homemade bread, and the fresh lettuce from the farm. They sat around the kitchen table, the two men in shirtsleeves, Minnie in a housecoat.

"Well?" said Lyle, looking at his father. "Any miracles?"

"In a way," he said, "in a way."

They waited wordlessly.

Clarkson sliced himself off a piece of bread and buttered it. He added the lettuce and a slice of ham. "We're going to break the contract."

"What contract?" said Minnie.

"Our contract with the United Mine Workers."

"Can you . . . can you do that?"

He added another slice of bread on top, and then taking a large knife sliced the sandwich in two. "Well, we're doing it."

"Is it . . . I mean," Minnie fumbled with her thoughts, "isn't a contract binding? To break it . . . Is it legal?"

Clarkson put down the knife and looked at her. "The contract is completely unreasonable in the light of the collapse of the coal market. Ordinary horse sense shows we can't live up to it, pay those wage scales. So we're canceling it, notices are going up at the mines at midnight tonight, and any man who wants to work for what we can afford to pay can work, if — uh — we have a place for him. Needless to say, production is going to be cut, and when I say cut I mean cut."

"Bennettown?" she inquired.

"Shutting it down," said Clarkson briefly. "It's my most marginal operation."

"The men," said Lyle, looking across the kitchen table at his father. "If they went to war in nineteen twenty-one, what'll they do *this* time?"

"The men," Clarkson said judiciously, "can be militant and get stirred up by a lot of radicals like Frank Keeney, but they've got horse sense like everybody else, a lot of them do anyway. They can see the figures, they'll be in the newspaper tomorrow, they can read, most of them can. They can see that if something costs you twelve dollars to mine you can't sell it for six, not for long you can't. And if the price stays at six, why then you've got to bring down the twelve dollars' cost of mining it. How are you going to do that? Wages, the payroll, that's the big number-one expense. A lot of the other expenses are fixed, you can't reduce them much. Payrolls are going to have to come way down."

"Are we still going to move?" asked Minnie.

"Well," said Clarkson, "we're not going to move just yet. Not just yet. Maybe we've found the miracle."

"Destroy the union," she said quietly.

Clarkson looked at her. "That's right," he said.

An unsettling mingling of emotion had attacked Lyle all through this weekend, the weekend, he said to himself, when King Coal was dethroned. He'd have to remember when it was, the second weekend in April 1924, so he could tell his grandchildren. That vagrant thought, grandchildren, only added to the confusion of his feelings.

His father had been right Friday night to tell them of the direst possible consequences of the break in the coal market. Lyle had gone to bed that night feeling a weird sense of exhilaration, almost somehow of hope fulfilled, a wildest dream realized. Since it was nonsensical that he would really be thrilled and happy by the ruin of his family, there had to be, he figured, some other source for this strange surge of feeling.

But what else it might be Lyle couldn't imagine. Perhaps

it was just the excitement of a drastic new situation, a sudden and complete reversal of life-as-usual in the Castle and at the university, an eerie dive into the unknown. Who in his family or among his friends knew what being poor was like? They had heard about it and seen it around them, but they also saw hills around them, but who knew what it felt like to be a hill? Poverty-stricken: it had probably impressed something in his nature as a new adventure, Lyle decided. Maybe that was why he felt so stimulated, even well, *pleased* in a spooky way, by the collapse of coal.

But following the supper Sunday Lyle felt deeply confused, muddled, even depressed. Those men he'd ridden into the mountains approaching Logan with in the flatcar, those strong union men: they or men like them up here in the Middleburg field were now going to be crushed by the Cliftons, the Hayeses and the Catherwoods. Or rather, not so much by the owners' antiunionism as the owners' — what was his mother's word? greed — by their greed, mismanagement, shortsightedness. The privileged men in their mansions and Rolls-Royces and Packards had taken all these privileges and all the money and then failed the industry, the workers, and themselves. The reason society gave them the mansions and the limousines was that they were supposed to have better judgment and understanding and insight and *foresight*.

And the Cliftons and the Hayeses and Clarkson Catherwood and the Hundred Millionaires had failed, miserably, graspingly failed. So now, in the desperate crisis their greed and blindness had created, they were turning on and setting out to destroy the United Mine Workers.

By God, maybe Lyle would go over to the union's side again.

eleven

I.

A CHARGE of dynamite erupted inside the Company's Number Four mine two days after the union-breaking notices were posted. It caused a major cave-in which blocked the main entrance to the mine for an indefinite period. The blast had been set to go off at three o'clock in the morning, so there were no casualties.

It happened that Lyle Catherwood found himself alone in a room at the Farms with Marcus Clifton the next night. "Well anyway there were no casualties," remarked Lyle, looking for some encouraging side to the shock the dynamiting had brought down upon Middleburg.

Marcus Clifton was drunk. Lyle had often seen him "pleasantly lubricated" as the saying went, but never drunk. He did not believe anyone had seen Marcus Clifton drunk before. His face flushed so that an almost purple tinge appeared on it, Marcus said loosely, "Yes, there was one casualty."

"There was? I didn't know that. A watchman?"

"No." Marcus breathed heavily and shifted in his big

easy chair. "The coal business. That was the casualty. It died last night."

Lyle stared at him.

"The one chance we had," Marcus went on, nodding to himself, "was labor peace, no strikes, no violence. Well, when they dynamite one of my mines, *that's* violence. We'll get strikes, picketing, we'll get production cut off. And that, young Master Catherwood, is one of the big fat reasons we've been losing customers! Too damn much labor trouble down here! They can't always count on getting our coal. So, they switch! Oil. If we could've busted that UMW contract and still had *peace*, well, we just might've made it. But they blew that sky-high with that damnable charge of dynamite out at Number Four. Made headlines in New York. There go another three hundred big customers, right over to oil. *We're finished.*" The big red-purple hound's face mooned up at Lyle. "Get a job teaching school or something."

Teaching school, thought Lyle incandescently.

Macel Clifton came into the library, gave Lyle a set smile and bent down to encourage Marcus out of his chair. "Now you can't stay here in the library with the house full of guests. I want you to go out and mingle and not have anything more to drink. Coming, Lyle dear?"

He followed the coal industry's premier couple out into the capacious living rooms, pleasantly alive with fifty or sixty people, the pick of the Hundred Millionaires and their spouses and a few members of the younger generation.

Lyle went up to his parents, who had been talking to Macel Clifton outside the library door. A band out of sight was playing bouncy music. "Mr. Clifton just told me I ought to teach school, or something."

The family looked at him.

"He said," went on Lyle "that the coal industry is dead, the explosion, labor problems, all that killed it last night. Said I should teach school."

"Well," said Minnie, "there are worse callings. People do have useful and secure lives that way. Look at that Mrs. Pence. I believe she's doing well in Washington." She glanced casually at her husband. "Isn't she, Clarkson? Wasn't she wise to get herself out of all our turmoil and uncertainty down here, to get a teaching job there and *keep* it." She blinked once or twice and smiled agreeably.

Lyle had soundlessly gasped: what in the world had ever made his mother think of Doris Lee at a time like this! Of all people, why Doris Lee!

And then, like a cave-in in some mine, the possible meaning of his mother's words and her glance at his father collapsed its full rocklike mass upon Lyle. He was too stunned to be sure what had hit him or what it meant or what state he was now in. Removed from them and from the room, Lyle drifted over to the punch bowl and accepted a glass, gulped it down, and accepted another. Nothing had any meaning and his own existence was problematical and he felt strangely happy, because of the unreality and impossibility of it all. *Got a job teaching in Washington and kept it. Wasn't she wise.*

She kept it. Very wise of her. Didn't give it up, even though she had a . . . had a . . . lover, Clarkson Catherwood. Wise because Clarkson Catherwood was about to become penniless and Doris Lee Pence in her wisdom had not allowed herself to be completely — what did they call them? Kept woman. She'd not allowed herself to be that, not completely, not completely kept by her lover, that would be Clarkson Catherwood, that is, not completely one hundred percent kept by him. Made love to, yes, over and over and over and over, but not completely kept.

Lyle was tingling from head to foot. Malaria must feel like this, he thought. Or going down the rathole to the funny farm.

He remained completely silent for the rest of the party,

or wake, as he saw it, the Cliftons' traditional spring party held over the corpse of King Coal. He said nothing during the short ride home. No one seemed to notice his silence. Everyone, after all, was acting unpredictably and uncharacteristically during these days. Lyle went to his room, undressed, noisily ran the water in his bathroom, ostentatiously turned out the lights in his quarters and, with a bottle of Canadian whiskey, got into bed. This bottle of Canadian whiskey had cost him twenty dollars from the River Street bootlegger. He didn't suppose he'd be able to afford many more of them. Well, corn liquor, white lightning, moonshine, there was plenty of that around and dirt cheap.

The next morning, not particularly suffering from a hangover, Lyle waited until he heard his mother pass his door and continue upstairs to her sewing room.

He got himself shaved and combed, and then, holding a cup of coffee, wandered casually up to join her there. Such confidential talks between them in this room had been an off-again on-again custom all through the years of his growing up. At her sewing machine Minnie was working on a blouse. He began a desultory conversation about the strained atmosphere at the Clifton party, then turned to the dynamiting and compared conditions to those preceding the Armed March three years earlier. And then Lyle slipped in his question:

"So Mrs. Pence is doing okay in Washington?"

"So I hear, yes."

"How did you hear that?"

"Oh people, you know, someone, well, Ophelia I believe, ran into her at the National Theater in Washington one night."

"Who was she with?" Lyle suddenly asked gruffly.

"Goodness, I don't know, or yes, I think Ophelia said it was some other member of the faculty at that school."

"Man faculty, or lady?"

"Why, I believe it was a lady. Why?"

"Just wondered." Lyle took a sip of cold coffee. It tasted awful. "Why did you think that . . . Dad" — his voice miraculously remained steady — "would know how Mrs. Pence was doing in Washington?"

"Did I suggest that?"

"Yes."

"Why I — parties, that punch had rum in it. I guess I was a little tiddly, and also, yes, upset, seeing Marcus drunk, and all those men so *nervous* about what's happening. I rather just said whatever popped into my head. And, you see, your father away so very much and it must be lonely —"

Here a knell tolled inside Lyle's head, fatal or insane or liberating.

"— so that I" — her voice very reasonable — "understand it if he seeks out some pleasant company to entertain at dinner once in a while in these strange cities where he has to spend so much time."

"And he —" Lyle's voice lacked some basic force but she appeared not to notice.

"Your father has entertained Mrs. Pence once or twice at dinner, yes." Minnie went on with a tinge of defiance, "Why shouldn't he? The widow of a former employee, a man whose life was lost serving Clarkson personally, herself alone in a new city. I believe he saw it as part of his duty, just as he gives — gave — more money than anyone will ever know to the families of men injured or killed in his mines."

Lyle obliterated these other actions by his father from his consciousness. "He told you about having dinner with her?"

She looked up over her sewing machine. "Why do you wish to persist in this, Lyle?"

"I just do," he said steadily. "He told you about it?"

"No," replied Minnie in a tone suggesting the unreasonableness of that assumption, "because he just — it just was

[317]

simpler not to." She bit off a length of thread. "One or two . . . friends, or friends of friends, happened to notice them once or twice in, you know, hotel restaurants."

So that, Lyle's freezing brain recorded, was it. What more was he going to have to be put through?

His father was the man Doris Lee had taken in place of himself.

Why hadn't he killed himself when he cracked up the Stutz on that crazy road from Morgantown? There was no place for him in this world, never had been, never would be.

Suicide: old Mr. Jeffries had blown his brains out, Miss Harriet Tarlton had jumped off the high bridge over the river. You read about famous people in the paper doing it. Some said President Harding had, to escape all the financial scandals of his administration.

And each one of the suicides he had heard of, near to his life or remote from it, now in this moment seemed to Lyle to appreciably weaken his own wish to live. He could feel that. Others had gone that way, many others. He had often seen Mr. Jeffries taking his constitutional down Middleburg Avenue, as sedate as you please. He had been at the Castle for several big parties: pleasant-seeming man. Blew his brains out.

Miss Tarlton taught piano. Fanny Carstairs had studied under her for a couple of years as a child. Strict, Fanny said she was, a disciplinarian. Jumped off the high bridge.

Well, and was Lyle going to fall in behind that line of self-created dead? Was that what Reverend Roanoke had seen that had so disconcerted him? A lost, damned soul, someone who killed himself by his own hand, and so of course was condemned eternally to Hell.

But of course he already was in Hell. Doris Lee giving herself to his father . . . over . . . and over . . . and over . . . again. Doris Lee, pure beauty, the voice that freed him, her swaying walk, forthright Doris Lee, his if there had been any sense at all in life and in human feelings, belonging to his father.

Then Lyle decided to shoot himself. He couldn't live with these facts, the image of those two beings nude in each other's arms. It was chaos, that picture, it was the end of his life. He knew where he could get a gun on River Street.

Lyle started to leave the room, and then the thought that he would never reenter it, never see this rare woman, his mother, again swept over him and he turned toward her, the April glow from the window shining behind her, her face, a pure face too, no betrayal of anyone there. Overcome, ripped to tatters, Lyle came over and pressed her hand. "Going back to Morgantown, dear?" she asked, her intuition, this above all times, failing utterly to tell her of the forces in the room. My face must be like stone, thought Lyle. I am turning to stone. She can't feel me through it. No one could.

Oh why can't you say to me what I can always keep, he begged inwardly. And why can't I say something like that to you! Tongue-tied forever, everyday words right up to death's door, tinfoil words till the world ends: "You're a wonderful woman," he mumbled.

"Why Lylie," she said beaming, "I didn't know you ever thought of me as a woman."

Lyle went out, bounded quickly down the stairs, down to the gallery above the octagonal hall. Nice house, he thought automatically. I wonder how much they'll get for it when it's sold?

Oh my God, he suddenly thought as he hurried down to the ground floor, people will think I'm doing this because we're going broke!

Only she will know better. Doris Lee might know better. And my ma might too. But *he* will be able to believe it, his weakling son weakling to the end, unable to take it, being broke, being nobody, one of the passé Catherwoods, the threadbare ex–coal barons.

Let him.

Although it was a balmy, clear day Lyle grabbed a raincoat and put it on.

The house shone and sparkled as he passed through it. The rich rugs, spring flowers everywhere, the mirrors and chandeliers, the polished woodwork and floors, the heavy side door all reflecting and adorning and proclaiming easy and ample wealth, and so did the driveway and, finally, his mammoth Pierce-Arrow in the barn.

How unbelievably springlike everything smelled, the new grass and flowers and leaves, tender-smelling, bursting out, as fresh as, well, young love.

Young love, he repeated to himself, grinding his back teeth, and turning the key and pressing the starter he exploded the big engine into life. Its deep-throated reverberation rattled the rafters. He backed the car out, and proceeding through the porte cochere turned for a quick glance at the Castle, a fake of course, a Castle Pretend built on a mountain of what they called black diamonds. But the coal was immeasurably newer, softer rock than real diamonds. That had just been a romantic phrase, an expression of the exuberant optimism of the boom: King Coal, black diamonds, an exuberance like the Castle and the Manor and the Farms. And now the coal was turning into dust; real diamonds never did that.

He drove out through the gates, the solid wooden steering wheel in his grasp pervading him with a sense of power, a very real sense. Quite a car. Detroit was one of the most booming centers of the boom, which continued unabated there as everywhere else in the country except back here in this backwater, which alone was falling into this sudden, strange silence.

The Pierce-Arrow plunged with its usual high-wheeled authority down the avenue, other motorists tending to make way for it, as though fearing it would grind their cars into steel filings if they did not.

Reaching Main Street Lyle realized that his route led past the First National Bank Building where his father had his offices. It suddenly seemed inevitable that he speak to him.

Lyle managed to find a place large enough for parking the Pierce-Arrow, and he entered the office building, into the familiar small rotunda with its spittoons, newsstand, smell of tobacco. Lyle got into the little wire cage of an elevator with the usual familiar colored man operating it. George, he was called. All colored porters and doormen and elevator operators were always called George, so that the important men they served would not have to be bothered learning new names. When the news of the collapse of the coal market really got around, thought Lyle, I'm going to propose that all the coal barons be called by one name: Joe. There'll be Joe Clifton and Joe Hayes and Joe Catherwood. He started a conversation with "George" and learned that his name was Sylvester.

The elevator reached his father's floor. In the hallways were tile floors, little white octagons of tile. He entered the headquarters of the Clarkson Coal Company. His father's secretary, Miss Matthews, told him to go in, Mr. Catherwood was down the hall but would be right back.

Lyle went into his office, a medium-sized room, business-like. On the wall there was an old photograph of a group of shirtsleeved men standing in front of a tipple. Squinting, Lyle made out that one of the men was a very young version of his father. He looked at this tall, broad-shouldered young man. *That* guy could have been Doris Lee's lover, but not the memory of him, which must have been what propelled his father into pursuing her. All of these thoughts left Lyle in a daze. At the bottom of the photograph had been printed in white: OPENING NUMBER THREE MINE, CLARKSON COAL COMPANY, BENNETTOWN, WEST VIRGINIA, MARCH 4, 1897.

On the desk, which Lyle had never seen in such disarray, there were two small photographs in linked frames: a very pretty one of Minnie in her early twenties, probably newly married, her hair in an old-fashioned swirl around her head; and one of himself, taken when he was about ten, in a cowboy outfit.

One happy family.

Except that Minnie was some kind of nervous case and odd religious zealot and seer; he himself was a half-crazy drunken suicide-bent no-good; and Clarkson was a philandering failure.

The swivel chair facing the desk had a padded bottom and back, heavily worn. Here his father had swiveled and worried and dictated letters and made decisions, all for the benefit of the family, and one or more young ladies on the side.

Behind the chair two big windows gave a panoramic view of busy downtown Middleburg, the railroad tracks and station, the river with the two bridges across it, River Street on the opposite bank, and the hills beyond. Not a mine, a tipple, a slag heap, even a miner's house, in sight.

Well it was all over and the fact that the telephones were ringing and the typewriters clicking in the outer office had no more meaning than a chicken running around with its head cut off.

That image shook Lyle: that was what he himself was like now.

Get out of this office, he ordered himself. Outside the door Miss Matthews at her desk said, "I'm sure he'll be back any minute."

"It doesn't matter," said Lyle. "Just say good-bye."

That was cruel, he supposed. These would be the last words his father would hear from him, secondhand, from his secretary. Well, too bad. What wasn't cruel?

He took the elevator down to the ground floor, said, "Thank you, Sylvester," as though that would make the man's day — what would Sylvester care what the Catherwood squirt called him?

Outside in the street Lyle climbed behind the wheel of his automobile. What a ridiculous, bogus piece of machinery! What in God's name was it for? He guided the car down the steep hill to the lower bridge and River Street.

In a room back of all the other rooms, behind the grocery store, behind the saloon, behind the poker and crap room, past the stairs leading to the whores, Lyle found Angelo Sacvucci, and Angelo, who sold everything, sold him a Colt .38 revolver and a box of bullets.

The feel of the revolver in his hand was similar to the feel of the steering wheel of the Pierce-Arrow: sturdy and powerful and deadly.

Holding the weapon transmitted something terribly provocative into Lyle's imagination: his father had driven him to this. Why shoot himself? Why not shoot his father and then himself?

Nothing meant anything, the image of his father and Doris Lee, their nude bodies locked together, negated all reason or control or sense, there was no meaning and he would simply blast the source of all this irrationality into kingdom come.

Climbing back behind the steering wheel, in command of the big piece of machinery, with the very professional, very real revolver in the pocket of his raincoat, Lyle headed back across the river and up the steep hill to Main Street. He parked the car and walked toward his father's office. Pete Hayes was coming toward him. "Think it's going to *rain*," joked Pete, "or what?"

"I'm carrying a gun in the pocket of this raincoat," said Lyle.

Pete laughed, said, "Things aren't *that* bad, not yet anyway," and walked on.

Lyle stepped into the little rotunda where the newsstand was. He looked over the papers.

UNIONS REJECT OPERATORS' CONTRACT BREACH
Leaders Vow "Fight to Finish"
Pickets Block Entrances to Major Mines

and from the other side of the conflict:

COAL OPERATORS FIRM
Contract "Inoperable" in Present Market

There was also an interview with Marcus. Lyle was too rattled to read it. He stepped through the glass doors and into the adjoining bank. A public telephone was on the wall there. Lyle pretended to place a call, his eyes on the rotunda through the glass door. It was 12:13 P.M. His father would soon pass through there on his way to the inevitable lunch at the inevitable table with the other inevitable executives at the inevitable Middleburg Hotel. The difference was that another inevitability awaited Clarkson today.

Clerks, secretaries, telephone operators were being released by Sylvester from the elevator each time it came to the ground floor. It wouldn't be long now before the executives descended. Some of the men were already wearing their summer straw hats.

The next descent of the elevator released Pete Hayes's father and uncle. They looked very glum and were not speaking to each other or anybody else.

Probably his father would come down with the next group of passengers. Lyle would fire and then put the gun in his own mouth and pull the trigger again. There were six bullets in the revolver. He would fire through the glass door because the shattering glass would be the right accompaniment.

He watched the arrow above the elevator door. It had gone to the top of the building, the sixth floor. Then it stopped at the fifth, and waited there, it seemed to Lyle, forever. Perhaps Sylvester was having a heart attack. At long, long last it crept down to the fourth floor, his father's floor and stopped there. Lyle imagined his father stepping in, wearing his fedora, saying "George" cordially enough to Sylvester. Then the needle moved downward again to three, then on past three, it was not going to stop at two either — obviously the car was full and Sylvester was coming directly to the ground floor and it was all happening too quickly for Lyle, his timing was thrown off, his mind out of synchronization, it was all rushing up to him like the tree he had smashed into with the Stutz, impossibly suddenly. The doors of the elevator parted, several young women stepped out and then his father stepped from the elevator into the rotunda.

Lyle's right hand locked around the gun handle, his index finger was against the trigger; he began to raise the gun inside his raincoat to bring it in line with the advancing figure.

What an old man: not knowing he was being watched, he had let his face hang; Lyle saw the long, tired lines in it.

Then a young man just behind Clarkson spoke to him and Lyle watched as his father's face lifted and lit up swiftly, almost hopefully. He wanted, it was nakedly visible, to ingratiate himself with the unimportant young man. He's doomed, thought Lyle in amazement, done in.

I could never shoot him.

Lyle started to lower the gun and then it jumped in his hand, there was a deafening blast, the window shattered, and the man in the newsstand let out a shout.

Everyone in the rotunda froze, staring first at the newsstand, then at the shattered glass door and then, in amazement, at Lyle with a hole burned in the outthrust pocket of his raincoat.

The uniformed guard of the bank, old retired Officer Prichett of the police force, who used to supervise Lyle and other schoolchildren crossing streets, now came up to Lyle, pulled his hand out of his pocket and relieved him of the revolver. Lyle's father was standing in a sea of shattered glass in front of him, speaking. Ears ringing, Lyle could not properly hear what he or anyone else was saying. He had not shot his father and he had not shot himself.

II.

"Your mother mustn't be told anything. She hasn't had a spell in years. This is one thing that could bring it on again. You should have thought of that before you started wandering around town with a goddam loaded gun. She keeps telling me how devoted to her you are. Some devotion."

Lyle said, "What about the newspapers?"

"I believe it won't be in the newspapers, except a little police court notice that you were fined for carrying an unlicensed weapon. She won't see that."

"Aunt Ophelia will."

"I'll fix her."

"You can't fix every gossip in town. Ma's bound to hear."

Clarkson drew a breath and swung around on his stool at the worktable in the barn to look at Lyle, in a wooden chair tilted against the wall next to a mining map. "Anyway, we'll minimize it. I'll take care of that. I've already spoken to the papers. And the police." Gosh you're competent, Lyle reflected sourly. "And now, maybe you'll tell me what you were doing with a loaded gun in the First National Bank!"

I was fixing to shoot you, Lyle drawled mentally. He looked at the exposed beams in the roof, suitable for someone hanging himself.

"It's just the purest chance you didn't hit the man in the newsstand . . . or even me!" His father's eyes widened at the unthinkability of this last.

Well, it was unthinkable, Lyle had to admit: stalk and shoot his own unsuspecting, unwarned, unarmed father. What he had really wanted to do was attack him, accuse him. Everything was lost, gone, ruined, life and hope and love and even money, but Lyle was still able to attack. "Can you tell me, Dad," he said in an even voice, his control of it surprising himself, "something about your relations with Mrs. Pence? Just man to man. This is something else we can not mention to Mother or Aunt Ophelia or anybody." Lyle flicked an appraising glance at his father's semistunned face after he had said this.

"My relations with Mrs. Pence?" he responded with an overtone of incredulity. "What're you talking about?"

"Oh well," said Lyle carelessly, "if we're just going to pretend things don't exist, then never mind."

After a stern and contemplative silence his father said, "See here, Lyle, what has a private social engagement of mine to do with you, armed in the First National Bank!"

Everything, of course, everything, he reflected. Aloud he said, "Private? Who from? Aren't we your family?"

"I have lunch and dinner with all kinds of people on business trips."

"Yes," said Lyle pleasantly, "but Mrs. Pence isn't married and some people think she's a beautiful lady. Some people want to know, well, what kind of relationship you have with her."

"That's nobody's business," snapped Clarkson, and then quickly reconsidering, added, "She's just . . . it was a social, friendly dinner, or two."

"Because you see," said Lyle, now more or less ignoring what his father was saying, "Doris Lee is someone who has meant a lot to me, ever since she was widowed and I got to know her. I don't think you ever noticed. Well, she did mean a lot to me. Does. That's why I would like to know about your relations with her."

His father regarded him appraisingly. "You're talking like a schoolboy, daydreaming. I saw Mrs. Pence because I was in Washington frequently and felt a certain responsibility for her, for her widowhood. And now that everything's changing so fast, I don't suppose I'll see her again." Clarkson said with a certain distant wistfulness: Lyle was a little touched in spite of himself. His father was having to say good-bye to quite a few things, all at once, many of them, Lyle surmised, things he had counted on to see him on toward and into old age. Abrupt, impoverishing farewells were being forced upon him this beautiful spring.

"Not see her again?" inquired Lyle.

"I don't suppose so."

"But did you — were she and you," Lyle began intensely, having to, "were you — I mean were you ever lovers?" Asking that was like diving to the bottom of the sea.

His father looked stern, Lyle awaited an onslaught, but instead his father simply and sternly replied, "No, of course not."

Do I believe him, Lyle asked himself. I don't know. I don't think so. I don't know.

"What has all this to do," his father demanded after a silence, attacking in his turn, "with your coming out of the bank into the rotunda with guns blazing!"

"Hardly blazing," murmured Lyle. "I didn't mean to fire it. I don't really know how to handle guns. I guess I got excited or nervous and accidentally squeezed the trigger."

"But *why* did you have a gun, and *why* was your finger on the trigger?"

"I was drunk," he mumbled.

"You were *not* drunk. And even if you had been, that's no explanation. Tell me the truth. Why!"

"Oh — I" — his mind wandering — "I guess, with all the violence, blowing up the Clifton mine, Baldwin-Felts guys coming in here — I hear they are, is it true?"

Clarkson reluctantly nodded.

"And I guess I thought of Logan and all and so, well, I got myself a gun."

"Where?"

"River Street."

"That was very foolish. This isn't going to be like Logan."

"How do you know?"

His father looked at him. "We aren't going to let it be."

Gosh you're tough, Lyle reflected sardonically.

III.

A few weeks later, when the university adjourned for the summer, Lyle packed a few things in a suitcase in his room in Morgantown and then set out in the Pierce-Arrow, heading north.

His route passed through Poundville, where Doris Lee Pence had been a little girl. At the entrance to the mine, outside the high wire fence with barbed wire along the top, pickets were out in force. They lounged or walked slowly back and forth, unarmed as far as the eye could see, but Lyle was certain that the eye could not see very far. They were the men on the flatcar all right, same kind of mixture of backgrounds, same kind of closed faces. They all stopped dead at the commanding sound and plutocratic sight of his Pierce-Arrow Raceabout. Lyle reached to the gearshift on the running board and shifted into a lower gear; if they rushed him he did not want to run into anybody. The men continued to stare and glare; remarks were passed back and forth among them. Lyle could imagine their general gist. It was offensive, when times were bad, to see an owner in a Rolls-Royce, but a playboy son in some kind of a racing car, that was a pure provocation. Back in the rear of the group someone reached for a rock. Lyle saw it come sailing out of the crowd. He gunned the engine, the rock bounced off the rear fender and he roared up the road, took a sharp curve upward, barely staying on the road, and was out of Poundville.

Pulse throbbing, he tried to figure out whether he had to pass any other mine entrances on this road. But where did this road lead to, anyway? Where exactly was he going?

This road led, he reminded himself, north out of the West Virginia hills — the hills of black diamonds, fabled stronghold of King Coal — to United States Route 40, that proud national turnpike, from there to Route 50, and *that* led to our nation's capital, Washington, D.C.

Up out of Poundville Lyle kept the car under strict control. It had never been built for these curving dribbles of roads, with their interesting West Virginia width of one and a half cars. Holding back the sixteen cylinders from running away with him, Lyle steered the monster northward into beautiful, untouched, highland wooded country, the freshness of June sweeping across it in delicate shades of green. He plunged through covered bridges and over pure mountain streams, through little farm hamlets where the handful of people on the road stopped to stare as the picketing miners had, but this time in, it seemed, awed admiration at this thundering manifestation of the auto age suddenly lurching into their midst. He had not noticed the Mason-Dixon Line marker but nevertheless speculated that he was now in southwestern Pennsylvania. The country rolled on, and he followed the blacktop country road over stone Revolutionary War bridges and past little farms. Rather suddenly, he emerged from the woods to see a broad, fully two-lane turnpike of white concrete ribboning across his way: National Route 40.

Lyle halted at the Stop sign and adjusted the windshield, his gray pragmatic driving clothes, smoothed down his red hair under his cap, shifted into first gear and roared eastward.

The Pierce-Arrow cut through the fresh June air with all its aromas of farms and forests. There were few cars on the highway and with the lack of curves on this stretch Lyle's visibility was such that he was usually able to pass eastbound cars without slowing down. White sprays of dogwood speckled the hillsides. I'm happy, thought Lyle. It's insane or something but I'm happy.

IV.

Doris Lee Pence had been given a wire-haired terrier by Clarkson the previous summer for her little boy. Every day when she returned to the apartment from teaching she took the dog for a walk in a deep ravine a block away, a part of Rock Creek Park just behind the Shoreham Hotel. A steep walk led down to the bottom of the ravine, and once there, the big city just above gave way to an illusion of woods and country meadows. A road wound through the park here, a bridge high above spanned it, but with the trees and shrubbery and grass, and a little brook, Doris Lee thought this provided the dog with a good place to stretch his legs. It gave her an opportunity to walk and get fresh air too. Many days Goldie brought Virgie down here too at an earlier hour.

It was such a warm and balmy day that she was wearing, neither coat nor hat, just a white blouse and a tan skirt. A man in a gray jacket and pants and wearing a cap was coming toward her. He had red hair. There was something familiar about the set of his shoulders: it was Lyle.

Doris Lee stopped in her tracks. The dog tugged at the leash to continue walking. Lyle came up to her.

"Hello, Doris Lee."

"Lyle," she said a little breathlessly. "How funny, I mean odd, always running into you in *ravines*."

"This didn't just happen accidentally. I've been watching where you live since yesterday and figured out you always come down here about this time."

"Oh not always," she lied swiftly, not exactly sure why, "just some days."

He looked at her steadily. "You look wonderful, Doris Lee."

"Thank you. You — you've filled out a little, Lyle. It's becoming."

"I'm older."

"Yes," she said, "and so am I."

"You don't look it. You beautiful women are different from other people, aren't you. I mean when you're eighteen you sort of look thirty, and when you're thirty there's something eighteen about you."

She tried to give him her best smile. "Well, I'm glad if that's all true."

"About your being beautiful? Oh, you're beautiful all right. All of us Catherwoods saw that."

She blinked. "How *are* your family?"

"Mother is okay. The old man is going bankrupt." He looked at her. "Has he told you that yet?"

Doris Lee tugged at the dog's leash. It was such an innocuous, harmless little beast. Goldie had said two women and a little child living alone should have had a German police dog.

Finally Doris Lee nodded affirmatively to Lyle's question.

"You're his mistress, aren't you?"

"Oh *Lyle* —"

"You took him instead of me."

"Lyle, I didn't *take* anybody. Your father and I —"

"Oh if you're going to lie —"

"We dined once in a while."

"How much money did he give you?" Seeing her stricken face at that question some pain knifed into him so deeply that he barely avoided a cry. "I'm *sorry*, Doris Lee, please forgive me for saying that. I'm . . . just not in my right mind one hundred percent today. See, we're going to be penniless. I had it straight from Marcus Clifton. This thing may straggle on for a while, some months, even a couple of years, but the coal industry as it used to be is dead and all our fortunes are dead or dying with it."

She looked at him. "I know," she said quietly.

"Dad tell you?"

She nodded faintly.

"You really didn't love him, did you?"

After a while she shook her head.

"You never did, did you."

She said softly, "No."

"Do you love me, or I mean could you, ever?"

"I —" Her delicate face was knit with perplexity, unresolved feelings. "I'm too old for you, Lyle."

"My grandmother was seven years older than my grandfather."

Doris Lee bent down to disentangle the dog's leash. She turned her head to glance up at him. "Were they happy?" she asked.

I think I've got her, Lyle's mind tensely recorded. *That question: "Were they happy?" What she's really asking is: "Shall we give it a try?"*

She doesn't even realize it herself yet, but that's what she just asked me.

I've got her.

An unimaginable sense of peace then settled over him.

V.

In Middleburg the Cliftons, the Hayeses and Clarkson, with the hearty concurrence of the fast-fading Hundred Millionaires, began negotiations with the Baldwin-Felts Detective Agency to send its men into the Middleburg field, to protect their mines, tipples and other property. They would also protect nonunion miners who were going to work at the new lower wage. The agency was also instructed to send in undercover agents to infiltrate the ranks of the recalcitrant miners and single out the ringleaders, as well as get any available information about violence.

Clarkson Catherwood, as he watched his balance sheets fluctuate wildly, became, along with his colleagues, increasingly indifferent to the methods used to curb union violence, protect his property, and safeguard what men would now work in the mines.

In September the Packard was sold to an undertaking establishment. The top floor of the Castle was sealed off for the winter. "God knows it's not to save on the cost of coal, selling at what it is," Clarkson observed dryly.

It had been Minnie's idea. "We don't need the space so why should we have it?" Thomasina was let go; so were the laundress, the heavy-work man, and Thomasina's helper, Zorida. George and Tot inside, and Angelo outside, would have to keep things together as best they could, Minnie explained to them. She, Clarkson, and Lyle when he was home would help by creating as little work as possible and by doing many things for themselves now that formerly had been done for them.

What Minnie missed most was having her hair washed and brushed. Thomasina had been expert at this and had seemed to enjoy it, and to enjoy the conversation which went along with it. During the years of tending Minnie's hair Thomasina had undergone conversion to the Church of the

Last Judgment without ever having been able to attend a service, Reverend Roanoke having been long gone from the neighborhood. But the summer just after the war, in 1919, Minnie had financed a trip by Thomasina to Arkansas where Reverend Roanoke had prayed with her and, sure enough, Thomasina was among the Saved.

Now soft-spoken, soft-handed, soft-eyed Thomasina had to be discharged, and there was no one now in Middleburg to hire her to do the kind of domestic work she did so well. "Where will you go?" asked Minnie, close to tears.

"I don't rightly know, Miss Minnie. Maybe to my sister, in Charleston."

"Things aren't any better in Charleston, I don't believe."

"I don't rightly know," said Thomasina mechanically.

What in heaven's own name is going to become of them, Minnie implored the air around her. The charity organizations were all drying up, because no one could contribute to them. And who else was there to look after the destitute? Out-of-work men had begun drifting to downtown Middleburg and there slumping on the rather grand stone steps leading up to the Corinthian entrance to the courthouse, as though the temple of government would somehow send out aid, manna, jobs, a guardian angel, something to care for them and give them hope. But within the courthouse there was no one, there were no resources, no programs, no ideas about how to do anything for the accumulating shabby, jobless men on the steps outside. Winter, which they all knew could get very cold indeed in the mountains of West Virginia, lay ahead.

What is going to become of Thomasina, Minnie implored her Savior, of these men, of their families — wherever they may be? What in the end is going to become of us?

Then she thought of her farm — pigs, those beautiful healthy pigs, the hens laying eggs, the cows giving milk. Driving the Model T it did not cost much to go out to the farm, and bring that nourishment back to the table in the Castle. How foolish she had been, during the several years before the collapse of coal, not to have built a modest house on the land. Now she supposed they could not afford to and also living far out of town would be impractical for many reasons. They would have to hang on to the Castle, to a part of it at least.

Minnie did not mind the dramatic simplifications of life going on around her. Beside Thomasina's likely fate, next to the bums on the courthouse steps, she saw their losses as almost negligible. But she did miss that one thing: Thomasina to wash and brush her hair.

One day when she was struggling with it in her bathroom Tot came in and asked if she could help. Minnie told her what to do, and after her hair had been thoroughly washed and dried Minnie took her accustomed place at her dressing table and Tot took up the elegant brushes with their handles of English silver and began to do her hair. Clarkson had bought the brushes in London just before they had set out on their Mediterranean cruise. As Minnie remembered, they had been remarkably expensive. These were something, she resolved that afternoon as her Aunt Tot stroked her hair, that she would not sell. The fur coats, jewelry, whatever, yes. Her English silver brushes, no.

I have my boy and my sewing and my farm and my God, reflected Minnie as her scalp pleasantly tingled from the brushing. And now I have my husband again. My life, my own life, is really becoming better as the weeks pass and the money fades away. But everyone else is now going to suffer, Lyle, Clarkson, my poor Thomasina, those hopeless courthouse men, and thousands and thousands of others in West Virginia. And now that I will have no money I can do even less than before to help.

Well, she said quietly to herself, I shall pray and I shall sew and I shall learn to drive the Model T against the day,

God forbid, when George must go, so that I can go to the farm and work with Mr. Eubanks. That farm must not just feed us, it must pay.

VI.

Lyle sold the Pierce-Arrow in Washington for $11,250. He could live for three or four years on that if he lived in a new way, like a poor student or workman. He visited the University of Maryland and learned that his credits at West Virginia University would be accepted if he transferred there, which he arranged to do.

He found a job in a hardware store in downtown Washington, and rented a one and a half furnished room nearby.

All this was done in three days' time. Lyle telephoned Doris Lee and asked her to have dinner with him. She agreed.

At that long dinner, in a small, inexpensive Italian restaurant, they discussed everything up to and including what she called her "association" with Clarkson. The fact that they had traveled to Europe on the same liner and stayed in London at the same time although at different hotels was not concealed.

"And how uh, how uh, intimate *were* you, anyway?" he finally blurted.

"We weren't *intimate*. He was a father or an uncle to me, what they used to call a protector."

Much later that night, when Lyle took her home, he came into her little apartment and very quietly in the dark living room he explored at long last her body with his hands and his mouth — it was far more hypnotizing than he had imagined — and she promised that they would go away from Virgie and Goldie, for a night, that they would be lovers.

When he left her Doris Lee went slowly, very faintly smiling, into her bedroom. And so she was to share her body with a man who could complete her as Virgil had done. And she was going to be able to do for him what she had for Virgil.

In her bedroom she went to the closet, fished around and found the picture of Virgil. She could look straight into his face now. In her mind she said to him, I've found a new father for our boy.

After leaving her, Lyle strolled through some park or other near the Potomac, water which came down out of West Virginia to wind through the capital, amid the great illuminated monuments, and he thought: There are so many tales that aren't going to be told. I'll never tell my father I raised a gun to him. And he'll never know I wanted to kill myself.

And I'll never really know whether he and Doris Lee — ugh! ugh! oof! — were ever naked locked in each other's arms and bodies. Neither one of them will ever tell me . . . if it ever happened.

Maybe not to know is the only thing that makes life work sometimes.

God, I have a lot of deep feelings, he thought. It's something running right through me, very deeply, a vein or seam, all these feelings and caring and falling so deeply in love, it's what I've really got, what I've always really lived for, and I guess always will live for.

He wandered back to his cramped little furnished room. He liked it. It was his own. He liked getting up very early and going to work in the hardware store. He liked his new inexpensive clothes. He liked calling the customers "sir" and "ma'am." He liked waiting on them.

Most of all he was made confident by the fact that no one here had ever heard of the Catherwoods and the Castle, and that in fact being a Catherwood didn't make any difference anymore anywhere.

Lyle realized he had always wanted to be free of his family and the artificial prestige he acquired from being a member of it. That was one of the reasons he had been so wild and mercurial and drunken. He wanted to break free of what was not himself. The Catherwood money and prestige stood in the way of his finding out who he was and what he himself was really worth.

But now all that impressive, monied barrier was being swept away and he was filled with pleasure at finding out that he was an anonymous student at the University of Maryland, a clerk in a hardware store, and the lover of Doris Lee Pence.

These definitions calmed him.

Now I just have to figure her out completely, he told himself. The kind of man she's drawn to is not exactly rich, not necessarily, but he needs to be a man of substance. I will have to develop that. That's what she wants. That's what she shall have. I've got nothing false or inherited or grafted on me by my family to offer anymore. There's just me, student and clerk, anonymous, and it's funny but I never felt more substantial in my life.

VII.

Minnie and Clarkson accepted the accomplished fact that Lyle had set out on his own.

And Clarkson cut expenses and eliminated liabilities and simplified operations, pruning and economizing and finding his actions always too limited and too slow to overtake the crisis. His appearance became less impressive as his situation changed; George hadn't time to look after his clothes anymore. The changing structures of his life were reflected in everything about him. Clarkson began to look small-town provincial, to feel like that, to be it.

The Baldwin-Felts operatives were posted at the tipples.

Their undercover men were infiltrating the union. One of the Hayes Coal Company's mines was dynamited. Two Baldwin-Felts detectives were shot and killed from ambush. Thousands of coal cars sat idly on sidings. Marcus Clifton sold five hundred acres of the Farms to a land speculator. Sanderson Clifton closed off twenty-five rooms of the Manor. The number of bums on the courthouse steps increased.

"Look at us," Marcus said to Clarkson as they walked along Main Street toward lunch at the hotel. "The country is in its biggest boom in history and *we*, just us, coal, King Coal, are in the middle of a panic. The only place in the country. How could this happen? How could we be singled out from all the rest of American industry? Why, the stock market's never been better, and that's the great barometer. Here it is, the biggest prosperity in history, and we're dropped out of it."

"It does seem uncanny," Clarkson agreed.

VIII.

That evening he returned to the Castle and sank with a weary sigh into his wingback chair in the library.

Minnie came in, bringing him a glass of Scotch. "How much more of this have we got?" he asked after taking a grateful gulp.

"Oh, some. Well, not too much."

After a silence he said, "I never minded drinking beer."

"Clarkson?"

"Yes?"

"The tax bill on this property came today."

He rolled his eyes up at her. "I don't want to know how much it is."

"It's rather a lot. I never looked at one before. I didn't know we paid that much in taxes. It *is* a lot."

Clarkson rattled the ice in his glass.

"It isn't as though we *needed* all this space anymore," she went on, "what with Lyle gone, no big entertaining to do, not having the kind of help anymore we need to really keep it up."

He took a second gulp of Scotch.

"You're not thinking of selling it, I hope," he said. "Nobody'd buy this gray elephant now."

"Maybe one of these days we could find a buyer, a funeral home —"

He groaned.

" — or, well, a little private school. Nuns. I don't know."

"Nobody in his right mind is going to buy this place in these times."

"As a matter of fact," pursued Minnie, "I wasn't thinking of that so much as, well, moving out of here, going to live in something smaller, easier to run, cheaper to run. Then, if the taxes on this got to be just too much, why if we had to we could just let it be sold for taxes and —"

He looked across at her. "How can you talk so calmly, no, coldly, about things like that?"

She returned his look. "Because I have to," she answered, controlling her voice. "It's no time for breaking down or going all sentimental about things."

He continued looking at her. "By God you sure have changed over the years."

She drew a long breath, and then murmured, "Reverend Roanoke."

"That fellow did it, did he, with his praying over you? Well, I'll have to hand it to him. It's been almost some kind of miracle."

"Praying *with* me, not *over* me."

[341]

"I — maybe I — when he — um, when he left this part of the country, maybe I shouldn't have, well, encouraged him to go." He gazed fixedly at her.

"It didn't really matter." Minnie shook her head and blinked at her hands. "My . . . salvation had been accomplished. And he did just as good work in Arkansas as ever he did here, I'm sure."

There was a silence in the library. Crickets hissed outside in the lawns and gardens. A smell of skunk, pure summertime West Virginia, was wafted in to them. Neither minded: it was part of their life, their past, their happiness.

Then Minnie resumed firmly, "And *if* this house ever had to be sold for taxes we would be living somewhere else and it wouldn't be such a wrench."

"Where?" he asked in a tone suggesting that he could not conceive of any other roof over their heads.

"On my farm."

"Your farm? Are you serious? In the pigsty?"

"The taxes on that property are very reasonable. Couldn't we, Clarkson, *build* a little place, something snug, solid. We could live like that whatever came, with food growing at our front door —"

"It costs money to build a house."

"You know something about building, with your hands I mean, don't you?"

"Something, yes."

"Enough to supervise construction of a simple two-bedroom little farmhouse?"

"I suppose so."

"George is pretty good with his hands."

"Um-hum."

"If we're going to keep on paying him a while longer, let's set him to work on something that *really counts*. Then there's James, Youranie's James. He's been laid off at the mine, of course."

Clarkson nodded grim concurrence.

"He'll work for us," Minnie said.

"I've got some timber around the mines," Clarkson observed cautiously, "useless there now, we might be able to use. Maybe I could make a deal at Phelps Lumber Company for the other stuff."

"Higginbottom Plumbing will surely be reasonable."

Clarkson looked for a long time at her again. "You want us to pull through this thing, no matter what, don't you."

"Of course. There's so much to look forward to. No more trips to Europe or any of that, but much more fundamental things. Things that really mean a lot more. For example," she brushed back her hair with a graceful gesture, "I expect before too very long we'll be having a grandchild."

Clarkson frankly gaped at her.

"A lovely little boy . . . or maybe a beautiful, perfectly *beautiful* green-eyed girl."

"You know," Clarkson said rather hurriedly, "this idea of a little house on that land of yours. I think you've got something."

"Let's go out and have a look at it."

"Now?"

"There's two more good hours of sunlight. Come on."

Clarkson gulped down the remainder of his drink, and pushing himself with a will up from the chair, linked an arm through Minnie's. "Okay, let's have a look."

They strode out of the library, across the big octagonal hall, and through the side door to the porte cochere, where the Model T Ford was waiting.